Books in th

Book 1: Never Say Spy

Book 2: The Spy Is Cast

Book 3: Reach For The Spy

Book 4: Tell Me No Spies

Book 5: How Spy I Am

More books coming! For a current list, please visit
www.dianehenders.com

NEVER SAY SPY

Book 1 of the NEVER SAY SPY series

Diane Henders

NEVER SAY SPY
ISBN 978-0-9878188-2-9

PEBKAC Publishing
P.O. Box 75046 Westhills R.P.O.
Calgary, AB   T3H 3M1
www.pebkacpublishing.com

This book is a work of fiction. Names, characters, places and incidents are either the product of the author's imagination or are used fictitiously, and any resemblance to actual persons, living or dead, business establishments, events or locales is entirely coincidental.

First printed in paperback October 2011 by PEBKAC Publishing
v.5

Since You Asked...

People frequently ask if my protagonist, Aydan Kelly, is really me.

Yeah, you got me. These novels are an autobiography of my secret life as a government agent, working with highly-classified computer technology... Oh, wait, what's that? You want the *truth*? Um, you do realize fiction writers get paid to lie, don't you?

...well, shit, that's not nearly as much fun. It's also a long story.

I swore I'd never write fiction. "Too personal," I said. "People read novels and automatically assume the author is talking about him/herself."

Well, apparently I lied about the fiction-writing part. One day, a story sprang into my head and wouldn't leave. The only way to get it out was to write it down. So I did.

But when I wrote that first book, I never intended to show it to anyone, so I created a character that looked like me just to thumb my nose at the stereotype. I've always had a defective sense of humour, and this time it turned around and bit me in the ass.

Because after I'd written the third novel, I realized I actually wanted other people to read my books. And when I went back to change my main character to *not* look like me, my beta readers wouldn't let me. They rose up against me and said, "No! Aydan is a tall woman with long red hair and brown eyes. End of discussion!"

Jeez, no wonder readers get the idea that authors write about themselves. So no, I'm not Aydan Kelly. I just look like her.

Oh, and the town of Silverside and all secret technologies

are products of my imagination. If I'm abducted by grim-faced men wearing dark glasses, or if I die in an unexplained fiery car crash, you'll know I accidentally came a little too close to the truth.

Thank you for respecting my hard work. If you're borrowing this book, I'd very much appreciate it if you would buy your own copy, or, if you wish, you can make a donation on my website at http://www.dianehenders.com/donate.

Thanks - I hope you enjoy the book!

For Phill

Thank you for being my technical advisor and the most tolerant husband ever. Much love!

To my beta readers/editors, especially Carol H., Judy B., and Phill B., with gratitude: Many thanks for all your time and effort in catching my spelling and grammar errors, telling me when I screwed up the plot or the characters' motivations, and generally keeping me honest.

To everyone else, respectfully:
If you find any typographical errors in this book, please send an email to errors@dianehenders.com. Mistakes drive me nuts, and I'm sorry if any slipped through. Please let me know what the error is, and on which page. I'll make sure it gets fixed in the next printing. Thanks!

CHAPTER 1

French-kissing the hot guy in my fantasy seemed like a good idea at the time.

I could have really enjoyed it, too, if my head didn't hurt so damn much. When I touched the sore spot, my fingertips showed a little smear of blood, but I puzzled over that for less than a second before I returned my attention to the much more interesting subject at hand. Or hands, to be exact.

I ran said hands down his back and over buns of steel. We were making a creditable attempt to lick each other's tonsils when a furious voice erupted from inches behind me.

"What the hell do you think you're doing?"

I snatched my grip off the beefcake and spun around.

"Ow, sonuva*bitch!*" I clutched my head when the abrupt movement slammed pain through my skull, and tried to focus my watering eyes on the source of the interruption.

Okay, that was weird. I was pretty sure I'd never had a fantasy that included a short, pissed-off paramedic.

The paramedic locked eyes with Beefcake. "What the hell do you think you're doing?" he repeated.

Beefcake shrugged. "I'm not doing anything. She jumped me."

"Can't you see she's injured? You could have at least

helped her back out of the portal!"

...Huh? It was my fantasy, but I didn't think I was controlling the action anymore. I gaped at the two men.

The short paramedic dismissed Beefcake with a final glare and turned to me. "Ma'am, please come with me. We need to get you to a hospital." As he spoke, he took my arm and steered me away.

"Uh...?" I was about to demand an explanation when agony punched through my eye sockets. I jerked into a ball, arms clamped over my head until the pain diminished enough for me to sit up and start swearing. After a few moments of heartfelt profanity, I recovered enough to realize the paramedic was trying to convince me to lie down on the sidewalk again.

Wait a minute.

Sidewalk? Sitting in a puddle?

Red flashing lights. Ambulance. Right, that explained the paramedic.

He had changed his clothes, though. Instead of his uniform, he wore a brown plaid shirt and khaki pants. My aching brain struggled to catch up.

The fantasy faded as awareness returned. Right, March in Silverside, Alberta. A chinook thaw, slippery sidewalks, and now my ass was awash in ice water and my head hurt like hell. I didn't even remember slipping. You know you're a desperate case when you get so engrossed in a fantasy you don't even watch where you're walking.

Embarrassment suffused me when a handful of murmuring bystanders began to gather, and I hauled myself to my feet despite the protests of the paramedic.

"I'm fine," I mumbled, pulling soggy denim away from my butt as unobtrusively as possible.

"Better get checked at the hospital just in case," he advised. "You need to get that abrasion on your scalp cleaned up, too." He guided me firmly into the back of the ambulance while his two uniformed cohorts got in front.

Three paramedics and an ambulance for a bump on the head. Gotta love a small town. If I'd slipped and fallen in Calgary, I'd be lucky to rate a Boy Scout with an aspirin.

My royal treatment continued at the hospital. My khaki-clad saviour waved the other two away and escorted me into a cubicle in the tiny emergency ward. I perched on the bed, and he nodded reassuringly and withdrew, pulling the curtains closed behind him.

Moments later, I overheard his approaching murmur. "... found her in the portal so I brought her into B wing."

A white-coated doctor strode in. "I'm Dr. Roth. How's the head?" she asked as she briefly examined my scalp and flashed a small light in each of my eyes.

"Sore, but not worth a trip to emergency."

"I don't see any sign of a concussion," she said. "But I'd like to ask you a few quick questions, just to make sure. Can you tell me your name and age?"

"Aydan Kelly. I'm forty-six years old. I know it's March. I know I'm in Silverside Hospital. I know it's Thursday, but I have no idea what the date is, which is normal for me. You're not going to flunk me for the date, are you?"

As I spoke, the doctor's eyes had begun to twinkle. She was a striking blonde about my age, and she smiled as she answered, "No, we'll let you away with that one. I'd normally suggest a quick MRI, but it's a very minor injury, and I think you'll be fine."

I laughed. "There's no such thing as a quick MRI. And I don't feel much like driving two hours down to Calgary to get one."

"No, we'd use ours..." She trailed off at my incredulous expression.

"MRI? In Silverside?" I demanded. "Population what, five thousand? No way."

"The MRI is privately and anonymously owned," she replied. "The hospital is allowed to use it for diagnostic procedures when it's available."

"Wow, who's your celebrity hypochondriac?"

She smiled. "I'll send Linda to clean up that abrasion for you. It should only take a few minutes, if you'd like to call your husband to pick you up."

I stared at the plain gold band I still wore on my left hand and cranked on a smile. "That could be a little tricky. He's been dead for two years."

Dr. Roth looked horrified as she apologized, "I'm so sorry, I saw the ring and just assumed..."

"It's okay. I guess it's time I stopped wearing it. Just habit at this point." I slipped the ring off my finger with only a slight pang. I'd come a long way since Robert died. What a shock that had been.

Given the graphic fantasy I'd just had, it was probably time I got back on the horse. So to speak. Too bad there wasn't anybody in real life who was built like my fantasy horse... er... guy.

Realizing the silence had stretched a bit, I refocused. "No need to call anyone. I'm fine. I'll just drive myself home."

The young nurse arrived shortly afterward, and we chatted like old friends while she cleaned the injury on my scalp. As I got ready to leave, I remembered the odd fragment of conversation I'd heard, and spoke up.

"Hey, Linda, what's the significance of Wing B?"

She paused, then smiled. "It's opposite to Wing A. That's all."

For a moment, my overactive imagination suggested she was being evasive, but whatever. My head still hurt, and I was in a hurry to get out of there in case the roads iced up in the evening.

Back in my farmhouse, I surveyed the disarray while I assembled a meal of leftovers. Three weeks after my big move, the kitchen was mostly organized. My ancient furniture looked right at home in the graciously-proportioned though shabby living/dining area, but my unpacking was far from complete. I gobbled my supper and went to work on my computer, ignoring the boxes still piled in the corners.

A couple of hours later, I dragged my headache into the small bathroom off the master bedroom. I eyed the dark stain in the floor at the base of the toilet while I brushed my teeth. Leaky seal for sure, and the floor would be rotten underneath. Time to break out the renovation tools.

Sliding into bed, I touched the handle of the crowbar under the other pillow for reassurance. I was probably perfectly safe in my new country home, but city instincts die hard.

I live alone. If somebody breaks into my house in the middle of the night, what am I going to do? Hit them with a pillow?

I don't think so.

A day spent tearing out crusty plumbing and rotten, smelly flooring left me looking forward to my trip on Saturday. I bounced out of bed at six thirty, keeping my fingers crossed for an offer on my Calgary house by the end of the day.

Hoping to make a good impression on the prospective buyer, I overcame my normal slobbish tendencies and put on my best-fitting girly jeans and a stretchy T-shirt that clung enough to make my boobs look good without revealing too much of the muffin-top that overflowed my waistband. I brushed out my long hair and examined it in the light from the bedroom window. Still more red than grey. So far, so good.

I hit the road in high spirits, belting out the songs on the radio with far more enthusiasm than talent and happily anticipating my regular Saturday afternoon lunch date with the group of ex-basketball friends that was the closest thing I had to family. Two hours later, I strolled into Kelly's Bar and Grill in Calgary, letting the familiar shabby ambiance wrap around me with the same welcoming warmth as my friends' greetings.

We lolled on the broken-down couches at the back of the bar, enjoying the excellent food and bantering with the waitress who'd served us for so many years she was almost part of the gang herself. I soaked up the wisecracks and off-colour jokes until we finally dispersed a couple of hours later, lingering and laughing on the sidewalk outside the bar.

When I pulled into my driveway a few minutes before our meeting time, I swallowed a bubble of hope at the sight of my real estate agent's cheery wave. Just a meeting with a potential buyer. No guarantees.

"Hi, Aydan, great to see you!" Cheryl's usual upbeat greeting made me smile, and we wandered into the house to lean against the wall in the empty living room, chatting. After fifteen minutes, she called the buyer's cell phone number, but it went directly to voicemail. We made desultory conversation for the next quarter of an hour, when Cheryl tried again.

She snapped her phone shut with a scowl. "Well, I guess he's not going to show. What a waste of time this was."

"No kidding. Especially after he insisted I come down." I blew out a sigh. "At least I got to have lunch with my friends. And I've got a bed here so I don't have to go back today."

We said our goodbyes in the driveway, and I attempted an attitude adjustment while I cruised down the gentle hill toward the nearby strip mall. Maybe Cheryl could set up something for later in the evening. And I'd get to pick up the low-flow toilet I'd ordered, and maybe a few other...

A flash of movement jerked my eyes up to the rearview mirror. Shock jolted through me at the sight of the dark-haired man pushing through the collapsible back seat from the trunk.

I whipped around to stare at Beefcake from my fantasy. Disbelief paralyzed me for an instant before I recognized the black object in his hand.

Gun.

Shit!

I stomped both feet on the brake. The car jerked to a stop with a tortured squeal of tires, hurling Beefcake's body between the front seats to crash headfirst into the dash. His gun discharged with a deafening bang. In mindless panic, I punched the seat belt release, snatched the door open, and flung myself out of the car.

The vehicle was picking up speed again on the downhill slope and the ground flew out from under my feet. I crashed to the pavement, rolling frantically to avoid the rear tires as they crunched by. My feet scrabbled for purchase on the gravel-strewn asphalt as I scrambled up, my hysterical panting whistling in my throat. After a couple of eternal seconds, I gained traction and fled up the hill like a demented rabbit.

A rusted-out Chevy Suburban skidded and rocked to a stop crosswise in the street with the driver's side facing me. The driver's door started to open, and I used the little breath I still had available to scream, "Gun! *Gun!*"

I dashed for the Suburban, its bulk looming only a few yards away like a bastion of safety.

A gunshot exploded from behind me. A tall, broad-shouldered man swung out of the Suburban. In a single fluid motion, he drew a gun as his feet hit the pavement.

He aimed directly at me and fired.

CHAPTER 2

I let out a strangled shriek and dodged sideways, trying to swerve around the front of the truck.

I wasn't going to make it. I was too close, going too fast.

A bullet thudded into the Suburban. I jumped and rolled at the front fender, caroming over the hood. As I tumbled past the windshield, I glimpsed the passenger's young face, his mouth stretched open in a 'O'.

Something plucked at my pant leg as I went over. Then I was on my feet on the other side, sprinting across two lanes of traffic while vehicles screeched to a halt with a chorus of honking horns.

Sobbing for breath, I did a broken-field run between the stopped cars. I couldn't hear any more gunfire behind me, but the hammering of my heart would have drowned it out anyway.

All eyes jerked toward me when I cannoned through the door of the nearest coffee shop. I doubled over, gasping, "911! Call 911!"

After a moment of shocked paralysis, the patrons surged to their feet in a babble of voices. Struggling for air, I braced my elbows on my shaking knees, brainlessly repeating "911" with every breath. A knot of people converged on me, offering a chair and jabbering questions and advice.

A woman's voice rose in a squeaky tremolo. "Oh my God, she's bleeding!"

I collapsed into the proffered chair and followed her white-eyed gaze to the blood-soaked rip in my jeans just above my ankle. When I pulled up my pant leg, I discovered a short, shallow gash in the skin just above my sock. It began to throb as I eyed it with the detachment gained from occasional renovation-related injuries.

Minor.

It looked impressive, though. My exertion had encouraged the bleeding. My sock was soaked down one side, and my shoe was squishy. A few drops leaked out onto the floor while I watched. I dropped the pant leg back into place, unable to summon up enough energy to care at the moment.

One of the baristas, an older woman, pushed through the crowd to pat me on the shoulder with a motherly hand. "Police and ambulance are on the way. Would you like a hot drink? Or some juice?"

"Orange juice, please," I quavered gratefully. When it arrived, I needed both trembling hands to raise it to my mouth. The bottle clattered a calypso rhythm against my teeth.

A few minutes later, the juice started to work its magic on my blood sugar. I drew a long, shaky breath, stretching out my hand to gauge the diminishing tremor. I wouldn't want to run a marathon or anything, but I could probably stand up without collapsing.

Most of the customers were still crowded around the windows, riveted on the scene in the street. The remainder drifted back to their tables, leaving me some welcome space.

When the barista offered to bring a first aid kit for my leg I accepted with thanks, and she disappeared through a door behind the coffee counter.

I swallowed the last of the juice, staring anxiously toward the street and straining my ears for sirens. At last, I heard the welcome wail, and I slumped back in the chair with a sigh, letting my shoulders ease down from around my ears. Thank God.

A few moments later, a disturbance in the bystanders outside the coffee shop made me sit up again to crane my neck. The police must be arriving.

Adrenaline slammed into my bloodstream. Shit, no!

The big gunman from the Suburban moved purposefully toward the door of the coffee shop, head and shoulders taller than the still-gawking crowd.

Goddammit, where the hell were the police?

I hauled myself to my feet to hurry in the direction of the bathroom, but my movement caught his attention through the glass. He met my eyes as he began to shove his way through the onlookers into the shop. His lips were moving, but I didn't wait to find out what he was saying.

With a fresh surge of panic, I bolted into the open door behind the coffee bar, nearly colliding with the barista as she returned. She held out the first aid kit as I passed, as if maybe I would stop and doctor my leg on the fly. I rocketed past a small table and chairs, then past storage shelves, frantically scanning for a back exit.

Thank God, there it was, equipped with what architects call 'panic hardware'. How appropriate.

I crashed into the door lever with a grunt and burst through the doorway only to be confronted by a beanpole of a young man, his eyes wide in his white face. He flung out trembling arms to stop me, but I recognized the telltale 'afraid of the ball' flinch as his face turned partly away, eyes squeezing.

I passed beyond fear. My mind clicked into the magical state basketball players call 'the zone' and time slowed, my mind analyzing and my body reacting without conscious thought.

He was a good three inches taller than me, maybe more. His reach was too long to avoid, but he was ridiculously skinny. I was five-foot-ten and a hundred and sixty pounds. I had a lot of momentum and a lot of motivation.

I could take him.

Disconnected, I saw the fear flood into his face at the sight of my maniacal grin. I didn't even try to dodge around him.   Instead, I dropped my shoulder, took two hard accelerating steps, and slammed into his gut. At impact, I jerked upright, flinging my arms upward. A tangle of bony limbs catapulted over my shoulder, accompanied by the explosive bark of air leaving his lungs. I dimly heard the thud when he hit the pavement.

The orange juice was wearing off already. I forced my rubbery legs to accelerate again, but I had only taken half a dozen strides when a voice boomed behind me.

"Stop, police!"

With a hiccup of relief, I skidded to a halt and swung back to face the coffee shop.

It wasn't the police.

The big man stood beside his fallen accomplice, his gun trained on me. The bore looked enormous, but it was probably only a 9mm. I'd always liked guns. Until now.

His eyes and gun remained locked on me as he reached out one foot and nudged the kid on the ground none too gently. "Breathe, Webb."

The beanpole twitched and drew in a wailing breath, then another. If I hadn't been so terrified, I'd have felt sorry for him. I'd had the wind knocked out of me once or twice. Those first few breaths were no picnic.

The kid took a couple more breaths, and then retched and vomited. That had to hurt. He curled around his stomach and lay still, but I could see the rise and fall of his rib cage. At least I hadn't killed him outright. That would probably upset the big guy.

"oh-shit-oh-shit-oh-shit," a small voice chanted in my mind. I wondered how many people's last words were 'Oh, shit'. It made me think of that joke, how did it go? 80% of people's last words were 'Oh, shit', except in Saskatchewan, where the usual last words were 'Here, hold my beer'.

Too much adrenaline. Focus.

I shook my head, rattling my brain back into action. Stay alert, stay smart. Get him talking.

"What do you want?" I quavered. Not very inspired, but at least it was a start.

"I want to talk to you," he responded evenly. "Don't run away. Calm down and talk to me."

"Nine millimetres of hot lead is a hell of a conversation-starter. Why are you trying to shoot me?" I asked, attempting a calm and conversational tone while my heart tried to punch through my ribs.

"If I'd tried to shoot you, you'd be dead," he said. "And it's a .40 cal."

I digested that. There was some logic there. Not the part about the .40 calibre; the other part. Earlier, he'd fired from such close range he'd have to have been completely ham-fisted to miss me. And the way he handled that gun, I was pretty sure he wasn't ham-fisted. I belatedly realized he was still talking, his voice steady and soothing.

"Let's start again. My name is John Kane. I'm with the RCMP." He jerked his chin toward his companion on the ground, his eyes never leaving me. "This is Clyde Webb. The man who was in your car was of interest to us. We want to ask you some questions. Don't run away."

I sucked in a trembling breath and studied him more closely, trying to ignore the firearm still pointing at me. My first impression of 'really big guy' hadn't just been frightened exaggeration. He nearly filled the back doorway of the coffee shop.

Short dark hair with a shading of grey at the temples, in a military-looking cut. Well-fitting dark jeans, black T-shirt stretched over wide shoulders and a muscular chest, loose-fitting black jacket open over top. Steady grey eyes never left mine. He stood completely still, no sign of tension in his posture.

"Why should I believe you? Your buddy doesn't look like he could have passed a police physical, and you don't have a uniform or a badge."

He one-handed the gun and reached into his jeans pocket to withdraw a wallet, which he flipped open and held up. "Here's my identification."

"Yeah, right. I can't read it from here, and even if I could, I wouldn't know whether it was real or out of a Crackerjack box."

His expression stayed calm, his deep voice unhurried. "What proof would you like to see? What would make you feel more comfortable?"

My legs quivered uncontrollably. I wasn't going to last much longer. But the more I thought about it, the more I was inclined to believe him. If he'd actually intended to shoot me, he could have done it many times over. And if he was a criminal, he wouldn't be patiently negotiating with me.

But I couldn't afford to be wrong.

"I'd feel a whole lot better if I saw some uniforms. I heard the police cars on the street earlier, so where are they?"

Without turning, he took two steps backward and thumped a couple of times on the door with his fist. "Come on out!"

The door opened and two men in body armour emerged, followed by two uniformed city police officers, their hands hovering near their weapons.

Officer Kane nodded toward his partner, who was still slumped on the ground. "Check on Webb."

One of the uniforms bent over him while the others ranged themselves beside Kane to watch me.

My mind reeled. They called in a SWAT team to chase me?

Shit, I've just assaulted a police officer.

Oh thank God, I'm safe!

My knees gave up and I sat abruptly and heavily on the pavement. Long tremors rolled through my body. I'd left my jacket inside the coffee shop when I fled, and although the temperature was above zero, it was hardly shirtsleeve weather. I wrapped my arms around myself, shaking.

In seconds, Officer Kane was standing over me, patting me, which seemed odd until I realized he was searching me for concealed weapons. The only place I could have hidden one was at my ankles where the legs of my jeans flared, and he briefly examined the gash in my leg before waving one of the uniforms over.

"Bring an ambulance around," he told the man. "Have them look at Webb, too."

A few minutes later, I was sitting in the back of the ambulance, enveloped in a warm blanket while a paramedic treated my ankle. He finished cleaning the wound, which was still sluggishly oozing blood.

"This could use a few stitches," he said. "We can take you in to Emergency now if you want."

"It hardly seems worth it," I responded. "It's just a scratch. I think I must have snagged it on a piece of sharp metal or something."

"You got snagged all right, but this is a gunshot wound. We have to report these, and you were very lucky to get away with such a minor injury."

"Please tell me I don't have to go to Emergency," I begged. "It's a total waste of my time and the hospital's resources. Can't you just patch me up? I'll be making a police report anyway, so that should cover your reporting requirements."

While we talked, the bony Webb had crept to his feet. He insisted on walking to the ambulance under his own power, rejecting the stretcher that had been wheeled over for him. Surrounded by all the machismo in SWAT gear and uniforms, he seemed to feel as though he had something to prove. He stood obstinately outside the vehicle while the paramedic examined him.

A couple of other men in body armour came around the side of the coffee shop, greeting Officer Kane with rough humour. One of them slapped him on the back and said, "Nice to see you've still got your edge after retiring to your cushy INSET job!"

"What part of this looks cushy to you, Archer? I'm out

there getting my ass shot up, and you ERT ladies come prancing in with your body armour once all the shooting's over," Kane groused back without rancour.

I caught Webb's eye. "I'm really sorry," I began. "I was so scared, and I didn't know who you were..."

"It's okay," he interrupted. "I should have identified myself. It was my fault."

Kane had arrived in time to hear the last of the exchange. He closed his eyes briefly and pinched the bridge of his nose. "Webb, I only wanted you to identify yourself. Just say who you were and get her to calm down..."

Webb shuffled his feet, blushing. "I'm sorry. I got so scared I forgot. She was running right at me and I'm no good at physical stuff. I was afraid she was going to kill me."

Kane went still. "No, I'm sorry," he said quietly. "I should never have put you in that position." One of the uniformed officers signalled for his attention and he turned away.

One of the ERT men, Archer, I thought, sidled over. "Shut up, Webb," he said in low tones.

Webb turned a hurt expression to him. "What?"

Archer muttered, "How do you think he feels? Why do you think he's got a skinny, useless analyst for a sidekick instead of real partner?"

Webb evidently took no offence. "That wasn't his fault," he murmured. "Everybody knows Kane is the best of the best. He couldn't have done anything to change what happened."

Archer sighed. "Yeah, try telling him that. So don't rub it in, okay?" They both clammed up as Kane returned.

"Are you finished here?" Officer Kane asked the paramedic.

"Both of them have declined a trip to the hospital."

"Fine," Kane responded. "The other team is doing the cleanup over on the street, so you can head out." He turned to me. "I'd like to take your statement now and ask you some questions."

I made a vague gesture that encompassed Webb along with the uniforms, ambulance, armoured men, and general chaos in the parking lot. "I'm really sorry about all this."

He regarded me gravely. "I don't think you have anything to apologize for at the moment. Let's go and sit in the coffee shop and you can tell me what happened."

Kane, Webb, and I trooped back into the building and appropriated one of the quiet corners. A couple of uniformed city police officers were finishing up with the last of the witnesses, and they waved a casual goodbye to Kane as they left.

Kane sent Webb to get writing materials from their truck, and I tried not to squirm guiltily in my chair while we waited in silence.

CHAPTER 3

What the hell was taking Webb? I shifted in the chair again before forcing myself to lean back and feign composure.

God, what if they arrested me for assaulting a police officer? But dammit, it wasn't my fault I got carjacked by some nutcase. Surely they couldn't blame me for being a little panicky. And my squeaky-clean record had to be good for something. Only one little speeding ticket in my entire life...

Shut up, already.

I shook off my anxious ruminations and straightened as Webb rejoined us, dropping into the chair across from me.

Kane regarded me neutrally as he opened the notebook Webb had brought. "Let's start with your name and address."

I told him my name and spelled it out. "I've been living near Silverside, Alberta since the beginning of the month, but I haven't done my address change from Calgary yet," I added.

At the mention of Silverside, Webb glanced at Kane, his mouth opening. Then he snapped it shut, his gaze returning to me. Kane's face remained expressionless while he wrote down my Silverside and Calgary addresses, along with my phone numbers and other identification.

When I told him my date of birth, Webb's face lit up. "Oh, hey, that's exactly the same as my Mom's! I didn't think you were that old. I mean..." he fumbled, "You look great! I can't imagine my Mom taking somebody out like that. You were like, Madame Rambo or something!"

I winced. "Thanks for that, I think. But Madame Rambo sounds a little too much like a 1-900 number for my taste."

Webb turned pink and I thought I caught a glint of amusement in Kane's eyes, but it passed too quickly to be sure. Kane brought us back to the business at hand by asking for a chronological list of events.

"You were right behind me, so I think you saw most of it," I told him. "That guy was hiding in my trunk, and he came through the back seat with a gun in his hand. I slammed on the brakes and jumped out, and that's when you arrived. But I don't know how he got in there, because I bought some stuff at the hardware store earlier and put my bags in the trunk. He wasn't in there then. And I went straight to my house after the store."

I pondered that for a moment. "So he must have sneaked in while I was inside the house."

"Yes," Kane confirmed. "We've had him under surveillance since Friday afternoon."

"What!" I squawked. "You watched him crawl into my trunk and you didn't *do* anything?"

"We've been watching him for several months now, both here and in Silverside. His name was Samir Ramos. We suspected him of espionage, but we couldn't find solid proof. We thought you might be his contact. We were a little surprised when you jumped out of the car."

I opened my mouth, but nothing came out. Deciding that open-mouthed gawping was probably not an attractive look for me, I closed it and sat for a few seconds, assimilating this new information.

"But," I said, and then shut up, trying to organize my thoughts.

"Okay," I tried again. "So you and Officer Webb are working on a case, and you think this Samir guy is a spy?"

Webb let out a whoop of laughter. "*Officer* Webb! I like the sound of that!"

At my look of utter bafflement, Kane explained. "Webb is a civilian. He's an analyst with CSIS."

He must have noticed my unenlightened look, because he went on to explain, "CSIS stands for Canadian Security Intelligence Service. Their role is to protect Canada's national security. Webb and I are part of an INSET team. INSET stands for Integrated National Security Enforcement Teams, and our role is counterterrorism. We believe that Ramos was attempting to steal classified information and deliver it to a terrorist group."

Webb spoke up again. "So I'm not 'Officer' anything, just plain old Clyde Webb. But you can call me Spider. All my friends do. Get it? Spider Webb!"

I smiled and nodded. Quite apart from the wordplay on his name, his lanky arms and legs did make him look spiderish. "Got it." I turned back to Kane, still trying to figure it all out. "But you're RCMP?"

"Yes, INSET teams can be made up of police, military, and civilian members."

"Okay... So who were the other acronyms?"

He raised an inquiring eyebrow.

"You said ERT earlier, I think?"

"Yes. ERT stands for Emergency Response Team. It's Canada's answer to SWAT."

I rubbed my aching temples. Already I'd forgotten what INSET meant. I moved on. "So back to the spy. Were you able to catch him, or did he get away? Can you question him? Why was he trying to shoot *me*?"

"We'd very much like to know why he was trying to shoot you. Or, more likely, capture you. If he'd wanted to kill you, he would have shot you as soon as you got into your car."

I shuddered. Which was worse, a bullet in the brain, or being captured by a creepy spy for purposes unknown?

"Unfortunately," Kane continued, "We can't question him because I killed him. There were too many bystanders in the vicinity, and I couldn't let him keep shooting."

Oh. I flashed back to Kane's comment to the paramedic about doing the cleanup on the street. Wet cleanup on Aisle 3. Eeuw.

I wrenched my mind away from the inappropriate humour when I realized Kane had asked me another question. "Sorry, what?"

"Did you know Ramos? Have you ever seen him before?"

"Uh," I said, my mind working furiously.

Yes, Officer Kane, I met him in a steamy fantasy. Bad, bad answer, on so many levels.

"I think... I saw him in Silverside," I ventured.

"When and where do you think you saw him?"

"It's... a little confusing."

Kane was watching me intently, and it took all my self-control to keep my eyes from shifting away from his steady gaze. Lying was probably a very bad idea, but telling the truth would make me sound at best, like a crackpot, and at worst, like a pathetic slut.

Hell, my fantasies were nobody's business but my own. I went with simple, true, and incomplete.

"I slipped and hit my head. I guess I was knocked out for a while. I think I saw him about the time the paramedics arrived."

"Exactly where and when was this?"

"Thursday. Around 12:30 in the afternoon. I slipped on the sidewalk in front of the ice cream shop on Main Street."

"So there should have been a few witnesses," Kane said.

"Um, I don't know. Maybe the paramedic saw him."

The paramedic sure as hell did see him, but I'd be damned if I knew how. How did he get inside my head, anyway?

"Maybe I hallucinated the whole thing," I added. "I was a little disoriented."

"Are you sure the man in your car today was the same one you saw in Silverside?"

"I... think so. But that wouldn't make any sense. If I saw him in Silverside, how could he possibly show up at my house here in Calgary? It's not like he would have had my name and address."

...Because I'd been too busy sucking face with him to exchange names...

Gah. Focus.

Kane exhaled wearily. "I'm sorry to ask you this, but will you look at the body and see if you can be positive about whether it's the same man?"

My stomach lurched, but I nodded. Looking at dead people wasn't high on my list of favourite activities. And I didn't think I was going to like seeing somebody freshly dead from a gunshot wound.

"I'm going to have to eat first, though," I said.

Webb spoke up. "You may want to wait until after we visit the medical examiner's office."

"No, I'll definitely want a full stomach."

Both of them regarded me doubtfully. "Okay, whatever you say," Webb replied.

"When should I go? And where's the morgue? Oh, and I forgot to ask, what about my car? Were you able to get it stopped before anybody got hurt? Where is it?"

"Ramos had to stop it before he could get out and start shooting," Kane responded. "Leaving it in gear probably saved your life. The car will be impounded until our team gets a chance to check it for possible clues, but that should only take a few days. Your insurance may cover the repairs."

I felt the blood drain from my face. "Repairs? How bad?"

My poor little car.

"Just a couple of bullet holes. You can ride with us to the medical examiner's office, and then we'll call you a cab to get back to your house."

Just a couple of bullet holes. Bullet holes were not minor in my world. I faked calm.

"Okay. I'll grab a sandwich and a drink to go and eat them on the way, if you don't mind me eating in your truck."

Kane shrugged. "It's a surveillance vehicle. It's already full of fast-food wrappers."

I rose to go to the sales counter and stopped as a thought hit me. "Oh, crap! I forgot, all my overnight stuff is in the car. I have nothing at the house. Can I get my backpack out of the car, or is that impounded, too?"

"It's part of a crime scene, so technically it should stay. But you can get a few things if I supervise and catalogue their removal," Kane replied.

"Good, that'll work."

Lucky I'd worn my waist pouch as usual. Someday the fashion police were going to take me down for wearing it in public, but it was convenient and impossible to leave behind. I might not be stylish, but at least I still had all my money, credit cards, and other essentials despite my wild flight.

I paid for my food, and we left the coffee shop to head toward the cordoned area in the street. The ambulance had departed, but there were still two police cruisers and a fire truck parked in the street along with Kane's Suburban and my Saturn. As we approached, a television van drove away, and I thanked my lucky stars they'd given up moments too soon. I could imagine the TV reporter slavering over an interview with a carjacking victim.

I glanced up at Kane pacing beside me. He had to be at least six-foot-four. It was unusual for me to have to look up at anybody, and it was a nice change. He noticed my glance and returned a questioning look.

"I was wondering about the media coverage," I explained. "How did you get rid of them without a whole round of interviews?"

"Part of the clean-up crew's job is to deal with media questions. Tonight on the news, they'll report that there was a shooting this afternoon, and that it was probably drug-related. That keeps the public calm, thinking it can't happen to them. In a couple of days, it will be old news."

"Drug-related? Jeez, I hope nobody recognizes my car."

Kane flashed his ID at the uniformed officer and lifted the police tape for Webb and me to duck under. Webb winced when he folded his skinny torso, and I offered him another repentant 'sorry'. He waved a magnanimous hand.

When we arrived at my car, I sadly regarded the bullet

hole in the trunk. With the white topcoat cracked away and the grey primer showing underneath, it looked very much like the gunshot decals the kids put on their cars to look cool. I wasn't feeling very cool at all.

I brushed my fingers over the hole and murmured, "Poor little car."

Realizing Kane and Webb were watching me, I reached into my waist pouch for my keys and encountered empty space in their usual pocket. "Oh, my keys are still in the ignition."

Kane strode to the open driver's door and reached in around the steering wheel. I started to follow him, but jerked to a halt when I noticed the ugly splatter at the top of the rear passenger door and over the roof. I looked away quickly. Maybe their evidence team would clean it off.

Kane handed over my loaded keychain, and Webb raised amused eyebrows. "How many keys do you need, anyway?"

"All of them. Believe it or not, I actually know what each of those keys is for. My friends call it the janitor's set."

"I know janitors that don't even have that many keys," he chuckled as I unlocked the trunk.

Before I could touch anything, Kane reached in and retrieved my small backpack. "Is this it?"

I nodded, and he opened the zipper. "Tell me what you need from this," he said as he began to withdraw items and lay them out in the trunk.

"I'll need everything in there," I blurted, hoping to forestall the unpacking process.

He continued without comment, and I felt a blush spreading up my face when he pulled out my bright yellow thong underwear. Webb strolled away with heavy nonchalance, his face scarlet.

Yeah, that was probably more than he wanted to know about me.

As Kane extracted the matching yellow bra, I took myself in hand. Dammit, I was pushing fifty. Surely I was past adolescent simpering over my undies. Kane's face showed nothing but professional detachment, so I stood a little taller and watched in silence while he completely unpacked my few items from the backpack and checked the pack itself over thoroughly.

He laid the pack in the trunk before taking a small camera out of his inside pocket to photograph the trunk and its contents. He made a note in his notebook, then methodically repacked the bag and handed it to me.

"What's in these other bags?" he asked.

"Oh, just my winter survival gear," I responded, glancing at their familiar lumpy bulk. "I always take it when I'm driving the highway. You know how fast the weather can change around here in March."

As I eyed the bags, a dark spot on one of them caught my eye. No, it was a hole.

"Oh, no," I said as I reached in before Kane could stop me. I gazed up at him. "You killed my sleeping bag."

CHAPTER 4

When we got into the battered Suburban, Webb offered me the front passenger seat while he got in behind. I'd noticed a couple of bullet holes in the driver's side of the truck, but apparently nothing vital had been hit. Kane pulled smoothly into traffic and we headed north.

I devoured my sandwich while Kane drove in silence and Webb chattered incessantly from the rear seat. In short order, I discovered he had two older sisters, still lived with his parents, had a computer science degree, and was a fan of World of Warcraft and Star Trek.

"You like the new Star Trek best, I suppose?" I asked.

"No, I love them all. The original ones are the best," he enthused. "Besides, you can't get all the in-jokes in the new movie unless you've seen the originals."

"I can't believe you're into a show that started, what, twenty years before you were born?"

"I'm a serious movie and TV buff," he replied proudly. "I watch everything."

We spent the rest of the short drive debating the merits of the latest Star Trek movie. When we arrived at our destination, Webb grew increasingly subdued while we waited for the medical examiner in the reception area. When the examiner arrived and we began the walk down the long hallway, silence reigned.

I swallowed nervousness. Death didn't disturb me and I'd never been squeamish, but I hoped I didn't throw up or pass out. That would be an embarrassing show of weakness.

The medical examiner led us into a room containing a drape-covered gurney. Kane glanced at Webb's pale face.

"You stand over here by the door," he said. "I've already got your puke on my pants; I don't need any more of it."

I glanced reflexively at Kane's legs, and sure enough, there was a splatter on his right shoe and pant leg. I averted my eyes. Didn't need to see that just now.

Kane took me gently by the arm and the medical examiner led us to the gurney. "Ready?" he asked.

I nodded, and the examiner lifted the sheet away from the dead man's face.

Clearly, Kane was an excellent marksman. There was a neat dark hole in the forehead. There was very little blood on the face, but I was glad I couldn't see the back of the head. I'd seen what a .22 bullet would do to a two-by-four as it went through. Tiny entry hole, total devastation on exit. Kane had said his gun was a .40 calibre. I really didn't want to see the exit wound.

Holding onto composure, I concentrated on the face, trying to see it as it would have been in life. I'd only seen Beefcake for a short time, and I hadn't been paying much attention to his face. And death changes even your dearest loved ones into remote strangers.

"I'm pretty sure it's the same guy," I said as I turned away from the table.

Kane's hand was still under my elbow. He came around in front of me without letting go of my arm and looked down into my face. "Are you all right? Do you need to sit down?"

I shook my head. "I'm fine," I lied.

A tremulous voice floated from the vicinity of the doorway. "I think... I might need to sit down."

We turned to see Webb propped against the wall. His pale face had taken on an unflattering greenish cast, tastefully highlighted with a sheen of sweat.

Kane let go of me and grabbed a handful of Spider's shirt, lifting and swivelling him into a chair. He shoved Webb's head down between his bony knees and held him in place with a hand on the back of the young man's neck.

"Breathe," Kane said. "Slow and easy. That's it."

I turned to the medical examiner, who had by now mercifully covered the damaged face on the gurney. "Could we get him a glass of water?"

He nodded and wheeled the gurney out of the room. By the time he returned a minute or two later, Webb was sitting up again, and he sipped shakily at the water.

"Are you going to be okay now?" I asked, and he nodded and rose tentatively from the chair. I noticed Kane didn't put a hand out to steady him. I guessed it was a guy thing. Besides, Kane had moved remarkably fast for such a big man. He could probably catch Webb before he hit the ground if necessary.

It seemed Spider was sufficiently recovered, though, and we proceeded uneventfully back to the reception area. When we arrived, Kane sprawled into one of the chairs in the deserted room, indicating with a wave of his hand that we should do the same. Webb and I sank into chairs of our own.

"Let's talk this back," Kane said, and I wondered if he was being considerate, tactfully allowing us to recover without fuss, or whether this was just for his own convenience.

Kane turned to me. "You're reasonably sure this is the same man you saw in Silverside."

"Yes."

"How could you... How could you just *look* at him like that?" Spider burst out, apparently still reliving the grisly vision. "Like he was a... a... piece of meat in the supermarket."

"He *is* just a piece of meat now," I replied as gently as I could. "There's nobody left inside. Whoever he was, he isn't in there anymore. Besides," I added, mostly to myself, "It's not the worst thing I ever saw."

The memory of tortured screams echoed again in my mind. I shook my head slightly and banished the ghost with the competence of long practice.

Returning to the present, I realized something must have shown on my face. Webb was staring at me, and Kane was frowning subtly. Why the hell had I said that out loud?

Kane apparently decided to let it go. "So when you saw Ramos in Silverside, was that the first time you'd ever seen him?"

"Yes."

"So Ramos sees you, once, in Silverside, on Thursday. Instead of tracking you down in Silverside, where he saw you, he travels two hours to Calgary to stake out an empty house with a For Sale sign on it."

I shrugged. "I don't get it either. First, how would he know who I was, and second, if he did know who I was, why would he come to Calgary instead of Silverside, and third, why the heck would he want to find me anyway?"

I could think of one reason, but I was pretty sure that hadn't been lust in his eyes.

"Oh, and fourth," I added. "How did he know I was going to show up at an empty house at all?"

"That one's easy," Kane replied. "See a For Sale sign, call a realtor."

"That makes sense." I sat up straighter. "My realtor called me and said she had a hot prospect who wanted to meet me in person. We both thought it was unusual, but she set up the appointment – and then the guy never showed."

"He showed, all right," Kane said. "You just didn't see him until it was too late."

Webb chimed in, "But it still doesn't make sense to lure you down here. Unless... he was planning to kidnap you and take you somewhere in Calgary."

My skin crawled at the thought. "Maybe he was just some nutso stalker, and it has nothing to do with your case at all," I said. "But that still doesn't explain why he would lure me here instead of just snatching me in Silverside. And anyway, that brings us back to... how did he find out who I am?"

"Think back," Kane urged. "Was your name ever mentioned in his presence? Could he have asked somebody your name and looked you up? You said you hadn't completed all your address changes yet."

That rang a faint bell. I sat still, trying to sneak up on the thought. Who had I discussed address changes with recently?

"No. Crap. Not that I can think of. The only place I've given my name and address recently was at the Silverside Hospital, and they wouldn't give that record out to anybody."

"You saw Ramos for the first time around twelve thirty on Thursday. You were admitted to the hospital on Thursday afternoon, correct?"

I nodded and Kane continued his analysis. "Ramos must have discovered your name and address sometime between Thursday afternoon and early Friday morning, because he left Silverside around eight AM Friday morning. That's when we started following him." He shook his head. "The hospital records are still the most likely source of his information. Records confidentiality wouldn't stop a spy."

"Oh!" I bolted upright. Kane and Webb both sat up fast.

"What?" Kane snapped.

"You're right, it had to be the hospital records! I just remembered the Silverside hospital had my Calgary address. They took it off my driver's license, and I forgot to tell them it had changed."

Kane relaxed back into his chair. "Okay, so now we know when and how. Which leaves us with why. Think. Did he do or say anything to give you a clue?"

My guilty conscience twinged again. I hate lying. The few times I've told white lies, the consequences turned out to be worse than if I'd told the awkward truth in the first place.

Well, too late now. I took a deep breath.

"Like I said earlier, I was pretty confused. It might help to talk to the paramedic who attended me, though. Maybe he saw or heard something."

Or more likely, he'd look at me like I was crazy and ask what man I was talking about.

"Do you know the name of the paramedic?" Kane asked.

"No, I haven't got a clue, but he shouldn't be hard to track down in a town that size. I'd like to talk to him, too. Just to find out what really happened."

Kane eyed me, apparently considering. "I think that's a good idea. Can you be ready to leave for Silverside tomorrow morning? Your car won't be released yet, but we're going up anyway, so you can ride with us."

"Okay, that sounds fine," I lied again.

Two hours of driving, cooped up in a car with strangers. Not fine.

"We'll pick you up at your house at nine o'clock tomorrow morning. If you think of anything else in the mean time, please give me a call." He scribbled a phone number on one of his notebook pages and tore it out to hand it to me.

"Um... do you think I should be concerned about staying at the house tonight?"

Kane regarded me solemnly. "If you feel uncomfortable, by all means go and stay with a friend, or have someone stay with you. If you see or hear anything that makes you nervous, call the city police non-emergency line, and if you feel you're in danger, call 911 immediately. Don't hesitate. Better to have a false alarm than to not call in something potentially serious."

"Okay, thanks," I replied, not significantly reassured. He hadn't exactly answered my question.

"One more thing," he added. "Since we're not sure whether there's a connection between our investigation and your run-in with Ramos, please don't mention details to anyone. If you have to discuss it, you can tell people that you were carjacked and the police are working on it, but leave out any mention of INSET and spies."

I shuddered. I didn't even want to think about INSET and spies.

CHAPTER 5

I willed myself not to shriek and lunge for the wheel when the cab driver turned yet again to make eye contact with me in the back seat, waving both hands and driving with his knee while he delivered a philosophical monologue.

By the time I stumbled out of the taxi and paid the driver to go away, it was all I could do not to collapse into a blob of quivering jelly in my driveway.

The wound in my leg throbbed, my head seemed trapped in a slowly-tightening vise, and every single muscle I owned ached. In fact, I was willing to swear I had brand-new, previously-undiscovered muscles that were also aching.

I dragged myself up the front steps and let myself in the door, automatically going to the security panel. I had almost finished punching in my code before I realized the panel wasn't beeping with my keystrokes, and all the lights were dark.

Dead.

"Nooooooooo," I whined.

I shuffled to the phone, half-expecting no dial tone, but it buzzed reassuringly when I picked up the receiver. I paced while the security company's on-hold music abraded my already-raw nerves.

Dammit, could this day get any worse? First some wacko tries to abduct me at gunpoint and then my security system mysteriously packs it in. By the time the dispatcher answered, I had switched to yoga belly breathing, willing calm.

"When can you have someone come out and look at this?" I asked anxiously after explaining the situation.

"Our techs go off duty at six o'clock."

I glanced at my watch. Seven-ten. Shit.

"We could have someone there at nine o'clock tomorrow morning."

"I'm leaving at nine o'clock tomorrow morning. I really need this fixed now. Is there anybody there who can help me?" I begged.

"'We'll do the best we can for you tomorrow morning," he assured me. "But we just don't have anyone available now."

Translation: You are completely hooped.

I said goodbye and hung up in despair. Maybe I should go to a hotel.

But even a cheap hotel by Calgary standards would strain my budget. I could stay with a friend, as Kane had suggested, but the thought of all the explanations and exclamations made my head ache even more fiercely. I'd had more than enough human contact for one day.

I jittered back and forth in the echoing living room. With the walkout basement and three glass-panelled exterior doors on two levels, the place was a security nightmare. I didn't even have my crowbar with me. I wouldn't sleep a wink without some kind of warning system.

I blew out a long sigh and locked the door behind me before forcing my protesting muscles into a semblance of a brisk walk to the nearby dollar store.

Characteristically, I realized as I arrived that I was still wearing my bloodstained jeans and sneakers. I endured looks that ranged from curiosity to alarm, and bought tape, string, pins, and some cheap tins.

Trudging back into the house, I set up a booby trap inside each exterior door, feeling foolish. On the latch side, I stuck a pin between the trim board and the wall. I taped several tins onto the end of a short length of string and tied the free end of the string to the doorknob. Supported only by the sagging pin, the tins would slide off and clatter against the door at the slightest movement. I hoped it would be enough to wake me.

As I considered it, I threw in a hope that the pin wouldn't let go on its own in the middle of the night. I'd probably have a heart attack if it did.

I double-checked all the deadbolts on the doors and windows before stiffly climbing the stairs to the master bedroom. It had a privacy lock on the door, so I locked that behind me. It wouldn't stop anybody, but it might buy me a few seconds in a pinch.

Lying in bed, my eyes refused to close despite my best relaxation exercises. At last, I blew out a tense breath and rolled off the bed to get dressed again. After a few moments of thought, I removed the window screen and disengaged the crank mechanism, just in case I needed to make a quick exit.

I gazed down at the long drop to the back yard. If I had to go out the window, I'd have to be careful to go over the tiny section of roof that projected out from the bay window directly below me. It slanted toward the deck, so it was only an eight-foot drop. I thought it would be doable if I slithered over and clung to the rain gutter to break my fall.

I felt increasingly ridiculous as I made my elaborate plans, but hell, I'm a bookkeeper. We tend to get anal about details.

I rehearsed my plan while I changed into my black yoga pants and a T-shirt and pulled my baggy navy blue hooded sweatshirt over top. I surveyed my bloodstained jeans and shoe irritably. I needed the shoe. At least it wasn't squishy anymore. The jeans were ruined. Dammit, that was exactly why I wore crappy clothes most of the time.

Granted, I didn't usually ruin my good clothes by getting shot and bleeding all over them. That was a first.

I threw the jeans in the garbage and put the shoes back on with clean socks underneath. It wouldn't be the most comfortable sleep I ever had, but if I had to run or fight, I'd be ready.

"This is stupid!" I said aloud. "Why didn't I just go to a hotel?"

Nobody supplied any useful answer, so I sighed and lay down again.

The faint clanking of tin woke me from a fitful doze. I was wide awake and rolling off the bed before the sound ceased. I snatched up my backpack and dove for the window, my stiffened muscles screaming in protest.

As I lunged out the window onto the roof, heavy footsteps pounded across the floor below me. Slinging my pack on my back, I flopped onto my stomach and slid feet first over the edge of the roof. As I slithered by, I caught the rain gutter with a wild one-handed grab, throwing myself completely off balance. With a wrenching squeal, the eavestrough pulled loose from the house. I dropped onto the deck below and landed hard on one foot before falling on my butt.

"Shit, shit, shit!"

I scrambled up and dashed across the deck. Frantically blessing my long legs, I hopped over the deck railing onto the shed roof, then down onto the top rail of the fence. I dropped to the ground and scuttled across the front of my neighbour's house, concealed by her tall hedge.

As I turned the corner, the sound of my outside door opening triggered a fresh burst of fear. I cut across the neighbouring tree-filled yard as stealthily as I could on shaking legs, trying to stifle my panting.

In the corner of the yard, I hoisted myself over the back fence and into the unlit strip of parkland that wound through the neighbourhood. I flew along the path, heart hammering, and dodged around the first turn. Trying to pant silently, I flattened myself against someone's back fence to listen for sounds of pursuit.

Nothing.

Squatting down in the deepest puddle of shadow near some shrubs, I pulled my cell phone from my backpack to dial 911, my shaking fingers fumbling at the tiny buttons. When the display illuminated, I discovered a serious flaw in my planning. My cell phone battery was almost dead.

Dammit!

As soon as the police dispatcher answered, I babbled my address and told him that someone had broken in.

"Get out of the house!" the dispatcher barked. "Get out immediately!"

"I'm already out of the house," I whispered. "I'm calling from my cell phone, and the battery is about to die."

"Stay with me on your cell phone," he commanded. "Go

to a neighbour's house and call me from a land line as soon as you get there."

I was about to agree when it occurred to me that if I was being stalked by spies and/or nutcases, there was no way I wanted to involve some innocent bystander. And I had to talk to Officer Kane before I talked to the city police.

And the thought of getting cornered inside a strange house made my skin crawl.

"I can't do that." My voice shook with the beat of my heart. "I'll wait until I hear the police sirens, and then I'll go back to my house."

The dispatcher argued forcefully and tried to keep me on the line, but I remained adamant, told him my battery was dying, and hung up. I spared the poor man a pang of guilty sympathy as I imagined him cursing my idiocy, but I didn't feel guilty enough to do as he'd told me.

Straining my ears and scanning warily, I still couldn't detect anyone trailing me, but I moved on anyway, vibrating with tension.

I hugged the fence and shrubbery, getting further away from my original location. I hadn't heard any police sirens yet. I hunkered down behind some bushes and brought up Kane's number.

God, please let it be a manned message centre, and please let somebody be there at... I squinted at my phone's display. Shit, three o'clock in the morning.

The phone rang once before a deep voice snapped, "Kane."

Oops. I hadn't realized it was his personal number. He sounded alert, but judging by the raspy edge to his baritone, the phone had awakened him.

Any other time I would have taken a moment to

appreciate that sexy bedroom voice. Hell, who was I kidding? I appreciated it anyway. You know it's time to get laid when you start calling guys at three o'clock in the morning just to hear a husky voice.

I herded my strung-out brain back to the situation at hand. "Officer Kane, it's Aydan Kelly calling. I'm so sorry to bother you at this time of night. But somebody has broken into my house and-"

"Get out of the house!" Kane interrupted. "Get out now! Go!"

"That was the first thing I did," I reassured him. "I'm on my cell phone."

"Hang up and call 911."

"Already did that, too. The police should be on their way to my house now." I heard a surge of noise in the background at Kane's end, and realized that he had turned on a police scanner to track their progress.

"Go to the nearest house and knock on the door. Tell them you have an emergency, and call the 911 dispatcher on their land line."

"I don't want to do that," I argued. "If this is related to the carjacking this afternoon and you say this guy, what's-his-name, Ramos, was a spy, then I could be putting innocent people in danger if I go to their house in the middle of the night."

I didn't add that I felt safer outside where I could run. Claustrophobia isn't exactly a logical argument.

"If you stay on the street, you're a sitting duck," he snapped. "Go to a house, now!"

"That's not going to happen, Officer Kane. I told the 911 operator I'd meet the police at my house. My battery is about to die, so that's what I'm going to do."

"No! Do not approach your house! Dammit!" I heard him take a deep breath. When he spoke again, his voice was even. "If you go near your house, you're in danger if the intruder is still in the vicinity, and you're making the officers' jobs much more difficult. Also, if we're dealing with organized criminals, they could be listening in on your call or using your cell phone signal to track you."

A wave of dread washed over me. I peered wildly into the darkness, straining my eyes and ears.

"If you won't go to a neighbour's house," he paused hopefully, and when I didn't respond, he continued, "I want you to listen to my instructions, and then leave your phone where you are. Meet me... where you ran through the spider web. Got it?"

My mind raced. Spider web? What?

Spider. Web.

Oh! Spider Webb. Where I ran through the Spider Webb. That would be the back of the coffee shop.

"Got it."

"Turn off your phone. Throw it away. Run. Do it now!"

"Roger that," I said smartly. I turned off the phone, pitched it under a bush, and ran down the path as quietly as I could.

CHAPTER 6

I zigzagged through the park until I was close to another neighbourhood access path. Dodging into the cover of a copse of trees, I hunched over, gasping and trembling.

How long would it take Kane to get to our meeting place? I had covered a lot of ground, and I'd been veering gradually toward my destination. I was only about five minutes away if I took a direct route.

I was soaked with sweat, and by the time I'd caught my breath, I couldn't tell whether my shivering was from fear or the chilly wind. I delved into my backpack for my old, baggy jeans and pulled them on over my yoga pants. My winter coat was still back at the house, but I pulled the hood of my fleecy jacket over my head and moved out into the well-lit residential street.

Setting a leisurely course for the coffee shop, I kept my head down to hide my face and adopted a slouching swagger. With the baggy pants and hoodie, I hoped to pass for a skinny teenage boy returning from a late-night party. With any luck, my intruder would be looking for a woman with long red hair walking fearfully through the streets.

The residential area was silent and deserted, but a few cars moved on the streets as I approached the small strip mall that housed the coffee shop. The roar of a Harley split the night. Some biker must be enjoying the ice-free roads and chinook temperatures.

A few minutes later, I slouched against a light pole within sight of the parking lot to scan for Kane's beat-up Suburban.

No luck. The only vehicle in the lot was the Harley propped on its kickstand, its beefy rider leaning against it. The tip of his cigarette glowed as he sucked in smoke. When I circled closer, I could just make out the lettering on the back of his leathers: 'Hellhound', accompanied by a large illustration of a snarling black beast. The orange of the streetlights made its red eyes glow with life-like savagery.

Great, just great.

I wandered across the street, moving closer to the parking lot and ignoring its leather-clad occupant. The cluster of newspaper vending machines on the boulevard seemed like my best bet, close to the parking lot but somewhat concealed from the street.

I meandered over and lowered myself to the cold ground behind the machines, leaning my back against one of them and facing the parking lot. The biker glanced my way, but I dropped my head to dig in my backpack, coming up with a cereal bar. I tore off the wrapper and chowed down, resting my elbows on my drawn-up knees and keeping my head hanging to hide my face.

Just a drunk kid hanging out. Nothing to see here.

Booted footsteps approached, and I caught a whiff of cigarette smoke.

Shit.

The boots stopped inside my peripheral vision, but I didn't look up as I stuffed the last of the cereal bar in my mouth.

A rough whiskey voice rasped, "Get the fuck outta here, kid."

I slouched to my feet and turned away, still hiding my face. In my best sullen-teenager voice, I mumbled, "Yeah, man, whatever," somewhat muffled by the last of the cereal bar.

A violent shove to my back sent me stumbling away. "I got shit goin' down here," the biker growled. "Fuck off before I kick your fuckin' scrawny little ass to hell."

"Okay, chill, dude!" I whined, and beat it down the sidewalk fast, head down.

That was all I needed. What were the chances this loser would pick this exact spot for his drug deal?

On the up side, my disguise seemed to be effective. People see what they expect to see. Nobody expects a middle-aged woman to hang out in a parking lot at three A.M. Or so I hoped.

That put a serious crimp in my plans. As I turned the corner, I chanced a quick glance back at the biker. He had resumed his position, and I realized he had chosen his vantage point as carefully as I had chosen mine. He had a clear view of the entire parking lot, including all the driveways and access points.

Shit, shit, shit!

What would Kane do when he arrived and realized what was happening? If this was a bike gang dealing drugs, things could get ugly fast. I had to find a spot where I had a clear view of the back door of the coffee shop, but was invisible to the biker. Then if Kane drove up and decided not to stay, maybe I could signal him and follow him to a new meeting place.

I strolled across in front of the coffee shop, making sure I was in plain sight as I walked away. As soon as the buildings blocked the biker's view, I turned the corner again to get at the back of the other wing of the L-shaped mall. There was a space between two of the buildings, probably a loading dock. I should be able to sneak in there undetected.

All I had to do was get over the eight-foot-high stucco wall.

I smothered a groan and surveyed it with a decided lack of enthusiasm, rubbing my stiffening legs with shaking hands. Limping closer, I eyed the pillars that decorated the wall. Each pillar had a projecting base at the bottom. If I stood on the base and hopped from there, I should be able to catch hold of the top of the wall where it met the pillar.

I managed the jump, banging my kneecap painfully in the process. The stucco scraped my skin but at least its deep texture provided a secure handhold. I hauled myself upward, scrabbling up the wall with my feet. At the top, I squirmed around until I was hanging by my midsection, my feet on the mall side. Slithering down, I clung to the stucco with sore fingers until my arms were fully extended.

The ground sloped away from the wall on the inside, and I lost my balance when I landed on the short grade. I rolled and tumbled onto the paved laneway behind the mall, trying to bruise as quietly as possible and clenching my teeth on the profanity that begged for utterance.

Whose goddamn stupid idea was this, anyway? To hell with altruism; next time I was going to do just as the nice policeman told me and go to a neighbour's house.

I picked myself up and hurried for the gap in the buildings. Sure enough, I had a clear view of the back of the coffee shop, but I couldn't see much of the rest of the parking lot.

Had Kane arrived? I skulked toward the opening. I still couldn't see much. If I went any closer to the parking lot, there was a good chance the biker would see me, if he was still there. I hadn't heard any other motorcycles, so I suspected he was.

I peeked out of the gap, scanning the empty parking lot. The big biker was still leaning against his Harley. He made no move or outcry, so I assumed he hadn't seen me.

I blew out a short breath between chattering teeth. Nothing to do but wait.

I withdrew into the shadows again, watching the coffee shop.

Come on, Kane. Hurry up, for chrissake.

Minutes dragged past while I shifted from foot to foot, trying to still my shivering with both arms wrapped tightly around myself. I hissed impatience, rubbing my goosebumps.

Maybe he'd arrived and I couldn't see him from where I was standing.

As I leaned toward the gap again, a vicious grip clamped onto my neck and nearly wrenched my head off with a hard jerk backward. The impact of my back against the building knocked my hood off and left me momentarily breathless.

The beefy biker's fist was already on its way to my face. In the fraction of a second I had left, I registered a leather skullcap on a shaved head and a ferociously scowling pockmarked face largely obscured by a grizzled beard and moustache.

The punch never landed. Instead, his expression changed to astonishment. The flat of his hand hit the wall beside my head with a smack, bringing his ugly face too close to mine.

His full beard split in a grin, revealing incongruously white, even teeth. "Well, hell-lo pretty lady," he breathed. "Ya must be Aydan."

His grip loosened, but he didn't let go while he reached into his pocket to extract a cell phone. Punching a speed dial button, he waited a moment before rasping, "Got her."

CHAPTER 7

One of his hands was occupied with the phone and his attention was divided by the call. I wouldn't get a better chance.

I grabbed his wrist with both hands and lunged forward, diving between his arm and his body and turning toward the parking lot. As his arm bent behind him, he lost his grip on my shoulder. He let out a startled shout that turned into a grunt when I jerked his arm up behind him and slammed all my weight into the small of his back. Letting go as he bounced off the wall, I dashed for the parking lot, my trembling legs barely cooperating.

Only a few strides later, pain and adrenaline slammed through me when a powerful grip on my wrist yanked me to a halt. I jerked and twisted, but it was futile. That arm might as well be caught in a bear trap.

He shouted, "Wait! Stop! I..."

I gave another titanic jerk away from him. As I'd expected, he responded by yanking me back. Instead of resisting, I borrowed his momentum to twist and step hard toward him, creating maximum force for the fist I'd aimed at his throat.

His eyes widened as he recognized my ploy and at the

last second he dropped his chin and threw up his other arm to deflect my punch. He was partly successful, and my knuckles struck his chin hard before hitting his Adam's apple. The jolt of pain as my fist hit bone made me yell and spontaneously kick out. My foot thudded into his knee, and he finally let go of my wrist as he dropped, both hands going to his throat.

I wheeled and ran for the parking lot.

Two strides later, I crashed into an unyielding wall of chest. I rebounded away, but powerful arms locked around me, pinning my arms to my sides.

And I lost it.

Blind rage flooded me, and I threw back my head in a berserk roar. My captor started, his grip loosening. I bent my knees to drop my body and flung my arms up with all my strength. The restraining grip fell away, and I lunged past his legs. Tripped over his foot. Tucked and rolled on the hard pavement.

As I scrambled to my feet, I heard Officer Kane's welcome shout, "Stop, police!"

I froze in my defensive crouch, panting like a steam engine, fists clenched. My blurred vision slowly cleared, and I realized to my chagrin that it was Kane himself who'd grabbed me.

His gun was in his hand, but it wasn't pointed at me. That was a nice change. He wasn't pointing it at the recovering biker, either. In fact, he didn't seem to know where to point it. His gaze snapped around the parking lot and alleyway.

The biker struggled up onto one knee. He coughed a couple of times and then croaked, "'Bout time ya got here, Cap. I was gettin' my ass kicked."

CHAPTER 8

I rounded on Kane, anger and adrenaline boiling in my veins. "Don't tell me this is another one of your... your... minions!" My fists jerked at my sides, all ready to fight and nobody to hit.

Kane eyed the man on the ground. "If you were getting your ass kicked, Hellhound, I'm sure you richly deserved it." He turned to me. In what I was beginning to recognize as his 'Everybody Calm Down' cop voice, he said, "Aydan, tell me what happened."

"I... He..." I was still too furious to speak coherently. I breathed deeply, forcing myself into yoga belly breathing.

In, out, slow like ocean waves.

I gradually unclenched my fists, flexing my fingers and admiring the slow ooze of blood welling up from the torn skin on my right knuckle. Kane waited in patient silence. Smart man.

Finally, I got my temper under control. "I came out through the park to the north," I began, realizing with discomfiture that my voice was shaking. I hoped he didn't think I was about to burst into tears. Nothing could be further from the truth. I still needed to hit somebody. Hard.

I drew another breath, steadying my voice. "I checked

out the parking lot, but I didn't see you, so I decided to wait."
I nodded toward the biker, who had regained his feet to limp
back and forth as if trying to get his knee working again. "He
was waiting, too, I guess. I sat down behind those vending
machines." I stabbed a finger in the direction of the
machines on the boulevard. "He ran me off from there."

"Ran you off?" Kane interjected.

"Shoved me down the street and offered to kick my ass to
hell."

Kane glowered at the biker.

"Ya said there might be some bad shit goin' down,"
Hellhound protested. "I saw this kid hangin' out, an' I didn't
wanna take a chance on civilian casualties, so I ran him off."

Kane gave him an incredulous look. "Him? What part of
this looks like a boy to you?" he asked, gesturing toward my
tangled hair.

"She had her hood up, an' she never showed her face,"
Hellhound explained. "I see this skinny kid in the middle of
the fuckin' night in a parkin' lot, what was I s'posed to
think?"

Kane sighed. "Go on," he said to me.

"He's right, I kept my hood up," I said. "I didn't want to
be too visible, and I was purposely trying to disguise myself.
So I gave him some teenage attitude, and then went down
the street and turned the corner. I sneaked up the back of
the mall and went over the fence. Lucky it was stucco. I
think." I surveyed my abraded fingertips ruefully.

"I was trying to get a view of the coffee shop and the
parking lot," I continued. "I peeked out, and I didn't think
he'd seen me, but I guess he did."

I shot a questioning look at the biker and he nodded. "So
I was hanging out in the shadows waiting for you when he

grabbed me from behind and just about punched my lights out."

Kane frowned at Hellhound.

"Well, shit," Hellhound justified himself. "I saw this dude scopin' out the lot, an' when I went to check it out, it was the same fuckin' kid I just ran off. So I figured it ain't just some kid. Thought I'd see if he felt like tellin' me who he really was."

"And what part of 'Do not engage under any circumstances' was unclear to you?" Kane grated. There was an edge to his voice that instantly made me think 'Drill Sergeant'.

Hellhound must have felt the same, because he straightened, feet coming together and chin going up in a classic 'Attention' position. It should have looked ludicrous, the grizzled, leather-clad biker standing at attention in his faded AC/DC T-shirt, but the tension between them negated any humour.

"Sorry, Cap," he said, looking unrepentant. "But what was I gonna do, let some fuckin' dirtbag grab this pretty lady here, an' maybe blow ya away, too? I don't need another fuckin' phone call like the one I got two years ago."

"Go on, Aydan," Kane said to me, his voice still harsh but controlled.

"Well, he slammed me up against the wall and started to throw a punch, but my hood fell down," I explained. "And then, instead of saying something useful like, 'Hi, Officer Kane sent me', he cuddles up, calls me 'pretty lady', and then phones somebody and says 'got her'! What the hell was I supposed to think?"

I glared at Hellhound, who was still standing rigid and expressionless. "So I tried to get away. And he grabbed me.

You saw the rest." I was mad all over again. "So is he another member of your team, or what?"

Kane's face was unreadable. "No," he said quietly, seemingly more to Hellhound than to me. "Mr. Helmand is a civilian. According to what you have told me, he has committed assault tonight, and if you want to press charges, I will arrest him." Hellhound's chin lifted a little higher, but he made no protest.

"Also," Kane continued, "Involving him in this situation was a serious lapse of judgement on my part. If you want to file a complaint and initiate an inquiry, I'll provide you with the contact information for my commanding officer."

I gazed from one man to the other, my anger draining away. Their faces were both impassive, but something about their silent tension made me think of soldiers fighting a losing battle, too proud to give up. I shuddered violently.

"I think... I'd like to get the whole story first," I said. "Somewhere warm, with food." I wrapped my arms around my trembling body.

Kane took in my shivering, dishevelled appearance. "All right. The diner on the corner is open all night." He ushered me to a shiny black Expedition. "Meet us there," he commanded Hellhound, who nodded silently and limped toward his Harley.

"What, no POS Suburban?" I joked, trying to lighten the mood.

"Another team member needed it for surveillance," he responded expressionlessly. "This is my vehicle."

Inside the SUV, he cranked up the heat before taking out his cell phone to dial.

"This is Kane. What's the status on the break-in?" He listened for a few minutes. "I have her. Wrap it up and head out. We'll coordinate reports in the morning." He disconnected and put the vehicle in gear.

"The uniforms went over your house." He spoke without looking at me, focused on the road. "The back door had been jimmied. Your bedroom door was kicked in, and the window was open. They combed the area on foot and with HAWCS, the police helicopter, but they didn't find anyone suspicious. They didn't find any witnesses tonight, but they'll go back and canvass your neighbours tomorrow to find out if anyone heard or saw anything."

"The window was open because that's how I went out," I said.

"From three storeys up."

"Yeah, I went over the roof down onto the back deck."

He sighed and scrubbed a hand over his face. "I'll get a complete statement from you at the diner." We rode the rest of the way in silence.

When we arrived at the restaurant, Kane motioned for me to precede him to a table. I chose one at the back, close to an exit, and sat down with my back to the wall, giving the room my habitual once-over. Kane slid into the chair beside me and we sat silently scanning the room until Hellhound appeared a few minutes later.

"Hadta take a leak," he informed us when he reached the table. He appraised the two remaining seats with obvious dismay. "Sure, take the good seats," he groused. When neither Kane nor I volunteered to give up our positions, the burly biker squeezed into one of the chairs facing us.

"Watch my back," he urged Kane. He winked at me and smiled, but I could tell he was serious.

"Always do," Kane replied.

The waitress arrived, and Kane and Hellhound both

ordered coffee. I was ravenous, so I went for huevos rancheros with home fries, a cup of hot chocolate, and a glass of milk.

"Ya gonna eat that shit at this time a' the night?" Hellhound demanded, his gravelly voice rising incredulously. "That shit'll rot your gut."

"You're getting old," Kane ribbed him.

"I'm gettin' smart," Hellhound rejoined.

They fell silent again as the drinks arrived, the momentary levity having done nothing to decrease the tension.

When the waitress departed, I turned to Kane. "So what happened?"

Kane rubbed his forehead as if it ached. His short hair was tousled, and his chin bore a heavy growth of stubble. The restaurant's harsh lighting accentuated the lines around his eyes and mouth, making him look as tired as I felt. God, I must look like the hag from hell.

"As soon as you hung up, I talked to the 911 dispatcher," he said. "I told him you wouldn't be going back to the house, and that I had set up a meeting place with you. But I live deep in the south end of town, and I knew it would take me fifteen or twenty minutes to get here. None of my team members were available except Webb, and I didn't want to put him in the line of fire again. You did a pretty good number on him earlier, so I imagine he's very stiff and sore."

Hellhound regarded me with interest. "Ya took on Webb, too?"

"Took out Webb is more like it," Kane said. "Anyway, I needed someone at our rendezvous point as quickly as possible in case you arrived before I did, and I also wanted to make sure we weren't walking into a trap."

"I guess introductions are in order," he continued. "Aydan, this is Arnie Helmand, a.k.a. Hellhound. He's a private investigator."

I must have looked sceptical, because Helmand grinned, showing those even white teeth again. "I clean up good," he said modestly.

I tried to picture him in a suit with his beard and moustache trimmed. It wasn't convincing.

"He helps me out now and then, and he lives close to here," Kane continued. "So I called and asked him to go to the parking lot and keep his eyes open for trouble. Surveillance only." He glared at Helmand. Helmand glowered back defiantly. "I also described you to him. Then I got on the road as fast as I could."

"I was the one he called after he grabbed you," he went on. "I was actually in the parking lot by then. I saw his bike, but I couldn't see him, so I was getting out of the SUV to look around. Right after he said 'Got her', I heard all hell break loose on the line, and I thought you'd both been attacked. I heard scuffling in the alleyway, so I ran in that direction. I arrived just in time to see you take him out."

The waitress arrived at that moment with my platter of food, and I dug in enthusiastically. The men watched in silence while I devoured about a quarter of the eggs, salsa, sour cream, and greasy fries. I'd finished my hot chocolate, and between the overheated restaurant, the extra calories, and the spicy food, I was warm at last. I paused my feeding frenzy long enough to peel off my jacket before getting back to work on the plate.

"Oh, hey," Arnie rasped softly from across the table. "I'm sorry, darlin'." I glanced up in puzzlement to see his contrite expression. Kane was frowning at me in concern, too.

I followed their gaze to the livid welts on my left wrist and forearm. There was a distinct reddened imprint of a Hellhound-sized hand, the creases of his fingers clearly visible as white lines. Various other scrapes and scratches glowed on my pale skin.

"Oh." I touched the burning area on my neck where he'd grabbed me first. That was probably fiery red, too. "Don't worry about it," I reassured him. "When they were handing out skin, I accidentally got into the 'Princess' lineup. It only looks dramatic. It'll be gone in an hour, no harm done."

"Are you sure you're all right?" Kane asked.

"Yeah, I'm fine. But, Arnie, what the hell possessed you to grab me without telling me who you were? You're not exactly a reassuring-looking guy, you know."

Helmand shifted uncomfortably in his chair. "Yeah, I pooched it all right. I was so surprised when your hood fell off, I forgot ya didn't know what was goin' down. Then ya slammed my face into the wall, an' I didn't want ya to run out into the parkin' lot an' maybe get shanghaied by some dirtbag, so I grabbed ya. I was tryin' to tell ya when ya punched me in the throat."

It was my turn to look shamefaced. "Sorry about that."

"Darlin', don't worry about it. Last time I wanted it that rough from a chick, she made me pay extra." He winked.

"Clearly I'm not charging enough, then," I retorted. "Maybe I should write you and Webb an invoice."

Hellhound shouted with laughter, then choked and coughed. "Try expensin' that one through the department," he croaked to Kane, massaging his throat.

Kane remained grave. "Getting back to the point of this meeting." Helmand sobered immediately, and they both looked to me.

"It was just a misunderstanding," I assured them. "I'm not interested in any arrests or disciplinary actions. You were both doing the best you could, trying to save my butt, and I appreciate it. If you'll forgive me for beating on the good guys, we'll call it even."

Neither man reacted visibly, but the air pressure around our table lightened by several tons. "No harm, no foul," Kane replied.

I frowned. "Yeah, that's bothering me a bit." A tense pause made me hasten to explain. "Maybe I should think about some self-defence classes or something. I was fighting for all I was worth, and I did no serious damage at all. I barely managed to get away from a guy who was actively trying *not* to hurt me. Aydan Kelly, Lethal Weapon."

Hellhound chuckled hoarsely. "Darlin', if ya did any more damage, they'd be haulin' me off in the fuckin' bone wagon."

Kane regarded me seriously. "You did fine. You escaped from an assailant who was much larger than you. You hit hard, and then you ran. Those were the right things to do. In fact, the only way you could improve on what you did would be to make more noise and try to do as much painful damage as possible. You should be screaming and scratching."

"Screamin' an' scratchin', an' moanin', 'Oh, Hellhound, oh, baby!'" Hellhound added dreamily, batting his eyes at me.

"You're out of line, Helmand!" Kane snapped.

But the ridiculous leer on Hellhound's ugly face made me laugh out loud. The sheer relief of being warm and safe had made me giddy, and I couldn't resist.

I shook my hair back sensuously and leaned across the

table to give Hellhound the full bedroom-eyes treatment. I made my voice throaty and breathy as I purred, "Oh, Hellhound, oh, baby! Are you done *already*?"

Kane barked out a guffaw as Helmand's jaw dropped. At his look of frozen shock, both Kane and I started to laugh in earnest. After another moment of paralysis, Hellhound joined in, bellowing like a laryngitic bull while we all convulsed with mirth, blowing off stress.

When we subsided, Helmand wiped his eyes. "Darlin', if ya gimme those big brown eyes an' say my name like that one more time, I will be done already!"

It had to be done. "Oh, *Hellhound*," I breathed, giving it all I had.

He threw back his head and let out a guttural grunt. Then he winked at me. "Darlin', I'm done for the night." He got up and laid a couple of toonies on the table for his coffee.

"Ride safe," I told him.

He looked surprised. "Always do, darlin'. Later, Cap," he said to Kane, and left. We listened to the Harley erupt to life and roar off into the night.

CHAPTER 9

"Why does he call you Cap?" I asked, emboldened by our shared laughter. "I get the feeling you two go back a long way."

"We were in the Forces together. I dared him to join the army when we were both eighteen, and he couldn't back down," Kane responded.

"So I take it you made Captain."

'Yes, that was as high in the ranks as I wanted to advance. The upper ranks have too much paperwork and bureaucracy."

I shot him a quizzical look. "I could have sworn I heard a drill sergeant back in the parking lot."

Kane chuckled. "That would be my dad."

I laughed and shook my head. "I can't imagine Hellhound saluting anybody."

Kane laughed, too. "He has issues with following orders, as you may have noticed. He used to keep his nose clean for a while and advance a rank, and then he'd get in trouble and get busted back to Private again. By the time he got out, he'd made Corporal for about the third time."

"How did he ever end up as a private investigator?"

"I left the Forces a year or so before he did and went into

RCMP training. It was a good fit for me, so when he got out, he tried it, too. But there's no room for Hellhound's maverick brand of independence in the police force."

Kane drank some coffee and continued, "He took away what he'd learned from the training and set himself up as a private investigator instead. He marches to his own drummer, and as long as he doesn't overstep his civilian rights, he gets along fine."

"Speaking of the military, there's something I want to ask you," he added. "Just before you hung up earlier, you said 'Roger that'. Were you in the Forces, too?"

I laughed. "God, no. You think Hellhound has a problem following orders? I've got him beat. They'd shoot me for insubordination before the first day was over."

"What then?" he persisted. "You usually don't hear that phrase from a civilian. Pilot's license? Ham radio?"

"No, Uncle Roger."

Kane shot me a baffled glance. "What?"

"Uncle Roger was a radio operator in the Navy. It always tickled his funny bone to be named Roger and say 'Roger' on the radio when he got a message. Now, you had to know his wife, my Aunt Minnie. She was... tough. Think, cross between drill sergeant and wolverine."

Kane grinned. "Most drill sergeants I've known have been part wolverine."

"Put one of them in a dress, and you've got Aunt Minnie. She had a short fuse. She'd ask nicely, once, and if Uncle Roger didn't hop to it, she'd belt out an order at the top of her lungs. And Uncle Roger would snap to attention and throw her this magnificent salute and bark out, 'Roger that!' And then he'd cackle like a hyena."

I smiled at the memory. "You had to hear Uncle Roger

laugh. You just had to laugh yourself. So it became a family joke. Any time somebody rapped out an order, we'd straighten up and say, 'Roger that!' I hadn't thought of it in years, but when you ordered me to drop the phone and run, out it came."

He chuckled. "Your Uncle Roger sounds like quite a guy."

"He was," I replied, still smiling.

He sobered. "The night's getting old. I need to take your statement, and then maybe we can both get a bit of sleep before our drive tomorrow."

I looked at my watch. "Yikes, a quarter to four. Can we start our trip a little later tomorrow morning?"

"Yes, I think we should make it ten o'clock. I'll need to file some paperwork before we leave." He opened his notebook. "Tell me exactly what happened."

"When I got back to the house from the morgue, I realized my security system wasn't working," I began.

Kane glanced up sharply. "Has that ever happened before?"

"Once or twice. I phoned the security company and they said there was no trouble indication on their end, but it obviously wasn't working at my end. That was strange. Usually they can tell from the control centre if there's a problem. Anyway, I felt pretty paranoid about it. At the time I thought it could have been just coincidence, but I knew I wouldn't sleep unless I had some kind of warning system."

"That explains the tins on strings," Kane interjected. "The uniforms at the scene were wondering about that. Why didn't you just leave and stay with a friend?"

"I just couldn't bear the thought of having to explain everything. And I was too cheap to go to a hotel. And I honestly thought I was probably over-reacting. I felt silly, and I didn't want to give in to fear."

"Sometimes it's smart to trust your gut," Kane said. "This time it was."

"Yeah. I guess it doesn't count as paranoia if you actually need all your elaborate preparations. Then it just looks like clever advance planning," I joked.

Kane smiled in response. "So walk me through your elaborate plans. The tins were your warning system. Then what?"

I described my activities, pausing only to gulp down the last of my cooling eggs.

"Too bad I didn't think to charge my cell phone," I continued. "Oh! Can I get my phone back? It's a smartphone, and it's got my entire schedule and contacts list in it."

"Tell me where you left it."

I did my best to describe the location, and Kane made a note in his notebook. "I'll ask the officers to check for it tomorrow morning when they're back in the neighbourhood," he said. "We'll retrieve it if we can, but you shouldn't carry it or use it until we know for sure what we're up against. You should buy a disposable cell phone tomorrow. Carry on with your story."

"Um... where was I?"

"Walking through the neighbourhood."

"Right," I mumbled. My stomach was full, I was warm, and my entire body felt like lead. I struggled to organize my thoughts. "So I walked out into the neighbourhood like I owned it. I didn't want to attract attention, and the only plausible thing I could think of was a teenager coming home from a party. That's how I got to the mall, and that's how the misunderstanding with Hellhound happened. I think you know the rest."

"Yes. Let's wrap this up," he said, closing his notebook. I delved into my backpack for my wallet, but Kane stopped me. "I've got it," he said, handing the waitress a twenty.

I was too tired to argue. "Thanks."

"You're welcome." We rose, and he waited while I pulled on my hoodie again and moved toward the door. I stopped at the pay phone near the entrance.

"Who are you calling?" he asked.

"I'm going to call a cab to take me to a hotel and see if I can salvage some sleep."

"I've got a better idea," he countered. "Until we know more about who's targeting you, I'd prefer to take some precautions. I'll drop you at a hotel myself. It'll be faster, and I'll know where you are so I can pick you up in the morning."

"Okay, thanks." My head felt stuffed with cotton, and I was glad to let him call the shots. All I wanted was safety and sleep.

I sleepwalked out to his SUV and we drove in silence to Macleod Trail, where there were a number of hotels. Kane chose one seemingly at random and pulled into the parking lot.

"I'll come in with you," he said, rousing me from my stupor. "I'll register under my name, and I'll come up with you so it doesn't look like you're alone. Can you pretend to be Mrs. John Kane for a few minutes?"

Something about that question seemed like it needed a smart-ass response, but I was too tired. I nodded mutely and followed him into the lobby.

The desk clerk was far too perky for four-thirty in the

morning. "Where are you folks coming from this late at night?" she chirped when Officer Kane stepped up to the desk.

"We're driving through from B.C.," Kane lied easily, handing over his credit card. "We had planned to be in by supper time, but we had car trouble. My wife's asleep on her feet." He laid a casual arm around my shoulders and snugged me gently against him.

Memory stabbed me in the heart. I'd almost forgotten what it felt like to be held like that. A flash of pain must have shown in my face, because the clerk was immediately solicitous.

"Ma'am, are you all right?" she inquired.

Kane glanced down at me with concern, and I forced myself to sound wry. "Just a back spasm." I slipped my arm around Kane's waist and let my head fall against him. "Are we done yet, Hon?"

The clerk handed us two card keys and gave us directions to a room on the fourth floor. We disengaged ourselves and wandered to the elevator, hand in hand. Once the elevator doors closed, we stepped apart, not speaking. My exhaustion temporarily forgotten, I tried to settle my whirling thoughts.

Sneaking a glance at his profile, I swallowed hard and looked away quickly. This man rang all my bells. He'd never make the cover of GQ. His nose had been broken at some point and re-healed with a bump in the bridge. When we'd sat in the coffee shop after my carjacking, I'd noticed the scar that sliced across his left eyebrow. Combined with the broken nose, I was reasonably sure he'd played hockey, sometime before face guards became mandatory in the sport.

His face and jaw were square, striking but not classically handsome. That was fine with me. I'd never been attracted to those well-groomed 'metrosexual' types. But I was a sucker for broad shoulders and a fabulous chest. There was no spare tire around that taut midsection, either.

The floor indicator dinged, rousing me from my lustful reverie. I stepped out without meeting Kane's eyes and admired the rear view while I followed him along the hallway. When he stopped at the room and slid the card key into the slot, my overtired brain made a detailed suggestion that I firmly ignored.

He opened the door and stepped into the room, towing me behind him. "Stay here," he said, placing me just inside the door while he matter-of-factly checked the bathroom and then the rest of the room. He crossed to the window and looked outside before closing the drapes.

"All right," he said. "You should be fine. Relax as much as you can and get some sleep. Nobody knows you're here. Don't leave the room. Don't even open the door until I come to get you at," he checked his watch. "Ten o'clock." The words came out on a poorly concealed sigh.

"What about breakfast?" I asked with alarm. "I can't function without breakfast."

He looked perplexed. "You just ate an enormous platter of eggs and french fries."

"But five hours is a long time, and then we've got a two-hour drive," I replied in my most reasonable tones.

"You're right," he said with a hint of a smile. "We'll grab something on the way out of town."

"Okay, thanks. See you in the morning."

He turned to leave, but hesitated at the door. "Thanks for cutting Hellhound some slack earlier. He's the best friend you could ever ask for, but he can be..." he paused, obviously searching for the right word.

"Rude, crude, lewd, vulgar, obscene, and generally offensive," I supplied. "I like him. He reminds me of Uncle Roger."

Kane grinned. "Thanks. Lock the door behind me. I'll take the stairs so it looks like I'm still here."

He went out, pulling the door closed behind him. I threw the deadbolt and the privacy lock, and listened until the sound of the stair door told me he was gone.

CHAPTER 10

I was rank with sweat and shivering again in my damp clothes. All my muscles ached even more fiercely than before, and my bruised butt throbbed in time with the gash on my leg. The frightening sight that confronted me in the bathroom mirror convinced me I had to have a shower, no matter how tired I was.

I stripped off my clothes and crept into a hot shower, soaking under the spray until I was warmed through. Dressed again in my last clean clothes, I called the front desk to request a wakeup call before falling into the bed to alternate between restless sleep and panicked jerks into wakefulness.

The ring of the phone convulsed every muscle, making me yelp. Completely disoriented, I floundered across the bed in a blind search for the source of the sound. A cheery wakeup message answered my slurred 'hello'.

The bedside clock read 9:45, and I blearily registered the presence of daylight behind the heavy drapes as I flopped back onto the bed and lay waiting for my heart to regain its normal rhythm.

I dragged myself out of bed and into the bathroom, where I used the facilities and brushed my teeth and my still-damp hair. Sleeping on it wet had emphasized its curls, and I tugged uselessly on the piece in the front that persisted in sticking straight out. Finally I doused it with water, hoping to subdue it. I'm such a fashion model.

On the dot of ten o'clock, there was a tap at the door, and Officer Kane's soft call came from the hallway. "It's John, honey. Open up."

I unlocked the door and stood back. He filled the doorway for a moment, his eyes flicking over the room before he stepped inside.

Yeah, you can fill my doorway any time, big fella.

He was freshly shaved and dressed in a snug black T-shirt that emphasized his broad chest and bulging biceps. I dragged my eyes back up to his face with an effort and gave him a smile.

"'Morning, Officer Kane. Or should I say, Honey?"

Kane grimaced. "Sorry. If you invent a cover story, it's best to stick with it. If you forget the details, they can come back to bite you later on. And just call me John. 'Officer Kane' isn't completely accurate anyway."

I waited to see if he would elaborate, but he said nothing further, so I said, "Okay... John," experimentally.

"Let's go," he said.

I put on my shoes and grabbed my backpack, and we headed for the elevator.

He put his arm around me again as we crossed the lobby to the checkout desk, and I felt my body react. Lucky I was wearing a good bra. Hate to flash the high beams at the morning staff.

I bumped against his hip and smiled up at him, playing the good wife. Huh. I'd rather be the naughty girlfriend.

When we got to Kane's SUV, Clyde Webb looked up from

the back seat. "Hey, Aydan," he greeted me cheerfully.

"'Morning, Spider. How's the gut?"

"Fine," he said dismissively, and I let it go.

Kane pulled out into the light Sunday traffic and navigated to a drive-through restaurant, as promised. Spider ordered pancakes and sausage, and I went for my favourite sausage and egg sandwich, along with milk, orange juice, and yogurt. Kane ordered black coffee.

I stared at him in disbelief. "Don't you ever eat?"

The corner of his mouth crooked up. "I ate breakfast at home."

Spider spoke from the back seat, his mouth full of pancake. "No, RoboKane never eats. His system is fuelled entirely by black coffee and baby food. He uses the baby food for target practice."

I got the movie reference immediately. "Didn't Robocop come out in the eighties?" I asked. "Were you even born yet?"

"1987," Webb said proudly. "I was three."

"You watched Robocop when you were three," I teased him.

"No, when I was sixteen. I told you, I'm a serious movie buff."

"Does that mean you only watch serious movies, or..." I goaded him.

"Yeah, yeah, you picky grammar types are all the same," he griped good-naturedly. "What are you, an English major or something?"

"Worse. Bookkeeper."

We reached the highway and settled in for the long drive. Kane was in silent driving mode. As before, Webb chattered incessantly from the back seat. He had intelligent and refreshingly different views on a wide range of subjects, along with a buoyant personality and an offbeat sense of humour. His conversation was liberally sprinkled with movie references, most of which I found completely obscure. That troubled him not at all, and he blithely described the movies and their plots in detail.

As we approached Drumheller, Spider broke off his flow of talk. "Kane, I need a rest stop and some snacks," he said.

Kane pulled off at a gas station. "Grab me some beef jerky," he said as Webb got out of the car.

Spider poked his head back inside. "Aydan, do you want anything?"

"No, I'm fine." I turned to Kane. "Assuming there's going to be time to eat when we get to Silverside?"

"Definitely."

Webb departed, and I sighed and rested my aching head against the headrest, massaging my temples.

Kane eyed me with sympathy. "Sometimes he shuts up if you ignore him."

I smiled through my pain. "He's an interesting conversationalist, but a little goes a long way."

"Don't let his babble fool you," Kane advised. "He's a brilliant analyst. He graduated at the top of his class, and CSIS recruited him right out of university."

"Oh, I certainly didn't get the impression he was stupid," I agreed as I opened the door. "I need to stretch my legs."

Kane nodded, and we both got out. He paced around the car stretching and flexing his neck and shoulders while I did some leg stretches, trying to persuade my stiffened muscles to relax. When Spider returned a few minutes later with his snacks, we all piled back into the SUV and got back on the road.

Webb struck up another conversation almost immediately. Kane glanced at him in the rearview mirror.

"Shut up, Webb," he said mildly.

Spider smiled and shrugged, unabashed. But he did mercifully shut up. He plugged his earbuds into his ears and turned his attention to his phone, texting at the speed of light.

CHAPTER 11

We pulled into Silverside shortly after noon. Without discussion, Kane drove directly to Fiorenza's, a little Italian restaurant.

When we entered, Kane chose a table in the back with a commanding view of the rest of the tiny dining room. I slid in beside him with my back to the wall, giving the restaurant my usual once-over and noting the exits.

Spider's humorous scrutiny made Kane ask, "What?"

Webb laughed. "You guys are two peas from a very scary pod. You're both sitting with your backs to the wall, doing that room scan thing."

Kane turned to me with a faint frown. "Habit," I told him self-consciously. "I told you I was paranoid." He gave me a half-smile and turned his attention to the menu, but continued to watch me surreptitiously.

Great, he thinks I'm a nut case. But surely I could be forgiven a little paranoia after the last twenty-four hours.

We ordered, and Spider's cheerful conversation filled the silence again. I chatted with him as pleasantly as I could and Kane let the patter flow over him, responding noncommittally only to direct questions. The food was excellent, and even Spider quieted to give it his full attention.

When the bill arrived, I appropriated it and handed the waitress some cash. "My turn," I said to the men's protests. "Thanks for driving me."

"What do you mean, your turn?" Spider inquired.

Guessing that Kane hadn't had a chance to fill him in, I gave him a quick recap of the night's events while we waited for the waitress to return with my change.

"So you met Hellhound," Spider said, quirking his eyebrows. "What did you think?"

I laughed. "I like him."

"You're definitely scary," Spider said with a grin.

We trooped back out to the SUV. "We'll go to the hospital first," Kane said. "Your paramedic might be on duty, but if he's not, we should be able to get a name and contact information."

Trepidation squirmed in my belly. This had seemed like a good idea at first, but as I thought it through, I couldn't foresee any positive outcome. If the medic said he hadn't seen Ramos, I could fall back on the 'I bumped my head' excuse, but I could hardly claim I'd been mistaken at the morgue, too.

And if the medic said, yes, he'd caught me in a clinch with Ramos, how would I explain that? I couldn't even explain it to myself. I blew out a miserable sigh. Kane glanced over, but made no comment.

When we arrived at the hospital, Kane showed his police ID to the hospital administrator. "We're looking for a paramedic who was on duty on Thursday at twelve thirty," he informed her. As she glanced up in alarm, he added, "He treated Ms. Kelly, and she wanted to talk to him to get a clearer picture of what happened."

Relief eased the administrator's face. "I'll bring up the

duty roster." She clicked keys on her computer for a few moments and frowned at the screen. "There were no male paramedics on duty on Thursday," she said. "Both were female."

Kane turned to me, his face expressionless.

"He changed his-" I stopped and reconsidered what I'd been planning to say. "He wasn't wearing a uniform when we got here. But he talked to Dr. Roth."

The administrator's face cleared as she brought up another record. "Yes, here it is. That was Mike Connor. He works part-time and he wasn't on duty that day. But he saw you fall, and he rode in on the ambulance with you. He's probably at his regular job today."

As we watched her write out Connor's phone number and work address, Spider glanced sharply at Kane's unreadable cop face before looking away, elaborately casual. I wondered what that was about, but neither man seemed likely to explain, and I had enough troubling thoughts of my own.

Information in hand, we left the hospital and returned to Kane's vehicle. I took a few deep breaths, trying to calm my nerves while we drove the few blocks to the address we'd been given.

The building turned out to be located right beside the place I'd slipped and fallen on the sidewalk. A nondescript square two-storey, it sported a bland stucco facade with a discreet sign beside the front entrance: 'Sirius Dynamics'.

We entered a small, hushed lobby that contained nothing but four chairs and what was obviously a security window. The thick bulletproof glass slightly distorted the uniformed man behind it. Sirius Dynamics had some 'serious' security, I joked feebly to myself. The pathetic joke did nothing to relieve my nervousness.

The man behind the glass looked up as we approached. "Afternoon, Kane, Webb," he said, his voice crackling through the speaker. He placed a clipboard and two security badges on the turntable inside the cubicle, activating it so that it spun around to the outer lobby.

Kane and Webb each signed the clipboard and picked up a badge displaying their respective photos. That explained Spider's reaction to the address, anyway.

"We need to see an employee named Mike Connor," Kane informed the guard. "Will you call and get him to meet us in the second floor meeting room?" He waved a hand toward me. "We'll need a visitor's pass, too."

The turntable whirled around again, disgorging a badge along with the clipboard.

"You're vouching?" the security guard asked Kane. At his nod, the guard addressed me. "Full name, address and phone number, please."

I filled in the blanks and replaced the clipboard in the tray, to be spun back into the security booth. I clipped on the badge and followed the men to the secured glass doors that gave onto a corridor lined with offices.

What on earth could Mike Connor's second job be? I couldn't imagine this kind of security being needed for any role that a paramedic might fill. Maybe he did on-site medical for oil and gas exploration or something. Those companies tended to be security-conscious.

Spider waved his badge at the panel beside the door, and the latch released to allow us into a hallway lined with offices that stood vacant on a Sunday afternoon. Reaching the end of the hall, we went through fire doors into a stairwell. At the top of the stairs, Spider used his badge to let us through another secured door.

As we walked down the corridor, we passed an employee lounge. A man in oddly matched clothing sat on a sofa, staring blankly ahead. He neither moved nor spoke as we passed. If not for the security badge clipped to his collar, I would have taken him for a vagrant who had somehow wandered in off the street. That was a little strange.

I rubbernecked as unobtrusively as possible at the vacant rooms as we strode along. None of them seemed to be offices in the conventional sense. There were no computers on the desks, and many of the rooms had some sort of soft seating. Strange indeed.

We entered a meeting room and took places around a modest oval table. Spider had brought a laptop, and he opened it and began to type rapidly. Kane sat relaxed and immobile, and I suppressed the urge to fidget.

A couple of minutes later, Mike Connor arrived. Apparently his second job didn't require a paramedic's uniform, because he was again clad in khaki pants and casual shoes, this time paired with a blue button-down shirt. He entered the room eyeing us each with curiosity. He showed no sign of recognition to Kane or Webb, but he frowned when he saw me.

Then his face lightened. "Oh, hello. How's your head?"

"Fine, thanks," I replied. "I guess I'm a tough nut to crack."

He laughed. "We haven't been formally introduced. I'm Mike Connor. What can I do for you?"

"I'm Aydan Kelly, and thanks for picking me up off the sidewalk last week."

Kane rose and shook hands. "I'm John Kane, and this is Clyde Webb. We're on temporary assignment with Security division."

No mention of RCMP or INSET. That was odd. Connor's pleasant face smoothed into a watchful expression. After a slight pause, he sat down.

"How can I help you?" he asked, sounding not quite as helpful as he had earlier.

Kane opened his notebook and withdrew a photo, which he slid across the table to Connor. "Do you recognize this man?"

I held my breath.

"Yes, I've seen him around the building," Connor replied.

That wasn't the answer I was expecting.

"Have you ever spoken with him personally?"

Connor darted an awkward glance in my direction. "Once."

"Where and when?" Kane asked.

I tensed. Here we go.

"I... can't answer that," Mike Connor said uncertainly.

Kane turned a hard gaze on him. "Can't, or won't?"

"I... It's classified," Connor replied. "Sorry."

This was past weird. Was he covering for me? Or for himself? And why would he? And who says 'It's classified', like it was a big secret spy thing?

"Webb and I have top-level clearances," Kane told him. "Ms. Kelly can step outside, and you can feel free to tell us whatever you want."

"No, she's fine," Connor said hesitantly. "I'll need to check your clearances with my department head before I can talk to you, though." He got up. "This will just take a minute," he added as he picked up the phone from a credenza in the corner.

Spider and Kane both snapped their heads around to

stare at me. "You have a security clearance at Sirius, and you *didn't mention it*?" Kane grated.

I closed my open mouth while I struggled to find my voice and organize my thoughts. "I haven't a clue what you're talking about," I stuttered finally.

Spider dove into his laptop to type furiously. He surfaced in a few seconds, his forehead creased with bewilderment. "No personnel record. And I have access to all of them, even the black ops personnel."

I felt a distinct drowning sensation. Black ops? I was in so far over my head...

"I don't work here," I protested weakly. "I've never been here before. I only moved to Silverside a few weeks ago. I don't know what you're talking about."

Connor finished his conversation and hung up. "Okay, you're clear," he said, not sounding very relieved. "My department head really doesn't like you, though."

Kane shrugged. "What can you tell us?" He kept a penetrating gaze on me as he spoke.

"I saw your guy in Portal D," Connor said.

Spider and Kane exchanged a hard look, and Spider blurted, "But he's a janitor! There's no way he should have portal access."

Connor's eyes widened. "Are you sure?"

"Of course I'm sure, I have the personnel records right here," Spider replied.

"Exactly when did you see him? Did you notice what he was doing in the portal?" Kane asked. I detected a tight note in his normally even voice.

What the hell was a portal? Connor had mentioned a portal when he rescued me. But the question I had dreaded was on the table.

Here it comes...

Connor glanced at me again, clearly ill at ease. Kane observed him, watchful and expressionless.

"I saw him on Thursday afternoon, around 12:30. He was, uh, meeting someone," Connor said.

"Who?" Kane snapped.

"Ms. Kelly," Connor said apologetically.

CHAPTER 12

Kane's gaze swivelled slowly back to me, pinning me to my chair. Spider's eyes were like saucers.

"Show the record," Kane said to Spider, not breaking eye contact. His voice had a distinct edge.

What record? Oh, please, God, tell me this isn't happening. It's all a bad dream. I'll wake up soon...

Spider turned back to his keyboard and typed for a few seconds before swivelling the laptop around so we could all see the screen. He pressed a key, and the display opened to a rear view of Ramos, just as I'd first seen him in my fantasy four days ago.

No, no, no...

I appeared in the frame as if from nowhere. The camera's vantage point was behind me, but my long red hair was a dead giveaway.

"Rotate," Kane growled. Spider pressed a key, and the camera angle changed to a front view of me, grinning lasciviously.

"How did you get inside my head?" I whispered.

The whole humiliating sequence played out, the uninhibited kissing and pawing, my guilty start as Connor arrived, the whole agonizing enchilada. Long, mortified minutes slunk past while the video ran. Mike Connor yelled at Ramos, and then led me out of the frame, both of us winking out of existence. After a few seconds, Ramos followed us, disappearing from the same location. The video ended.

A heavy silence settled while Kane's stare burned into me. I could feel the flush on my face deepening as I looked back at him helplessly. Connor studied the tabletop with intense concentration. Spider's face held a kicked-puppy expression of betrayal.

The silence stretched. At last, Kane said coldly, "It's a very bad idea to lie to me."

I had felt comfortable and safe with him earlier. Now I had a vivid impression of the suppressed energy of a nuclear warhead. Aimed at me. With the timer counting down.

Shit, shit, shit!

"Let's start at the beginning," Kane continued in the same deadly voice. "Maybe you could try the truth this time. How do you know Samir Ramos?"

"I don't... didn't know him. That was the first time I ever saw him." My voice sounded guilty and scared, even to me.

Kane gazed at me with biting contempt. "So you jumped a man you'd never seen before, in a portal which you have no clearance to access in the first place. Does that about cover it? How did you get the fob? Who are you working for?"

He might as well have been speaking Swahili. I stared at him open-mouthed. After decades of scrupulously obeying every law, I'd managed to commit a crime without even knowing I was doing it. If only I knew what I'd done...

"What... I never saw a portal. I don't have a fob. What's a fob?" I stammered.

"Don't play games with me," Kane grated. His

expression smoothed into his cop face. "You've committed an offence under the Criminal Code of Canada. You have the right to have a lawyer present before you answer any questions. Would you like me to call a lawyer for you?"

He was arresting me.

The bad guys were trying to kidnap me, the good guys were going to put me in jail, and I didn't even know what I'd done.

I would go crazy and die in jail.

I hadn't had a panic attack for years, but I felt one coming now. Adrenaline spiked into my bloodstream and my hands started to shake, my breath coming shallow and fast. I held onto control with grim determination. Breathe, belly breathe. In, out. I deliberately slowed my breathing, reaching for calm. Think about something else, something absorbing.

What did I need to finish up in my bathroom at the farm? I mentally stepped into the bathroom, surveying the gaping hole in the floor around the toilet stack. I knelt beside the hole and pulled experimentally on the drain. There was enough play in it, good. I'd be able to replace the cracked flange and bring it up to the correct floor level.

Blocking. I was going to need some wood blocking to stabilize the new plywood floor. I put on my safety goggles and earmuffs and picked up the piece of two-by-two. It fit perfectly between the floor joists, and I smiled, pleased with my accuracy. I picked up my air nailer. Bang, bang. The wood was secured in place, and I reached for the next piece. I moved to the side of the hole to get better access while I positioned it against the next joist and brought the nailer up to it.

My bathroom door crashed open and I leaped to my feet

with a scream, nail gun brandished in front of me.

Kane flowed through the broken doorway with the same smooth, fast motion I'd noticed when he first jumped out of the Suburban. He loomed larger than life in green combat fatigues, and this time he held a much larger firearm. I didn't know anything about automatic weapons, but it was big, and it was pointed right at me.

Behind him, Mike Connor looked ridiculously short, clad again in his paramedic's uniform. Wide-eyed Spider Webb was incongruous in a Star Trek uniform from the original series. He was wearing a red shirt. A hysterical giggle bubbled from my throat. Ensign Expendable.

I was insane. At least I knew that now. I hadn't realized insanity was so frightening.

"Put the weapon down," Kane commanded.

"It's not a weapon, it's an air nailer," I quavered. "What are you doing in my bathroom?"

"Put it down! Do it now!" he roared.

My brain flipped into overload. I was clearly nuts anyway, so what did it matter? I copped an attitude.

"So shoot me already. Put me out of my misery. You're a figment of my fucked-up mind anyway, so whatever." I squatted down beside the hole again and nailed in the strip of blocking. Bang, bang.

I reached for the next piece and positioned it. Bang, bang.

I decided I liked doing construction work while I was insane. I didn't even have to cut the pieces of wood, they were just there at hand when I needed them. And they fit perfectly. This was easy. I smiled and reached for the next piece.

There was a large black boot on it. I tugged, but the

wood didn't move. My gaze tracked from the boot up the camo-clad leg, 'way, 'way up to Kane's face. He was frowning, but at least the gun wasn't pointed at me anymore.

"Why are you still here?" I complained. "This is my delusion. I don't want you here." I glanced past him to where Webb still hovered in the doorway in his red shirt. I giggled and turned back to Kane. "But if he's Ensign Expendable, why aren't you dressed like Captain Kirk?"

"Where do you think we are?" Kane asked cautiously.

"Well, duh, in my bathroom. If you're going to hang around, would you pass me that piece of plywood?"

He glanced over to where a square of plywood had appeared, leaning against the wall. Removing his foot from the two-by-two, he stepped over to pick up the plywood. I snatched up the blocking and nailed it into place. Bang, bang.

"Thanks." I took the plywood from him and test fitted it over the opening. As I'd expected, it fit perfectly. I laid it aside and reached for the cordless drill that hadn't been there a second ago. Materializing a piece of steel strapping out of thin air, I screwed one end of the strapping to the top of one joist, then passed the other end of the strapping under the stack drain.

"Hold this." I placed the end of my level on the floor next to me, extending past the stack. I shot an impatient look up at Kane. He was frowning down at me, clearly puzzled.

"Come on," I said, wiggling the end of the steel in his direction. He squatted down warily and grasped the end of the strapping.

"Pull up a bit. Bit more. Good, hold it," I ordered when the top of the flange reached floor level. I reached over and screwed in the end of the strapping he had held.

"Stop," he said firmly. "Look at me."

When I did, I discovered he'd changed his clothes. Now he was clad in the T-shirt and jeans he had worn in the morning. Assuming it was still today in la-la land. I giggled again, teetering on the edge of hysteria.

"You look good in black," I told him. "That army uniform wasn't a good colour on you."

"Aydan," he said. "Come with me." He stood and held out his hand.

I rose, too. Why had I ever thought he wasn't handsome? He was amazingly hot. I stepped closer, unconsciously reaching for his extended hand. Then I remembered that getting busy with a hot guy was what had gotten me into trouble in the first place.

It was a trap!

I sprang back and my foot dropped into the hole in the floor, throwing me off balance. I flung up my arms in an attempt to right myself, but I was too close to the wall. I staggered back and struck my bruised head as I fell.

Blinding flashes of agony coursed through my skull, and I swore loudly and continuously, tapping into my considerable store of invective. The pain began to subside around the same time I ran out of fresh curses, so I stopped swearing and groaned wordlessly instead, rocking back and forth.

At last, I stopped moaning when the pain receded to bearable levels. An overly loud voice from above inquired, "Are you done?"

I cracked one eye open. Kane towered over me. "Can you clean it up a bit? There are ladies and children present," he said, waving a hand toward Webb and Connor, now back in their original clothing. Kane seemed to be having difficulty keeping a straight face. His lips twitched, and he ran a hand over his mouth and chin.

I opened the other eye. Connor's face was pale, his eyes wide. "You kiss your mother with that mouth?" he stammered.

"Not recently. She's been dead for thirty years," I snapped.

"Oh..." he sounded shell-shocked.

Spider Webb's eyes were wide, too, but with awe and delight. "Wow," he was saying, "Wow! I've never heard anybody swear like that, not even Hellhound! 'Snot-gobbling fuck-pig', I've never heard that one before." His lips continued to move silently as if practicing his new vocabulary.

Kane turned his back to me, his broad shoulders quaking as if in laughter, but when he turned back, his face was composed. I crawled across the carpet and shakily propped myself against the wall, discovering as I did that we were back in the meeting room at Sirius Dynamics.

I propped my elbows on my bent knees and rested my aching head in my hands. "Sadly, I can't take credit for the originality of the material," I addressed Spider. "My Uncle Roger was an equal-opportunity thinker well before his time. He thought little girls should learn to swear just like little boys. I always loved him for that."

I massaged my aching temples, fear gnawing at me. I was crazy. They were going to put me away. Just when I thought I was getting a new start. I'd been so excited about my new farm.

"We need to talk," Kane said.

"Okay," I mumbled, holding onto my fraying composure.

"Aydan, I want to search your waist pouch."

"Okay." I handed it to him.

Stay calm.

He went through it systematically, laying out its contents much as he had done with my backpack earlier. When it was empty, he turned the pouch inside out and examined it, too. Then he turned back to me.

"I'm going to need to search you, too. I'm sorry there isn't a female officer here to do that, but it needs to be done right now."

"I'm not carrying any weapons," I told him. "The only sharp object I had was the jackknife in my pouch."

"That's not what I'm looking for," he said, and helped me to my feet. I held my arms out from my sides and he patted me down thoroughly but impersonally while the other two looked on.

Shit, I get felt up by a hot guy for the first time in friggin' years, and I'm stuck with an audience and about to be incarcerated.

"You can sit down now," Kane said a few minutes later. I let my trembling knees drop me into a chair and mechanically began to repack my waist pouch. "Nothing," Kane said to the others, his face showing bewilderment.

"That's not possible," Spider said. "We need to try the RFID scanner."

"I'll get it," said Connor, rousing himself from his trance to go out the door.

Spider sat down at his computer again, rapidly clicking keys. "That's impossible," he said again.

"What?" Kane asked, moving over to look at the screen.

"I just reviewed the data record, and there's no RFID signature for her."

They put their heads together, muttering over the laptop, and I slumped in the chair. Nothing mattered now. I was nuts. I'd be in an asylum, or in jail. My beloved cars would end up in someone else's garage. My dream of living in the country, my bright new life, all shrivelling away to dust and ashes.

Mike Connor returned, bearing a handheld electronic device. Spider took it from him and waved it over my body, much like the metal-detecting wands in airport security. I sat still, staring blindly into middle distance and clamping down panic. Stay calm.

Maybe the insane asylum would let me go outside with supervision. Maybe they'd let me paint. Painting was nice.

Don't panic. Think about painting.

I stepped up to the big easel and opened the can of liquid white paint. With my one-inch brush, I applied an even coat over the canvas, just the right amount. I squeezed out a dab of cadmium blue on my palette and barely touched the brush to it. With short criss-crossing strokes, I applied the blue paint, darker at the edges, fading toward the middle. A nice, translucent summer sky...

A large hand reached out and held my wrist securely. I tried to move my arm away, but the hand didn't let go. I looked up. Kane again. He was still wearing civilian clothes. Nice to know he'd heeded my wardrobe advice.

"Come with me," he said.

"Where are we?" I implored. "We were just in the meeting room. We can't be here. I don't even know where here is."

I waved a hand at the white void around us. It reminded me of a blizzard whiteout. Suddenly I was freezing, snowflakes whipping by on a rising wind. The easel was gone, but Kane was still there, holding my wrist.

"Come with me," he repeated, pulling me toward him. This time I didn't resist. I just let him tow me into the whiteness.

CHAPTER 13

"Unnngghh," I said, or words to that effect. I rested my elbows on the meeting room table and cradled my throbbing head in an attempt to prevent my eyeballs from exploding. At least I wasn't on the floor this time. I breathed through my teeth for long moments until the pain subsided a fraction.

"Well, that's better," Kane said unsympathetically.

"Define better," I gritted.

"You didn't make Connor's ears bleed, and you didn't pass out this time."

"Marvellous. I wish I had."

"Which do you wish you'd done?" Spider asked, getting back some of his own.

"Both. Not necessarily in that order."

"Aydan, I need you to stay with us," Kane said.

"I presume you mean mentally. That would definitely be my preference," I agreed. "Any hints on how to accomplish that?"

Kane shrugged, looking frustrated. "If I knew, we'd all be happier," he said. He turned to Connor. "We need to get some input on this. I want to meet with you and Sandler at," he consulted his watch, "four o'clock. Set it up, would you?"

"Today?" Connor objected. "It's Sunday. I already had

to call Mr. Sandler at home for your security clearances, and he wasn't pleased at all. Can't we do it tomorrow?"

Kane skewered him with a look. "He's the head of security. We have a major security breach. If you'd reported it right away, we'd have two suspects to question." He glanced at me. "Now we only have one. Get on it."

"We'll need Smith, too," Spider added.

Kane nodded. "And Smith. Four o'clock," he repeated. Connor trailed out.

Kane turned his attention to Spider. "We've got reasonable cause now. Call down to Calgary and get a search warrant for Ramos's place ASAP. Get search warrants for both of Ms. Kelly's places, too, while you're at it. Get Wheeler and Germain to bring up the Silverside ones. I'm going to need them to do the searches up here right away. Get Richardson to do the search at Ms. Kelly's place in Calgary. And get digging for anything that relates to this. I'll need your expertise in this meeting."

"Right. I'll talk to Larkin, too, and get all the fob records from last week forward." Webb headed for the door. "Oh, those records checks came up while you were in the... gone," he added obliquely. "Chief Petty Officer Second Class Roger Kelly, served with the HMCS Bonaventure 1958 to 1970, when the Bonnie was decommissioned and he left the navy. The other check came up completely empty. I'll dig deeper, but so far it looks like what you see is what you get."

"Thanks," Kane said. Spider waved and followed Connor out the door.

"Checking up on me?" I asked.

Kane frowned. "There's a lot about you that doesn't add up. It was nagging at my subconscious before I ever saw that data record, and now... now I want some answers."

"So do I," I snapped. "I want to know how the hell you got inside my head and filmed my private thoughts. From all angles, I might add."

"You're not in a position to demand answers," Kane said flatly. "If you cooperate with me now, things might go easier with you in the long run. It's your choice."

"I didn't do anything," I stammered. "I don't even know what I did." I leaned my head in my hands, massaging my still-aching temples.

"Really." Kane's voice was hard. "Here's how I see it. You and Ramos collaborate. You succeed. You... celebrate."

He eyed me coldly. "Then, you have a falling out. Maybe you disagree over where to sell your information. Or maybe one of you wants a bigger cut. He follows you to Calgary to eliminate you. I conveniently show up and shoot him for you. And you pretend to be an innocent victim. It almost worked, too."

"I'm not a spy! I'd never seen him before. I was just having a fantasy..." I felt my face heat up and babbled on. "I was inside my own head. I don't know how you recorded it, but I didn't know him, I don't know how I imagined his face, I was just..."

"You're not a spy," he mocked. "In the last twenty-four hours, I've watched you jump out of a moving vehicle, shrug off a gunshot wound, be completely unfazed by a corpse with a bullet hole in its head, develop an elaborate rooftop escape plan, scale a wall, and fight off a biker. Let's see, did I miss anything? Oh, yes, whenever you enter a public area, you scope out all the exits and choose the seat with the best defensive advantage. And you coincidentally show up unauthorized in a secured facility. But no, you're not a spy."

The terror rose again. Jail. Captivity.

I breathed.

In. Out. Ocean waves. Think ocean waves.

The waves rolled in, soaking my shoes. Seagulls cried in the gray sky and rain misted my face. The briny ocean smell surrounded me.

Completely disoriented, I froze for a moment before giving in to panic. I bolted along the deserted shoreline, kicking up sand and pebbles. An enormous tumble of boulders loomed up in front of me as if from thin air, and I flung myself into their shelter, scrambling over their shifting bulk. My overused muscles burned with the effort while I burrowed deeper into the rubble. At last, I found a dark cave and curled into it, my breath sobbing in my chest.

As my breathing steadied, I took stock. Kane was nowhere to be seen. This probably counted as resisting arrest. Not good. Staying around to be arrested... also not good. Talk about a rock and a hard place. I shifted uncomfortably. Too bad rocks weren't soft and warm.

Obligingly, the rock around me warmed to a cozy temperature, and I relaxed into cushy comfort.

Wait a minute.

I gathered my scattered wits and thought over my experiences thus far. As far as I knew, insanity didn't conform to logical parameters. But as I reviewed each episode in which I'd departed the reality of the boardroom, some rules seemed to apply.

In the bathroom, events had proceeded logically and sequentially. With the exception of the costume changes for the men, everything had occurred just as I'd expected. Want a piece of wood; there it was, just the right size. Need a piece of strapping; pull it out of thin air.

And the painting episode. I'd been thinking about

painting, and then suddenly, there I was, painting. Hmmm, come to think of it, I'd been thinking of working in the bathroom earlier, too, right before it appeared. I'd thought about calming ocean waves, and here I was, listening to ocean waves. Go figure.

So far, if I'd concentrated on something specific, it happened. I wonder...?

I concentrated on a pink hippopotamus in a tutu. Sure enough, one popped up on the rocks in front of me, pirouetting gracefully.

Okay, the pink hippo was a little disturbing. I banished it with a wave of my hand.

What if I wanted to be hiding in a forest instead of a rock pile?

From my seat on a fallen log, I breathed in the moist, spicy forest air, cedars swaying above me. The vividly green ferns nodded in the breeze. I straightened, smiling. Being crazy wasn't so bad after all.

With a dramatic sweep of my arm, I painted the forest floor with daffodils and snowdrops. Another wave of my hand, and a waterfall appeared, its cascading stream just below my feet.

I could create anything. I laughed in sheer delight. I made it rain, then made the sun come out, lighting up the forest. With a grand gesture, I dried my wet shoes and removed the bloodstain. As an afterthought, I dried my clothes, too.

Something crackled in the undergrowth behind me and I turned, expecting, *creating* a deer. Sure enough, there it was. It bounded away in alarm. No wonder.

My mouth opened, but no sound came out.

"Nice forest," Kane said.

A cage blinked into existence around me, shrinking rapidly. My first whimpers started as the cage contracted, its bars thickening. I flung myself against my shrinking prison, battering my hips and shoulders. Mindless wails escaped me.

I tried to close my ears to the hoarse cries of agony from my familiar nightmares, but the apparition loomed closer, horribly visible through the remaining gaps between the bars. Screams ripped my throat while the broken body writhed, impaled on the post. The cage crushed inward, constricting my lungs. My screams stifled, I wheezed fast shallow breaths in my terrified fight for air.

"Aydan!" Kane's voice cut through the horror. "*Go somewhere else!*"

I burst free to collapse onto a park bench, frantically gulping the crisp spruce-scented air. Echoing silence surrounded me while I stared across the long valley, concentrating on the distant peaks beyond. I wrapped my arms around myself, gasping and shuddering and willing the open space with everything I had.

As panic receded, I realized Kane was standing silent and motionless a few yards away. My breath caught in my throat, but he made no move toward me. I wrestled for control and focused again on the view.

A couple of yards from my feet, the shoulder of the mountain fell away in a breathtaking sheer drop. Almost a thousand feet lower, the lake glittered blue, reflecting the vivid sky. A wispy cloud drifted below us, dissipating quickly in the autumn sun.

"Where are we?" Kane asked, his voice quiet and conversational.

"Mount Indefatigable. Kananaskis Country," I quavered.

"In the fall, about twenty years ago. This bench isn't there now. Here now. Whatever."

"Why don't you come away from the edge?" The same low-key, non-threatening tones.

"This is where the original bench was. And I don't think I can stand up just yet."

"Is it all right if we go somewhere else?"

"No."

"Okay." He lowered himself to the ground, propping his arms behind him and stretching out his legs.

We sat in silence for a while.

Finally, Kane spoke again. "What did I see, back in the forest?" he asked mildly.

"Dream. Memory. Some of each."

I studied my scuffed running shoes. The bloodstain was back.

"Which was which?"

A gust of wind tossed my hair and tangled it in the needles of the spruce tree that leaned over the bench. I concentrated on freeing it, avoiding the question.

"I think I understand why you told Hellhound to ride safe."

I chanced a look in Kane's direction. He was still sitting relaxed on the ground, watching me.

"What happened?" he asked quietly.

I sighed. "The biker pulled out to pass me. Not a lot of room, but he could have made it. Drunk driver pulled out from behind an oncoming car. The biker tried to cut back in and overcorrected. High-sided. Landed right on top of the fencepost."

I fell silent. The fresh bloodstain spread slowly across the toe of my shoe, glistening brilliant crimson. I suppressed a shudder.

"Were you injured?"

"Minor stuff by comparison. Pinned by a compound fracture in my left leg, traction for six weeks. Some soft-tissue injuries."

"What happened to the drunk?"

"Those assholes never get hurt. And this was before they toughened up the drunk driving laws. Nobody died, so..." I looked up in time to see his look of incredulity. "Yeah, the biker survived. That poor bastard was conscious the whole time." A shudder rocked my body. Raw-throated cries of agony echoed through the mountains, getting louder...

I breathed, concentrating on the lake, and the sound faded away.

"And the cage?" he asked.

"Just a dream. Thanks for yelling at me, by the way. I forgot I could change things here. I usually just have to wake up screaming."

"Do you dream it that often?"

"Not since I divorced my first husband," I said lightly. I glanced over. He wasn't smiling. I sighed again. "I only have that dream when I feel trapped or helpless in some part of my life. I'm claustrophobic, so it's just my subconscious mind's way of expressing anxiety."

"What are you feeling anxious about?"

"Gee, I don't know, where should I start? Carjackers, gunmen, home invasions, and now you want to put me in jail." My voice wavered on the last word, and faint bars appeared around me again. I took a deep, steadying breath and looked out over the valley.

"I don't even know what I did," I added.

"And yet, here we are," Kane said.

I glared at him. "Would you stop being so goddamn cryptic?"

He gazed at me, silent.

I knotted my fists in my hair and tugged a couple of handfuls. "Why am I even talking to you? I'm crazy, and this is a delusion. You're only going to tell me what I already know myself, because you're a figment of my deranged mind. I don't know why you keep showing up, though. Must be my fear of captivity. You're just another metaphor for a cage. Go away."

I waved a banishing hand at him, but he stayed, watching me. I leaned back and closed my eyes to block him out.

"I'm not a figment of your imagination."

"Yes, you are. Go away."

"Okay, suppose I am your metaphor for captivity. Talk to me. If you resolve your issues with me, maybe I'll go away. Convince me you're not guilty."

I opened my eyes to give him another glare. "You know I can't do that. It's logically impossible to prove a negative."

"Well, at least let's go somewhere warmer to talk about it. It's chilly up here."

I conjured a warm jacket for myself out of thin air. "Problem solved."

"Okay, problem solved," he echoed.

I glanced over. He was reclining on a sandy beach, the wavelets of a misty blue lake lapping in front of him while the sun beat down. Vertigo swirled through me when I glanced from his reality to my own, the beach and the mountain peak, side by side. I closed my eyes momentarily, recovering.

"Where are you?" I asked.

"Shuswap Lake."

"Oooh, I love the Shuswap," I breathed. My mountain peak faded into the other half of the beach. I slipped off my jacket and wadded it under my head for a pillow, letting the sun-warmed sand bake my back.

A few seconds later, I bolted upright. "Wait a minute! You altered my reality! How did you do that?"

"I altered my reality. Yours stayed the same until you saw the wisdom of my choice," he said smugly.

I stuck out my tongue at him. If you can't win an argument, always take the high road.

He looked startled, and then laughed. "Let's talk."

I flopped back down and stared at the sky. "So talk."

"As I said earlier, there are some things about you that don't add up," he began. "I'd like to know more so I can fill in some blanks."

"You're inside my head. You already know everything I know," I said peevishly.

"Humour me."

"Fine. What do you want to know?"

"Why do you always sit with your back to the wall and scan a room?"

"Habit. I don't like being in a position where people can sneak up on me."

"Who would sneak up on you?"

"I don't know! That's the whole point. I just hate having my back exposed."

"Why?"

I blew out a frustrated breath. "When I was younger, I used to go to some tough bars. I never knew who would come in, or when I might want to leave in a hurry. I always sat where I could see everything and I always knew where all the exits were. I just never lost the habit."

"Why not?"

"Because, that's why. Same reason you don't forget how to ride a bike. Once you've done it, you do it forevermore. Or maybe I have trust issues. So sue me."

"Is that where you learned to fight?"

I grinned. "No, I learned that in Grade One. I was always in trouble for beating up the bigger kids."

He grinned back. "Why does that not surprise me? Tough school?"

"Not at all. It was a very nice school in a very nice small town filled with mostly nice people. I just had a powder-keg temper and a serious aversion to bullies. Still do."

"Those moves you put on Hellhound didn't look like Grade One."

"No, I took a few Tai Chi classes at one of the community centres 'way back when. One of the things they emphasized was using your attacker's momentum to help you instead of trying to use brute force to oppose someone. And I watched a few self-defence videos on the internet."

"Why did you move to Silverside?" His voice remained pleasant and conversational, but I knew there was nothing casual about these questions. He wasn't the least bit interested in my Grade One escapades. He was a cop working on a case.

I squirmed a little on the warm sand and suppressed the urge to tell him it was none of his damn business.

I hissed a long breath of resignation. "I'm a country girl. I've lived in the city all my adult life, and hated it for most of that time. My husband was a city boy with a city job. Being with him made it worth living in the city. When he died, there was nothing holding me there."

"But why Silverside in particular?"

"Pure chance."

He frowned. "Really."

"Really."

"So here's another thing that's been bothering me. Why are you in such good shape?" Something in his voice made me glance over at him. He was eyeing my body, not my face.

I looked down at myself. I had changed into a skimpy bikini, and I was pleased to see I'd lost those stubborn pounds. My abs were softly defined in the mellow light, and the jiggly bits were nowhere to be seen. Gotta love insanity. I stretched and flexed luxuriously, just because he was watching.

"Did you do the wardrobe change, or did I?" I asked.

His voice had a husky edge. "I'm pretty sure you're the only one who can change your clothes. They're part of your reality."

Now that was a sexy voice. Mmmmhmmm, very nice indeed.

I concentrated briefly. "Yup, you're right. I just tried to put you in a Speedo."

He looked down at himself. "That would be emb-" He shook his head slightly, apparently regrouping. "Getting back to the point. Most women your age couldn't run across a parking lot. They struggle to carry grocery bags. You're hanging from rooftops and fighting bikers."

The stereotype flooded me with irritation. "Listen, buddy, you obviously haven't been to my gym. There are little old ladies there who blow me off the running track. There are all kinds of super-fit middle-aged women running marathons and doing triathlons and winning bodybuilding contests."

He sighed. "I didn't mean to imply otherwise. What I meant was, it's just one more unusual thing about you. And too many unusual things in one place make me suspicious."

"Well shit, if I'd known it was a crime to stay fit, I'd have sat on my ass eating potato chips all day long until I weighed four hundred pounds," I snarled.

"And how do you explain your escape planning skills and your blasé attitude toward gunshot wounds?"

I threw up my hands. "I'm a bookkeeper! I plan things! I'm anal about details! And I'm lousy at being a good little victim. You wanted to know why the bullet hole in the corpse didn't upset me too much, well now you know. It was clean and merciful compared to what that poor biker went through. And as far as that so-called gunshot wound on my leg, I've hurt myself worse than that doing home renovations."

I glared at him. "I've explained everything. I can't prove to you I'm not a spy." I flopped back onto the sand. "I guess you'll just hang around in my head and torment me forever. At least as a metaphor, you're better than the cage."

"I'm not a metaphor. I'm not in your head. You're not insane. I'm the real John Kane, and we're really having this conversation."

"Prove it."

"How can I prove it?"

"Tell me something I can't possibly know, and that I wouldn't be able to imagine."

He sat in silence. I stared at the sky some more.

"Hellhound crochets afghans in his spare time," he said.

I jerked upright, staring at him. "Bullshit!"

"No word of a lie."

"No, you're just messing with me."

"Seriously." Kane grinned. "He broke his leg in a training accident right after we joined the army and ended up in traction for six weeks. He was bored, hitting on this pretty nurse, and he figured he could make time with her if he asked her to teach him to crochet. It worked, too."

"And he still crochets because...?"

"It gets him in touch with his feminine side."

I gaped at him. "Now that is a truly scary thought."

"Actually, I am messing with you on that one. Hellhound doesn't have a feminine side. He says he still uses crocheting as a ploy to get the chicks."

"Thank God," I sighed. "The thought of Hellhound's feminine side was just..." My voice died in my throat.

Hellhound minced toward us in high heels and a white Marilyn Munroe halter dress, the light fabric contrasting appallingly with his full beard and hairy, tattooed body.

He came to a stop in front of us, simpering while the dress blew up around his legs and he held the front down á la Marilyn. Then he winked. Gave us his trademark leer.

And turned and mooned us.

"Aaaaagh!" I shrieked, shielding my face with both hands. "My eyes! I'm blind! Make it go away!" I flopped back and caught a glimpse of Kane, who was prostrate on the sand, laughing helplessly.

"You!" I pounced on him, belabouring him with my jacket while he feebly defended himself, tears of mirth rolling down his cheeks. "I'm scarred for life because of you! That was all you! That was... that was horrible!" I collapsed in laughter beside him.

He gasped for air, wiping his eyes. "It wasn't me! That dress... I would never... in a million years... Admit it, you did that."

"Well, I did feel a sense of impending doom," I conceded, giggling. "But the rest of it had to be you! I had no way of knowing he had a tattoo there. And I would never have imagined it in such... such detail!"

He propped himself weakly on one elbow. "Okay, that part was me. I've seen him moon so many people over the years... that's how he earned his first demotion." We laughed some more. "It's all about expectations here," he added.

We lay on the sand a few minutes more, recovering. Then I turned to face him. "Okay, then, if it's really you, tell me this. I have a right to know what I'm being charged with. Exactly what did I do? Exactly when, date and time?"

"You hacked into a secured, classified government network. The first time was this past Thursday at 12:30 in the afternoon."

"That's impossible. I was flat on my back in a puddle of ice water then."

He sat up slowly, watching me. "I have the data record."

I sat up, too. "It couldn't have been me. I was lying on the sidewalk. You saw the ambulance records yourself."

"It was you," he insisted. "Maybe you slipped and fell as you left the building and you're trying to use the ambulance as an alibi, but it was definitely you. You saw the record yourself."

I stared at him, wheels turning in my mind. "I've never even been inside the building before today. Review your security tapes if you don't believe me."

Pieces fitted together slowly. I was so close to figuring this all out...

Expectations. Expectations create reality. The data record. Which was a video of what had been happening *in my head*. The data record was evidence that I'd hacked into the network. This beach was all in my head.

My mouth dropped open. "This is virtual reality! This *is* the network you're talking about! Isn't it? I'm accessing the network right now!" Suddenly, it all made sense.

"Oh thank God, I'm not insane!"

A slightly frantic giggle escaped me. "I'm not insane. This is all logical and rational, we're together in a networked virtual reality simulation that's being generated by our own brainwaves. I didn't know this was even possible. This is so cool!"

I stopped as I recalled the conversation in the meeting room. "And so classified..." I added slowly.

I turned to Kane. "Your network security *sucks*."

CHAPTER 14

Kane rested his arms on his bent knees, frowning. "So it would seem. How did you get in?"

"I don't know. I just... did. Honestly, I wasn't even in the building. There was no login, no password, nothing, not even a 'No Trespassing' sign. All of a sudden, I was just... here... inside... and there was this guy. I didn't have any idea I wasn't safely inside my own skull. I'm never going to have a personal thought again, ever."

I rubbed my burning face and changed the subject. "Next thing I knew, I was flat out on the sidewalk. So how does it work? Why isn't there any security? If this is all inside my mind, what's my body doing right now, back in the boardroom?"

"To answer your last question first, your body is sitting in the boardroom, staring off into space. So is mine."

"That explains the guy with the vacant stare as we came in. He was accessing the network."

"Probably," Kane agreed. "As far as your other questions go, it's complicated, and it's classified. I can't tell you anything without clearing it with my C.O. You already know too much for my taste."

I eyed him uneasily. "That statement is usually followed

by 'now I have to kill you'."

The corner of Kane's mouth quirked up. "You've been watching too many movies. This is Canada. Now I have to make you sign a non-disclosure agreement."

"I love Canada," I said with feeling.

He looked at his watch. "Time to go. I have to check in with the higher-ups before I do anything further, and our meeting is in half an hour." He stood.

I rose, too. "Great, how do we get out? It's been fun and all, but..."

"You mean you don't know how to end the session?"

"Hell, no! I didn't even know I was in a session. If I'd known how to end it, I wouldn't have been doing the funky chicken in that goddamn cage!"

He stood silent for a moment, probably deciding how much he could tell me without putting his neck in a noose with his superiors. "There's a portal," he said finally.

"Aha!" I exclaimed. "When he brought me to hospital, Connor said he'd found me in a portal. Which makes sense, because I didn't move far from where I'd appeared the first time." I felt a flush climbing my cheeks again and continued hurriedly. "So how do you find the portal from the inside?"

"Can't you see it?"

"I don't even know what I'm looking for. Hold on." I waved a dismissive hand at our lakefront vista. Now that I knew I could control it with my mind, the hand gesture probably wasn't necessary, but it seemed to help. Whiteness surrounded us.

I turned in a circle, studying the void and seeing, appropriately enough, nothing.

"Hmmph." I waved my hand again and the whiteness resolved itself into the Star Trek holodeck in its inactive state. "There we go," I said, pointing to the door. "Am I right?"

"Trekkies," Kane said with resignation. "Are you sure you're not a computer geek, too?"

"I was," I said, ignoring his sharp glance. I walked over to the door and pressed the control pad beside it. The door swooshed open, and I stepped through it into the boardroom.

I had a second of disorientation as my point of view switched from looking into the boardroom to sitting at the table. Pain lanced through my brain again.

"Son of a *bitch*," I spat, holding my head together with both hands.

Kane regarded me from across the table. "Interesting. Whatever gets you into the network seems to exact a price. My head doesn't hurt when I go in and out."

"Bully for you," I snarled through my pain.

"So you're a computer geek," he said, ignoring my ungraciousness. "You see, this is what I mean by suspicious coincidences."

"I said I *was*," I grumbled. "That was in the '90s. My knowledge is so out of date, I'm a dinosaur today. I know DOS, for chrissake!"

He let that pass. "Stay here," he commanded, and I knew he didn't mean my physical body.

"I don't know how. Every time I think about something, I get sucked into the network again."

"Then stay focused on this boardroom. Or try reading." He tossed me a dog-eared magazine from the top of the credenza.

I obediently opened the outdated magazine and began to read, forcing myself to concentrate on the words. After watching me closely for a few moments, Kane lifted the telephone receiver and dialled a number. Pretending to read, I listened to his end of the conversation.

"It's Kane. Give me General Briggs. It's urgent." He waited on the line, then spoke again. "General Briggs, John Kane. We have a situation. Unauthorized access to the Sirius net."

"Yes, sir, we know who. One is dead, and I have the other in custody. She claims it was accidental and she knew nothing about it."

"I realize that, sir. That's what I originally thought, too."

"I'm inclined to, sir. There are a number of things that just don't make sense, given the circumstances."

"No, this just came to light in the last hour."

"Yes, sir. I may need to disclose some information in order to get the whole story."

"Standard NDA? I'll get it done ASAP. Yes, sir." He hung up, rubbing his forehead.

"You'll need to sign that non-disclosure agreement as soon as possible," he said. "It's nearly four o'clock, so as soon as the others get here, I'll have someone print it up."

I squirmed. "Um. I really need to go to the bathroom."

"I can't let you out of my sight."

"How about if you just stand outside the door?"

He shook his head. "I'd have no way of knowing if you were accessing the network."

"Can't you just monitor the portal? If I show up somewhere on camera, you'll know."

"That will work," he agreed. "You'll have to wait until Webb gets back, though. I'll need him to set up the simultaneous feeds."

"Okay." I gazed at him pleadingly. "You know I'm not

doing this on purpose, don't you? I really don't know how or why this is happening."

He shrugged, rolling his shoulders tiredly. "I don't know what to think. There's so much here that doesn't make sense. Some of that works in your favour, some of it doesn't. I need more information."

"What could I do to prove I'm innocent?" I begged.

He eyed me levelly. "I don't know."

CHAPTER 15

Connor and Webb arrived a few minutes before four o'clock, immersed in a debate over World of Warcraft. Kane broke into their conversation as soon as they sat down.

"Webb, will you set up a simultaneous real-time feed from all of the portals? We need to be able to monitor them."

"Sure, no problem," the young man responded. He fired up his laptop again, fingers flying. After a short delay, he turned the screen toward Kane.

Kane nodded. "Good. Watch these feeds and yell if Ms. Kelly shows up in any of them."

He stood, and I rose, too, taking the magazine with me. He walked me to the door of the ladies' room and leaned against the wall outside the door.

Once settled inside, I immediately opened the magazine and began to read with fierce concentration. There was no way I wanted Kane to have to crash in here and find my zombie body sitting on the toilet while my brain went who-knows-where.

I did what I had to do, and we made our way back to the meeting room. Two other men had joined Webb and Connor in our absence, and I studied the new arrivals as we entered.

They were a study in contrasts.

One man was short and meticulously groomed. He wore a dark suit over a crisp white shirt and a quiet tie, looking much too formal for a Sunday afternoon at home. His sandy, thinning hair was precisely trimmed and parted, and his shoes shone like dark mirrors.

The other man was also sandy-haired, but there the resemblance ended. He was completely bald on top and his remaining lank hair dangled in too-long strands. He wore a rumpled shirt that didn't conceal the soft roll of belly fat beneath. The front of the shirt was tucked in, exhibiting what looked suspiciously like food stains, but half of the tail dangled outside the waistband of his green pants. The pants were too short, exposing white socks with black shoes.

As I walked by them, my nose was assailed by a wave of body odour from the unkempt man, and an almost equally nauseating wall of sweet cologne from the dapper one. I held my breath and sat as far away as possible.

Kane took a seat opposite the two men. "Sandler, Smith," he greeted them evenly.

"Kane," the dapper man replied. He infused the single word with the disgust of a man who'd just stepped in dog shit with his shiny new shoes. "Who is this?" he continued distastefully, indicating me. The other man sat in silence.

Kane indicated the well-dressed man. "Aydan Kelly, this is James Sandler, head of security for Sirius Dynamics. And this is John Smith, head developer." He indicated the slob.

I nodded to Sandler, disliking him immediately. "Nice alias," I said to Smith.

He tensed, his nostrils flaring. "*What?*"

I backtracked hurriedly. "Sorry, it was just a joke. I went to university with a guy named John Smith, and we nicknamed him 'The Alias' because it was such a common name, it was like he was trying to hide something. Sorry, bad joke, I'm just a little nervous."

I realized Kane was watching us intently. I shut up. Jeez. This is why I don't go out much.

"Why is this... person... here?" Sandler addressed Kane.

"As Webb informed you, we discovered a security breach in the network. The first instance that we know of was this past Thursday at 12:30. Ms. Kelly claims she was able to access the network from outside the building. She has subsequently been able to gain access several times from within the building, without the use of a security fob," Kane said.

Sandler and Smith stared at me. "That's impossible," they said almost in unison.

"We have data records," Kane said. "In all cases, Ms. Kelly is clearly identifiable. In several instances, some or all of us," he indicated Webb and Connor, "...saw her access the network and followed her in. There is no RFID signature for her in any of the records."

Sandler replied, sarcasm dripping from his voice. "I hardly think you are qualified to analyze the data records. You have undoubtedly misinterpreted the data, creating a crisis where none exists. Allow Smith to review them."

Kane nodded shortly. "Webb, bring up the first record."

God, not again. I shrank in my seat and stared at the table while the humiliating video played. In the silence at the end, I continued to study the table, my face on fire.

"How very... edifying," Sandler sneered. "I must compliment you, Ms. Kelly, on your theatrical aspirations, however, I suggest to you that this is hardly an appropriate venue for an amateur pornographic production."

"I didn't know I was in your network," I muttered. "It was completely unsecured. I wasn't even in the building."

"Let me see it again," Smith said to Spider.

I groaned. "Why don't you just post it on the internet so everybody can watch?"

"Why, Ms. Kelly, surely you have not been stricken by a sudden case of modesty," Sandler derided me. "If you choose to conduct your sexual escapades in the middle of virtual road, you can scarcely bemoan the attentiveness of your subsequent audience."

Anger and humiliation frothed into a potent cocktail in my veins. I bit my tongue to keep from saying anything that would get me into any deeper trouble, mentally throttling Sandler until his face turned purple...

"*Aydan!*" Kane snapped. I jerked upright, startled. "Stay here," he said forcefully.

"Right, sorry."

Shit, that was a close call. I'd almost slipped into the network again. I wondered if a person could be charged with virtual assault. I shook myself. Stay here.

I frowned around the table, defiantly meeting their eyes. Smith was looking speculative. "Kane and Webb are right," he said. "There is no RFID signature for Ms. Kelly." He turned to me. "How and when did you reverse-engineer the fob?"

"I *didn't*. I don't have a fob. Ask Kane."

"She's telling the truth," Kane agreed. "I searched her myself. She has no fob anywhere in her belongings or on her person."

"Oh, I'm sure you searched her *thoroughly*," Sandler sneered.

A flush climbed Kane's neck and he opened his mouth to

reply, but Spider interjected indignantly, "Kane followed proper procedure to the letter! Connor and I were both witnesses, and he did everything by the book!"

Sandler smiled. "Yes, it's clear that Ms. Kelly prefers an audience."

"Enough," Kane overrode him. "The issue here is Ms. Kelly's access to the network. She has no fob. She shows no RFID signature. She is capable of accessing the network at any time, completely bypassing security."

Smith addressed me again. "How are you doing it?"

"I don't know. Any time I start thinking about something and stop focusing on my present environment, I get sucked into the network."

"You can't get *sucked into* the network," he scoffed. "Accessing the network requires intent and two-factor authentication, along with a complex algorithm to modulate your brainwave frequency."

I threw up my hands. "Apparently not for me."

"Show me," Smith commanded.

I looked to Kane for approval, and he nodded.

"Remember, you told me to do this," I said. "I'm not trying to sneak around and spy."

"Duly noted," he agreed. "Webb, Connor, stay behind and monitor the feeds. Sandler and Smith, get ready to follow her."

Sandler snorted, but I noticed both he and Smith were fingering their security fobs. I leaned back in my chair, breathing deeply.

Oh God, what if I couldn't do it now?

I pushed the thought from my mind and concentrated on being somewhere else.

I stepped into the vacant bay in my garage, remembering

with a pang that my poor little bullet-ridden Saturn was still in Calgary. Seconds later, Kane, Sandler, and Smith popped into being beside me. Sandler was scowling. Smith regarded me as if I was a strange new bug that had just appeared under his microscope. Kane remained impassive, but I thought I detected a faint air of vindication about him.

"Fascinating," Smith said. "Where are we?"

"My garage."

Kane's face lit up. "Nice wheels," he breathed, approaching my Corvette convertible with the reverent appreciation of a fellow car fanatic. "Is that the '67?"

"'66. The only real difference in the body styling was the side air intakes."

"Can I see under the hood?"

"Yeah, it's got the 427 big-block, with a three-barrel racing carb," I told him as I popped the hood. We stood side by side and admired the gleaming engine. It looked even better than real life.

I shot a fond glance around my garage. In my loving rendition here in virtual reality, it was even bigger and brighter, and the smooth concrete floor was pristine. Even the oil stains under my half-finished '53 Chevy sedan had vanished.

Smith wandered over. "Fantastic detail," he commented. He drifted to my shiny floor-standing tool chest, opening drawers and lifting out tools.

"Hey," I snapped. "Put those back where you got them."

"How far does your control of detail extend?" Smith asked.

"What?" I wasn't sure whether he was making a crack about my compulsive neatness or asking a question about the simulation I'd constructed.

"How big a simulation can you create while sustaining this level of detail?" he rephrased.

"I don't know. I'm not putting any effort into this because it's so familiar. I guess if I expect something to be the way I know it to be in real life, then it'll just be there. Other than that, if I'm not expecting something, there's just a white void."

"What other areas of the network can you access?" he asked.

"I don't know. I haven't tried to access anything, because I didn't know I was in a network."

"Try," Smith urged.

I looked to Kane for guidance again. "This feels like a witch hunt. Tie her up and throw her in the water. If she sinks and drowns, oh, oops, she was innocent. If she floats, she's a witch, so you can fish her out and burn her at the stake."

"This session is being recorded, and Webb and Connor are monitoring the live feed," he reassured me. "Your cooperation will help you in the end."

I thought about that for a moment. The 'in the end' part didn't reassure me much, but my options were severely limited.

I sighed and waved my hand, dissolving the garage into white nothingness. The others studied me while we stood in the void. Sandler seemed to have suspended his pique for the moment, and was eyeing me as intently as everyone else. I gazed around at the blankness, considering. How would I go about accessing the actual structure and files inside a network?

My antiquated computer knowledge resurfaced grudgingly. Network topology, God, that was so long ago.

Okay, if I followed the network structure, it might look like corridors. A large room appeared around us, corridors branching off in several directions.

Choosing one at random, I walked down it until it ended in a brick wall. "Firewall," I thought out loud. "Wonder if I can get through."

I frowned at the bricks, willing them away. Nothing happened.

"Hmmph." I reached out to touch the wall, which still looked as solid as ever. My hand went through it as if through thin air.

"Yikes!" I jumped back, staring at the bricks. "Can you guys get through this?"

"I should think so, we all have top-level clearance," Sandler snorted.

"I don't want to step through unless there's somebody on the other side," I said. "I've had enough accusations of spying for one day. Do you want me to go through or not?"

Sandler stepped through the firewall. "Try," he said from the other side, his voice muffled only slightly by the seemingly solid wall.

Once again, I eyed Kane, and he nodded. The illusion of brick was so convincing that I put my hands out to protect my face as I stepped through the wall. Kane and Smith followed behind me.

Sandler's expression changed from contempt to consternation. "You should not have been able to do that."

I sighed. "I tried to tell you. I'm just bumbling through here like it was mist. Could any of you have accidentally granted me access somehow? You said your fobs use RFIDs. That's radio-frequency identification, so it broadcasts a signal, right? Could your fobs have overlapped to let me in or something?"

Sandler's natural personality reasserted itself. "Surely you don't think the DND uses garden-variety RFIDs. These are highly modified, technologically advanced units that are biometrically keyed to an individual. Our fobs couldn't possibly allow you access."

I did my best to ignore his snotty attitude. "Should I leave now?"

"No," Smith said. "Keep going. See if you can access any files."

"I really don't think I want to do that."

"It would help us if you would try," Sandler said, clearly attempting civility.

I frowned up at Kane. "I have to trust you on this. And I don't trust anybody. Tell me now, am I making things worse for myself?"

"No," he replied. "If you cooperate with us to figure out what's happening here, you may be able to escape charges."

Charges. Jail.

Bars rose around me again, and I closed my eyes and breathed deeply, willing them away. When I opened my eyes again, Sandler and Smith were peering at me with curiosity.

"Never mind," I told them, and walked away down the corridor.

Okay, looking for files. Where would they be stored? I studied the featureless corridors. I needed some signs.

Obligingly, signs appeared on the walls, and I smiled. Just like the Enterprise's guidance panels.

"What files do you want me to look for?" I asked.

"Keep it simple. See if you can access my personnel file," Kane advised, and the other two nodded agreement.

"Take me to Personnel Files," I addressed the panel on

the corridor wall.

A blue directional light appeared in the floor in front of me, receding down the corridor. As I followed it, I heard Smith's quiet voice behind me.

"Oh, crap."

The light guided me through a maze of corridors and a couple of firewalls, the men following behind me in silence. The trail ended at a door marked 'Personnel Files'. How helpful.

I turned to my rapt audience. "Do I go in?"

They nodded as one, and I opened the virtual door to step into a room full of tabbed files on shelves. I found my way to the 'K' aisle, and reached up to pull 'Kane, John' from the shelf. I handed the folder to Kane.

"I have to know if you can open it and read it," Smith said.

Kane handed me back the folder, and I opened it. "Kane, John Wyatt," I read. "Mother, Ellen Ann Yates. Father, Douglas Anson Kane." I scanned down the file, idly noting he was two years older than me. There were a lot of military-looking records and a long list of medals and commendations.

"I can read the whole thing, no problem," I said. "Should I read the rest?"

"No."

I closed the file and handed it back. "Let's get out of here."

The others nodded wordlessly, and I waved my hand to bring back the holodeck. I went straight to the door, swooshed it open, and stepped through.

This time I was expecting the pain. It didn't help.

"Aaah! God... dammit... Son of a..." I locked my hands

around my skull and rocked back and forth with my eyes screwed shut, breathing heavily through my clenched teeth.

When the pain subsided, I squinted my eyes open. The five men watched me warily.

"Full access," Smith muttered. "How did she *do* that?"

Sandler rounded on him. "I thought you said the network security was foolproof. Two-factor authentication, and even then access is only possible through the portal interstices with the aid of a brainwave frequency modulator."

"As I reminded you when we discussed the initial design spec," Smith responded caustically, "...the algorithm modulates the frequency to a specific band, which still falls within a normal range of human alpha waves. I told you from the beginning that some individuals may naturally use that range. Ms. Kelly is clearly one of them."

"English, please," Kane demanded.

Spider spoke up. "Aydan can match up with the portal's frequency naturally. Her brainwaves just happen to fall into the right range. But she still shouldn't be able to get access without a login and a specially-generated password."

"Besides, I could get into it from outside, too. Don't you have some sort of physical security?" I asked. "You're just broadcasting this network out into space?"

"No, of course we have shielding and jamming devices," Smith replied condescendingly. "The network is fully enclosed in this secured building. Which brings us to the next question. How did you get into the building?"

"I didn't! I told you, I was out on the sidewalk. Check your building security tapes. Today is the first time I've ever been inside this building."

Sandler gave a patronizing chuckle. "We have advanced in our monitoring procedures somewhat beyond magnetic tapes."

Spider's fingers were already racing over his keyboard. "Facial recognition..." he muttered. "Correlate with log data and search..." There was a short pause. No one spoke. "She's telling the truth," he said at last. "The only record of her being anywhere in the building is today."

"That's not p..." Smith bit off his denial. "Let's go outside," he said instead.

"Connor, Webb, stay here and monitor," Kane commanded. "Let's go."

We trooped downstairs to the main lobby. "Taking our fobs out to the sidewalk for a few minutes," Kane told the security guard.

The man looked startled. "That's a policy violation..." he began.

"I authorize it," Sandler said, and the man nodded, placated.

An alarm squealed behind us when we stepped out of the building.

"Ignore it," Sandler said. "It triggers if a fob is removed from the building."

"Where were you when you fell?" Kane asked.

I walked down the street about fifty yards and stood in front of the ice cream shop. "Here."

"Try the network."

I concentrated. Nothing happened.

I altered my breathing, slow and deep, focusing on my garage. The three men watched me, hands on their security fobs.

"I can't get in," I admitted at last.

"Ha!" Smith barked. "I told you it wasn't possible."

We retraced our steps back inside the building and up to

the boardroom in silence. I racked my brain.

What could have changed? Why did I get into the portal effortlessly from outside the building on Thursday, but not now? How could I convince them I wasn't lying?

Spider and Connor looked up from the monitor as we re-entered the meeting room. "Nothing in the portal," Connor said with obvious relief.

Wait a minute. Connor. Paramedic.

"You said you had jamming devices to contain the network," I ventured. "Could those devices fail? Or be compromised for a short time?"

"Of course not. They're on a UPS," Smith replied as if addressing a simpleton. "And even if there was an interruption, it would appear in the security event log."

I noticed Kane watching me while I watched Connor. Connor looked distinctly nervous.

"Could you check the logs for Thursday?" I asked. "Because I don't think I was the only one who accessed the network from outside the building that day."

CHAPTER 16

Kane followed my gaze to Connor. "That's right, you appeared in the portal's data log, too, Connor. In fact," he paused in thought. "Webb, show us that record again."

I sighed audibly, massaging my forehead. "We don't need the whole thing," Kane said mercifully. "Just the first few seconds."

I averted my eyes while the video ran again.

"Freeze it. There." Kane pointed to the screen. In the frozen frame, I was staring at the smear of blood on my fingertips, looking puzzled.

He addressed Connor. "Aydan entered the network *after* she fell. She was already injured, lying on the sidewalk outside the building. You came into the portal to retrieve her, so you must have known she was in the portal when you found her on the sidewalk. So what really happened?"

Connor's eyes darted sideways. "I, uh... slipped out for a smoke. I forgot I had my fob."

Kane's gaze sharpened. "You forgot. And you didn't remember when the alarm went off."

Connor's face paled. "Um... I didn't go out through the front door," he muttered, not meeting Kane's eyes.

"Where did you go out?"

"Through the fire exit at the side."

Sandler leaned forward in his chair. "The side fire exit is alarmed. The alarm will sound if the door is opened for any reason."

"I... disabled it," Connor whispered.

The tense silence around the table made me feel sorry for the young man. He had helped me even though he hadn't been on duty as a paramedic, and now it had landed him in trouble.

"Why did you disable it?" Sandler barked.

Connor shifted in his chair, his gaze slipping up to the corner of the room. "It was just such a pain to have to go down and turn in my fob each time and then sign for it when I came back in. I was just trying to save time and be more productive. I didn't mean any harm, and I kept my fob hidden so it would be safe."

"You were surely aware that you were committing a serious policy breach," Sandler admonished. "Those policies exist to safeguard our security."

It looked like the beginning of a long lecture, and Kane broke in. "Let's focus on the issue at hand. Did you access the network from outside the building?"

"Yes..." Connor hesitated. "I didn't even think about it at the time. I was around the side of the building having a smoke, and I saw Ms. Kelly fall and then she just lay there. I knew she'd hit her head. I called the hospital to send the ambulance, and then I ran over. She had her eyes open, but she had that thousand-yard stare, you know? I knew right away she was in the network, so I went in after her. And then I had to ride along to tell Dr. Roth to put her in B Wing. The paramedics on duty wouldn't have known, and I couldn't disclose anything because they weren't Sirius employees."

There was B wing again. "What's so special about B Wing?" I asked. "I heard you mention it at the hospital, and when I asked Linda about it, she blew me off."

"Classified," Sandler snapped.

Kane brought us back to the point again. "So the jamming system had to have been disabled."

Smith appropriated Spider's laptop and typed rapidly with two fingers. He looked up after a few moments. "The security event log shows a ten-minute interruption in the power to the jamming devices at 12:30 on Thursday. Why was this missed? This was your responsibility, Mike!"

"I checked the logs as soon as I got back from the hospital," Connor defended himself. "I found the log entry, and I checked over the entire system from the electrical riser to the wall current, through the UPS, to the jammers. Everything was operating normally. No sign of trouble. And there hasn't been another interruption since."

"But you didn't report it," Kane said.

"It looked harmless," Connor whispered.

"And you needed to cover your ass, didn't you?" Kane's voice was edged. "And a suspected terrorist was able to access the system undetected, until now." Catching my look of panic, he added, "Samir Ramos, not you, Aydan."

He pinned Connor to his seat with a hard look. "And as a result of your actions, Aydan's life was endangered and she was wounded when Ramos attempted to abduct her at gunpoint."

Connor's face was ashen. "I'm sorry, I'm sorry!"

Kane ran his hand wearily over his eyes. "Sorry doesn't cut it. If this had gone unnoticed..." He shook his head. "I need to review what we've discovered to date. I'll talk to you again later. Don't leave town."

Sandler regarded the young man coldly. "You can expect disciplinary action. I will escort you down to security to turn in your fob. We will discuss this in detail tomorrow morning."

He turned to Kane. "This does not, however, explain Ms. Kelly's ability to browse freely through our secured... *supposedly* secured network. We will discuss this tomorrow, also. Keep us up to date with your findings. Michael, come." He turned and left the room with Connor trailing meekly behind him. Smith got up and left, too.

"Does this mean you believe me?" I asked tentatively.

"Your story is beginning to sound more convincing. I still need more information." Kane picked up the telephone, then paused and shot me a stern look. "Stay here. Out of the network."

I sighed. "Talk to me, Spider."

Kane made several calls. At last he hung up the phone and turned back to us in time to interrupt Spider's lengthy exposition of the plot of 'Jane Eyre'. Thank God.

"Warrants are on the way," Kane informed us. "Wheeler and Germain should be here in half an hour or so. Webb, get a copy of a standard non-disclosure agreement for Aydan to sign. I'll take over babysitting duty."

"I want out of here so badly," I said. "I just want to go home."

Kane shook his head. "Not so fast. You don't think I'm going to let you back into your house before we search it, do you?"

I stared at him, horrified. "But that'll take hours! I'm starving! Oh, please tell me I don't have to sit in here all that time trying not to think!"

"No, we all need to eat, and I don't want you within

striking distance of this network for any longer than absolutely necessary." He exhaled tiredly. "I wish I knew if you're telling the truth about not being able to access the network from outside the building."

I straightened with indignation. "Of course I am! I haven't lied to you!"

"Except that you didn't tell me where you'd seen Ramos in the first place," he said quietly.

"That was omission, not lie. I didn't know what to tell you. As far as I knew, I'd been having a private fantasy. When Ramos showed up in the flesh, I didn't know what was happening. I thought maybe I'd seen him earlier and then dreamed him, or something. Would it have helped if I'd told you then?"

"No, probably not," he admitted. "But it's still suspicious that you looked so friendly with him."

I dropped my head into my hands. "Haven't you ever had a fantasy where you get to skip all the preliminary bullshit and just get laid?" I mumbled.

When I looked up, he was regarding me with an unreadable expression. "Rhetorical question," I added as heat rose in my face again.

Spider returned with the paperwork, and I signed my life away. "Can we go now?" I pleaded.

"Yes."

CHAPTER 17

Once again, there was no discussion over where we would eat. I hadn't tried any of the town's restaurants except the burger joint, so I was happy to go anywhere as long as it was far away from Sirius Dynamics.

When we entered Blue Eddy's Saloon, Kane motioned me ahead and I selected a table in the corner near the exit, with a full view of the rest of the bar. I sat with my back to the wall. I didn't see any point in pretending I was comfortable doing otherwise.

With a quirk of his mouth, Kane sat beside me, leaving Spider with his back to the room. The young man shot us a knowing grin and sat without comment.

On a Sunday evening, only a couple of other tables were occupied. A stage in the corner held a piano and a sign promising live music on Saturday nights, open jam on Thursdays. Gritty blues music played in the background, and I settled into my chair. This was as good as Kelly's.

The bartender made his way over, apparently waiting tables as well as tending the bar on such a quiet evening. "It's been a while," he greeted Kane. "The usual?"

Kane shook his head. "I'm working tonight. Just club soda with lime. Thanks, Eddy."

"How about your friends?"

"I don't drink," Spider said. "Coke for me, please."

Eddy turned to me. "Would you like a drink?"

"I would love a drink until death did us part." I beamed at him. "Corona, please. Oh, and a glass of water. And a menu. Thanks!" He withdrew with a smile, and I turned to Kane. "What's good here?"

"I've never had anything bad."

We'd only enjoyed the blues for a minute or two before Eddy returned with the drinks and the menus. My bottle was ice-cold, and I squeezed the lime down into the beer and took a long swallow.

"Thank God," I breathed, and opened the menu. It offered the usual pub grub, and I decided on hot wings, potato skins, and a Caesar salad.

Closing the menu, I tipped up my beer again, lowering the level past the bottle's shoulders. I let out a long sigh and slid down in my chair, stretching my legs out.

Spider shot me a grin. "I don't think I've ever seen anyone enjoy a beer quite that much."

"You've probably never seen anyone who needed a beer quite this much," I replied, slugging back another swallow. "Besides, for once in my life, I'm not driving, so I can actually have a beer. This is a treat."

"So why the water?" he teased.

"Slows me down between beers."

Eddy arrived to take our food orders. After he left, Spider was silent for once, evidently deep in thought. I sat enjoying the music, and I caught myself swaying my shoulders to the beat. I looked over to see Kane's fingers tapping along with the music, too, and we exchanged a small smile.

"Blues fan?" he asked.

"Yup."

The food arrived promptly, and Eddy raised an eyebrow at my empty bottle. "Dead already?"

"Yes, it was a brief but passionate relationship," I assured him.

"Another?"

"Yes, please."

I dug into my food with a rapturous moan. The wings were hot but not suicidally spicy, the potato skins loaded with cheese, the salad fresh and crisp. By the time Eddy returned with my beer, the chicken bones were already piling up, and the beer quenched the fire in my mouth.

Eddy lingered, apparently killing time. "Slow night."

"Not quite as busy as Thursdays and Saturdays," Kane agreed.

"So you're working late on a Sunday. What do you do, anyway, John?"

"Energy consultant," Kane said. "You know these oil and gas companies, you sign the contract and they think they own you."

Now that was interesting. Why would he lie?

Eddy turned to me, sticking out his hand. "I haven't seen you around here before. I'm Eddy Carlson, but you can call me Blue Eddy. Everybody else does."

I wiped the wing sauce off my fingers and accepted the handshake. "Hi, Eddy. I'm Aydan Kelly, but tonight you can call me Hungry and Thirsty."

Eddy chuckled. "I can see that. Where do you put all that food?"

I grinned at him and slapped my belly. "Right here."

"And what do you do for a living, Hungry Aydan?"

"I'm a bookkeeper."

"No, really?" Eddy's eyes widened. "Are you taking new clients?"

"Actually, I just moved here, so I'm actively looking for new clients."

"This is my lucky day!" Eddy crowed. "Yesss! When can you start?"

I smiled at his enthusiasm. "Are you sure you don't want to get some of my references, maybe talk about the software I use or something?"

"Hungry Aydan, I don't care if you count on your fingers. I'm desperate. Can you come tomorrow morning?"

I laughed. "Why so desperate? Maybe I should ask for *your* references. What's wrong?"

"My bookkeeper moved away three months ago. There's another lady in town who does bookkeeping, but she won't do mine, so I've been doing it myself. I'm no good at it, and I hate it."

I felt a moment of misgiving. "Why won't the other bookkeeper do your books?"

Eddy frowned. "She's a nice lady, but she's very religious. She didn't try to stuff the Bible up my nose or anything, she just said she didn't feel right doing books for a business that she didn't believe glorified the Lord."

I eyed him, straight-faced. "I have some strong religious convictions myself," I said, watching his face sober. I started grinning as I quoted Ben Franklin. "I believe beer is proof that God loves us and wants us to be happy."

Eddy roared with laughter. "Then we're going to get along just fine! Can you come tomorrow morning around ten-thirty?"

"I'll be here," I assured him.

As I turned back to my food, two men entered the bar. They stood near the entrance, scanning the room before heading for our table. Kane nodded to them as they approached.

"Wheeler, Germain," he greeted them. "Join us?"

The tall, blond man he'd addressed as Wheeler shook his head. "No, we ate on the road."

Wheeler was handsome and thirty-ish, well-groomed and clean-shaven. He wore an expensive-looking brown leather coat over perfectly tailored slacks and a sweater. As he moved closer, I caught a whiff of subtle cologne.

His partner, Germain, was very dark, almost as wide as he was tall. He wasn't fat, just broad and solid, about my height. He wore a scuffed black leather jacket over a plain black T-shirt and cargo pants. His five o'clock shadow looked about ten hours past due. Crisp black curls brushed his ears and forehead, emphasizing black brows and keen brown eyes. I couldn't estimate his age. Somewhere over thirty and under fifty. Something made me want to like him immediately. Maybe it was the laugh lines at the corners of his eyes. I was a sucker for those.

Kane had those sexy laugh lines, too. I studied his face surreptitiously while he conversed with the two men.

"Searches on Ms. Kelly's car and her house in Calgary came up empty," Wheeler reported. "Richardson called me about an hour ago to let me know, said he couldn't reach you."

Kane nodded. "We were in Sirius."

I stored that information away for future reference. Apparently Sirius blocked cell phones. That explained why everyone used the land line there. And Sandler had referred to DND. Department of National Defence. Hmmm.

"We also retrieved Ms. Kelly's smartphone," Wheeler added, handing it to Kane. "We've been through it, it's clean. Her car should be released on Tuesday."

"You two might as well get started then," Kane said. "Wheeler, you can search Ramos's place. It's just an apartment, so it shouldn't take too long. You can head out to Ms. Kelly's farm as soon as you're done. Germain, you can ride with us out to Ms. Kelly's place."

Both men nodded, and Wheeler left. Germain slid into the chair beside Spider, seemingly unconcerned about exposing his back to the door.

"You're not really planning to search my whole place tonight, are you?" I asked. Germain's eyebrows went up.

"Germain, this is Aydan Kelly. Aydan, Carl Germain," Kane said.

Germain's sharp eyes took in our food and my beer. He frowned.

"Ms. Kelly's status is unclear in this," Kane told him. "Earlier in the day, I had reason to believe that she was spying at Sirius. Now I'm not sure. We're going ahead with the searches so that we can gather as much information as possible."

"If you have to get this search done tonight, it's going to be a long night," I said.

"What makes you say that?"

"It's a farm. A hundred and sixty acres. A house. A garage. A workshop. Sheds."

"We'll get the house done tonight," Kane said. "We'll see how that goes, and decide from there."

I sighed. "Well, I guess I had to unpack those boxes sometime."

CHAPTER 18

We drove down the dark road in silence, listening to the crunch of gravel under the tires. At my gate, I gave Kane the combination, and he got out and opened the padlock, leaving it dummy-locked behind us so that Wheeler could get in later. I handed over the keys to my house, and Kane punched in the security code I gave him.

"Where do you want to start?" I asked.

"I want you to sit at the table without touching anything," he said. "We'll carry on from here."

"Do you want the password for my computer?"

"That would help. Give it to Webb."

I perched on the edge of a dining room chair, determinedly suppressing the urge to jiggle my knee while I watched. Spider went directly to my office, where I had no doubt he'd turn my computer inside out in short order. Kane and Germain split up and began to search the main level thoroughly and efficiently.

I sighed as they began to open boxes and spread the contents systematically across the floor. I had my work cut out for me to get everything put away afterwards, assuming they didn't find anything that made them arrest me on the spot.

Another sigh escaped me, and I smoothed down the tattered cuticle I'd been picking despite my best effort to appear calm and composed. God, what would they find to incriminate me? As far as I knew, there shouldn't be anything suspicious in the house, but I hadn't known I was a spy until a few hours ago, either.

I swallowed and clasped my hands together. Do not fidget.

Spider emerged from my office. "Computer's clean. Nothing in the paper files, either."

"Fine," Kane replied. "You can start in the basement, then."

Spider descended the stairs and disappeared from view. Kane moved into my bedroom, and I wondered if police officers got an illicit thrill from pawing through women's underwear drawers. Probably not, I decided. It was probably as routine to them as flipping through the pages of a well-read book.

Kane emerged, raising a questioning eyebrow. "Why is there a crowbar under your pillow?"

There was no way I was going to admit to the intent of bashing somebody in the head. "As you can see, I'm working on my bathroom. I probably just put it down and forgot about it."

"It was under the pillow, and the bed was made."

I gazed up at him, keeping my expression as bland as possible. "I'm absent-minded like that sometimes."

"Well, now you know where it is."

"Gee, thanks."

Spider's strained voice floated upstairs. "Kane! I found ammo!"

Kane's voice was expressionless, his gaze steady on me.

"Bring it up."

Spider came up bearing my box of ammunition, which he placed on the table in front of me.

"That's a lot of ammo," Kane said, beginning to lift out boxes. "Let's see what you've got." He began to lay it all out on the table, organized by type. "Where are your guns?"

"In the gun locker under the stairs. Legally stored and registered. I store the ammo separately. I have a possession-only license, in the lockbox under the stairs. The keys to the gun locker and lockbox are on my keychain." I handed him my keys again.

He disappeared down the stairs, returning with my license and guns. "Check these," he said, handing the license to Spider, who nodded and headed for my office again.

"Nice guns," Kane said. "Why do you have them?"

"The .22 is just for target practice. The .410 is for trap shooting. The 12-gauge and the .22-250 are in case I need to kill a rabid skunk or something."

"Are you a hunter?"

"No, I don't like killing animals. I just like target shooting."

Spider returned and gave me a reassuring smile. "All checked out."

I breathed a sigh of relief as unobtrusively as I could.

"Good, we'll put these back where we found them," Kane said, and took everything downstairs again. Spider followed him, and Germain resumed his search on the main level.

A few minutes later, Kane was back, this time carrying my bow case. "Well armed, aren't you?"

I sighed again, then internally berated myself for sighing so much. Fake calm, dammit.

"It's a target bow," I explained, showing him the shiny,

blue anodized bow and arrows. "Look at the length of that stabilizer. It's not exactly a stealthy weapon."

Germain came over. "I've seen these compounds do some serious damage. They'll shoot 90 metres no problem, and I once saw an arrow go right through a bulletproof vest."

I shuddered. "I hope there was nobody in the vest at the time."

"No. It was draped over a plywood chair. The arrow went through the vest, through the plywood, and came out the back of the vest."

"That must have been some pretty high poundage," I said. "And if they used a broadhead, it would cut through Kevlar like a hot knife through butter. Mine is only set up for a forty-pound draw weight, and I don't have any broadheads, just practice points. I'm just a target shooter."

"You have answers for everything, don't you?" Kane asked.

"Innocent people generally do," I responded, keeping my voice level. "If you don't believe me, keep looking. You should find my target medals in one of those boxes."

"So that's what those were," Germain said, turning back to the boxes. He picked his way through the clutter and came up with a handful of ribbons and medals.

Kane examined them briefly before turning to me. "Any other weapons you want to explain away before we find them? Some throwing knives? A garrotte? Maybe a small grenade launcher?"

"Very funny. The only other things you'll find will be a couple of hunting knives. Oh, and a machete. Don't give me a hard time about that, I use it for chopping up stuff for my compost bin."

The corner of his mouth quirked. "Right. Why didn't I

think of that?"

I said nothing and he turned away, carrying the case back down the stairs. After another half hour of faking serenity, I begged for a book and forced myself to lean back in the chair, my eyes scanning the lines while my brain steadfastly refused to absorb the story.

Germain finished on the main floor and joined the other two in the basement. At least they didn't seem to consider me a threat so far.

At last, they emerged from the basement, empty-handed. "Well, that's the house done, anyway," Germain said cheerfully.

"Can I move around and start cleaning up now?" I asked.

Kane nodded permission. "We'll start on the garage next."

"Maybe I'd better come out to supervise," I said, feeling relieved enough to joke a little. "I don't trust just anybody with my Corvette, you know."

Kane seemed to have relaxed, too, and he gave me a half-smile. "You can come along if you want to sit in the empty bay and read your book."

Germain gave Kane a sharp-eyed glance. "Have you been here before?"

"In a manner of speaking," Kane replied. "I've been in a simulation of the garage." Germain's eyebrows rose, and Kane went on, "I'll give you and Wheeler a full briefing tomorrow."

We were donning our jackets when the doorbell sounded, and Kane opened the door to Wheeler. Wheeler's fair cheeks were flushed, his eyes sparkling. He grinned broadly, reached into his coat pocket, and wordlessly pulled out a Sirius Dynamics security fob.

Spider pounced on it. "Ooh, I can hardly wait to open this up and see what's inside," he crooned.

Kane grinned, too. "Let's go roust out Sandler and Smith. Wheeler, Germain, can you finish the buildings here tonight?"

"It'll be a long night, but we can split it," Germain replied.

"Good, do it." Kane and Spider turned and left.

Germain turned to Wheeler. "Flip you for the first shift."

"Tails."

Germain flipped the coin. "Looks like I get the first shift. Go get some sleep, and trade me off around two." Wheeler nodded and headed for the door. Germain turned to me with a grin. "Let's go have a look at that 'Vette."

CHAPTER 19

I groaned my way out of bed at six o'clock the next morning. Germain's search of the garage had turned into a gabfest about my cars, and it had been a late night. At two A.M., I'd woken to the sound of car doors slamming as Wheeler traded shifts with Germain.

While I waited for my toast, I peeked out the window. Wheeler crossed the yard, on his way to my shed. As I watched, Germain drove up and joined him, their breath rising in wisps of vapour. The temperature had dropped overnight, and I didn't envy them their chilly task.

Breakfast finished, I took a stab at organizing the mess until 9:45, when I stood in front of my closet for a long moment, scowling at my business clothes.

I hate dressing up.

I shrugged and decided to skip it. Eddy was so delighted to have a bookkeeper, he wouldn't care if I showed up naked and covered in mud, with a bone in my nose.

I snorted amusement. Hell, he was male, who was I kidding? I could probably charge extra if I showed up naked and covered in mud. I compromised with a pair of girly jeans and a nice sweater. March weather isn't compatible with nudity.

When I stepped out onto the porch, Germain and Wheeler emerged from the shed empty-handed, looking grey and tired in the morning light.

I called across the yard, "I need to go into town. Is it okay if I arm the alarm system?"

"No problem, we're done here anyway," Wheeler responded.

"So I'm in the clear?"

"Looks like it so far," Germain said. "Have a good day."

They got in their car and drove off, and I went out to my truck, shivering in the biting north wind.

In town, I drove directly to the tiny computer and electronics store that doubled as the local outlet for telephone and satellite services. I left the store with a disposable cell phone, and tested it by dialling Kane's number.

"Kane." His deep, husky voice tickled my eardrum.

"Hi, it's Aydan Kelly. Did I wake you again?"

"No. I just had a late night and an early morning. I haven't had enough coffee yet."

"I'm calling to let you know I picked up a disposable phone. I wanted to give you the number because I'm going to be seeing clients today and I won't be at home."

"Good. We may need you to come over to Sirius again this afternoon. I'll be in touch."

Oh, lucky me.

I drove over to Blue Eddy's and parked in the empty lot. The doors were locked, but I went around to the back and knocked as we'd agreed the previous night. Eddy let me in with a jubilant smile and led me into a cramped office, where I eyed the ledger book, folders, and shoeboxes full of receipts with trepidation.

"I'll need a few minutes to look this over, and then we can talk and figure out what you need done," I told him.

"Take your time." He left the office with obvious relief. A few minutes later, I heard someone playing a boogie-woogie piece on the piano. The rollicking bass line made me grin, swaying my body and tapping my toes. When I peeked out the door, Eddy glanced up and stopped playing. "Sorry, is this bothering you?"

I beamed my delight at him. "If you keep playing like that, I'll have to pay you for the privilege of doing your books."

"Well, in that case, let me run up your bill," he chuckled, turning back to the keyboard.

I went through the books and discovered his previous bookkeeper had been accurate and efficient. Everything was in order until three months ago. After that, chaos reigned. I went to the door again. "Okay, I think I've got the big picture. Let's work out what you need me to do here."

After hashing out a plan and agreeing on a fee, Eddy left me to sift through his paperwork and decide what to take with me to begin his conversion to a computerized system.

When he returned about fifteen minutes later, he set a plate down in front of me with a flourish. The aroma of the big burger and home-cut fries made my stomach roar its eagerness.

"It's lunch time, and I've seen you eat, Hungry Aydan," he said. "On the house. Thanks for saving my butt."

I grinned. "You want to be careful, Eddy. You know what happens when you feed a stray cat. She keeps coming back looking for more."

He laughed. "That's what I'm hoping."

My cell phone rang, making me jump. When I answered,

Kane's voice dragged me back to reality. For the past couple of hours, I'd been happily immersed in normalcy, and it was an unpleasant jolt to remember I was still in trouble with the law.

"Aydan, can you come down to Sirius?" he asked. "Smith has been tweaking the security, and he needs you to test it."

I blew out a long breath. "I'm just finishing up with a client, and I need to eat lunch. I'll get there as soon as I can."

"Check in at the security desk on the main floor, and they'll call me to come and get you from the lobby."

I hung up with trembling hands. What if I couldn't convince Kane of my innocence? I'd lose my delightful new client, my new farm, my new life.

"Is everything okay?" Eddy asked.

"Fine. I've just been a little sleep-deprived lately, and I guess it's catching up with me." I secretly crossed my fingers to dilute the lie. "And my next client is pretty demanding."

Eddy shot me a smug look. "Glad I snapped you up early. You're busy already."

I summoned up a smile. "Nice to be a hot commodity."

CHAPTER 20

My feet dragged as I approached Sirius's bland stucco facade. I could think of a number of things I'd rather do than go back inside that building. Things like dropping a bowling ball repeatedly on my toes.

I squared my shoulders and went in. At the security cage, I requested Kane, then sat in one of the lobby chairs and tried to concentrate on staying in the present reality. I wasn't feeling hopeful about Smith's security tweaks.

Kane appeared to collect me within minutes, apparently not trusting me to stay out of the network any more than I trusted myself. When we arrived at the meeting room, Smith and Spider were waiting. Smith was still wearing the same shirt, although I detected some fresh food stains. If possible, he smelled even worse than the previous day.

"What took you?" Smith demanded. "Don't you realize how critical this issue is?"

"Sorry." I attempted to sound regretful. "I got tied up with a client."

"Well, don't just sit there. See if you can get in."

As before, I looked to Kane for confirmation. "Go ahead, Aydan," he encouraged.

I rubbed the frown lines between my eyebrows,

procrastinating. The three men eyed me expectantly.

Smith straightened, smiling. "You couldn't get in, could you?"

"I haven't tried yet."

His face fell. "Well, hurry up!"

I sighed again. I wanted to be anywhere but here. I wanted to be home...

I stood on the hill above my house, looking out over the rolling land. A chilly wind sifted fine snow over me, and I shivered, pulling a warm jacket out of nothingness and putting it on. Seconds later, Smith and Kane materialized behind me.

"Dammit," Smith snapped. "How are you doing that?"

"I wish I knew."

Another man popped into existence beside us, staring incredulously around him. "What the...?" he said, and then shivered. "What the hell are you doing creating a construct in the portal?"

Smith stared him down. "We are performing network security tests," he said haughtily. "You might as well go right back out, because I'm going to close all network sessions in fifteen minutes anyway."

"How am I supposed to get anything done? You've been locking us out every half hour all day," the man grumbled, but he turned and vanished through the portal.

Smith turned to me. "Will you turn off the damn snow?"

"Sorry." I waved a hand to dissolve my simulation.

Construct, the man had called it. And apparently it was a no-no to create a construct in the portal. In my corridor simulation yesterday, the hallways had been lined with doors. Maybe that's what they were for.

Smith interrupted my speculations by speaking in a loud,

firm voice. His voice seemed to surround us as he announced, "Attention. All network sessions will be terminated in fifteen minutes. Please conclude your work and exit the network immediately. Thank you."

Seconds later, my corridor simulation reappeared, but I didn't think I'd been the one to create it. Several people emerged from the doors that lined the virtual hallway and straggled toward us, griping. They all gave Smith hostile looks as they went through the portal, which I could now see as a doorway marked 'Exit'. Guess I wouldn't need the holodeck simulation any more.

Smith turned to Kane and me. "You might as well go out, too. I'm going to give a five-minute warning, and then I'll come out and shut the whole thing down. Again."

"All right," Kane agreed. He turned to me. "Let's go."

I gritted my teeth and stepped through the door. Sure enough, the pain hit me instantaneously. Resigned, I swore as quietly as possible.

When I pried my eyes open, Spider was looking disappointed. "Not your finest work."

"It's been a long day," I growled. "Next time somebody shoves your brain through a cheese grater, remind me to critique your vocabulary."

I rubbed my temples while we waited for Smith to come out of his trance. This was the first time I'd been able to observe someone at close range while they accessed the network, and I watched him curiously. He sat immobile in his chair, staring straight ahead. The thousand-yard stare, Connor had called it.

"What if there's a fire alarm or something?" I asked. "Does his body retain any consciousness or physical sensation at all?"

"Oh, yes," Spider responded. "Any sudden sound or touch in the physical reality will bring people back out of the network. It's just like waking up someone who's sleeping."

"So here's another question. What would happen if I created a construct in the network, let's say, a cliff, and then I fell off the cliff in my simulation. And I believed it was really happening to me, so I fell to my death. In the simulation, I mean. What would happen to my real physical body?"

"Unless you had a heart condition and you gave yourself a heart attack out of sheer terror, you'd probably just wake up back in reality," Spider said. "Just like a nightmare."

"But I never actually die in my nightmares," I argued. "I always wake up right before I die."

"That would probably happen in the simulation, too."

"Let's hope so. It'd be a little tricky to explain to the Workers' Compensation Board otherwise."

Smith blinked and straightened. "Okay," he said. "In five minutes, I'm going to bring down the entire network. Then I'm going to lock it down so it accepts only my login and excludes everybody else, even those with administrator privileges. I'll block everything but my own biometric ID. We'll see if that keeps you out."

"I'm sure it will," I said hopefully.

He pinched the bridge of his nose and grimaced. "We'll see."

Ten minutes later, Smith looked up from his laptop. "Try it now."

I took a deep breath and let it out slowly. And stood back on my hilltop, shivering.

Smith popped into existence. "Dammit, this is impossible!" he yelled, waving his arms. "This can't be happening! You aren't me! Our biometric information is completely incompatible!" He seized me by the shoulders and shook me violently. "How are you doing it? How? Tell me!"

I twisted free and backed away. "I told you, I don't know!"

He churned his hands in his lank, greasy hair. "You must have a fob. A skeleton key. Something that totally overrides all security protocols. Where is it? Where have you hidden it?"

"I don't have anything. Kane searched me himself yesterday."

"Kane searched you. I think I need to search you." He made another grab for me, but I darted away and dove through the portal.

Brilliant agony slashed me while the world looped end over end. The sound of my own screams was deafening. My body thrashed and jerked beyond my control, mindlessly struggling to escape the torment. A tumult of noise slowly resolved itself into a voice shouting, "Aydan! Aydan, hold still! It's Kane, you're safe, hold still! Aydan!"

I went limp, still keening while waves of pain hammered my head. Black splotches began to overtake my blindness. The splotches lightened and I glimpsed Kane's face above me, shot through with brilliant flashes of colour.

His voice was quieter now. "Aydan, stay with me. You fell, but you're going to be all right. Just stay with me."

I blinked furiously, willing the spinning colours to subside. Gradually, the pain receded and the meeting room swam into focus. I lay on the floor. Kane was on his knees, supporting my head and shoulders while Spider and Smith hovered on each side of me, white-faced.

"Ow," I croaked. "Fuck." Something tickled my nose,

and I pawed at it clumsily, generating fresh pain. "Ow," I repeated.

"That seems a little inadequate," Spider quavered.

I squinted up at him. "Always with the criticism." My voice shook with the tremors that still vibrated my body. I swiped at my nose again, a little more carefully this time. My hand came back smeared with red.

"You hit your face when you fell, but I don't think your nose is broken," Kane reassured me.

His arms felt so good I had to resist an inappropriate urge to snuggle a little closer. I reminded myself that blood and snot probably wasn't an alluring look for me, and the momentary desire trickled away into embarrassment.

"I'm okay now," I mumbled. "Other than I probably need to wash my face." I struggled upright, and Kane helped me into a chair.

"What happened?" he asked. "Was it the beefed-up security that caused such a bad reaction?"

I scrounged a tissue out of my waist pouch and dabbed at my nose with a shaking hand. "Hard to say. It could have been that, or it could have been that I hit the portal at a full run."

"Why were you running?"

I jabbed my chin toward Smith. "He attacked me."

Kane turned to Smith, frowning.

"She's lying," Smith snapped. "I caught her trying to access the restricted files, and I chased her out."

I erupted from my chair, fists clenched. "You filthy lying s-" I bit off the epithet and jerked my scowl over to Spider instead. "Show the data record!"

"The portal monitoring was disabled for the test," Smith said smoothly.

I took a step toward him, rage swelling inside me. "How very convenient for you," I whispered, not trusting my voice. Kane's large hand wrapped around my arm. I shook him off. "I'm going to wash my face," I hissed, and stalked out of the room.

Kane was right behind me. "Aydan, you know I can't-"

"Can't let me out of your sight, I know. You can come into the ladies, or I'll go into the men's, I don't care. I'm just going to wash my face. Your choice."

"Men's," he decided, stepping into the room ahead of me and scanning it briefly for occupants. "Come in."

I went straight to one of the sinks and started running the water. In the mirror, I saw Kane prop the door open with the garbage can. "Yeah, maybe you should get Spider to chaperone," I snarled. "You wouldn't want me to falsely accuse you."

He met my eyes in the mirror. "I don't believe you'd do that."

I regarded him for a moment. "Thanks."

I splashed water on my face, cleaning away the smeared blood. Kane handed me a paper towel, and I patted my face dry, checking the mirror to make sure I'd got it all. My nose was red and puffy.

I plucked at the smears of blood on my good sweater and growled frustration. "I'm never going to dress up again."

Kane leaned on the counter beside me. "Aydan." I met his serious grey eyes. "Were you hurt in the simulation?"

"No. Smith was upset that I'd gotten in, and he got a little physical. Then he decided I hadn't been adequately searched, and tried to take matters into his own hands. So to speak. That's when I left."

Kane's face darkened, and a muscle jumped in his jaw.

"I'm sorry."

"Not your fault. Let's finish this." I turned and left, and he followed me back to the meeting room.

I took my seat. "Okay, we need to find out whether it was the extra security or the speed of the exit that caused the problem for me." I glared at Smith. "Shall we step into the network and find out?"

"No," Kane said. "This time I'm coming with you."

"You can't," Spider countered.

"Yes, I can. Set it up."

"No, that's not what I meant," Spider explained. "In order to properly test this, all the parameters have to remain the same except the way Aydan exits the portal. If we change anything, it could change the outcome. We'd never know whether it was a valid result or not."

I nodded agreement.

"Aydan, you don't have to do this," Kane said. "I can't ask you to put yourself through that again."

I summoned up some bravado. "Yes, I do have to do this. I want this resolved. It would be nice to avoid another faceplant, though, so if you could prop me up in my chair, I'd appreciate it. I'll go into the network first. Smith can follow me. If I don't come out within fifteen seconds of him going in, wake me from here." I gave Smith a hard look. "Let's go, Smith."

Smith fiddled with his collar, his gaze sliding away from mine. "This really isn't necessary. We've established that she can bypass the security. That's all I needed to know."

"That's not all I need to know," I growled. "Come on." This time I willed myself into a white void, not bothering with a simulation.

A few seconds' delay made me think Smith wouldn't

come. When he finally popped into existence, he was looking fearful. Rightly so. My fist was already on its way to his face.

Pain shot through my knuckles as his nose squished sideways under them. I followed up with a solid kick to his nuts and watched while he folded. Then I turned back to the portal, taking a deep breath.

The memory of the devastating agony was so fresh I hesitated for a long moment, swallowing the tightness in my throat. Smith's strangled groans reminded me I couldn't afford to stick around until he recovered. I clenched my teeth and stepped through.

Pain crashed over my head, and I slumped down in the chair, holding my skull with both hands. Kane's powerful arm supported me, and I leaned into him for a few seconds before straightening slowly.

"I guess speed kills," I croaked. "I took it slow, and this time was no worse than usual." I looked up at Kane's concerned face. "Thanks, I'm fine now." I massaged my eyes and temples, trembling with relief while he went back to his seat at the table.

Spider eyed Smith's vacant face. "What's taking him?"

"I guess he had a few things to work out," I muttered. I caught myself unconsciously flexing my fist. The knuckles didn't hurt anymore. Gotta love simulations. Kane gave me a sharp glance, but made no comment.

A few moments later, Smith's eyes refocused and he sagged, then pushed himself up straight, palms on the table. "She assaulted me!"

I gave him a deadly look. "Play back the data record."

"You know it wasn't being monitored," he snapped.

I shrugged. "Oops. I forgot."

Smith scowled at Kane. "Arrest this woman. She's a spy,

and she attacked me." He turned back to me. "Admit it!"

I maintained silence.

Kane gave me a level look. "Aydan, you didn't respond to Smith's accusation that you assaulted him," he said carefully.

I stared at him. I couldn't believe it. Mr. By-The-Book had left me a loophole. I took it.

"I didn't," I agreed.

Spider spoke up. "Which didn't you..." He intercepted Kane's look. His eyes widened and he shut up.

"She lies!" Smith cried.

Kane's baritone was silky, and I shivered. That voice bypassed my intellectual processes and went straight to sensation, like velvet on skin. "You have each accused each other of assault, and you have each denied it. I have no possible method of determining whether either of you is lying. This issue is closed."

He turned to Smith. "Get the monitoring back up, and open up the network," he said, his velvet voice turning rock-hard.

CHAPTER 21

Smith reached sullenly for his laptop and began to type. Kane appraised me from across the table, and I met his eyes squarely.

"We need to resolve this search issue once and for all," he said at last. "I checked with the Drumheller RCMP detachment this morning. They have a female officer on staff. Aydan, will you consent to a thorough body search?"

Oh, joy.

"Yes," I said firmly. "I want this resolved as much as you do. Probably more."

He made the call. When he hung up, he turned to face us again. "The officer will be here in about forty-five minutes. Smith, arrange for a meeting with Sandler in an hour. You and he will check Ms. Kelly's clothing and belongings to make sure I didn't miss anything."

I recoiled. "I don't want either of those creeps whacking off with my panties!" Spider and Smith both blushed scarlet.

Kane sighed. "This is the only way I can be sure nothing has been missed." He added in a steely voice, "There will be no impropriety." His look scalded Smith.

"If he even touches my underwear, burn it," I said. "I'd rather go without."

"I'll supervise the entire search," he reassured me. "Now, I have some more questions for you." He turned to Smith. "Go set it up with Sandler."

Smith packed up his laptop and shuffled out of the room, and Kane returned his attention to me. "Does the name Kasper Doytchevsky mean anything to you?"

"No, should it?"

"I wanted to ask you about your comment to Smith yesterday about the alias."

I scrambled to catch up with the non sequitur. "Um... Yeah, I was out of line. Sometimes my mouth starts up before my brain is in gear."

"Really. Because after the way he reacted yesterday, I decided to check into it. He changed his name to John Smith about five years ago. His real name is Kasper Doytchevsky," Kane said. "Did you know anything about that?"

I internally cursed my inappropriate sense of humour. "No, I was just running off at the mouth."

"Okay," he agreed without inflection.

I resisted the urge to beat my head against the table. What sadistic fate kept putting me in these situations?

"I don't know what to make of you," he said. "You claim this is all coincidence, but you drop these hints that tell me that you know more than you should."

I threw up my hands. "It's all just stupid coincidence. That's all I can tell you."

He assessed me, his brow furrowed. "But I wonder if there's something you can't tell me. Aydan, are you under duress of some sort? Are you trying to communicate something without telling me directly?"

"No, I'm not under duress. I'm not trying to tell you anything. I'm not spying. It's all just coincidence."

"I don't believe in that many coincidences," Kane said. "Let's go over the list, shall we? First, we suspect Samir Ramos of spying. You coincidentally meet him in the portal, which you accidentally accessed during an implausibly small window of opportunity. Then you coincidentally fling yourself out of your car right in front of us, drawing attention to yourself. You were the one who suggested talking to Mike Connor. Why would you do that if you were trying to hide your access to the network?"

I shrugged. "I told you, I didn't know what was happening."

"Let me finish. We check the data record, so Ramos's access to the network is revealed. We would have missed it due to Connor's cover-up, if you hadn't suggested the meeting. But why cast suspicion on yourself?"

I kept silent, realizing it was a rhetorical question.

"Then, you access the network right in front of us, proving once and for all that our security has been and still is compromised. Why? If you're a spy, why would you do that?" He frowned at me.

"We search you and find nothing, proving it's not a simple security breach. It's complicated and potentially disastrous. Again, you draw suspicion. You make an apparently casual joke that uncovers a name change you should have no way of knowing about. Which, by the way, was in his personnel file."

He rubbed his forehead and continued. "We beef up security and bring you in again to test it. You break through, and you make no effort to hide that fact. If you were a spy, why wouldn't you just lie about it and tell us you couldn't get in? But you don't. You tell us. Now you've consented to an invasive search that anybody in their right mind would prefer not to undergo."

He frowned at me, frustration written on his face. "If you're a spy, you're the stupidest, most incompetent spy I ever met."

I gave him a half-smile. "Lucky I'm not a spy, or I might take offence."

"I don't believe for an instant that you're stupid or incompetent," he said flatly. "So that leaves me with limited possibilities. The first is to accept a ridiculous and improbable string of coincidences. You know how I feel about that. Another possibility is that you're working deep undercover for our government, and we're both working toward the same goal of identifying and eliminating threats to national security. That's equally far-fetched. Both Webb and I have top-level security clearances, and along with our best analysts, we've spent most of today and half of last night digging into everything about you. We've found nothing."

I stared at him, open-mouthed. Far-fetched didn't quite seem to cover it.

"The last possibility is that you're a super-spy, and you've developed a complex plan to manipulate us somehow, for purposes I can't even begin to fathom. There's no logic to that possibility, either. Accessing the network right in front of us would be insane."

"I'm not a spy. Please believe me," I implored.

He shook his head. "I don't know what to believe."

The phone on the credenza rang. Spider picked it up and listened for a moment before passing it to Kane.

Kane gave me a severe look. "Stay here."

"Yessir, roger that," I sighed. Kane turned away to his call.

I jerked upright in my chair as a thought occurred to me.

"Hey, Spider, if you can pull somebody out of the network by touching them or making a loud noise, why didn't you just pull me out the first time I went in?"

"We needed to know what part of the network you were trying to access." He grinned. "We weren't expecting a bathroom renovation."

I eyed him curiously. "Here's something I've been meaning to ask. Why did you show up looking like Ensign Expendable in my bathroom?"

Spider looked sheepish. "It's a quirk of the network. If you don't consciously control your physical appearance in the sim, then you appear exactly as your self-image dictates. People with a poor self-image look uglier. People with a strong, realistic self-image look just like real life. You looked like yourself, except you were wearing old, baggy clothes." He dropped his eyes. "I looked like Ensign Expendable because that's how I feel around Kane when he goes into combat mode."

"So if somebody identifies themselves strongly with, say, a profession, that's how they'll appear," I deduced. "So Mike Connor was wearing his paramedic's uniform, because that's how he sees himself. And Kane was wearing combat fatigues because he really was in combat mode."

"That's about it. If you concentrate, you can change your physical appearance, but it's hard to hold it while you do any other kind of simulation."

"So if I wanted to, I could be a cute little five-foot-nothing blue-eyed blonde," I speculated.

Spider frowned. "You could. But... it wouldn't suit you."

I laughed. "Thanks, I think. But other than the fact that a brainwave-driven network is cool, what do you use it for?"

Spider hesitated. "Research and development," he said

at last.

"But what good is it?" I prodded. "If your expectations drive the sim, you couldn't use it for research. You could run a test, but you'd just get whatever result you expected."

He eyed the table while he ran his thumbnail back and forth along a joint in its surface. I knew I'd pushed the limits, and I was surprised when he finally responded.

"You can create external parameters that remain constant inside the sim regardless of your own input. That way you can physically interact with your theoretical models, and they respond strictly according to the data you've pre-programmed."

He looked up to meet my eyes with a strained expression. "I probably shouldn't have told you that. This is all classified."

Kane ended his call and was turning back to us when the phone rang again. "Kane." He listened, then replied, "Good, I'll be right down."

He hung up. "The RCMP officer is here. Everything we've discussed here is highly classified. We can't disclose any details at all to this officer." His eyes bored into me. "You will recall that you signed a non-disclosure agreement."

"Of course."

"I'll get Smith to bring down the network completely. It won't be accessible, even to you, Aydan. Officer Peters will conduct your search in the ladies' washroom. There are no surveillance cameras there, so you'll have complete privacy. Webb and I will wait outside. The officer will give us your clothing and your waist pouch. Webb will stay. I will take your personal effects to Sandler and Smith for analysis. As soon as they're done with your clothes, I'll bring them back to you. Is everything clear?"

"I meant what I said about burning my underwear," I told him.

"I'll make sure that's not necessary."

I sighed. "Okay."

Kane picked up the phone again and dialled. "Sandler, it's Kane," he said. "Have Smith bring down the network now." He hung up and turned to us. "Let's go."

I hid my nervousness as best I could. A strip search. What a great way to end my day.

The RCMP officer was mercifully quick and competent. She had even brought a blanket for me to wrap up in while we waited for my clothes to be returned. We made stilted conversation, but Sandler and Smith were quick, too, and Spider tapped at the door in short order. The officer handed me my clothes and tactfully withdrew so I could get dressed.

Once clothed, I hovered in the bathroom for a few seconds. This was embarrassing. Everybody knew where that officer's hands had just been.

I shook myself and squared my shoulders. What the hell, it wasn't like I had anything none of them had seen before. Except maybe Spider. I smiled to myself at the thought and stepped out of the bathroom. Spider blushed and averted his eyes.

"I need to walk Officer Peters down to the lobby," he mumbled. "You'll need to come, too, because I can't leave you alone."

"Okay, no problem," I replied, and followed them down the hall.

By the time we saw Officer Peters out the door and walked back to the meeting room, Kane had arrived bearing my waist pouch.

"All clear," he said with obvious relief. "Now we can

concentrate on figuring out what's really happening here. Aydan, you can go, for now. This network access issue isn't dead, but I need to track down some other leads. Webb will walk you down to the lobby."

As we rose and moved toward the door, he spoke again. "Oh, one more thing, your car will be released tomorrow afternoon from the police impound lot in Calgary."

"Great, I'll go down on the bus tomorrow morning."

He nodded, and was on the phone before we left. "This is Kane. We need to look at Ramos's place again."

In uncharacteristic silence, Spider walked me to the lobby to turn in my visitor's badge. As I opened the door to leave, he burst out, "Aydan, I'm sorry about... about... today. I believe you, I just don't know what's happening or how to make it right."

I gave him a smile, warmed by his vote of confidence. "Thanks, Spider, that means a lot to me. Call me if you need me again. I'll help any way I can."

The icy air took my breath away when I stepped out onto the sidewalk. The chinook was over and the temperature had dropped rapidly while I'd been inside the building. I shivered my way to the truck. Its engine turned over reluctantly before firing.

At least it wasn't snowing. I turned the heater to high and blasted it all the way home, shivering with reaction after my harrowing afternoon. On my way into the house, I checked the thermometer. Minus 20. And dropping fast, by the feel of it. I scurried inside and locked myself in.

CHAPTER 22

I crept miserably out of bed the next morning at five A.M. I hadn't slept well, and I wasn't looking forward to waiting for the bus in the frigid darkness. A glance at the thermometer compounded my self-pity. God, minus 30. It was March, for chrissake. We were supposed to be done with this crap.

I pulled on long johns under my jeans and layered a T-shirt under my sweatshirt. My truck started easily after its warm night in the garage, but I knew it would be different story when I came to pick it up later.

When I parked at the gas station and coffee shop that doubled as the bus pickup point, an opaque mist of exhaust from the idling vehicles rose in the dark air. I scooted into the building and bought a one-way ticket to Calgary.

The bus arrived promptly at six A.M., and I climbed aboard carrying my small backpack. As usual, the overnight passengers sprawled across the pairs of seats, heads and limbs protruding into the aisle. I threaded my way through the maze as carefully as possible to find a vacant seat.

The Silverside-to-Calgary route was a milk run, stopping in every little town along the way. I tried to doze, but failed. Every time the door opened, a blast of arctic air blew across my ankles and the smell of diesel coiled my stomach into a queasy ball.

At nine-thirty, I levered myself out of the uncomfortable seat and limped into the Calgary bus depot, trying to stretch out my cramped muscles. My car wouldn't be released until after four, so I bought a transit day pass and took the bus downtown.

I treated myself to a toasted bagel with cream cheese and a cup of herbal tea at the downtown mall's food fair before heading for the bookstore. Happily ensconced in the Mystery section, I browsed through the shelves, reading the first couple of chapters of each potential purchase.

The day dragged, and I did my best to fill it by dawdling over lunch and planning the convoluted bus route that would carry me to the impound lot. The weather had warmed marginally, so I wasn't too chilled by the time I finally arrived at my destination.

I was glad to get my little car back, and at least they'd cleaned off the blood spatters. I mourned the bullet hole in the trunk, though. When I started to drive, I discovered to my chagrin that a second bullet hole on the driver's side below the dash created an unpleasant draft on my leg.

Creeping along bumper to bumper through rush-hour traffic, I reflected that this was why I had such a potty mouth. The snarled-up mess was enough to make a saint blaspheme. Maybe I'd learn to swear less once I'd lived in the country for a while.

By the time I finally parked in my driveway just before six o'clock, I was starving and if I'd had to choose between air to breathe or beer to drink, it would have been a toss-up.

I growled aloud in sheer irritation. I never drank and drove. I'd developed a permanent allergy to impaired drivers. But I really, really wanted a beer.

I locked up the car and left it in the driveway. What the hell, I was warmly dressed and it was only a short walk to Kelly's.

I dropped my backpack on the floor between my feet and sank gratefully into my usual spot on the broken-down sofa, my back to the wall. Alanna, the waitress, stopped at my table.

"What's this?" she asked. "It's not Saturday, is it? You're totally messing me up by coming in on a Tuesday night!"

I grinned back at her. "You're right, I'm just messing with you. Can you grab me some hot wings and a Corona, please?"

"Where's the rest of the gang? You want to wait for them before you order the rest of your meal?"

I shook my head. "Just me tonight."

"And you're having a beer? I'm shocked!"

"I left the car at home."

She smiled and made an 'Aha' face before heading for the bar to put in my order. She returned in seconds with my beer, and I savoured the first few crisp, delicious swallows while I scanned the room, seeing none of the Saturday regulars.

I relaxed into the couch and stretched out my legs while I sipped, trying not to overdo it when my stomach was so empty. Nevertheless, I was a bit buzzed by the time my wings arrived. I set the beer aside and switched to water while I finished the wings, giving them my full attention.

When I came up for air to survey the patrons again, I hid my sudden pang as a man wearing an outback hat sat down at the other side of the room. Robert used to wear a hat just like that. This man's heavy build didn't look anything like my husband, but I felt melancholy all the same.

Usually I enjoy my solitude, but I suddenly felt very alone. I couldn't tell anyone the truth about what had happened to me, and I couldn't think of any plausible lies. The good guys thought I was a spy, and as far as I knew, the bad guys, whoever they were, were still looking for me. And I really didn't want to stay at my house alone again. I frowned and pitched the last chicken bone into the basket.

Alanna hurried over to remove the plate. "Is everything okay?"

"Fine. I'm just struggling with the momentous decision of what to have for supper. How about a Monte Cristo?"

"Good choice. Do you want another beer yet?"

"No, thanks, but you could bring me a fresh one when my sandwich is up."

I slouched back on the couch and finished off my bottle. The man in the hat talked busily on his cell phone. I pulled a book out of my backpack and started to turn pages, but the story didn't draw me in, and I put it away without regret when my food and beer arrived.

I ate the delicious sandwich without giving it the attention it deserved. Even my beer didn't seem as tasty as before. Alanna cleared away my empty plate, and I nursed the last of my drink. I didn't want to go out into the cold and darkness, and I didn't want to go back to my house. I pulled out the book again with a sigh.

A shadow fell across the pages. The man in the outback hat stood in front of me, silhouetted against the lights behind him. "What's a pretty lady like you doin' drinkin' alone?" inquired a gravelly voice.

"Hellhound?" I asked in surprise, shading my eyes against the glare.

"None other, darlin'. But I'm just Arnie tonight. It's too cold for Hellhound."

I grinned up at him, feeling ridiculously cheered by a familiar face, ugly as it was. "Actually, I'm eating alone. The drinking is incidental. What are you up to? I didn't know you came here."

"I'm workin' tonight," he said. "Mind if I sit down? I'm watchin' somebody, an' it'd be less obvious."

"Well, sure, pull up a couch," I invited. I didn't ask who he was watching, and he didn't volunteer the information.

He sat down on the sofa beside me, his back to the wall. "Best seat in the house. Now, darlin', am I interruptin' anything? Are ya meetin' somebody?"

"Nosy, aren't you?" I teased. "No, I'm by myself. Just sitting here with all my friends tonight."

He smiled back at me, flashing those even white teeth. "I can't believe ya got no friends."

"No, I have friends. Just none I can talk to at the moment."

"Talk to me, then, darlin'. I got time to kill."

I sighed. "Things have gotten... complicated... since the weekend."

"What could be more complicated than gettin' chased across hell's half-acre by some fuckin' nutjob?"

I sighed again. "I can't tell you. Like I said, it's complicated." We sat in silence for a few moments. Then I turned to him. "Arnie, have you ever done something where you didn't even know you were doing it, but you found out later it was really, really bad?"

"Darlin', that's the story a' my life," he chuckled.

"What'd ya do that was so bad?"

"I can't tell you. But it was really, really bad. Kane arrested me." My voice trembled a bit on the 'arrested' part and I slugged back a swallow of beer, not looking at him.

His voice was cautious when he spoke again. "Kane arrested ya? When? What charge?"

"On Sunday."

"How long were ya held? Are ya out on bail?"

"No, he didn't take me to jail. Yet," I said uncertainly.

"Then ya ain't been arrested, darlin'. Ya hafta go in an' get processed, fingerprints an' photographs. Did that happen?"

"No, but he said what I did was a crime. And he said I could call a lawyer. But I didn't mean to do what he said I did. I didn't even know I was doing it. I'm not making any sense, am I?"

I dropped my head into my hands. "This is why I didn't want to talk to anybody. And I'm not allowed to talk to anybody, anyway."

His tone was still cautious. "I got a friend, hadta sign a non-disclosure agreement 'cause a' somethin' he got involved in with Kane. But he can't even talk about the agreement, let alone the stuff he got mixed up with."

I looked up at him. "How close is this friend?"

"Close."

"I have a friend like that, too," I said, and hung my head again.

Hellhound reached over to lift my chin with gentle fingertips. "Darlin'," he said gravely, "You're right, it sounds complicated. But if Kane didn't take ya to jail, then ya ain't been arrested, and if ya ain't been arrested, then he doesn't think you're guilty."

"He knows I'm guilty," I burst out. "My guilt has been observed and recorded and replayed repeatedly in front of an audience! The only question is whether he believes I really meant to do it or not."

"Did ya kill somebody?" Hellhound asked.

"No!"

"Then anythin' else can be fixed."

"I don't think this can," I whispered.

"Trust me, darlin'. Kane's the best. He'll find out what really happened, an' you'll be fine."

I rubbed my hands over my face, trying to wipe away the despair. "I hope so, Arnie."

Alanna arrived at the table and appropriated my empty bottle. She turned to Arnie. "Would you like a drink?"

"Just coffee," he replied. "I'm drivin'."

Alanna turned to me. "Do you want another?"

I summoned up a smile. "Yeah. One more for the road. Thanks."

Arnie turned to me, frowning. "Ya ain't drivin', are ya?"

"Hell, no, it's a joke. Alanna knows I never even have one if I'm going to drive. I walked tonight."

"Ya walked? In this weather?"

I shrugged. "I wanted beer more than I feared frostbite." Alanna arrived with our drinks and I took a long swig. "Ahhh, liquid courage." I toasted Arnie with the bottle.

"Don't think ya need any more courage, darlin'," he observed. "Ya ain't afraid of much that I can see."

"Are you kidding? I'm afraid of lots of things. I'm afraid of carjackers with guns. I'm afraid of wacko home invaders. I'm afraid of politicians. I'm afraid of music played by 80's boy bands."

Hellhound chuckled. "Well, that ain't nothin' to be

ashamed of. All sane people're afraid a' those things."

"Well, there you go. It's nice to know I'm sane. That was in question for a while this weekend, too." I gulped more beer.

Two was usually my limit. The third was probably a bad idea, but what the hell, maybe it would help me sleep.

God, I was tired.

I slouched down on the couch and stretched my legs out, and we sat in silence for a while. I drank more beer and laid my head back.

"Don't pass out on me, now," Arnie teased.

"That'll never happen. I've never been that drunk, and I never will be. Just in case I have to run for my life again."

His coffee cup paused halfway to his lips. "Why would ya have to do that?"

"I'm kidding. I hope."

He frowned. "Where're ya stayin' tonight?"

"At my house."

"Did they catch the guy that busted in yet?"

"Not that I know of."

"Darlin', I know you're strong, an' you're brave, but that really ain't a very smart idea," he said gently.

I sat up. "Well, I can't just go running away and staying at a hotel every time I feel nervous. I don't know how long it'll take for them to catch this guy, if they ever catch him. And I'm not going to go snivelling to my friends every time something goes bump in the night, either."

"Ya ain't snivellin'. Somebody broke into your house an' ya barely got away. That was what, two days ago, for chrissakes? It's okay to be nervous, darlin'."

I blew out a breath of frustration. "I'm not saying it's not normal to be nervous. I'm just saying, I can't let it rule my life. I live alone. Yeah, I'm nervous. The best way to stop being nervous is to go and sleep in the damn house and get over it."

"An' I'm sayin' it ain't a smart idea. Let Kane find out what's goin' on. What if ya sleep there tonight an' some fuckin' dirtbag breaks in again?"

I threw up my hands in irritation, rapidly adjusting the gesture when my beer sloshed. "What if?" I demanded. "What if I get hit by a bus walking home? What if a chunk of frozen shit falls off an airplane toilet from 40,000 feet and lands on my head? You can't live your life constantly worrying."

Hellhound regarded me intently, his ugly face creased in concern. I swigged some more of my now-foamy beer and leaned back in the couch again while he drank his coffee, frowning into middle distance. After several minutes of silence, he turned to face me again.

"Come home with me tonight," he said quietly.

I searched his face, trying to read his mood. "Is this an invitation to come up and see your etchings?"

He grinned. "Hell, yeah, if ya want it to be. The ladies tell me I got the finest etchin's they ever did see." He winked, then sobered. "No. Seriously. No pressure, no strings attached. I don't think ya should be walkin' home alone, an' I don't think ya should be stayin' there."

"Thanks, Arnie, I really appreciate the offer. But I'll be fine. And anyway, I can't stand cigarette smoke."

"I don't smoke."

"Bullshit! You were smoking the night I met you!" I retorted. "What was that, you didn't inhale?"

He chuckled. "Part a' the character. What's a biker do with his hands when he's hangin' in a parkin' lot? He don't play games on his cell phone, that ain't cool."

I sat back and drank some more beer while I considered him. There was more to Arnie than met the eye. Kane trusted him. That had to say something. Kane didn't strike me as a man with poor judgement. And I really didn't want to stay at my house alone.

"Please tell me you're not riding the Harley tonight," I begged.

Hellhound shot me a mischievous grin. "Is that a yes?"

"Only if you sit on the P-pad. The only way I ride a bike is if I'm driving."

He laughed. "Don't worry, I got the Forester tonight. I don't put my knees in the breeze when it's thirty below. I might freeze off somethin' dear to me."

I blew out a long breath. "I must be crazy. Okay."

"Finish your beer, then, an' let's go."

I chugged back the last of the bottle and threw some cash on the table.

CHAPTER 23

It was just a short drive to Hellhound's place, but by the time we arrived, my beer-fuelled courage was wearing off. I didn't know this man at all. I'd only met him once before, chaperoned by an RCMP officer. What the hell was I thinking, going home with him? Once we were alone, there was no telling what he might do.

He pulled into a numbered parking stall in front of a block of apartment-style condos, and we got out. I closed the passenger door and hesitated, wrestling with my better judgement. The newspapers were full of stories about women who'd made such ill-advised choices.

Which was worse? Suffering and death at the hands of a total stranger who might break into my house, or at the hands of a man I barely knew?

Arnie walked around the front of the SUV and stopped, surveying my face. "Aydan, I know ya been through some bad shit lately. If ya want me to take ya to a hotel or call ya a cab, I'll do it, no questions asked, no hard feelin's. Just say the word."

I stood there for a long moment. I've never been good at trusting people. I should probably go to a hotel.

Kane's voice came back to me: 'He's the best friend you

could ask for.' I sighed.

I was tired. I was a bit drunk. And I hate being scared.

Kane trusted him.

"Fuck it," I said.

I followed Arnie inside and up the stairs. He unlocked his door and cracked it open cautiously with one foot jammed in the opening. Then he slipped inside, stooping as he went. When he turned to face me, he was holding an enormous battle-scarred cat.

"Hope ya ain't allergic," he said. "I forgot to mention Hooker."

I laughed, sounding more nervous than I wanted to. "I should have known you'd have a hooker in your apartment." I stepped inside and closed the door behind me, leaving it unlocked.

Arnie put the big cat down and kicked off his boots. He shrugged out of his parka, expertly tossing it and his hat past me to land atop the leather jacket already draped over the half-wall beside the door.

"He ain't that kinda hooker," he growled good-naturedly. "This here's John Lee Hooker."

"Oho!" I knelt down to the cat's level. "Boom, boom, boom, boom," I sang softly to Hooker.

He stared back at me with round yellow eyes. "Mmow, mow," he replied hoarsely.

Arnie and I both laughed. "Sounds just like John Lee," I said.

I extended my hand slowly. The scarred nose travelled the length of my fingers, and then Hooker pushed his broad face against my palm, begging for attention. I petted him and rubbed under his jaw. His eyes slitted with pleasure and a booming purr filled the room. I chuckled, relaxing. "Hey, big guy. Do you like to be picked up?"

"He loves any kinda attention," Arnie said. "The cat an' I have a lot in common."

I slipped off my jacket and shoes and carefully scooped up the big cat. When I rose holding him against my chest, he squirmed up until he could push his face under my hair. As his cold, wet nose tucked under my ear, his purring reached a rapturous crescendo. He squirmed some more, then placed one paw on either side of my neck, hugging me tightly while he purred in my ear.

"Aaaww," I said, my heart squeezing. I buried my face in the long, tickly fur.

"You're special, darlin'," Arnie said. "He won't hug just anybody. I'm gonna make some coffee. Want some?"

"No, thanks."

He disappeared into the kitchen, and I wandered around his shabby but clean living room, still cuddling the cat. The decor consisted mostly of tall shelves sagging under hundreds of record albums and CDs, interspersed with speakers and stereo components.

With secret amusement, I noted the crocheted afghans folded on the battered end tables and draped over the back of the well-worn couch. When Kane had mentioned crocheting, I'd automatically thought of fussy old-lady ruffles, but the clean-lined designs were masculine and contemporary, the colours masterfully selected. There was more to Arnie than met the eye, indeed.

He returned to the living room bearing a steaming mug of coffee and sat down, moving slowly and circling me widely. I recognized the technique. I used to use the same one with feral kittens.

"These afghans are beautiful," I complimented him.

"Where did you get them?"

"Oh, that's what I do to keep my fingers nimble," he said as he reached down beside his chair. He pulled up a guitar and played a blues riff.

I stared at him in surprised delight. "You're a musician!" I sat on the sofa across from him, still cuddling Hooker. "I'm feeling blue. Play me some blues, baby," I sang.

He grinned and launched into a piece I didn't recognize, a classic Chicago blues style. He sang along with the guitar, his rough-edged voice a perfect tool for the music. By the time he finished, I was beaming.

"You're an artist!"

He inclined his head modestly. "I do some jammin' sometimes."

"Will you play some more?" I entreated.

He chuckled. "Hell, yeah, darlin'. Your problem is gonna be gettin' me stopped." Then he sobered. "Aydan, is it okay if I lock the door now?"

"It's okay. I have your character reference right here." I nodded down at the big cat, still purring and nuzzling under my hair. "Thanks for giving me space, though."

Arnie got up and locked the door, then resumed his seat in the chair. "First time I ever got a reference from a cat. How d'ya figure?"

"Here's my theory. First of all, a lot of men prefer dogs. It's all about possession and dominance. So if you have a cat, it's a point in your favour. But if the cat is friendly and cuddly, if he goes to a stranger, it shows he trusts you, and he trusts all your friends. Hooker knows you better than anybody. If you're good enough for him, you're good enough for me."

"Well thanks, darlin'." He bowed from sitting position,

smiling. Then he picked up the guitar again and began to play. "How d'ya like this one?"

I sank back on the couch, letting Arnie's music flow over me. Hooker purred hypnotically, a warm weight on my chest. Surrounded by safety, the stress of the past few days ebbed away, leaving me heavy with exhaustion. I gradually snuggled into a comfortable position and tucked my feet up.

I was barely conscious when Arnie laid aside the guitar and covered me with a soft afghan before turning off the light. I floated away in blissful slumber.

When my phone vibrated in the dark, I jerked awake, disoriented. Hooker's purring bulk immobilizing my right arm reminded me where I was, and I made a left-handed grab for my phone to avoid disturbing him. After a short fumble, I pressed the button and mumbled an incoherent hello.

Kane's voice crackled through the speaker, wide awake and urgent. "Aydan, where are you?"

"Wha...?" I croaked muzzily. "I'm at Hellhound's." I yawned hugely. "Get off me, big guy," I murmured to Hooker as I freed my arm and sat up.

There was a moment of silence on the other end of the line. "I see," Kane said neutrally.

"Huh?" My brain spun up to speed, replaying the conversation. "No! Jeez! No, you don't 'see'. I was talking to the cat. I'm sleeping on the couch!"

"I see." This time he sounded amused. He paused as if in thought. "Good."

"What do you mean, good?" I sputtered. "Since when do you get to judge my sleeping arrangements?"

He chuckled. "I meant, good, I'm glad you're at Hellhound's. That's a good place for you right now. Stay there."

"What, you woke me up at oh-dark-thirty to tell me to stay where I am? What time is it, anyway?"

"It's two A.M. We had some developments at this end today, and we just uncovered some new information that makes it look like you could be in very serious danger. I called Richardson to go over to your house and get you. He said your car was in the drive, but you weren't there. I tried your phone expecting the worst."

"Oh," I mumbled, trying to process the new information. "More danger. Fabulous. What do you want me to do?"

"Just stay there. That's the safest place for you right now. I'm going to call off Richardson, and then we can all get some sleep." I heard the tiredness creep into his voice now that the urgency was gone.

"I'll call Hellhound's place tomorrow morning at nine o'clock," he continued. "He should be approaching consciousness by then. If you want to do us both a favour, you could make some coffee around a quarter to nine. Otherwise, we'll have to listen to him complain for the first half hour."

"Will do, thanks. I'm sorry for the scare," I said. "Goodnight."

"Goodnight," he replied, and hung up. I held the phone to my ear for a few seconds longer. When a voice like that says goodnight in your ear, you can't help thinking about a good night.

I sat thinking lustful thoughts for a few minutes, then shrugged and gave it up as pointless. I snuggled back down onto the couch and pulled up the blanket again.

Then I considered what the words 'very serious danger' would mean to a guy like Kane and shuddered.

CHAPTER 24

I woke to sunshine streaming in the window. The cat had deserted me at some point in the night, but there was still an indentation on the blanket where he had curled up. I squinted at my watch. Eight o'clock. I sat up and stretched, trying to ease the kink in my neck. It was a comfortable couch, but it was still a couch.

Soft snoring emanated from the bedroom, and I got up quietly to carry my backpack into the bathroom. I washed and dressed, congratulating myself on my foresight in carrying the backpack along to Kelly's the night before. At the time, it had only been a convenient way to carry my books, but it had turned out well in the end.

I felt so much better. Amazing what a full nights' sleep could do. Kane's dark words seemed far away from the bright, cozy apartment.

I slipped into the kitchen to search for coffee and filters, trying not to clatter around too much. Hooker appeared, winding around my feet and demanding breakfast with hoarse meows, and I found the bag of dry cat food and put a few morsels in his dish.

Not being a coffee drinker myself, I wasn't too sure about the mix, but strong seemed best. Promptly at 8:40, I pushed the button to start the coffee maker.

A few minutes after the brew scented the air, I heard the bathroom door. Shortly afterward, Hellhound shuffled into the kitchen, eyes half-closed.

I averted my gaze.

"Darlin', I love ya. Will ya marry me?" he croaked, heading for the coffee pot.

"No thanks, I'm trying to quit."

He slopped some coffee into a mug and sucked back a swallow. "Goddamn, that's good," he groaned. "How'd ya know the way to my heart?"

"Kane called last night about two o'clock. He gave me the heads-up."

Hellhound glanced up warily. "What'd ya tell him?"

Something about his expression made me wonder. I decided to see what was going on.

"I told him I was here, and he did this 'I see' thing. I got pissed off and told him you and I had been doing the nasty all night long, and he was interrupting my seventh orgasm," I embellished cheerfully.

His jaw dropped. Shock, delight, and dismay chased themselves across his face. I had expected the first two. The third confirmed my suspicions. Hellhound was in trouble again.

He settled on a rueful grin. "Thanks for the boost to my rep, darlin', but a dead man can't enjoy it."

"Why should Kane care if you get lucky?"

"He couldn't care less if I get lucky. But if he thinks I got lucky with you last night, I'm in deep shit."

"Why?"

He hesitated, then gave it up. "I was s'posed to be watchin' ya yesterday. He told me to just watch, stay hidden."

I stared in disbelief. "You were following me all day?"

"Nah. That was my first fuckup. Kane knew ya were takin' the bus into town yesterday to pick up your car, so he called me to follow ya. I knew what time the bus came in, an' you'd be easy to spot."

He slurped some more coffee moodily. "So I got to the bus depot on time but I ate a bad burrito the night before an'-"

I held up a restraining hand. "Spare me the details."

"Anyway," he continued, "By the time I got off the shitter, the bus was there an' ya were gone. I pissed away a bunch a' time tryin' to find out where. The lady at the C-store remembered your gorgeous red hair, darlin'." He smiled at me. "An' she said ya bought a transit pass. So I was hooped. No fuckin' idea where ya went. Kane about tore me a new one when I told him."

He slopped some more coffee into his mug. "We knew you'd be at the impound lot in the afternoon, though, so I was waitin'. Saw ya pick up your car, but I lost ya in that goddamn traffic clusterfuck. Figured you'd go home, so I drove straight there. Found your car but not you. So there I was, up shit creek again."

"No offence, but if he was so wound up about having me followed, why didn't he get one of his team members to do it?" I asked.

"Half his team is up in Silverside, an' the rest was tied up here. He couldn't spare anybody for an all-day surveillance job."

"So how did you find me?"

"Well, I figured if ya were still in the wind, ya hadta be on foot. An' it was dinner time, an' I've seen the way ya eat.

So I started lookin' in all the restaurants an' coffee shops in walkin' distance. I'd about given up when I saw Kelly's. I figured what're the chances of Aydan Kelly goin' to Kelly's, so I walked on in an' there ya were. I called Kane an' sat down to watch. Finally."

I frowned puzzlement. "But after all that grief, why did you come and talk to me? I never would have spotted you. I looked right at you, and I didn't even recognize you until you came over."

He shrugged. "Ya looked so sad an' lonesome, I thought what the hell, I'll just go an' say hello. An' then I could find out if ya were meetin' anybody, kill two birds with one stone."

"So you risked the wrath of Kane," I paused to inwardly enjoy my Star Trek pun, "just because I looked sad. And then you brought me here, knowing it would land you in shit again."

"Well, what else could I do?" He gave me a wink and a devilish grin. "I'm a sucker for pretty ladies in distress. But now Kane thinks I broke orders just to get laid, he's gonna rip my dick off an' feed it to me."

He batted his eyes at me. "Don't s'pose you'd consider layin' some sugar on me for my noble sacrifice. Like a last meal for the condemned man." He hung his head and gazed up at me pathetically from under shaggy brows.

I grinned. "You're begging for a pity fuck?"

"I ain't too proud to take charity," he replied hopefully.

I laughed. "Don't worry, your dick is safe. I was just kidding. I actually told Kane I was sleeping on your couch, and he said he was glad I was here. Too bad I wasn't more awake, though. I could have told him that story just to rattle his chain."

Hellhound sagged back against the counter. "Christ, lucky ya didn't. Ya wanna be sure what's on the other end a' the chain before ya start rattlin'."

"Sage advice from a man in his underwear," I observed.

"No shit," he agreed, slurping coffee and scratching his hairy, tattooed belly. "An' the underwear's special for ya, darlin'. Had a helluva time findin' it. Usually I go commando."

The bearded, cross-dressed memory from the sim flaunted itself in my mind, and I bit my lip to hide the smirk that threatened. Something must have shown on my face, because Hellhound grinned, a wicked glint in his eyes.

Warmth surged to my face. "By the way," I blurted before he could speak.

The phone rang.

"Kane's calling at nine o'clock," I finished with relief.

CHAPTER 25

Hellhound cut his eyes at me and picked up the phone. "Yeah."

I listened to the one-sided conversation, trying to hide my smile while he defended himself. He was obviously being reprimanded, but I was pretty sure Kane wouldn't be too hard on him.

Eventually, he said, "Here she is," and passed the phone over to me.

"I hope you weren't too hard on Arnie," I said without preamble. "He was good to me." The man in question gave me a thumbs-up and a grin from across the kitchen.

"No, I cut him some slack," Kane replied. "This turned out a lot better than it could have. And I still need his help. I've asked him to bring you back to Silverside today."

"I've got my car now, I can just drive myself."

"No, I don't want you to go anywhere near your house or car right now," Kane said. "When we talked last night, you may remember I mentioned some new developments. One of them was a dead man on your property."

"Oh, shit. Please tell me you don't think I did that, too."

Across the kitchen, Arnie glanced up with a frown.

"No, definitely not," Kane replied.

I mimed wiping my forehead in relief, and Arnie's expression lightened.

"But when we identified him, we discovered that this situation may be a lot bigger and more dangerous than we originally thought," Kane continued. "I want you back here, where we can keep a close eye on you, and I need to brief you on what we know so far and see if there's anything else you can tell us. Remember, all of this is classified. All Hellhound knows is that you could be in danger and he's doing courier duty."

"Okay. When do you want us to leave?"

"Ideally, yesterday. Call me as soon as you're on the road."

"Will do. 'Bye." I hung up the phone. "He wants us there ASAP," I told Arnie. "Can I mooch breakfast? Have you got some toast or something?"

"Yeah, think I got bread."

He opened the cupboard and pulled out a bag. We both squinted at the furry, greenish object inside.

"Maybe not," he decided, chucking the bag in the garbage.

"Fruit?" I asked. At his blank stare, I shook my head and tried again. "What have you got in here?" I pulled open the fridge door and surveyed the cases of beer and the lone pizza box. "How old is the pizza?"

"Yesterday afternoon."

"Perfect."

He handed me a plate, and I plopped a couple of slices onto it and slid it into the microwave. A couple of minutes later, I sat down at the table and dug in. He filled Hooker's food and water dishes and sat opposite me, nursing the last of his coffee.

I took a breather halfway through, and Arnie reached over to touch the back of my hand where it lay on the table. "Your knuckles are healin' up."

I smiled. "Yeah, you've got a hard chin."

I expected him to withdraw, but he didn't. Instead, he stroked my hand, his lean guitarist's fingers barely touching me. Feathery caresses went straight to the pleasure centres of my brain.

I sat very still.

When he spoke, his voice had deepened to the rasping grumble of an idling diesel. "How 'bout we go an' see about givin' ya orgasm number eight?" He smiled, his eyes gentle. "I guarantee, ya do it with me, you'll never call it the nasty again."

I swallowed hard, suddenly breathless. This kind man had flouted orders to comfort me and keep me safe. He had reassured me and sung me to sleep. We were adults. How easy it would be to just take his hand and walk the few steps to the bedroom, no expectations, no strings attached.

My body responded hungrily to the thought, and to his slow, sensuous stroking. God, I needed to get laid. To feel those warm, light touches all over my body...

I shivered. Reached out.

Took his hand.

"Damn, you're good," I said as I put his hand back on his side of the table. "You were nowhere close on the pity angle, but you nearly had me that time."

He leaned back in his chair and laughed. "Someday you're gonna find out how good I really am, an' then you're gonna kick yourself for waitin' so long. I'm gonna go get dressed. Finish your pizza." He got up and headed for the bedroom.

We went out to the Forester, he carrying his guitar case and a duffel bag, I with my small backpack. I raised my eyebrows at the guitar case. "Don't leave home without it?"

He grinned. "She's the most faithful relationship a' my life. I take her everywhere. I might hang around an' jam at Blue Eddy's on Thursday." He mirrored my raised eyebrows, nodding toward my backpack. "That all ya got?"

"Yeah."

"Most women, that's the size of their makeup case alone."

I shrugged. "I'm not most women."

"I noticed."

His frankly appreciative gaze caused a slight hitch in my breathing. Damn, it had been too long since anybody looked at me like that. Maybe I should have accepted his offer.

We got in the SUV and Arnie took the fastest route out of town. As soon as we were on the highway, I borrowed his cell phone to call Kane and tell him we were on the way. After anxiously observing Hellhound's driving for a while, I mentally awarded him a gold star and relaxed.

We drove in silence while I turned over the past days' events in my mind, trying to make sense of them. What had Kane discovered that had made him concerned enough to call me in the middle of the night? And if he was willing to tell me about a dead man over the phone, what could he possibly be holding back? I frowned.

"Hey, are ya mad at me for makin' a pass at ya?" Arnie asked.

"What?" I shook myself out of my absorption. "Oh, hell no, you can't blame a guy for asking. As long he takes no for an answer." I smiled at him, and he smiled back, clearly relieved.

"Ya don't talk much," he observed. "It's like ridin' with Kane."

"Sorry. I've got a lot on my mind, and I was just thinking it all through. Do you want to talk?"

"Nah. Just wanted to make sure we're okay."

"We're okay," I assured him.

We had a pit stop in Drumheller, then got on the road again. When we arrived in Silverside, Hellhound drove directly to Fiorenza's.

Strolling into the restaurant, I spotted Kane at the table we had occupied last time, his back to the wall. Spider sat facing him. I smiled. Slipping in front of Hellhound, I walked over and sat beside Kane. Arnie surveyed the remaining seat with barely concealed dismay. I felt for him, but not enough to give up my seat.

Spider looked up at Hellhound as he hovered. "What, you, too?" he asked. "Are all you people paranoid?"

"Occupational hazard," Hellhound grunted as he slid into the chair, twitching it sideways so he could see part of the restaurant in his peripheral vision. "Watch my back," he told Kane.

"Always do," Kane replied, and I recognized what was surely a long-standing exchange.

Conversation stayed general throughout the meal. Spider chattered away as usual, the rest of us responding as needed. When the bill arrived, I turned to Hellhound. "I'm buying. I owe you big time."

"No way. I'm plannin' to take your debt out in trade later." He leered at me, bouncing his eyebrows.

I laughed. "You'd better take the dinner. It's a sure

thing."

We haggled amicably for a few minutes, but in the end we each paid our own way. Hellhound got up.

"She's yours for now," he said to Kane. "Ya take good care of her. I got hot plans for this lady."

"In your dreams, Hellhound," I said lightly.

"Darlin', if ya only knew," he growled. He flicked the tip of his tongue over his lips and winked at me before turning to leave.

Spider stared after him, open-mouthed. "He is so... Why do you put up with that?" he asked, turning to me incredulously. "If I said something like that to a woman, she'd slap me silly. Talk about politically incorrect." A pink flush climbed his cheeks. "Talk about sexual harassment!"

I gave him a half-smile and a shrug. "Unless somebody is deliberately insulting me, I'm pretty hard to offend. It's all in fun. If he was serious, it'd be a different story."

Kane gave me a level look. "Trust me, he's serious."

I flashed back to the heated memory of the morning. "Yeah," I agreed casually. "But he'll take no for an answer and laugh it off without getting hurt or mad, and he doesn't push it too far. He just lays it out there and waits to see if I'll pick it up. It's like the difference between fly-fishing and gill netting."

Spider shook his head. "I still don't get it."

I grinned at him. "Then I suggest you don't try his approach."

He looked shocked. "I wouldn't!"

Kane and I both laughed. "Let's go," Kane said. "We've got a lot of ground to cover."

CHAPTER 26

We climbed into Kane's Expedition, and he headed toward the centre of town. "Please, not Sirius again," I begged, reflexively clutching my head.

Kane's mouth crooked up. "No," he agreed. "Not Sirius this time."

"Thank God."

He steered the SUV down a side street and parked in front of a small house. Two unobtrusive signs at the gate read 'Kane Consulting' and 'Spider's Webb Design'. I followed them into the house, discovering that the living/dining room had been converted into office space. Down the hallway, we entered one of the former bedrooms that now housed shelves and a meeting table.

"Energy consultant." I raised an eyebrow at Kane as we sat. "I wondered about that at Blue Eddy's."

Kane nodded. "We need to bring you up to speed on a number of things. Our priorities have shifted based on what we've discovered to date."

I wondered what that really meant. Could it mean he was starting to believe me and I might not get charged? Or did it just mean he'd get around to arresting me when it was more convenient for him?

"I'll fill you in with some background information to start with," Kane said. "Then we can get into our latest developments."

Spider interrupted. "Do you want some coffee or a Coke or something?"

"I could use a coffee," Kane agreed, getting up.

Spider got up, too. "Aydan?"

"Just a glass of water, thanks."

They left to collect the drinks, and I sat quietly in the room, reflecting that their leaving me alone must indicate some level of trust. That seemed like a good thing.

Spider returned first, bearing my water and a Coke for himself. Kane brought up the rear with his coffee. He turned to Spider. "You did the sweep?"

Spider nodded. "Right before we left." He took a small device out of his pocket and walked around the room, eyeing its steady green light. "Clear."

Kane sat down heavily, leaning forward and propping his elbows on the table. "Aydan, everything we are going to discuss here is highly confidential. There could be serious repercussions if this information becomes public. I need to know you understand the importance of the non-disclosure agreement you signed."

"You keep reminding me of that," I said, feeling miffed. "I understand non-disclosure. I *live* non-disclosure. I'm a bookkeeper, remember?"

He nodded slowly. "This goes a little beyond the realm of bookkeeping. There's more at stake here than some public embarrassment and a potential lawsuit."

I studied his face. He was very serious. I felt a flutter of apprehension, thinking of what I knew already. Department of National Defence. Counter-terrorism. A brainwave-driven virtual reality network. Shit, and now he was going to tell me something *really* secret?

I took a deep breath and met his eyes squarely. "I understand the importance of the non-disclosure agreement."

He held my gaze for a few seconds. "Good."

He sat back in his chair. "I'll begin at the beginning. You noticed I introduced myself to you initially as an RCMP officer, to Connor as a member of the security division at Sirius, and to Blue Eddy as an energy consultant. All of those are true, but not complete. When it's necessary for me to identify myself in an official capacity, I'm an RCMP officer. All other times, I'm a consultant."

I eyed him. "And Spider is a CSIS analyst and a web designer. Mike Connor is a security analyst at Sirius and a paramedic. Does everybody lead a double life here?"

"No," Kane replied. "Officially, Sirius Dynamics is a research and development company for the oil and gas exploration industry. They maintain regular contracts with petroleum companies. That is public knowledge."

He leaned forward again. "Unfortunately, you stumbled upon Sirius's real role, which is as a government and defence research facility. We were hoping to hide that from you, but you discovered too much on your own. We now think it's safer for all concerned if we give you more information. If you're a spy, you'll already know what I'm about to tell you anyway. If you're just an innocent civilian, you could endanger us all simply through your ignorance."

"Not everyone who works for Sirius has a security clearance," he continued. "Those who do, take on additional roles to help protect the secrecy. That's why Mike Connor maintains his paramedic's credentials. If something happens to a Sirius employee, we have medical staff who can maintain confidentiality."

I pondered that. "Dr. Roth is one of them, isn't she?"

Kane looked up sharply. "What makes you say that?"

"Mike Connor told her to put me in Wing B. He rode along in the ambulance specifically to talk to her because he thought I was a Sirius employee. So Wing B must be reserved for Sirius employees to be attended by Sirius's own medical staff. And I bet Sirius is the anonymous donor of the MRI, too, right?"

Kane rubbed his forehead. "This is why we decided to fill you in. You're too quick to put together the clues you have. Why couldn't you just be stupid?"

"Sorry," I apologized insincerely.

"You have to realize you are our worst nightmare. You've discovered a highly classified network and you have complete access, seemingly without any external aid. My first instinct was to bury you in the deepest, darkest hole I could find."

My pulse quickened as I stiffened in my chair. Where was he going with this?

"However," he continued, "That wouldn't solve the problem. If you exist, and especially if this is all random chance as you say, then there's a very good possibility there are others like you. And if that's the case, our enemies are almost certainly actively recruiting them. The more we can find out about you, the better. And it's essential that you don't fall into enemy hands."

I shuddered as unobtrusively as I could.

Kane drank some coffee, still eyeing me. "Before I knew how deeply involved you were, I told you we suspected Samir Ramos of espionage and terrorism. We have confirmation of that now, thanks to you. Because you drew attention to that data record, we were able to get the search warrant. We retrieved the hacked Sirius security fob, as well as his phone records. And that led us to some information we didn't expect."

He leaned back in his chair, cradling his coffee cup, and directed a piercing grey gaze at me. "What do you know about Fuzzy Bunny Enterprises?"

"What?" I faltered. Talk about hitting them out in left field. "Fuzzy Bunny? I've never heard of them."

He watched me a few seconds in silence before explaining. "Fuzzy Bunny Enterprises is an importer and manufacturer of children's toys. They ship worldwide, selling retail and wholesale. For some time, we've suspected them of shipping arms, intelligence, and drugs with the toys, as well as laundering money. We've never been able to prove anything, but many times when we've uncovered an operation, Fuzzy Bunny has been peripherally involved. Nothing we can nail them for, but they always seem to be there."

"Fuzzy Bunny. You've got to be kidding."

Kane smiled. "What, you think all the bad guys name themselves something sinister like 'Evil Incorporated'?"

I laughed. "I guess you're right, that would be stupid. But Fuzzy Bunny just seems so... incongruous."

He sobered. "And that's why it works. We discovered Ramos had made calls to contacts within Fuzzy Bunny in the past week. And then things got a lot more complicated. We went back to look at Ramos's apartment again, and it had been trashed. Somebody had been there since we initially searched. We're guessing they were looking for the fob. If he had an arrangement to deliver it to Fuzzy Bunny, they may have decided to go and take it for themselves when he didn't show up for a meeting."

He put his cup down on the table and leaned further back, tipping his chair onto its back legs. The chair creaked ominously, and he leaned forward again, dropping it back onto the floor. "We found a call record between Ramos and Mike Connor, and also between Ramos and another security analyst at Sirius, a Eugene Mercer. Connor and Mercer both had simple explanations for the calls, but it makes them suspects for hacking the fob."

I thought that over. "So you think Mike Connor and this Mercer may be connected to Fuzzy Bunny?"

"If so, we haven't been able to find a connection so far. But Connor disabled the alarm system so that a fob could be taken out of the building unnoticed. And he concealed the network containment breach and the data record that showed Ramos in the portal. He's our prime suspect right now. We're still digging to get solid proof."

I frowned. "But what has all of this got to do with me? I don't know a thing about fobs, and I've never even heard of Fuzzy Bunny before now."

"That's where things get complicated. I told you about the dead man on your property."

I nodded.

"He died of hypothermia," Kane explained. "You know how cold it was the night before last, and there was a high windchill. The RCMP found his car parked beside the highway. There was still a bit of snow left, and they could see footprints leading away over the fields. They thought his car had broken down and he'd walked for help, so they followed his tracks and found him just about a quarter-mile from your house."

Sick dismay tugged at my heart. "That poor bastard. If he'd made just it a bit further, he'd have been okay. I was home that night."

"Lucky for you he didn't," Kane said grimly. "He was armed, and he was carrying a stun gun and nylon ties."

A surge of horror washed over me. I had been home alone, as usual. I would have answered the door, letting the poor half-frozen man in. And I would have been captured, no one to know I was even gone until I didn't pick up my car at the impound lot the next afternoon. I breathed slowly and deeply, my hands shaking.

"It gets worse," Kane said, watching me closely. "We didn't discover that until late in the day. Once we found out, we started digging into the man's identity. He had connections to Fuzzy Bunny, too. Ramos or Connor must have told them about you. And it looks like they're serious about finding you. First Ramos tried to carjack you, then there was the failed abduction at your house in Calgary, and now this third attempt here in Silverside."

I closed my eyes. "Shit, shit, shit, shit," I chanted quietly.

"That's why I called you late last night. I didn't actually expect you to answer. I thought they'd have you for sure."

CHAPTER 27

I took a deep breath. "So now what?"

"Now, you don't spend another second alone until we get this resolved. For the next few days, Wheeler, Germain, and I will trade off staying with you. I feel like the pieces are coming together on this. Things have gone wrong for them, and that's when people start to get desperate and make mistakes. But if it drags out for much longer, you'll have to go into protective custody."

I sat rigidly, fists clenched, willing my breathing slow and steady. In. Out. Ocean waves.

"Aydan?" Spider's concerned voice brought me back to the meeting room. He touched my arm. "Don't be scared. Kane and Germain and Wheeler, these guys are the best. Nothing's going to happen to you. They'll keep you safe."

I faked calm with an effort of will. "Thanks, Spider."

My hands were still trembling, but I held my voice steady as I turned to Kane. "What does this mean in terms of my mobility?"

"For the next few days, you'll follow your normal routine. We'll tag along with everything you do. If you need to go somewhere, one of us will drive. We'll stay at your house at night, for now. If it goes beyond that, we'll work out the details with you then."

"Can I do anything to help?"

"If I think of anything, I'll let you know. I'll be with you today. Then Wheeler will take over for the night, Germain in the morning. We'll trade off every eight hours or so."

I let out a long, slow breath. "Okay. Are we done here?"

"I can't think of anything else, unless you have more questions."

"No. Can we leave, then?"

"Where do you want to go?"

I surreptitiously dried my moist palms on my jeans. "I need to go home and get some workout clothes, and then I need to come back to town and go to the gym. If I don't work off some of this nervous energy, I'm going to explode."

He smiled. "Your wish is my command. Webb, do you want me to drop you off at Sirius?"

"No, that's okay," Spider replied. "I'm going to get some work done here."

"I'll go and grab a change of clothes," Kane said. "If we're going to the gym, I'll work out, too. I'll be right back." He disappeared down the hall. After a short delay, he returned wearing sweats and carrying a duffel bag.

Staring through the windshield of the Expedition, my mind whirled, my heart still beating harder than necessary. I was the target of an international cartel of evil. I was in danger of being locked up by the good guys. I wasn't going to have a moment alone for the foreseeable future. I was scared, helpless, and... horny as hell, dammit.

After the sexual tension of the morning, my body wanted release and there was none in sight. Why hadn't I just taken

Hellhound to bed? I squirmed in the seat and sighed. Because there was no such thing as casual sex, that was why.

And now, big, hot Kane was going to be my shadow for the afternoon. I wished he hadn't said 'Your wish is my command'. That conjured up some extremely inappropriate scenarios in my imagination.

He glanced over. "Something on your mind?"

I snorted. "You really don't want to know."

"We'll catch these guys," he said.

"I hope so."

We drove in silence the rest of the way to the farm. He made me stay in the SUV while he opened the gate himself, then drove in and parked in front of the house.

I reached for the door handle, but Kane stopped me. "From now on, any time we come back here, we'll follow a procedure. You'll stay in the vehicle, sitting in the driver's seat with the doors locked. I, or whoever is with you, will circle the outside of the house once. If you see anyone other than Germain, Wheeler, or me, you will immediately drive away as fast as you can. You will call Webb, and he will meet you at our office. Is that clear?"

I nodded. "Got it."

"Once I finish the circuit of the exterior, I'll come back and get you. Stay in the vehicle until I do. We'll go up to the front door together. You will stay behind me. I'll open the door and check the house. You will follow me, stand where I tell you to stand, do exactly as I say until I tell you the house is clear. If anything happens to me or if I tell you to go, you will run to the vehicle as fast as you can and drive away. Call Webb, meet him at the office. You will not hesitate, and you will not try to help me in any way if I'm injured. You will just go. Got it?"

"Roger that." I gave him a weak smile. These guys weren't messing around.

"I know this may seem over the top, but we can't afford to lose you."

"It's good to be popular," I joked feebly.

He gave me a half-smile. "Slide over to the driver's seat as soon as I'm out." He got out and watched to make sure that I followed his instructions. I pressed the door locks, and he nodded, drew his gun, and started to circle the house.

By the time he retrieved me from the SUV and methodically cleared the inside of the house, I was wound so tightly I thought I might jump out of my skin if there was a sudden noise. When he gave the all-clear, I scuttled into the bedroom.

"Change here," he called after me. "I can't supervise you in the locker room at the gym."

I put on my workout gear and snapped on my waist pouch again before heading to the kitchen to snag an apple from the fridge. "Ready to roll," I said. "Too bad you had to go through all that just for me to spend thirty seconds in the house."

He shrugged. "Better safe than sorry. Oh, I just realized, you should bring a change of clothes. You can't change at the gym, but we can go back to the office afterwards and change there. I arranged to meet Wheeler at Blue Eddy's, and I don't want to do this again in between."

Back in the bedroom, I packed clean underwear, a nice pair of jeans and a flattering T-shirt into my bag. I really do try to dress a little better when I know I'll be out in public.

Kane preceded me out the door, scanning in all directions, and then hustled me back to the SUV, staying close. Shielding me with his body, I realized.

When we were back on the road, I turned to face him. "You must be hating your job right now. You probably didn't sign on for nursemaid duty, did you?"

He smiled. "I don't think of it as nursemaid duty. I'm protecting national security. It's a nice change that this time it comes in an attractive package. Usually I'm dealing with fat old men."

I laughed. "I aim to please." I thought wistfully about the double entendre before letting it go. We rode back to Silverside in silence broken only by me crunching my apple.

When we arrived at the community recreation centre, Kane stuck close while we walked across the parking lot and through the entrance. I'd signed up for my membership the week after I moved in, so I showed my card at the reception desk in the gym. Kane produced one, too.

I glanced up at him. "How much time do you spend here in Silverside, anyway? I wouldn't have thought it'd be a hotbed of crime."

"My time is about fifty-fifty between here and Calgary. It's not that there's so much crime here, it's just that I have access to certain tools here that I don't have in Calgary." He fell silent, and I let it lie. He probably couldn't tell me anyway.

"Do you want to split up and do your thing?" I asked.

"No. I need to stick close to you. Where do you want to start?"

I eyed him doubtfully. "You won't get much of a workout if you follow me around. I just do some strength training on the machines and then I run a bit or hit the elliptical trainer."

"Lead on. Anything's better than sitting at a desk."

"Okay," I agreed. "I usually do my core first. It's too bad they don't have those basketball machines here. Those are fun."

"We could toss a medicine ball."

"Sounds good."

At the mats, I picked out a six-pound medicine ball. "This is about all I can handle."

Kane nodded, and we sat down on the mats facing each other, knees bent. I lay back on the mat, holding the ball over my head, then sat up and tossed him the ball. He caught it and repeated my motion, tossing the ball back.

We did twenty reps, then varied the routine by tossing the ball to the side for another forty reps. I caught the ball on the last one and collapsed onto the mat.

"Okay, I'm done," I panted. He rose and came over, reaching a hand down to pull me up. He was breathing normally, and he hadn't even broken a sweat. Wow.

"Upper body next," I said, heading for the chin-up bar. I always did my chin-ups first, so I could get in as many as possible. Hey, when you're talking six chin-ups total, you don't want to let the count drop by one.

I hopped up. The first three were always easy, and I did them smoothly. By the sixth, I strained to the top with agonizing slowness, then dropped back to the floor, a little embarrassed. "Your turn. Show me how it's done." I gestured him to the bar.

He stepped forward, reaching the bar easily, and took a wide grip. Yeah, those were a lot more difficult than the kind I did. He surged up and down without apparent effort, his massive arms and shoulders flexing. I lost count of his reps and just stood there enjoying the show. Like me, he pushed his muscles to failure, and when he stepped away from the bar, he was sweating and breathing heavily.

Now, that was a good look for him. The parts of me that

weren't already sweating got hot and wet. I turned away.

What the hell had I been thinking? I'd planned to work out to reduce my tension, not increase it.

Oh, well. I stifled a grin. I could think of worse ways to spend a couple of hours.

I headed for the lat row. "I'm just going to do some lighter stuff here. Trade you off on the triceps pulldown," I offered.

The two machines were in close proximity, so I didn't expect he'd object. He stepped over to the pulldown and loaded up the stack. This was going to be good. I'd chosen the lat row machine because it faced where Kane would be working out. I'm not stupid.

I loaded my usual weight on the machine and pulled off my twenty reps easily, absorbed in Kane's flexing triceps. We switched, and I lightened his stack by over a hundred pounds before pulling my usual reps.

When I finished at the bench press machine, Kane eyed me. "Do you mind coming with me to the free weights? You're strong enough to spot me, and I like free weights better than the machines."

I shrugged. "I don't mind, but I don't have a clue what to do. I've seen what you've lifted so far, and I guarantee I'm not strong enough to do anything but run for help if you drop a weight on yourself."

He laughed. "I don't need you to be able to lift the weight. And I'm not going to push my limits today."

"Okay, it's your funeral."

At the bench, he pointed to the set of hooks near the bottom of the rack. "If I drop the bar for some reason, I don't want you to try to hold it up. Just yank the bar back toward yourself so that it lands in these hooks instead of on my head."

"You're nuts," I said flatly.

He grinned. "Don't worry, it's never happened. It's just a precaution."

"Okay..."

I positioned myself over the head of the bench. As he had directed, I took a wide stance with my legs flexed and back straight, placing my hands lightly under the bar, which was loaded with several huge plates. As he slid onto the bench, I realized with a shock that his face was almost in my crotch.

Not that I'd have any objection to that in private, but it seemed ridiculously intimate in the crowded gym. As he pressed the bar up and down, breathing rhythmically, it occurred to me that maybe I wasn't the only one enjoying our workout.

I managed to finish the rest of my weight workout without actually dissolving into a puddle of jelly, though I came close several times while I watched Kane's muscles in action.

"Elliptical," I said finally, heading for the machines. We chose a pair that stood side by side and I climbed aboard, setting the random program at high resistance. I really needed a hard cardio workout by that time. If you can't have sex, you've gotta have exercise.

The difficulty of the workout left me no time to appreciate Kane. At the top of each resistance spike, I bore down hard on the foot pedals, my breath coming in hard gasps. I grinned fiercely, enjoying the effort and sweating profusely. Not quite as good as an orgasm, but at least it took the pressure off.

When the 45-minute program ended, I set the resistance

back to minimal, cooling down. Kane must have set his machine to a high-resistance program, too, because he was sweating as much as I was. We glanced at each other and smiled, our breathing slowly returning to normal.

Shit, mutual virtual sex. Now that was just sad.

We got off the machines and headed back to the mats for cooldown stretches. I watched Kane out of the corner of my eye while I went through my usual routine. He was remarkably flexible.

Damn.

When we left the gym, Kane hovered closely again, scanning the parking lot. Once in the SUV, he drove directly back to the office.

Spider was at his desk in the shared office space, and he gave us a cheery hello when we walked in. "You guys look like you've been through the wringer. Better you than me. I'll never understand the need to go and push around heavy weights until I pass out."

Kane and I exchanged a glance and laughed. Both our T-shirts still showed sweat stains, and he pulled his away from his body. "I'm going to hit the shower. Webb, you're responsible for Aydan's safety until I get back. You know what to do."

Spider nodded, looking serious for once, and I wondered what they could possibly have worked out. Much as I liked Spider, I thought I'd probably fare a lot better in a fight than he would.

"Go ahead and keep working," I told him. "I'm just going to walk around a bit and finish cooling down. Can I get some water?"

He smiled. "The kitchen's just around the corner. Help yourself."

I went in and ran a tall glass from the tap, then walked slowly up and down the hallway, sipping water and cooling off. I had made several laps and was halfway down the hall when the bathroom door opened and Kane came out, his head muffled in a towel while he dried his hair. Fortunately, he couldn't see my reaction as I stopped dead in the hallway, my jaw dropping.

Oh. My. God.

He was shirtless, his jeans slung low on his hips. Men twenty years his junior would wish they had that body. The hair sprinkled over his massive chest was starting to show a little gray, but below his luscious six-pack abs, a dark, arrow-straight landing strip disappeared into his waistband, luring my eyes down to a magnificent denim-wrapped package.

With an effort, I retrieved my jaw from the floor and reinserted my eyeballs. By the time he emerged from the towel, I had what I hoped was a casual expression on my face.

"Your turn," he said, and I nodded, not trusting my voice.

In the bathroom, I stripped rapidly and got into the shower, thanking whatever merciful gods had decreed it would have a massaging shower head. I emerged some time later from the steamy bathroom, feeling much more relaxed.

CHAPTER 28

The men were waiting when I came out. I hadn't thought to ask what time Kane had planned to meet Wheeler, and we were a few minutes late when we arrived at Blue Eddy's. Eddy waved a welcoming hand from behind the bar as we walked in.

As usual, I scanned the room, spotting Mike Connor and another man at a table in the corner. Connor glanced in our direction and offered a friendly smile, which I returned, glad to see he apparently didn't bear me any ill-will.

Wheeler was already seated at Kane's usual table, and Kane took the seat beside him, his back to the wall. Spider turned to watch me, his eyes dancing as I perched uneasily in the chair facing Kane. Like Hellhound, I slid the chair slightly to the diagonal in an attempt to see more of the room. It didn't help much.

Kane leaned across the table. "I'll watch your back," he said quietly. I gave him a grateful smile, but remained distracted from the conversation at our table, hyperaware of the rest of the room behind my exposed back.

When the waitress arrived, I ordered my usual Corona and a glass of water. What the hell, if I was going to be chauffeured everywhere for the next few days, I might as well reap the benefits. I'd finished my first beer by the time our food arrived, and along with all the water I'd had earlier, it was time for a trip to the ladies' room.

Mindful of Kane's earlier warnings, I stood and said lightly, "I have to go and return some of Eddy's rental beer. Do I need an escort?"

Kane nodded. "I'll come with you."

"Never mind, I'll go," Wheeler said. "You just got your steak, and my salad isn't going to get any colder."

Kane gave him a grateful nod and dug into his steak while Wheeler and I went down the hallway to the washrooms. Wheeler leaned against the wall beside the door while I went in.

I was washing my hands when two tall women came in, chattering gaily. They moved uncomfortably close to me, and as I sidestepped to get them out of my personal space, a sudden jolt galvanized my body.

My muscles convulsed with the pinned-on-an-electric-fence sensation I remembered from childhood. Every nerve sizzling, I vaguely registered that I'd hit my damn nose again when I fell, but moments later the thought exploded into chaos while my body spasmed out of control.

Unmeasurable time passed, but it was probably only a few seconds later when I distantly heard one of the women at the door, her voice urgent. "Are you with this woman? She fell, and she's bleeding."

Through blurred eyes, I saw Wheeler's feet rush into the bathroom. Seconds later, his body crumpled to the floor beside me. A muzzy voice in my head sang, "Oh shit oh shit oh shit" as the two women lifted me up, one arm across each of their shoulders. My limp legs dragged while they lugged me briskly out of the ladies' room, down the hall, and out the back door.

My heart pounded furiously, pumping adrenaline. Utterly useless. I could neither fight nor flee.

A van waited in the parking lot. Its side door slid open, and the two women dragged me inside, letting me fall to the floor as the door closed. I felt the van accelerate.

It had all happened so fast. Kane wouldn't even know I was gone yet.

My face was crushed against the floor, my nose clogged with blood, and I tried to control my frantic panting. Breathe. Slow and steady. The rough carpet scraped my cheek and the vibration of the hard floor punished my aching nose.

Just breathe. Clamping down on spiralling panic, I forced my mind to focus on my predicament. I had expected my kidnappers to drive to the highway, but the slow speed and frequent corners made me think they must be staying close to the town limits. I tried to memorize the turns, but my terrified brain refused to cooperate.

After a short drive, the van stopped. The world spun as I was slung over someone's shoulder, and I caught a glimpse of a building that looked like a warehouse. A male voice grunted, "Christ, she's heavy!"

A steel door clanged and my captor's shoulder dug painfully into my stomach while my battered nose banged into his back with each stride. Blood trickled up into my eyes. I blinked furiously, trying to remember the twists and turns of the seemingly endless corridor.

At last he dropped me, my muscles finally cooperating just enough to prevent me from smashing my head. Someone yanked off my waist pouch. Rough hands dragged me into a chair and secured my arms and legs to it with nylon cable ties.

Fighting panic, I stayed limp and let my head loll forward, faking unconsciousness. I knew I wouldn't be able to break the nylon ties. I could only stall and hope for rescue.

Surely Kane would have noticed I was missing by now. Please, God...

Time passed while I bled and drooled. Pushing down terror, I breathed slowly and evenly through my mouth. Involuntary tears streamed from my eyes, as much from the impacts on my nose as from fear. At least they cleared the blood from my eyes.

Eventually, I quit drooling, and I was pretty sure the nosebleed had stopped, too. My face was itchy, my mouth full of the metallic taste of blood.

Using all my self-control, I let my head hang, playing dead for as long as possible and willing my pulse to slow. I tried to think of a better expression than 'playing dead'. I had a feeling these folks weren't much for the 'playing' part.

When a rough grip on my hair yanked my head back, I got a clear view the room for the first time. The man who'd grabbed my hair was dressed in jeans, but the other two men wore women's clothing. That explained the tall, strong women.

"I know you're awake," my captor growled. He aimed a savage slap at my face, and I ducked without thinking. The blow glanced off the top of my head.

Shit. So much for playing dead. I straightened to look him in the eye, holding onto composure with every ounce of my control.

"Now, Ms. Kelly," my captor said pleasantly, "I understand you have a special talent. Let's see it. We need you to access the network."

"I don't know what you're talking about," I mumbled, thinking frantically.

Network. They had a network connection! Maybe I could go in and broadcast an SOS the way Smith had broadcast his shut-down message. Surely somebody would hear me and come to my rescue.

A violent slap blasted pain through my face, rocking me back in the chair. I slumped forward, gasping around the new dribble of blood from my nose and desperately willing the network's familiar white void.

Nothing happened. I tried again. Then again.

Un-be-fucking-lievable! It had been all I could do to stay out of the network. Now when I finally wanted, no, *needed*, to get in, I couldn't do it.

He wrenched my head back by my hair again. "Let's try this again. We know you were working with Ramos. We know you have a hacked fob. Access the network. Pretty please."

"I'm trying! I can't!"

I tried to roll with the blow when his palm struck my throbbing cheek again, ripping pain through my neck and filling my eyes with involuntary tears.

"You can. We know you can."

"I can't!"

I had only a moment to tense my abs before he punched me in the stomach. The blow slammed an involuntary cry out of me and I doubled over the monstrous pain. Approximately an eternity later, I wheezed a single agonizing breath. Then another.

My mind floated up near the ceiling. Poor Spider. I know how you felt.

Dragged upright by my hair again, I slumped in the chair, fighting for breath and blinking away the streaming tears.

"Ms. Kelly," the man said in the same pleasant, reasonable tones.

I held myself rigidly against the shudders that rocked my throbbing body

"This is becoming tiresome," he continued. "And frankly, beating a woman seems a little, hmmm... crude. Let's try a different approach." From a sheath on his belt, he pulled out a large knife.

Pushing his face close to mine, he bunched up the front of my T-shirt in his fist and ran the flat of the knife blade over my cheek, the point just below my eye. I panted shallowly, my muscles locked in fear. He laughed.

"Ms. Kelly, access the network."

I clamped my teeth together to keep them from chattering. "I told you, I can't," I gritted, terror racing through me.

I flinched at his sudden move, but he didn't cut my face. Instead, he jerked the front of my T-shirt forward and slashed through it top to bottom in a single motion of the razor-sharp knife. The two halves of my T-shirt fell away to the sides.

"Look at that white skin," he murmured, tracing my cleavage with his fingertips. "I wonder if it's sensitive." He ripped clawed fingers down from my shoulder over the top of my breast, down into the V of the bra.

"I can't access the network!" I yelled. "I can't!"

"Isn't that too bad," he said sympathetically. He clawed across my chest in the opposite direction, leaving a grid of livid welts. I tried to jerk away, but the ties held me helpless in the chair. The scratches burned like fire.

My stomach squeezed into sick horror at his smile. "Look, Xs and Os," he said. He gouged an X in the top of the grid, near my shoulder. "X."

Moving down a square, his nails seared my skin again. "O."

The last of my control evaporated and I yanked desperately at my bonds, clenching my teeth to hold down the whimpers that tried to escape with every breath.

I recoiled when he leaned down to offer me a feral smile from inches away. "This is fun, but I'm going to get serious very soon. When I'm finished playing Xs and Os, I'm going to find a couple of your more outstanding features."

His fingers slipped inside my bra, pinching and fondling my nipples. I froze, my breath stopping in my throat.

His smile widened. "And I'm going to cut them off. And after that, I'm going to go looking for other tender pieces to cut off. You'll find it most unpleasant. Unless you access the network."

My whisper barely emerged through my trembling lips. "I told you. I c-can't."

My mind crawled sluggishly, numbed by dread. How long would they torture me before they finally realized I was useless? Mingled tears and blood dripped from my chin.

"X," he said.

As he bent over me again, I caught a flash of movement from just beyond the doorway.

Kane. Oh, thank God.

A cry leaked out between my teeth when my tormentor's nails dug into my skin again.

"O."

Then Kane was in motion. As he hit the first man, my

captor began to turn and straighten. With all my strength, I wrenched forward in the chair, my bruised abs screaming. My forehead cracked into his temple, and he staggered.

Hopelessly off-balance, the chair began to topple, and I jerked at it, trying to force it to fall toward him. I was partly successful, and it caught his leg on the way down. He sprawled on the floor, kicking at me as we fell. I did my best to pull my knee out of the way, letting the chair take most of the impact.

I'd only have a minor bruise there. If I lived.

I lay helplessly on my side, watching the fight from the floor. It was short and ugly, nothing like the movies. I couldn't tell if Kane had a weapon in his hand or not. One man already lay unmoving on the floor. The man I'd hit had lurched to his feet, staggering toward the table.

The second man fell bonelessly and Kane pivoted, his movements fast and smooth. I knew nothing about martial arts, but whatever he was using, he was good at it.

The last man wheeled around, a gun swinging toward Kane. There was a confused jumble of motion and the other man fell. His body hit the floor as if in slow motion, his head bouncing against the concrete with a sound like eggshells breaking. Dead or unconscious before he landed.

Kane knelt by my side. "Aydan," he grated. He grabbed the knife from the floor and carefully manoeuvred it between my arm and the chair to cut the ties that held me.

I drew a shuddering breath, trying not to sob. Another. Slow and even.

"I'm okay," I gasped.

He cut the last of my bonds and I rolled slowly onto my hands and knees.

"Can you stand?" he asked urgently.

"Yeah, give me a hand up," I whispered, trying to hold my voice steady.

His large hand closed around mine, and I crept to my feet, hunched over my bruised stomach. I straightened slowly against the pain, wiping the last of the blood out of my eyes and smearing the trickle away from my mouth and chin. Except for my nose, nothing seemed seriously damaged.

I rolled my aching shoulders and tottered over to the table to collect my waist pouch. Leaning on the table, I took a few long, deep breaths, willing the tremors out of my arms and legs.

In. Out. Ocean waves. Stay in control.

Kane stepped over beside me, glancing at the doorway. "Can you walk yet?"

"Yeah." I fumbled the pouch on and fastened it around my waist with a pained grunt when the twisting motion pulled my bruises. The dangling sides of my T-shirt interfered.

I reached out a blood-smeared hand. "Give me the knife."

Kane passed it over, still watching the door, and I made a slash in each side of the T-shirt, leaving two tails of fabric free. I tied them across my boobs, securing the shirt and attempting a bit of modesty at the same time. With my scratched, blood-caked cleavage emphasized by the tied-up T-shirt, the fashion effect was questionable at best. Daisy Duke meets Texas Chainsaw Massacre.

Kane shot me a tense frown. "Leave that. Let's go."

I wiped my hands on what was left of my shirt, forcing my brain into action again. "Right. Okay."

"Take this," he said, holding out the gun that he'd retrieved from the fallen man.

I stared up at him. "And do what with it? I'm already on the hook for an espionage charge. I'm not adding weapons charges to it."

"Aydan, we don't have time for this," he snapped. "The top priority is to get you out of here. There will be no espionage charge. There will be no weapons charges, even if you shoot somebody, and I expect and require you to shoot anybody who stands in our way."

I stood open-mouthed. "I thought you were Mr. By-The-Book."

"I am. Some days I use a different book. Take the gun, dammit, and let's go."

I took the heavy weapon from his hand carefully. I'd seen demonstrations, but I'd never handled a semi-auto handgun before. I ejected the full clip, quickly noting the capacity, and snapped it back into place. Kane reached over and worked the slide on the top, jacking a shell into the chamber. The gun had a long silencer and laser sight attached, and the balance felt off. I sighted, getting used to the feel of it. My hands shook, but I'd learned from long years of competition that I could shoot despite shaking hands.

Kane was watching me intently. "I'll go first. You watch our six. Shoot to kill, no questions asked. If anything happens to me, leave me and get out of here by any means necessary. Do not hesitate, do not try to help me. Copy?"

"Roger that." I attempted a smile at my feeble joke. I doubted if he could see it under the layer of blood on my face, but he gave me a wintry smile.

God, what if something happened to Kane? I'd never find my way out. I could really use a floor plan right now...

My mouth dropped open as I suddenly stood in front of a

table holding a set of construction drawings.

What the hell? How was I in the network now, without even trying?

It didn't matter. I shook off my paralysis and scanned the floor plans frantically, trying to figure out where we were. Pinpointing the most probable room, I identified a route and leaped for the portal, remembering just in time to stop and step through it slowly. This would be a very bad time to be incapacitated.

My eyes snapped open and I ground my teeth on a groan, fighting off the pain. A bobbing motion confused me for a moment until I realized Kane was carrying me.

"Put me down," I said in alarm. "You'll give yourself a hernia."

He stopped and lowered my feet to the floor of the corridor, one powerful arm still tight around me. "You fainted."

"No, I was in the network."

His eyes bored into mine. "I heard you swear under torture you couldn't access the network."

I frowned. "Apparently I lied. I found floor plans, and I tried to memorize the way out. But I don't know where we are now."

"No time," Kane snapped. "Follow me." He took his arm away carefully, making sure I could stand on my own before handing me the gun again. I took it from him reluctantly.

"Aydan." Kane gripped my shoulders and held my gaze with his. "If we don't get you out of here, our entire country's security could be compromised. And you will die. Slowly. These people will torture you until you give them what they want. I need you to do this."

I squared my shoulders and drew a deep, trembling

breath. "Okay."

He started forward cautiously, scanning the corridor ahead. I followed, watching behind.

CHAPTER 29

We crept through the corridors quickly and quietly. Thank God Kane knew where he was going. I was completely lost. At each corner, he paused and checked in all directions. I stuck close behind him, paying little attention to what was ahead.

Scuttle, pause, scuttle. Our rhythm continued through seemingly deserted corridors. My heart vibrated somewhere in the vicinity of my back teeth. Jesus, we had to be getting close to the exit.

A gunshot blasted through the corridor and Kane jerked back, swinging an arm around to push me behind him. I risked a quick glance in his direction and saw him lunge forward to return fire. He ducked back beside me, covering behind the corner of the wall.

I snapped my gaze behind us again, trying to control the adrenaline surging into my bloodstream. More shots exploded, and the tang of gunpowder scented the air. Two men ran around the corner behind us, guns in hand.

I had been holding my weapon in ready position. Their arms jerked up, but I was already in motion, sheer reflex kicking in. Lead the target. Just like trap shooting.

I fired once. The gun kicked in my hands, and one man

fell.

The other snapped off a shot that went wide and dodged behind a projecting wall. His shadow stretched across the floor, marking his position.

Drywall partition. It only looks solid.

It's not.

I jerked the laser dot onto the wall at chest height. It zigzagged wildly in my shaking hands, and my tournament instincts took over unbidden. I eased out a long, controlled breath and squeezed the trigger. A dark hole appeared in the wall and the body toppled over into the corridor.

I felt Kane move beside me and spared a quick glance his way. He was giving me that intent look again. "Clear," he hissed. "Run!"

We dashed down the corridor, my injuries screaming protest. Kane had been efficient. Three bodies sprawled across the corridor. We dodged around them.

"Door!" Kane barked, pointing. We burst through it and charged across the parking lot.

I gasped for air that didn't seem substantial enough, my heartbeat thundering in my ears. I stumbled on jelly-like legs, tripped and fell. I struggled frantically to my knees.

Shots rang out behind us and Kane lunged between me and the building, dropping to one knee. Firing one-handed, he fumbled his keys into my hand.

"Run for the truck. Leave me. Go!" He jabbed his chin in the direction of his SUV and fired toward the warehouse again.

The vehicle was only about a hundred yards away, but it might as well have been a hundred miles. I tried to scramble to my feet, but my knees wouldn't hold me and I fell helplessly to the ground.

I rolled over beside Kane, straining to raise the heavy gun, and fired toward the building from prone position. It was extreme range, and I was trembling so much I couldn't aim any more, but at least I could provide some covering fire.

"Is there a Plan B?" I yelled over the gunfire.

He ejected the empty clip from his gun, slamming home the fresh one he'd taken from his pocket. "Get to the truck!" he shouted. "Go, dammit!"

A stinging shower of asphalt sprayed us as a bullet ricocheted off the pavement only a few yards away. I squirmed backward toward the SUV. Kane moved with me, keeping his body between me and the warehouse while he returned fire.

More men rushed out the warehouse door, spreading out to fire on us. I couldn't move fast enough. We were going to lose. The SUV was too far away.

The icy pavement numbed my exposed skin. It was only a matter of time. Kane would get shot. It was a miracle he hadn't been hit already. And I would either die with him or be taken and tortured. I fired a couple more rounds, barely able to control the recoil.

"Move!" Kane bellowed. "We can't let them take you!"

With the clarity of despair, I realized there were no alternatives left. My mind refused to consider what would happen to me if I was captured again. Some things are worse than death.

I gulped back pure terror. "They won't take me." I gestured with my shaking gun. "Six shots left. Five for them. One for me. If it comes to that."

Kane spared me a fleeting glance. "Wait as long as you can. Backup's coming."

He fired and a man fell. I pulled the trigger again, and

again. My world shrank to the task of counting my remaining bullets.

Four.

Three.

I heard a vehicle approaching fast from our right, but couldn't spare it a glance. Kane was still shooting, and I fired again.

Two.

A dark van rushed into my peripheral vision and a din of automatic weapon fire erupted. The volley continued while the van skidded to a halt between us and the building. A hoarse voice bellowed, "Kane!" and the side door of the van slid open.

Kane scooped me up like a sack of potatoes. His shoulder slammed into my bruised stomach and my face smacked against his back. My cry of pain was drowned out by the gunfire.

Then we were inside, the square figure in the other side of the van still firing continuously at the building from the open side door. The vehicle accelerated hard.

Blessed silence fell as the weapons fire stopped and the door slid closed. I sprawled across the back seat, my ears ringing while I choked and sputtered blood from my freshly injured nose.

A tidal wave of relief threatened to sweep away my control. I was with the good guys. All my body parts were still intact.

I was safe.

I allowed myself the luxury of a couple of silent sobs in the darkness before clamping down hard again.

A beating sound thundered so closely overhead that I ducked reflexively. A brilliant light flashed through the van, fading as the sound diminished.

"That'll be JTF2," Germain said as he turned, slinging his sub-machine gun across his broad chest. He moved up to sit in the passenger's seat, extracting his phone from his pocket.

Kane bent over me in the dark. "Aydan?"

"I'm okay," I panted. I struggled to sit up, groaning, and his strong arm supported me into sitting position. "Goddamn son of a *bitch*," I whimpered, then choked again on the thick metallic taste and wiped at my throbbing face with the tattered remains of my T-shirt. "I am never, fucking *never* dressing up again!"

Kane's arm tightened around my shoulders. "You're going to be all right."

"Where to, Cap?" rasped a voice from the driver's seat, and I realized that Hellhound was the driver. Friend with a non-disclosure agreement, indeed.

"Hospital," Kane barked.

"Don't bother on my account," I said. "All I need is some food. And I need to wash my face."

"Hospital," Kane repeated firmly.

I subsided. Germain talked quietly on his phone in the front seat. Kane still had his arm around me, and I leaned closer, shivering against his warm bulk.

A few minutes' driving brought us to the hospital. Instead of going around to the Emergency entrance, Hellhound parked beside an unmarked but well-lit door at the back. The door swung open, and an orderly wheeled out a stretcher.

Hellhound swung out of the driver's seat to open the side door and Kane carefully helped me out of the van. When I finally stood unsteadily in the bright light, Hellhound's eyes widened.

"Aw, darlin'," he rasped as his fingertips grazed my matted hair.

"I'm fine. You should see the other guys," I joked.

My trembling knees buckled again and Kane and Hellhound each caught an arm, making me grunt at the jolt to my bruised stomach muscles.

I recognized B Wing as I was wheeled in. Doctor Roth appeared immediately, taking in my appearance with a practiced eye.

"Hi again," I said as she examined my head and face without comment, lifting my blood-caked hair to check for injuries. "I'm fine," I added. "I just took a couple of hits to the face and my nose bled."

"If that's so, why is your forehead covered with blood?"

"I was upside down for a while."

She frowned. "It looks like you took a couple of hits to the stomach, too." She indicated the purpling bruise showing through the tatters of my bloodstained shirt. "And somebody used you for a Tic-Tac-Toe board."

I picked at my T-shirt, peeling the sticky, stiffening fabric away from my skin. "Just one hit to the stomach. And the others are just scratches. All I really need is a facecloth and a bottle of orange juice."

"I'll be the judge of that," she replied. "Linda!"

Linda appeared, her eyes widening with horror when she saw me. "Aydan? Oh my God!" she cried. Dr. Roth gave her a stern glance, and she went quiet, her face pale.

"I don't see any serious injuries," Dr. Roth said. "Linda, bring a basin and let's get this mess cleaned up so I can get a better look." She eyed my shivering form. "And bring a hot blanket."

I lay wrapped thankfully in the blanket while Linda and

Dr. Roth cleaned away the caked blood. When they were done, the doctor looked down at me, her expression relieved. "That's better. You're going to be sore for a while, but you're fine. Your nose isn't broken, and we shouldn't have to pack it. The bleeding has stopped."

"Good. Can I get something to eat? That'll fix the shaking."

"Do you have hypoglycemia?"

"No, I just need food."

"Okay," she agreed. "We'll start you with some juice and see how it goes." She turned to Linda. "Could you bring it, please?"

"Sure," Linda replied, her smile buoyant with relief. She touched my shoulder. "I'm so glad you're okay. You looked so awful when you came in."

Dr. Roth waited until she was out of earshot before turning to me. "I'm going to give you the name of a psychologist who has experience helping torture victims. I hope you'll consider calling her."

I glanced up at her, startled. "I just have a few scratches and bruises. It's nothing serious. This was just the warm-up act."

She frowned. "You were hung upside down. You have ligature marks on your wrists and ankles. You were beaten and deliberately scratched. That looks like torture to me."

I shrugged, trying to hide the long tremors that still rippled through my body. "I'll be fine."

"Nevertheless." She handed me a business card, and I stored it in my waist pouch.

Linda returned with a glass of orange juice and a straw. I extricated one arm from the warm blanket to take the juice, and she propped up the head of my bed.

"Ready to meet your public?" she asked, pulling the cubicle curtain aside to reveal Hellhound, Kane, and Germain standing in the corridor.

"Come on in," I invited.

Hellhound and Kane sat in the two available chairs while Germain stood at the foot of the bed. I attempted to sip my juice, but my hand shook so much I couldn't get the straw in my mouth. Hellhound took the glass away and held the straw to my lips. I sipped thankfully, smiling at him. The other two watched in silence.

"So this is the spook wing of your hospital," I said. Kane and Germain twitched in unison.

"We need to debrief in a secure area," Kane said. "Until we do, nobody says anything. Clear?" We all nodded.

"Once I get something to eat, I'll be good to go," I said. They all regarded me doubtfully. "Jeez, I just need food," I insisted. "Arnie, give me some more juice, please."

As I sipped again, a sudden thought hit me, and I jerked up, wincing at the pain. "Shit, I forgot to ask. Is Wheeler okay?"

"He'll be fine," Germain replied. "They hit him with a stun gun, but they also injected him with an overdose of sedative. He's barely conscious right now, but Dr. Roth says we found him in time. He'll probably be released in the morning."

I sank back onto the pillow with a long breath. "Thank God. I'd feel awful if he'd been hurt."

With the juice in my system, I felt better almost immediately. I begged Linda to find me some food, and after clearing it with the doctor, she brought me a steaming plate of lasagne. The spicy smell made the saliva rush to my mouth, and my stomach rumbled. "That's the best looking hospital food I ever saw."

Linda smiled. "It isn't actually hospital food, it's my supper," she admitted.

I grinned at her. "You are such a sweetheart!" My hand tremor had diminished to a manageable level after the orange juice, and I helped myself to the lasagne, shovelling it into my mouth with no attempt at daintiness.

Germain's brown eyes crinkled with humour. "My God, she was starving."

"You have no idea," I assured him around a mouthful. I felt mildly embarrassed as the three of them silently watched me stuff my face, but I wasn't embarrassed enough to quit. At last, I set the empty plate aside with a sigh. "I owe somebody a really good lunch. When can I go?"

Linda fetched Dr. Roth, who shooed the men away so she could examine me again. At her request, I unfolded myself carefully, gradually stretching my sore stomach so I could stand upright. I walked back and forth in the cubicle a couple of times for her approval.

She nodded satisfaction. "You can go. Your only potentially serious injury is that hit to the stomach, and I don't think it's anything more than a bruise."

"No, I tensed up really hard before he hit me."

"Lucky you're in good shape," she replied. "I'll get Linda to bring the paperwork."

"Thanks. I'll try to avoid being your best customer in the future."

She smiled. "You'd better. Get out of here."

CHAPTER 30

Hellhound had insisted on giving me his jacket, and he hovered closely on the way to the door. I turned to him with a smile. "Relax, I've had my food. I'm not going to hit the deck."

"That's what ya said right before ya hit the deck last time," he growled.

"No, I just said I was fine," I argued cheerfully. "And I was. Would I lie to you?"

"Hell, yeah."

I laughed, and his shoulders relaxed at the sound.

The lights were on when we arrived at the small house-cum-office. Spider sprang up from his desk as we entered.

"Aydan, thank God you're okay," he blurted, but faltered when he took in my dishevelled appearance. I hadn't looked in a mirror, but I guessed that my nose was red and puffy again, and my hair felt crispy around my face.

"You are okay, aren't you?" he added uncertainly.

I nodded. "I'm fine, no worries."

"Thank God," he repeated.

"Thanks for driving," Kane told Hellhound. "You saved our butts. You can call it a night now."

Hellhound grinned. "Yeah, same old, same old."

I held out a restraining hand as he turned to go. "Wait, you need your jacket."

He waved it away. "Give it back to me later."

"Arnie, it's minus ten out. You need your jacket." I eased it off, babying my aching muscles, and held it out to him. "Thanks."

He eyed me, his face set in hard lines. My injuries were even more livid against my pale skin with most of the blood cleaned away. I followed his gaze and offered him a reassuring smile. "Don't worry, you know my Princess skin. It'll be all better tomorrow."

"Take your jacket, Hellhound," Spider said from behind me. "I brought Aydan's jacket with me from Blue Eddy's."

I turned to take it from him. "Thanks, Spider."

The young man's eyes widened as he took in my scratches and bruises and the slashed, blood-soaked shirt.

"Oh my God," he gasped. "Oh my God." He dropped into his chair and hid his face in his hands.

I slipped on my jacket to hide the mess. "Hey, Spider," I said gently. "It's okay, it only looks scary. I just had a nosebleed. Same as at Sirius."

"They..." He lifted a pallid face out of his hands, his eyes dark with distress. "They tortured you."

"Hey, Spider. Buddy. Relax," I comforted him. "I've been hurt worse than that playing basketball. With friends."

Germain frowned disbelief. "That sounds like a different kind of basketball than I used to play."

I grinned. "Yeah, we weren't too hung up on the rules." I held out my left hand and showed them the short, ragged scars on the back. "This is what happens when you try to steal the ball from a 250-pound steroid-fuelled ex-football player."

I was pleased to see Spider was becoming distracted by my story. "What happened?" he asked, examining my hand. "How did you get the scars?"

"Those were from his fingernails."

He gazed at me, open-mouthed. "He did that? Because you tried to steal the ball?"

I grinned. "It was an accident. He felt really badly afterwards." I paused for comic timing. "At least I think he did. It was hard to tell under that low, steroid-induced brow ridge." I mimed an ape-like gait, arms swinging, knuckles dragging.

Spider let out a half-hearted laugh. "You're crazy."

The other three men had been watching while I told my story, and Germain diverted Spider's attention with a question. As they turned away, I braced myself on the corner of Spider's desk, straightening slowly. That little show had cost me in pain, but it was worth it to see the colour returning to Spider's face.

Hellhound stepped to my side to wrap a strong arm around me, supporting me while I unbent. When I stood upright again, he moved away.

"I'm outta here." He jabbed a finger at Kane. "I told ya to take care of her. Don't fuck up this time. Anythin' else happens to Aydan, an' I'm gonna do some serious ass-kickin'."

Kane glowered at him. "Nothing else is going to happen."

"Better not," Hellhound growled, and went out the door, closing it with unnecessary firmness.

I sidled over to Kane. "Do you have a T-shirt I can borrow? I'm cooking in this coat, but I don't want to take it off." I nodded in Spider's direction.

"I've got some downstairs," he replied quietly. He spoke up so Germain and Spider could hear him. "We'll debrief downstairs. I've had enough surprises for one night." They both looked startled, but nodded and fell in behind as he led the way.

We followed Kane down the stairs into a cramped basement. The ceiling was so low that both Kane and Spider had to duck to avoid some of the beams. Kane headed for what looked like a furnace room at the back of the basement, the rest of us following single file. Nobody else looked as curious as I felt, so I assumed it was new only to me.

Kane went directly to the electrical panel, and I was surprised to see it was a 200 amp service, unusual for such a little old house. He threw some breakers in a seemingly random pattern, and as he pressed the last one, he put his face close to the panel. Light beamed across his face. Moments later, a door-sized section of the concrete basement wall swung soundlessly aside.

CHAPTER 31

This only happened in spy movies. It couldn't be happening in real life. I caught myself gawking and closed my open mouth.

Kane motioned us ahead, and we all went through the opening while he brought up the rear. As soon as we were all inside, he activated a switch, and the panel closed behind us. Spider and Germain were already on their way down the enclosed stairway, so I followed, my heart twitching into a hurried rhythm in the enclosed space.

Stay calm. Belly breathe. I eased out a long, slow breath, hiding a wince when my bruised muscles contracted.

At the bottom of the stairwell, Spider punched a code into a keypad and placed his face next to the scanner. The door released, and we all stepped into a large, brightly lit room with a table and chairs in the middle. Video screens lined the walls, and there was a lot of electronic equipment.

I gaped up at Kane. "Well, hello, James Bond."

Kane's mouth crooked up. "James Bond is a fictional character. And if you ask at any level in any department of our government or military, you will be assured that Canada doesn't employ anybody remotely like James Bond."

I surveyed him. "I have to agree. You're not remotely

like James Bond. You're too tall, and he never wore jeans. And I'm sure there's a perfectly plausible explanation for a secret underground spy cave."

"Fortunately, it's secret," he rejoined. "No explanation required, plausible or otherwise."

We shared a smile, and I cocked an eyebrow. "I have a feeling there's a really big non-disclosure agreement coming my way."

"The same one applies. And I'm not going to lecture you about it again." He gave me a grim smile. "After what I saw tonight, I'm inclined to believe you take non-disclosure seriously. Let's get something to drink, and then we can start debriefing." He led the way around the corner to a small kitchenette. "Coffee?" he asked as he went inside.

I waited outside the door of the tiny room. "Just a glass of water, please."

He filled a glass for me and a mug for himself before coming out so that the other two could help themselves. As they moved toward the kitchen, he guided me a short distance down the hall and opened a locker, handing me a neatly folded black T-shirt.

I eased out of my jacket and dropped the shirt over my head, covering the disaster that used to be one of my better T-shirts. His shirt was ridiculously big on me, drooping off my shoulders and hanging down to my thighs, but at least it covered most of the evidence of my misadventures.

When I slipped into a chair at the meeting table, Webb's face paled again as his gaze strayed to the red and purple marks around my wrists, but he made no further comment.

"Let's get started," Kane said. "Aydan, you go first. Tell us exactly what happened."

I gathered my thoughts. "I went into the bathroom.

Wheeler was standing right outside the door, in the hallway. I was washing my hands when these two tall women came in. I thought they were crowding me, so I tried to move away, and they hit me with a Taser or something. It felt like getting pinned on an electric fence. My muscles went completely haywire, couldn't do a thing."

"Stun gun," Kane explained. "Same idea as a Taser, but it's only good for close range."

I nodded. "Then things got a little mixed up. One of them called out to Wheeler and said I'd fallen. He came in and they knocked him out, too. They dragged me out, threw me in a van, and took off. They were actually men dressed as women. Carried me into the warehouse, tied me up, and the rest you know. Your timing was perfect, by the way. He was just about to get frisky with that knife. Thanks."

I had deliberately left out the gory details, and when I noticed Spider's face go even paler at the mention of the knife, I was glad I had. For Germain's and Spider's benefit, I filled in the rest.

"Kane came in and took out all three guys, cut me loose, and got me out. We made it to the parking lot, and then the cavalry showed up." I smiled at Germain. "Thanks for the fireworks."

He grinned back, his eyes crinkling. "I don't get much chance to play with that baby."

I turned to Kane. "How did you find me so fast? I thought I was toast for sure."

Kane smiled. "You can thank Webb and Blue Eddy for that. You remember I told you earlier about Fuzzy Bunny, and how they seem to have tentacles everywhere. When Webb was doing his research last night, he came across the fact that Fuzzy Bunny is the owner of that warehouse.

They're buried multiple layers deep in shell companies, but he dug them out. So we already knew there was a connection there."

He took a swallow of coffee and continued. "And you can thank Blue Eddy's sharp eyes. I was sitting at the table eating when I saw Eddy dash for the back door. You and Wheeler weren't back, so Webb and I followed Eddy in a hurry. He had recognized your hair, and he knew something was wrong when he saw you getting dragged out. He made it out to the parking lot in time to get a description of the van. He told me what direction it was headed, so I was reasonably sure about the warehouse."

Webb broke in. "Kane took off after you, and I called Germain right away for backup. Blue Eddy called the police. Then some lady went into the bathroom and found Wheeler, so I went to the hospital with him."

Kane took up the story again. "I got to the warehouse, and their van was there. Luckily."

I shuddered, thinking of what would have happened to me if he'd been wrong.

"I called Webb to let him know we were on target. I got in without too much trouble," he continued. "I'd hoped to be able to wait for Germain's backup, but when I got close enough to hear what was happening, I knew you were out of time. So I went for it."

"Thanks," I repeated.

Germain picked up the thread. "As soon as Webb called me, I scrambled JTF2. But I didn't know exactly how long it would take for them to get there, so I called Hellhound for my wheelman and we headed out."

I held up a questioning hand. "Who, or what, is JTF2?"

"JTF2 stands for Joint Task Force 2," Germain

explained.

"Well, that clears things up," I said with perhaps a touch of sarcasm.

Germain's eyes twinkled. "JTF2 is the counterterrorism unit of the Canadian Special Forces."

"Oh. Thanks."

He turned to Kane. "I talked to Blue Leader about half an hour ago. They've secured the warehouse and they're starting the cleanup outside. They've notified the RCMP that they're on a training exercise. That explains away the helicopter and the weapons fire."

Kane nodded. "Good. At least it's night. They shouldn't attract too much civilian attention, and the exterior cleanup should be done by morning."

"Will they do the parking lot, too?" I asked. "I dropped the gun there when you grabbed me to get in the van."

Spider looked up sharply and his mouth opened, but Kane talked over him. "By morning, there won't be a sign that anybody was ever there tonight. That leaves us with our own cleanup. Blue Eddy is a witness, and so is the woman who found Wheeler in the women's washroom. We need a cover story."

Webb spoke up. "Eddy thinks Wheeler got drunk and attacked Aydan in the bathroom and then passed out."

Kane and Germain both winced. "It's plausible, but it leaves Wheeler in a bad situation," Kane observed grimly. "I don't see how else we can explain it, though. Why else would he be unconscious in the women's washroom? And we still need a story for who abducted Aydan. We can't explain that away as a misunderstanding. Not after Eddy called the police." He massaged his forehead. "I suppose the search is still on."

"No," Webb said. "I called them as soon as Germain called me and said you had her. I told them you were an RCMP officer, and that you'd taken her to the hospital and you'd file a report with them later. So the search is called off. Oh, and I called Eddy and told him Aydan was safe and in the hospital. That's all I told him. And I brought the Expedition back from the warehouse."

"Thanks," Kane said. "At least that's covered. But what about the rest of it? We still need a story about the abduction, and why I took off like a bat out of hell after the van, too. Blue Eddy thinks I'm an energy consultant. That won't fly."

They all fell silent, frowning.

"How about this," I offered. "Tell Eddy my crazed stalker ex-husband and one of his low-life buddies attacked me, drugged me, and abducted me. Wheeler heard us struggling in the bathroom and ran in trying to save me. They attacked him and drugged him, too. You took off after the van so you could relay its position to the police. The RCMP set up a roadblock and nabbed my ex-husband and rescued me. I went to the hospital just as a precaution."

Three faces showed rising hope. "That might work," Kane said thoughtfully.

"I think it should," I agreed. "Everybody ends up looking like a hero, and you don't have to panic people with stories of random abductions. If anybody asks, I can tell them that I moved here to get away from my ex-husband."

Germain turned to me. "Do you really have a crazed stalker ex-husband?"

I grinned. "I have an ex-husband. But I'm pretty sure he's not a crazed stalker. I haven't seen him in years. I wouldn't want to spin a yarn like that in Calgary, but nobody knows him here, so it should be okay."

"Why would you worry about telling a story like that in Calgary?" Kane eyed me with curiosity. "Is your ex-husband in a prominent position?"

"No. But just because it was a shitty marriage doesn't give me the right to spread lies about the guy."

"That never stopped my ex-wife," Germain muttered.

Kane returned to the point. "Okay, that story covers most of our bases, but it's still a little thin in the part where the energy consultant rushes out after the van. To do what, exactly? And why?"

Webb spoke up, his eyes sparkling. "I know why. Because you're in love with Aydan!" He looked around at our open mouths. "Well, not really. Like, you know, as a cover story."

Kane shook his head slowly. "That creates all kinds of complications down the road. Aydan lives here. I spend half my time here. It would be too hard to maintain."

Germain's eyes crinkled with his mischievous smile. "You could have a torrid affair, and then have a spectacular fight and end it. Real Harlequin Romance stuff."

I made a gagging noise and shook my head. "Please. I have to live here."

There was a short silence. Then Spider said, "Ouch!"

I followed his gaze to Kane, who was looking a little disconcerted. "Nothing personal," I hastened to explain. "Not that I'd object to a torrid affair..."

Kane's eyebrows went up, along with the corner of his mouth. A quiet 'Oooh' came from Germain's end of the table.

"What I meant was..." I felt a blush starting and swung around on Germain, who was laughing openly by now. "You shut up."

I took stock of the three grinning faces around the table and started to laugh myself. "You know damn well what I meant. You ladies will have to get your fix from the TV. I don't do soap operas."

Kane chuckled. "Agreed. The soap opera scenario is off the table."

"Anyway, why do you have to explain it at all?" I asked. "So you take off after the van, so what? Sometimes people do irrational things in the heat of the moment. Stop thinking like a spy, think like an energy consultant. You didn't know it would hamper the police investigation, you were just trying to help."

Kane looked relieved. "Good point. No need to over-analyze this. We've got our story."

"What about Hellhound?" I asked. "Doesn't he need to know the story? Why isn't he here, too?"

"We'll tell him the cover story, but the less Hellhound knows, the better," Kane replied. "I told him in the beginning that you were an important witness, and that you were in danger. That hasn't changed as far as he's concerned."

"Does he know about your underground bunker and the fact that you guys are secret agents?" I asked.

"The bunker, definitely not. The other part, I'm sure he knows, but he doesn't ask and we don't tell."

"Nice to have a friend who'll turn a blind eye to spraying down a building with automatic weapons fire," I commented.

Germain grinned. "You've got that right. Speaking of which, are we done here? I need to check in with Blue Leader again."

"One more thing," Kane said. "We need to ID everybody

from the warehouse. We need to know who was there and how they're connected. Until we get this unravelled, we can't afford to take any chances. Aydan, you'll stay here tonight. We've seen how badly things can go wrong in an unsecured location."

He turned to the others. "I'll stay here, too. Germain, after you finish at the warehouse, get some sleep and then come and spell me off here around four A.M. By morning, Wheeler should be back in action. We'll meet here at ten o'clock tomorrow morning to strategize."

Spider looked up from his laptop. "What about me?"

"Get some sleep. Once the IDs from the warehouse start coming in, we're going to need your full concentration on putting the pieces together."

Spider nodded and packed up his laptop. He rose and turned to leave, but turned back to give me a troubled glance.

"Good night, Spider," I said gently.

"Good night." He bobbed his head uncertainly and left. Germain followed him out, leaving me alone with Kane.

I propped my elbows on the table and rubbed my hands over my aching face, feeling my hair crunch stiffly. "I need a shower," I said, repressing a shudder at the memory of my attacker's hands on my body. I wrapped my arms around myself. "I really need a shower. Can I go back upstairs?"

Kane gave me a sympathetic smile. "No need, we have showers down here. I'm sorry I can't offer you a change of clothes other than spare T-shirts, though. And we're not going back to the farm tonight."

"What about my workout clothes? I left my bag in your SUV. I could rinse them out and at least have something clean for tomorrow."

"Hold on," he replied, pulling out his phone to punch a

speed dial button. "Webb. You still here?" He paused. "Good, could you please bring Aydan's bag from the Expedition? Thanks." He hung up. "Webb will bring it down. The shower is this way." He rose.

I pushed my chair back and eased myself upright, leaning heavily on the table. He took a quick step toward me, his hands reaching out, but he stopped without touching me.

"Do you need help?" he asked.

"No, thanks, I'm okay. I just stiffened up from sitting still."

He nodded and led the way down another corridor, stopping at a doorway. "There's no surveillance in this room," he said. "You'll have complete privacy. Are you all right? Do you want me to wait outside?"

"I'm fine. Towels and shampoo?"

"Inside."

"Thanks." I went in and closed the door, sagging against it while I absorbed a few precious moments of safety and solitude. The tremors started again, and I wrapped my arms around myself, fighting off the need to sink to the floor in a quivering heap.

After a few long, slow breaths, I pulled myself up straight again and painfully pulled off the oversized shirt. When I turned to the mirror, I realized why Spider had been so upset. Even after my rough cleanup at the hospital, I still looked like hell.

The hair around my forehead was dark and spiky with dried blood, and there were rusty streaks at the sides of my face. My nose was swollen, and dried blood still clung to my skin here and there. Vivid red handprints splayed across my left cheek.

Below the neck, I looked even worse. My bra and the tattered shirt were liberally soaked and smudged with blood, now dried and darkened. My torso was smeared and streaked with rusty stains, and my jeans were spattered, too. The bruises and scratches looked like an overdone Hollywood makeup job. I could only imagine what I must have looked like before the cleanup. No wonder Linda had reacted with horror.

I sighed and picked at the knot holding my shirt together. After a couple of tries, I abandoned the effort as a waste of time. I pulled my jackknife out of my waist pouch and cut through the shirt. It wasn't like I was going to wear it again.

I eased out of the rest of my clothes and stepped into the shower, setting it hot. For a long time, I stood in the comforting spray watching the rust-coloured water swirl down the drain. When it ran clear, I reached for the shampoo and took my time.

CHAPTER 32

By the time I stepped out of the steamy shower, I felt almost human. I regarded my crusty bra with distaste and decided not to put it back on. It went into a sink full of cold water and shampoo instead. I combed through my wet hair and put on Kane's big T-shirt, then reluctantly pulled my stained jeans on underneath. I debated briefly before putting on my socks and shoes again, too.

I wasn't sure what to do next, so I made my way back to the main meeting area. Kane was working at one of the terminals that lined the walls, and he glanced up as I came in.

"You look better."

"I feel better. So, James, now what?"

He gave me a half-smile. "It's John, not James."

"John Bond." I grinned at him. "Nope, it's not working for me."

He leaned back in his chair, rubbing a hand over his face, and I wondered how much sleep he'd had in the past few days. "It's just John Kane," he said quietly. "And we need to talk. Why don't you sit down?"

I hovered indecisively. "First I need to ask you something."

He raised his eyebrows and gestured for me to continue.

"Am I a prisoner here?"

"No. You're not a prisoner."

I moved toward the door. "So I could walk through this door right now, and you wouldn't try to stop me." I rested my hand on the handle.

He went still, his face smoothing to an expressionless mask. Cop face. "I would try very hard to convince you that this is the safest place for you right now."

My pulse quickened, my muscles tensing. "So you would keep me here against my will."

"Aydan," he soothed. "You're not a prisoner. If you need to leave, you can leave. You don't need to escape."

I stood still for a long moment, staring at my hand clenched on the door handle. Common sense told me to stay here, protected and safe. Animal instinct screamed that I was buried underground, no windows, no light of day, no escape.

Trapped. My knuckles whitened.

"Aydan. Aydan, look at me." His deep voice was compelling, and I met his eyes. "You can trust me. I'll show you all the exits. Just stay here. Please. You have nothing to fear from me."

Common sense won. I took a deep breath and let go of the door handle. "I'm not afraid of you. I'm just claustrophobic. Normally I deal with it all right, but I'm feeling a little twitchy tonight."

The cop face faded. "Understandable."

"Will you give me the grand tour now?"

He nodded and rose from his chair, his movements unhurried.

I smiled at him. "You do that 'stay calm' thing very well."

He smiled back, his broad shoulders easing. "I'm glad it worked. I wouldn't want another wild chase tonight."

We walked through the complex and he pointed out the exits, three in total, explaining where they came out on the surface. We finished up back at the meeting room.

"Will you sit down now?" he asked.

I nodded, sinking gratefully into a chair when my knees wobbled. I must have been out of my mind to think about running away.

"I'm going to go and get a coffee," he said. "Do you want anything?"

"You must have an iron gut," I teased. "I can't believe how much coffee you drink."

He gave me a rueful grin. "Normally I don't drink this much, but I need to stay awake. How about it?"

"I'd love a hot drink, but nothing caffeinated."

"I think Webb keeps some herbal tea here."

"That would be great, thanks."

He headed for the kitchenette, and I reflected he must be taking a huge risk bringing me here. Maybe that meant he was starting to believe me? I pondered while I waited for him to return.

When he did, I inhaled chamomile scent from the steaming mug he placed in front of me. I picked up the mug and hugged it to my chest, breathing deeply and relaxing. When I looked up, Kane was watching me with a half-smile.

I smiled back. "You said we needed to talk."

He nodded. "First off, I need to ask you something personal. What happened between you and Hellhound?"

I stared at him, dumbfounded. "What does that have to do with anything?"

He ran a hand through his hair. "Normally, nothing. It

would be none of my business. But you're under my protection now, and Hellhound is a team member. I know you traded some innuendos with him earlier, and you stayed the night at his place. I need to know if he has done or said anything to make you feel uncomfortable."

I shrugged. "He offered. I declined. We're both fine with that."

His gaze searched my face. "I saw the way he touched you earlier. I've seen this happen before. It's all fine to start with, and then something happens and there's a sexual harassment charge. I don't want that to happen. It's my responsibility to make sure it doesn't. Say the word, and I'll talk to him and tell him to back off."

I met his eyes. "Are you telling me he might not take no for an answer?"

"No!" Kane shook his head, frowning. "No, I didn't mean that at all. He'd never cross that line."

"Then there's nothing to worry about," I said mildly. "I'm a big girl. I can take care of myself. If Arnie and I need to have a talk for some reason, I'll deal with it."

He exhaled slowly. "All right. I had to ask. Remember that if anything changes, you can come to me."

I nodded. "Got it. Can we move on?" He leaned back in his chair, his shoulders easing. "You really look out for him, don't you?" I asked.

"I try to look out for all my team members." Old pain flared briefly in his eyes. "Sometimes I do a better job than others."

I mentally replayed the conversation I'd overheard between Webb and the ERT guy, remembering Kane's insistence that I should leave him and escape.

"I have it on good authority that you couldn't have done

anything differently," I said softly.

His head jerked up. "What do you know about that?"

"I don't know anything. I overheard Spider talking to one of the ERT guys."

He frowned. "Webb talks too much."

"What happened?" I knew I was prying, but seeing his hurt, I had to ask.

He crossed his arms and sank his chin onto his chest, his eyes staring into the past. We sat in silence, and I didn't think he'd answer.

When he finally spoke, his voice was quiet and even. "Henry was one of my team. The two of us used to partner up for a lot of ops. One day the op went bad. I took a bullet. I was down for the count. I told him to leave me and get the hell out of there. Instead, he dragged me to the pickup site under fire and got me into the chopper. He was hit just as he was climbing in after me. He died instantly."

I closed my eyes for a moment, feeling the grief behind the unemotional sentences. "You would have done the same for him," I said with certainty.

He shrugged. "But I didn't."

"You had no choice in the matter. You try to take care of your team, but sometimes you have to let them take care of you. That's why it's called a team."

He met my eyes. "Look who's talking."

I straightened painfully in my seat. "Hey, this is me accepting help. I'm still here, aren't I?"

He laughed softly. "True enough. So let me help you. Tell me what your role in this really is. I think you're deep undercover, and I believe we're working toward the same goal here."

"I'm not undercover. I'm just a civilian."

He sighed. "All right, we'll play it your way. If you're just a civilian, why did you refuse to access the network, even under torture? Most women... never mind; most civilians, male or female, would be begging for mercy. You just sat there and swore you couldn't do it. Even when you knew what was coming."

I twitched an irritable shoulder. "I'm not most women. And if I'd thought crying and begging would have helped, I might have tried it."

"Might have," he echoed.

"That's what those guys get off on. I wouldn't give him the satisfaction if I could help it."

"So why not just access the network? You were already injured. You knew it was going to get worse. Why refuse?"

I stared at him. "That's a pretty funny question coming from a guy like you. Besides, I couldn't."

"Couldn't, why?"

"I just couldn't. I don't know why."

"I saw you do it seconds later," he countered. "When I asked you about it, you said you'd lied about not being able to access the network."

"It was just an expression. I really couldn't get in at the time."

He gazed at me, clearly unconvinced. "Really. And where did you learn to shoot like that? You looked very comfortable with that handgun. I didn't see anything in your firearms license about owning restricted weapons."

"I haven't shot a handgun since I was a kid. They weren't regulated then."

He nodded encouragement. "Because so many little girls play with handguns instead of Barbie dolls."

I gave him a dirty look. "Funny. I meant, since I was a

teenager."

"Uh-huh. Because so many teenage girls..."

I cut him off with an impatient wave of my hand. "I'm a freak. The sooner you get used to the idea, the happier you'll be. My dad liked guns. I like guns. He taught me how to shoot."

"What did you shoot?" he asked.

"Six-shot revolver. Smith & Wesson .357 Magnum."

Kane eyed me with curiosity. "What did you say your father did for a living?"

"I didn't say, but he was a farmer. Well, to start with. Later he worked for the government."

He frowned. "So your father, who worked for the government, also carried a .357 Magnum. And taught his daughter to shoot."

"Yeah. No! Jeez, when you say it like that... No, he worked for the Department of Agriculture. He just liked guns for fun."

Kane nodded. "And I'm an energy consultant. Tell me, when you haven't shot in thirty years, how you could miraculously pick off two men with a single shot each. And don't tell me it was just luck."

I didn't like the direction this was taking. "I never claimed it was luck, and I never claimed I hadn't shot in thirty years. I just haven't shot a handgun. I'm used to shooting moving targets when I shoot trap. When I'm competing in an archery tournament, I'm aiming at a spot that's a little smaller than a penny at twenty yards. I'm an instinct shooter. My first few shots are always my best."

He regarded me, his grey eyes piercing. "And how do you feel about those two good shots tonight?"

I met his gaze squarely. "I'm not going to lie to you and

say I'm devastated. That might come later, after I have a chance to process all this."

He held my eyes for a few seconds. "Aydan..." he said finally. "I... You realize I'm really out on a limb, here. I think we're on the same side, but all I've got to go on is my gut feeling."

"We're definitely on the same side," I assured him. "Just not in the way you think. I'm just a civilian, and I'm just trying to stay alive and help you get this figured out so I can go back to my normal life."

He sighed and scrubbed his hand through his hair. "If you're really just a civilian, then please explain something to me. I've seen people with military training who don't stay as cool as you did. Under torture. Under live fire. But we haven't been able to find any evidence of that type of training in any of your records."

I shrugged. "That's just the way I react. I told you I'm a freak."

"Aydan." He met my eyes, his expression strained. "Please. I'm not asking out of idle curiosity. I'm holding national security in my hands. Do you have any idea how many lives depend on me making the right decision here?"

I blew out a long breath and dropped my face into my hands as every old defensive instinct sprang up. But I couldn't lie to him. He was putting himself in a desperately vulnerable position.

I propped my elbows on the table and addressed my lap. "No, I don't have military training. But I have years of practice at keeping my emotions bottled up and hidden. When I was a kid, I was a tomboy. When you play with the boys, you never cry, and you never show pain if you get hurt. That's the way I grew up. Then I married my first husband."

I paused. So long ago now.

"What happened?" His voice was quiet.

"I was young and naive, and that was before emotional abuse had a name. I didn't understand what was happening, but I found out that showing any kind of reaction made things worse. So I learned to stay in control. Hide every emotion. And after years of practice, I got really good at it."

I met his eyes, and immediately looked down at the table again, swallowing hard. Nothing worse than sympathy. Didn't have much practice dealing with that.

"So the worse things get, the more you clamp down on your emotions," he said gently. "Because others can use your emotions to hurt you."

I lifted a shoulder and we sat in silence for a few moments while I avoided his gaze.

"Why did you stay with him so long?"

I laughed. "Sheer stupidity, as far as I can figure out."

"Aydan, I know that's not true. Really, why?"

"Because I promised!" The anger in my voice caught me by surprise, and I quickly tucked it away. When I spoke again, I kept my voice calm and even. "For better or for worse. 'Til death do us part."

I stood and turned away to escape the memory of all those desperate, unanswered prayers for death. Old instinct made my tone dispassionate as I wrapped my arms around my aching body and continued.

"Finally, I discovered he'd been cheating on me. For years. And I used that as an excuse to divorce him. So much for the honour of my promise."

"Aydan, nobody could expect you to stay in a situation like that." His voice was forceful behind me.

"I made a vow. I broke it." I shrugged. "I'm more

careful about what I promise these days. Anyway, it doesn't matter. Now you know why I don't lose control under pressure."

"And you don't fear death, but you're terrified of captivity. Because you were trapped for so long," he finished quietly.

I shrugged again and made sure my face was under control before I turned back to the table. I lowered myself carefully into my chair and sipped at the lukewarm tea. I could feel his eyes on me, and I steadfastly surveyed the table.

"But he's the one who broke your vows, not you," he murmured. "Didn't he promise to love, honour, and cherish?"

I sighed. "John, you needed to know this, so I told you. But I really don't want to talk about it."

"Aydan, I would never use this knowledge to hurt you. You have my word."

"Please don't promise. Just tell me you'll do your best."

"I'll do my best."

CHAPTER 33

I drained the last of the cool tea from my mug. "What are the sleeping arrangements here?"

"We have a couple of bunks," Kane replied, mercifully accepting the change of topic. "I've made up one of the lower ones for you. This way." He stood. "Oh, here's your bag, too," he said, handing it to me.

I rose stiffly, and we headed back down the hallway again, past the bathroom to the door of a small room containing two bunk beds.

"You'll have this to yourself tonight," he said.

"I thought you said you were staying the night, too. Is there another room?"

"I'll just nap in a chair down here tonight," he replied. "I need to be close to the action."

I shrugged. "Don't feel you have to take the chair on my account. Take the other bed if you want. Just be forewarned, sometimes I snore."

He laughed as he turned to leave. "Duly noted."

I went back to the bathroom and rinsed out my workout clothes. Most of the stains had soaked out of my bra, and I scrubbed until it was presentable and then hung it up along with my other things. I took off my jeans and did my best to clean the stains out of them, too, before padding barefoot back to the little bunkroom, enveloped in Kane's big T-shirt.

I crept into the bunk and tried to find a position that didn't strain my sore stomach. Once under the covers, I drifted, dozing and jerking awake. Each time I dropped off, bullets cracked past my head or I fell helplessly, my hands bound. Finally, my over-tired subconscious gave up, and I fell deeply asleep.

Opening my eyes in the dark room, I saw a bulky shape by the door. It moved quietly toward my bed while I lay motionless, straining to see. The big, black-clad man suddenly pounced, his vicious grip shooting pain through my wrist. He yanked it up to secure it to the bedpost with a nylon tie. His weight pinned me as he seized my other wrist, jerking it up to the opposite post. His teeth gleamed in a savage grin. I kicked and thrashed, but he was too strong. He crushed me onto the bed while I screamed and screamed.

I bolted upright, the last scream ripping my throat as Kane burst into the bunkroom.

"Aydan!" He slid to his knees beside my bed, close, but not touching me. "Aydan. You're safe. It was just a dream," he said urgently.

I stared blindly at him, still disoriented. A big black-clad man kneeling beside my bed. But not touching me. I clasped my bruised wrists against my aching stomach, panting. Gradually, reality separated itself from the dream, and I focused on my surroundings.

"Aydan," Kane repeated. "You had a bad dream, but you're safe. Don't be afraid."

I shook off the last of the dream. "Sorry," I croaked.

"Shit. I'm fine." I forced a shaky laugh. "I warned you about the snoring but not about the screaming. Sorry."

He sat back on his heels. "It's all right. You're entitled to some bad dreams." He took a deep breath and let it out slowly. "You scared the hell out of me. I'd turned off the surveillance camera in the room to give you some privacy, but I was watching all the other monitors. I couldn't imagine what could have happened."

"Sorry," I repeated, thoroughly embarrassed. "Better turn the camera back on. Then if it happens again, you can just ignore me. I always wake up pretty quick once the screaming starts. And anyway, I usually don't do it more than once a night. I should shut up for the rest of the night now."

He searched my face in the half-light from the open door. "You don't have anything to be embarrassed about. You went through a horrific experience tonight, and you never flinched. You have to allow yourself to deal with it somehow."

I concentrated on picking a few motes of lint off the blanket. "I prefer to deal with it privately, though, not by having a public meltdown and giving everybody heart failure."

Kane touched my hand. "I'm not public. I didn't have heart failure. And you have nothing to be ashamed of." He sat on the other bunk. "Go back to sleep. I'll sit with you a while."

"Don't bother. I'll be fine. I'll feel safe knowing you're watching the monitors."

He paused, his expression unreadable in the shadow. "Remember the conversation we had about letting your team take care of you?"

I blew out a half-laugh, half-sigh. "Thanks, but it actually kind of creeps me out if people watch me while I'm sleeping."

"All right," he said quietly. "Just call if you change your mind."

"Thanks," I said again, and he left, closing the door behind him.

I eased myself back down on the bed. God, how humiliating.

I squirmed a bit before giving a mental shrug and letting it go. It couldn't be helped. He'd seen me freak out in the network simulation a couple of days ago, so it should be old news to him. I just hoped I wouldn't embarrass myself again when Germain came on duty.

CHAPTER 34

I woke confused in the darkened room. As the events of the night seeped back into my memory, I tried to sit up, and let out an involuntary grunt when my bruised stomach muscles contracted. I carefully swivelled my feet around onto the floor and stood, holding onto the bunk bed while I gradually straightened and stretched my complaining body.

I shuffled to the door and squinted into the bright light of the corridor before padding toward the bathroom, yawning. When I turned the corner, I came face to face with tall, blond Wheeler. I let out an involuntary yelp and backpedalled, and he quickly put out his hands to steady me, his face creased with concern.

"Are you okay?" he asked anxiously.

I gave him a smile. "I'm fine, how are you feeling?"

He stared at the floor. "I feel terrible. Webb told me what they did to you... what happened last night. I'm sorry. It was my fault."

Behind his back, Germain appeared from the direction of the meeting room. I caught his eye and gave him a tiny headshake, and he faded back the way he had come.

"It wasn't your fault at all." I touched Wheeler's arm, and he met my eyes hesitantly. "You couldn't have done anything differently," I assured him. "And Spider was just upset last night because I had a nosebleed and it scared him. I'm fine. Just minor bruises and scratches."

Wheeler didn't look convinced. "You're forgetting I was at the hospital when they brought you in. I saw the nurse's face. I don't think Webb was exaggerating."

"They just freaked out because there was a bunch of blood on my face. That's all. If there'd been anything seriously wrong with me, they'd have kept me at the hospital. You were in worse shape than I was."

He searched my face. "Thanks for saying that. But I still feel terrible."

"Hey, it wasn't your fault. Shit happens. Don't worry, everything's fine."

"Thanks." He gave me a half-hearted smile and continued down the hallway.

Germain poked his head around the corner again as I arrived at the bathroom door. He gestured for me to wait as he came down the corridor, giving me a quick once-over with his observant gaze. "You look better this morning."

I grinned at him. "That's not much of a compliment. I looked like shit last night."

His eyes crinkled. "Oh, so you're fishing for compliments this morning. All right." He swept me a deep bow. "Milady, your radiant beauty astounds me..."

"Yeah, yeah." I laughed and turned for the bathroom.

He stopped me with an outstretched hand. "Thanks for being kind to Wheeler. And Webb last night," he said seriously.

I shrugged. "They're making a mountain out of a molehill."

"They're thinking of what might have happened."

I met his eyes. "If I spent my life being horrified at what might have happened, I'd be a basket case by now. I don't suppose there's any toothpaste in your luxurious bunker."

He followed my clumsy segue gracefully. "Check in the bottom drawer. There are usually some new toothbrushes and toothpaste in there." He smiled and walked away.

I locked myself in the bathroom and followed his advice. Sure enough, there were a couple of toothbrushes still in their packages and a tube of toothpaste. Thank heaven for well-equipped spies.

When I consulted the mirror, I was pleased to see that Germain was right. I did look better. The red marks were gone from my face and my nose was almost back to normal. My eyes were shadowed, but I couldn't tell whether it was bruising or just tiredness. My hair was curling wildly, and I pulled my brush through it with little effect. The bruises looked no worse, and some of the scratches had faded.

I dressed in my workout gear and emerged into the windowless corridor. My heart lurched into a quicker rhythm. Buried underground. No daylight. No air...

I sucked in a deep breath and eased it out slowly, willing away the twitchy urge to flee. Not trapped. I knew where the exits were. I could get out. I was okay. Not trapped. I held the mantra determinedly in my mind and forced my shaking legs into a decisive stride toward the work area.

Germain and Wheeler were working at a computer with their heads together, so I went on into the kitchenette, hoping to find something edible to distract me. The fridge held nothing but pop and juice, so I selected an apple juice and made my way back to the meeting table.

I had just eased into a chair and opened my juice when Spider came in, carrying a paper bag along with his ever-present laptop.

"'Morning, Spider," I greeted him, holding my voice steady.

"Good morning." He stared at me. "You changed your hair."

I forced a laugh. "I slept on it wet. Aydan Kelly's School of Hairstyling."

He laughed, too. "I brought you something." He placed the bag in front of me.

I gazed up at him inquiringly as I opened it. Then I gasped with delight. "Spider, you're a prince among men!" I reached in and extracted a toasted bagel, yogurt, and a fruit cup. Tension eased out of my shoulders at the homey smell of hot peanut butter.

Spider beamed back at me, and Germain glanced over with a grin. "There she goes again," he teased. "Now we all know the way to your heart."

I spoke around a soothing mouthful of bagel and peanut butter. "I admit it. I'm a pushover. Bring me food, and my heart is yours."

Kane came through the door as I spoke the last sentence. His short hair was rumpled and his chin was shadowed with stubble, making him look thoroughly delicious. I concentrated on my breakfast while he strode down the hall to the kitchenette and returned with a mug of coffee.

He dropped into a chair, leaning back and scrubbing his hands over his face and through his hair. He swallowed a slug of coffee before he spoke, his deep voice husky from lack of sleep.

"What's new, Germain?" he inquired, and I enjoyed his morning voice with a secret shiver.

"Exterior cleanup is done at the warehouse. They're still

working on the interior. They bagged eight bodies, no IDs yet. Captured six others, and get this. They found Eugene Mercer tied up in one of the rooms. He must have been taken yesterday late afternoon or evening. He'd been beaten and drugged. He's in the hospital, apparently with some unusual reaction to the drugs. He's not coherent yet."

Germain hesitated, eyeing Kane. "Interesting thing about the bodies. All your usual tidy work. But two of them, the slugs matched that cannon Aydan was shooting when we got to the parking lot last night."

I froze, watching Kane. Germain's sharp eyes observed us both, waiting.

Kane took his time replying. "Last night, I forced Aydan to take on a role that she didn't want. She saved both our lives. I take full responsibility for giving the order."

There was a short silence while three pairs of eyes appraised me. Then Germain cracked a smile. "Nice shooting, Aydan."

"Thanks," I mumbled.

Spider was wide-eyed. "You shot two people?"

I studied my lap so I wouldn't have to see the monster reflected in his eyes. "Yeah."

"Good." His voice was firm. I glanced up, surprised. "They deserved it," he said.

I gave him a half-smile. "Thanks."

Germain's phone rang, and he picked up and listened for a few minutes. "Good," he said. "I'll get Webb on it." He hung up. "Got some IDs coming through now."

Spider nodded and opened his laptop.

I spoke up tentatively. "Is there any chance I could go back to the warehouse today?"

"Why?" Kane eyed me with curiosity.

"There was something weird about that network. I want to see if I can figure out why my access was so sporadic."

Kane considered for a moment. "I'd prefer to keep you here where it's safe until Webb has a chance to do some analysis. We still don't know what we're up against. But on the flip side, if you can figure out something about the network, we'll gain important information that way, too."

"The cleanup crew and some of JTF2 are still at the warehouse," Germain offered. "It should be pretty well protected. If the three of us escort Aydan over there, she should be safe."

"That's what we thought last night, too," Wheeler mumbled.

Kane finished off his coffee. "Aydan, are you sure you want to take the risk?"

"I really want to know. The sooner we figure this out, the sooner I'll be safe." I gave him a pleading look.

"All right, let's do it," he agreed. "Here's how it's going to happen..."

CHAPTER 35

When we parked in the deserted parking lot, I could hardly believe what had taken place the previous night. The wall facing the parking lot looked freshly painted. There were no visible bullet holes, and the lot itself was swept fresh and clean. When we approached the newly painted steel door, I noticed some long gouges in the asphalt paving, but nobody would ever identify them as marks from bullets.

Germain stepped forward and banged on the steel door. "It's Germain," he called. The door was swung open by a large man with a submachine gun slung from his shoulder. He nodded us inside wordlessly.

I looked up at Kane. "You'll have to lead the way. I was upside down for this trip."

"Doesn't look like the cleanup crew has made it this far yet." Kane nodded toward the floor. "We can follow the same trail I did last night."

I regarded the intermittent rust-coloured splashes leading down the hallway. "How clever of me to leave you a trail of breadcrumbs."

We followed the droplets down a series of twisting corridors, and I thanked my lucky stars all over again that Kane had arrived when he did. I never would have found my way out, even if I'd somehow managed to escape my bonds.

Finally, the trail led into the room where I'd been held. The stained chair still lay on its side beside a small puddle of dried blood. Wheeler's face hardened as he took in the smears and spatters on the floor and the rusty smudges on the knife that still lay on the table.

I patted him on the shoulder. "It's okay. Never underestimate the dramatic effect of a simple nosebleed."

"What do you want to do here?" Kane asked.

"I want to work back from where I accessed the network," I said, moving to where I'd been when it had worked the first time.

"About here, I think," I muttered, concentrating on a white void. Sure enough, it materialized around me, and I nodded satisfaction. I braced myself and stepped out through the portal.

"Agh!" I clutched my head and clenched my teeth, eyes squeezed shut while I rode out the pain.

When awareness returned, I realized Kane was holding me tightly against him. All that hot, hard muscle felt very nice indeed, but it was definitely unexpected. I peered up at him, puzzled.

"I take it you accessed the network," he said as he set me back on my feet. I gave my head a little shake to settle my brain, realizing Germain and Wheeler were watching me with alarm.

"Right. Sit down before you access the network," I said dryly. "Thanks for catching me." He nodded, the corner of his mouth crooked up, but his eyes were grave.

I righted the chair approximately where it had been the previous night and sat in it, placing my arms on the armrests with a faint shudder.

Kane's voice came from behind me. "You don't have to do this."

"Yes, I do." I willed myself into the void and stood pondering. Last night I couldn't get in. I was in the same physical location now, and it worked fine. I sighed and stepped out, hugging my head and groaning involuntarily. I breathed slowly through my teeth for a few moments before straightening.

"Shit. That worked fine. Maybe I was just too scared last night. Or maybe it was the last of the stun gun effect."

I stood and circled the room again. What had changed since last night, other than the fear? I wandered to the door, mumbling to myself.

"Okay, carried in the door and dropped... here." I stood over the smeared mark where I'd landed. "Dragged into the chair." I walked over to the chair again. "It doesn't make sense."

The men stood patiently watching me while I paced and muttered. I sat in the chair again, accessing the network without difficulty. Stepping out, I tried to control a cry of pain that escaped anyway. I rubbed my temples, breathing my way through. Each time, it hurt a bit more.

I stumbled out of the chair. "Are you okay?" Germain asked, his brow furrowed. "Why are you hurting so much?"

"It's just my freaky way of accessing the network. I don't know why everybody else can just breeze in and out while I get spikes hammered through my brain each time."

I walked back to the doorway to retrace the route again. "Dropped... here. Dragged... What else is different, dammit?" I froze in sudden thought. "Hey, wait a minute."

I walked across the room and took off my waist pouch, placing it on the table. "They took off my waist pouch after they dropped me," I explained, and moved back to my seat in the chair. I willed the void. Nothing happened.

"Aha!" I bounced up, momentarily forgetting my bruises. "Unngh." I folded over my aching gut and breathed deeply for a moment. "Shit." I unbent more carefully and made my way over to the table, reaching for my waist pouch. "Come to Mommy."

I took it and sat down in the chair again. The network sprang into being around me the moment I made the attempt. "Ha! Gotcha!"

I stepped out again, grinning.

"Aaaagh!" I doubled over, hissing the obscenities that forced their way past my clenched teeth despite my best efforts. The pain went on longer than before, and I straightened slowly, hands braced on my knees.

Kane squatted in front of me, looking into my face with concern. "Aydan, your nose is bleeding again. I think you should stop."

I scrounged in my pouch for a tissue and swiped the trickle away. "Don't worry, it's just my brain liquefying. I've almost got it. We're almost there."

I dabbed at my nose as I struggled out of the chair and carried my pouch over to the table again. There, I unpacked, laying each item methodically on the table. The three men hovered behind me, watching with apparent fascination.

"What the heck have you got in there?" Germain teased as the pile grew.

"The usual wallet and change purse. Couple of jackknives. Measuring tape. Scissors. Reading glasses. Sunglasses. Ear plugs." I named the items off as I took them out. "Dental floss. Keys. Flashlight. Cough drops. Aspirin. Chequebook. Tissues..."

"What, no screwdrivers or power tools?" Germain prodded.

"I have Phillips and common screwdrivers. No Robertson or Torx," I replied absently, still unpacking as he laughed.

I dabbed at my nose again, but the bleeding seemed to have stopped, so I stuffed the tissue into my pocket.

When the pouch was completely empty, I carried it back to the chair and sat down. "Okay, let's do this systematically. I'll start with the empty pouch."

Kane frowned. "I searched it. Smith and Sandler searched it. You swore you didn't have anything."

I returned his frown. "We missed something. We all must've missed something."

I concentrated. No go.

"It's not the pouch." I tossed it to Germain, still standing by the table. "Give me something else."

One item at a time, I went through the contents of my pouch. I sighed and lobbed my measuring tape back to Germain. "Nope."

He tossed me my keys. "At least it doesn't hurt to try."

I smiled at him. "Literally. Thank goodness." I concentrated again.

And finally stepped into the network. Startled, I stared at the bundle of keys in my hand. The janitor's set. No way. I knew what each one of those keys was for. I'd had them for ages.

One by one, I flipped through them, identifying each. I came to the last one and frowned. All present and accounted for. The only things left were my ancient keychain disc and the amethyst pendant that decorated the key ring.

My breath caught as I held the amethyst up to the light.

It was the newest item on my key ring. I'd found it in my back yard several months ago and put it on my keychain.

That had to be it!

I did a quick, elated dance. I'd found it! This had to be the key! I did a final spin, enjoying my pain-free virtual body, and leaped for the portal. Kane was going to be so happy to find out. I was going to be safe again...

Too late, I remembered. Speed kills. I crashed through the portal into agony.

I shrieked and fell forever. Deafening noise, flashing lights. I felt screams coming from my throat and was powerless to stop them. Pain hammered my head and body while I thrashed helplessly. Gradually, my wordless wailing resolved into heartfelt swearing while I exercised my considerable vocabulary once again.

I embraced my skull, rocking on the floor. Firm hands held my shoulders.

A male voice spoke urgently above me. "Ma'am. Ma'am. You're okay now. You're safe."

I slowly uncurled and let my swearing run down. Cracking open one eye, I saw uniformed legs and booted feet.

"Ow," I croaked. "Fuck."

I pried open my other eye to squint up at the ring of men surrounding me, their expressions varying from grim to shocked to amused. Clearly I'd played to an appreciative audience again.

I choked, swiping blood away from my nose. That was really getting old. When I tried to sit up, my stomach muscles screamed their disapproval and I fell back again with a grunt.

"Ma'am, just lie still. You're injured. The medic's on his way." The man at my head tried to get me to lie back.

"No, I'm fine." I struggled to sit up. "Where are the men who were with me?"

"Ma'am, don't worry about them. They won't bother you again," he assured me.

I peered through a forest of legs to see the three motionless bodies sprawled face down on the floor.

"No-no-no-no-no," I gibbered as I struggled to my hands and knees, ignoring the pain. I scrambled toward the bodies, shoving my way past the legs of the standing men.

"Kane! Germain! Wheeler!" I floundered over, slithering to halt on my knees between Kane and Germain. My heart stopped at the sight of the blood caking Kane's dark hair. "John! Oh no..." I reached for him, hands shaking.

Kane's calm voice came out slightly muffled by the floor. "Aydan, please tell the nice men with the guns that we're your team."

I gasped relief, hyperventilating for a few breaths before I turned back to glare ferociously up at the cluster of standing men. "This is my team. You attacked my *team*!"

There was a general shuffling of booted feet and mumbling of apologies as Kane, Germain, and Wheeler rolled over and sat up. I gave them each an anxious once-over, but Kane's bloodied head seemed to be the only injury. When I crawled behind him to look at it more closely, I could see the bleeding was almost stopped. I was willing to bet it hurt like a bitch, though.

As the three men got to their feet, there was a disturbance in the group of armed men. The medic pushed through, immediately targeting me where I sat on the floor. My heart was still pounding, and I wasn't sure my trembling legs would hold me. My head ached fiercely, throbbing in time to my protesting muscles.

He knelt in front of me. "What happened here?"

"Nothing. I just had a nosebleed."

He eyed me suspiciously, taking in my bruised wrists and my hunched-over posture.

"I was in a bit of a scrap last night," I explained. "I got checked out at the hospital then, and I'm fine."

I could see he wasn't going to take my word for it, so I reached a hand up to Kane. He clasped it and pulled me to my feet. I clenched my teeth to bite back an involuntary groan and stood up as straight as I could, crossing my arms and lifting my chin. The medic rose slowly, watching me.

I looked him in the eye. "If you want to do something, you could look at his head," I nodded in Kane's direction.

The medic held me in his gaze for another couple of seconds. "Your nose is still bleeding," he said finally, and handed me a gauze pad. I took it and dabbed at the mess while Kane stooped tolerantly for examination.

Another disturbance in the crowd signalled the arrival of a uniformed man who was apparently a ranking officer, judging by the way the rest of the men straightened up. He came directly toward us, frowning as he took us in. "Germain? What the hell?"

"Just a misunderstanding," Germain assured him.

The commander turned to the nearest armed man. "What happened?" he snapped.

The man stiffened. "We heard screaming. We ran into the room, and they were struggling." He indicated Kane and me. "She was screaming and fighting, and there was blood all over her face. These other two were just standing there watching. I gave the big guy a gun butt to the head and put them all down on the floor until we could sort it out."

"I'm sorry," I said, stepping forward. "I was having a

seizure, and I must have banged my nose."

The medic stared at me with obvious disbelief. "I've never heard of anybody screaming while they have a seizure."

"I was disoriented when I started to recover," I extemporized hastily. "I didn't know where I was, and I panicked."

Doubtful looks greeted this revelation.

Kane stepped up beside me. "No harm done. We're almost finished here anyway. You can all go back to what you were doing."

"Thank you for trying to help," I added.

The officer frowned at us for a moment before nodding to his team. "You heard the man." The crowd dispersed, and the medic left with a final, suspicious glance. As the room emptied, the officer turned to Germain. "What really happened?" he demanded.

Germain met his eyes. "Classified."

The man grunted resignation and turned to go. "Your guys did good," Germain complimented him. "They're really sharp."

The officer nodded. "Thanks. I know." He left, and we stood in silence while I shakily dabbed at my nose.

"Sit down before you fall down," Kane said. He and Germain each took one of my arms and guided me to the chair, easing me down. I slumped into it and rubbed my aching head. "Jeez, I'm ready for this to be over," I muttered.

When I straightened slowly, I was grinning through my pain.

"What?" Kane demanded.

I dangled the amethyst. "I found it. I found the skeleton

key."

"Are you sure?" He bent to examine it.

"Pretty sure. I just have to run through the rest of the stuff to make sure, and then I'll go back and double-check it."

He shook his head. "You're done for the day. I'm calling this off."

"No way," I argued. "We have to know for sure, you know we do. And I don't want to have to do this again."

"No. You're done. You've had a worse reaction each time you've gone in. It's just not that important. Sandler and Smith can re-test everything."

"That last one was my fault," I explained. "I was stupid, I got excited and charged through the portal. Same as what happened at Sirius. You know I went in again right after that, and I was fine."

He appraised me doubtfully.

"Besides, I'm pretty sure this is it," I cajoled. "If this is the only thing from my pouch that works, I won't even be going in again."

He sighed. "All right. But if you have another reaction like the last one, it's over. End of story."

"Okay," I agreed. "Take this away and put it on the table. Pass me the next thing."

I worked my way uneventfully through the rest of the contents of my pouch. When we reached the last item, I looked up at their relieved faces.

"That's it," Germain said cheerfully.

"Good," I said. "One last test, then. Take the amethyst off the keychain and I'll try it by itself just to be sure."

He removed it slowly and passed it over, frowning. Kane stood close beside my chair, poised to catch me just in case. I popped easily into the network, holding the amethyst at eye level. I peered at it. It looked like an ordinary chunk of amethyst. I shrugged and stepped ever so slowly and carefully back through the portal.

Pain again, one last time. No worse than usual, though, and I managed not to swear while my breath hissed through my clenched teeth. I felt Kane's hands on my shoulders, and as I clutched my pounding head, his strong hands moved up to firmly massage my neck and temples. I groaned and relaxed, letting my head drop forward.

"You realize I'll just sit here as long as you keep doing that," I mumbled, eyes closed in bliss. I heard his chuckle behind me as he stopped rubbing, and I straightened slowly, mentally kicking myself for not just keeping my mouth shut.

I rolled my shoulders and flexed my neck. "Okay, I'm done like dinner." I handed Kane the amethyst. "You'd better take this. Don't concentrate on the network."

He grimaced and dropped it in his pocket. "Trust me, I won't."

CHAPTER 36

When we returned to the office, Spider was at his desk, his forehead puckered in concentration while he typed furiously on his laptop. He glanced up with a blithe hello as we entered, but his cheerful expression changed to startled concern when he noticed my face.

"What happened?"

"Nothing, I just had a nosebleed," I assured him. As he eyed me doubtfully, I gave him a tantalizing smile. "Kane has a little something for you. Want to guess what it is?"

"I'm afraid to," he replied warily.

"Downstairs," Kane said, and Spider's eyebrows went up. He rose and we all followed Kane down the basement stairs to repeat the previous day's security ritual. I held the knowledge of the exits determinedly in my mind, and managed the cramped concrete stairwell with only a minor acceleration in pulse and breathing.

Not trapped. Just breathe.

When we were seated around the bunker's meeting table, Kane extracted the amethyst from his pocket and laid it carefully in front of him. We all gazed at it in silence, and Spider's forehead furrowed.

"And?" he queried.

"I think it's the skeleton key," I said. "We did some experiments at the warehouse, and I could only get into the network as long as I had this amethyst in close proximity."

Spider reached out. "Let me see it." Kane passed it over, and he held it up to the light. "This shouldn't get you into the network. Amethysts are just a crystalline mineral. They don't have any properties that would provide the kind of access you're getting."

"Aydan tested it thoroughly," Kane assured him. "We can't find any other explanation."

Spider rose and carried the stone over to one of the desks, pulling out a sliding shelf that held a microscope. He positioned the amethyst under it and peered through the eyepiece.

"Whoa," he breathed. Everyone at the table sat up straight, eyes riveted on him.

He looked up from the scope. "Where did you get this?" he demanded.

"I found it in my back yard."

"You *found* it?" he repeated. "You're kidding me, right?"

"No. All kinds of weird stuff gets tossed over into my yard from the green space behind my house. Usually it's empty booze bottles, but I've had garden statuary, shoes, you name it."

"What is it?" Kane asked.

"I don't know for sure yet," Spider replied. "But there's micro-miniaturized circuitry inside this stone. The stone has been cut and hollowed to contain it, and the cut sections have been reassembled along the facet edges. The cuts and re-assembly are so finely done and the circuitry's so tiny that it's not visible unless you look at it under the microscope. I'll need to take it over to Sirius and get Smith to help me disassemble it and figure out what it really does."

"How long have you had this?" Kane asked me.

"I picked it up sometime last fall before the snow started, so maybe mid-October. I was just doing the fall garden cleanup so the yard would look good when the house went up for sale, and there it was. It was pretty, and its reputed magical properties appealed to me, so I put it on my keychain."

"Reputed magical properties?" Germain's eyes crinkled with amusement.

"Yeah, when I found out amethyst is supposed to protect you from drunkenness, it seemed like a must-have," I joked.

Spider was vibrating with impatience. "This particular amethyst is a lot more important than that. I need to get over Sirius with it right away."

Kane nodded. "Agreed. This could be the key to everything that's happened to date. Wheeler, go with Spider to Sirius. That stone doesn't travel anywhere without a security escort." Webb snatched up the stone and his laptop, and he and Wheeler left hurriedly.

"There's one more thing that's been bothering me," I said slowly. "Why is there an open Sirius network portal in that warehouse?"

"I questioned that, too," Kane agreed. "I got James Sandler out of bed last night while you were sleeping, and he was over at the warehouse half the night. It looks as though that network is not actually part of or connected to the Sirius network at all." He leaned back in his chair, rubbing his face tiredly. "That's a huge relief. If we'd been hacked, this would be a complete disaster."

"So Fuzzy Bunny has created a counterpart of the network?" I asked.

"So it seems," Kane replied. "That, in itself, is worrisome. It shows they have resources we weren't previously aware of. We need to dig more deeply into that issue. We also need to finish questioning Mercer and the detainees. Once Webb and Smith have cracked that crystal, we might know more, too."

"How are we going to do this?" Germain asked. "Aydan still needs to be protected, but we have a lot of research and questioning to do before we get to the bottom of this."

Kane sighed. "We're short-handed, as usual. I'll get some more CSIS analysts on it. This is so big, I should be able to pull priority. That'll cover Webb's role while he works with Smith to figure out the stone. Until we get this sorted out, Aydan stays here."

Alarm kicked my heart into high gear. "You mean here, underground?"

He nodded. "I'm sorry, there's no other option."

I took a deep breath and slowly released the fist I hadn't realized I'd clenched. "Is there something I can do to help while I'm here?" My voice came out tight, and I took another deep breath to steady it before continuing. "I'm going to need something to occupy me."

Kane gave me a sympathetic look. "You aren't a prisoner. If you really need to leave, one of us will go with you. But it would be best for you to stay here where it's safe. Maybe you should try to get some more sleep. You probably need the recovery time."

I nodded, the stiff muscles in my neck responding reluctantly. "Okay, I'll try. Just keep me busy if you can."

Kane turned to Germain. "I'll go over and carry on with the questioning. You can stay here and coordinate the research data as it comes in. I'll come back and join you as soon as I'm done. Call me if anything breaks."

He departed, leaving me sitting at the table with Germain. I realized my fists were clenched again, and deliberately relaxed my hands.

Germain regarded me with his keen gaze. "Everything okay?"

"I'm just a little claustrophobic." I drew a deep breath and willed calm. "I'll settle down as soon as I get distracted with something else. What can I do?"

"Why don't you go and get cleaned up first, and then try to get a nap? If you can't sleep, I'll find something to keep you occupied."

"Thanks." I got to my feet and went down the hall, walking slowly and staying calm. I was *not* trapped. I could leave any time I wanted. I clutched the thought like a life preserver.

In the bathroom, I discovered I hadn't done a very good job with the gauze cleanup. At least I didn't get any blood on my clothes for a change. I snorted. If I'd been wearing anything better than my workout clothes, I had no doubt I'd have managed to wreck the outfit.

I took my time cleaning up my face before making my way down the corridor to the bunkroom. Bending carefully, I crept back into the lower bunk and tried to relax. I breathed slowly and deeply, concentrating on letting my muscles soften. Time dragged by.

Dammit. I was hungry.

I rolled over, trying to ignore the sensation. Breathe. In. Out. Ocean waves. I scowled at my watch in the dimness. This wasn't working.

Lying tensely in the bunk, I reflected that my every move was controlled by someone else. I couldn't even eat without someone else's say-so. No food in the bunker, and I wasn't supposed to leave.

Unable to lie still any longer, I jerked out of bed, growling at the painful bruise. I paced the length of the room. Four steps. Back and forth. Back and forth.

I tried to control myself and calm down, but my turmoil kept building. I stopped beside the bed and lashed out a fist at the mattress on the upper bunk. The jolt of pain fed my growing frenzy.

Trapped. Hurt. Hungry.

I punched again, ignoring the pain. And then again, with some shoulder behind it. Punch. Punch. Left. Right. My fists made satisfying thuds against the mattress. My stiff muscles began to warm up while I hit harder and harder, pain and frantic effort escaping in animal-like whimpers and grunts.

A sound at the door made me whirl, fists at the ready.

"Aydan?" Germain asked cautiously.

I glared blindly in his direction, barely in control. My voice came out harsh and ragged around my panting. "Just... give me... a minute."

He nodded and left.

I pounded the mattress until my muscles rebelled. Gasping for breath, I doubled over the fiery pain in my abused stomach. My trembling knees dropped me onto the lower bunk, and I brought my breathing slowly under control while I examined my abraded knuckles.

I sensed rather than heard Germain at the doorway again. When I glanced up, he stepped into the room and handed me a bottle of orange juice before perching on the edge of the opposite bunk.

"Thanks," I muttered, not meeting his eyes. I twisted off

the cap and took a gulp, managing not to spill it down my chin only by clenching the bottle in both shaking hands.

I sipped in silence for a few minutes, staring at the floor. "I forgot about your surveillance system," I said finally. "I don't suppose there's any way to delete that little performance."

"The cameras are turned off in this room while you're here," he reassured me. "I was just coming down the hall and it sounded like somebody was taking a beating."

"Sorry to bother you," I mumbled. "I'm not normally this wacko. You should go back to what you were doing. I'll be okay now."

"Maybe, but I don't think that mattress is ever going to be the same."

The humour in his voice made me look up, some of the tension going out of my body. I gave him a weak smile. "Oh, so now I'm on the hook for abuse of government facilities."

He laughed. "It'll be our dirty little secret."

I gave him a real smile this time. "Thanks. I'd appreciate that."

He sobered, watching me closely. "Are you really okay?"

"Yeah. Just embarrassed."

"You don't need to be embarrassed. I've been known to punch the hell out of inanimate objects on occasion, too."

"Maybe, but I prefer to do it without an audience," I replied ruefully.

He stood. "Come on. Let's go upstairs."

"No, it's okay. I've blown off some steam now. I'll be fine for a while. You might as well get back to work. I'm sure you've got enough to keep you busy without babysitting me."

He grinned. "That's true, but it's lunch time, and Hellhound is going to be arriving with pizza any minute." He reached a hand down to me. "Coming?"

I beamed up at him. "I think I may love you. And him."

He shook his head in mock disapproval. "You're so easy."

"I know." I gave him a sunny smile. "That's why all the guys love me." I took his outstretched hand and he pulled me carefully to my feet.

CHAPTER 37

At the top of the stairs, Germain held out a restraining hand. "I'm sorry, but you'll need to stay away from the windows once we're up top. I don't want to take any chances."

"No problem," I assured him. "Just being above ground and getting some food will be great."

I stepped out onto the main level and sucked in a deep breath, stretching. Warmed by the exercise, my muscles felt looser, and even the bruises hurt less. I sighed relief and rolled my neck and shoulders, realizing Germain was watching me curiously.

"You really are claustrophobic, aren't you?" he asked. "How do you manage in elevators and cars?"

I shrugged. "Really tight spaces are bad, but I'm fine in elevators and cars because I know I can get out. It's not being able to escape that freaks me out. I'd feel claustrophobic in a football stadium if I couldn't get out. "

"But what if the elevator stops between floors?" he prodded. "Wouldn't that bother you?"

"No, you can always get out of an elevator. The hydraulics on the doors aren't that strong, and you can easily pull them open, both in the cab and on the building floor.

I've done it a few times. It's not very safe, though. If the cab starts to move while you're getting out, you're in serious trouble. I heard of a guy getting decapitated like that."

He winced. "Ouch."

A sound on the front porch made Germain hustle me around the corner into the kitchen. Seconds later, he said, "All clear," and I poked my head back out into the open area to see Hellhound arriving with pizza boxes and a grin.

The aroma drifted over and made me salivate. I sniffed the air theatrically and purred, "Oh, Hellhound, oh, baby, I *love* your cologne!"

Both men laughed, and Germain said, "She's so easy!"

Hellhound bounced his eyebrows. "I wish."

"C'mon, stop messing around, you guys," I urged. "Let's eat."

Hellhound led the way into the kitchen, dumping the boxes onto the table, and we dropped into chairs to chow down on the hot, greasy slices.

I finished my first piece and sat back in my chair, licking my fingers. "This is amazing. Where did you get it?"

"Fiorenza's does takeout." Hellhound shrugged. "I didn't know what ya liked, so I got one vegetarian and one loaded. Chicks always go for veggies."

I blinked at him. "I like everything."

He returned a leer, waggling his eyebrows. "Darlin', that's the only thing that gives me hope."

I laughed and snagged another slice. "Keep dreaming. You're right about the pizza gender divide, though. Any time I've ever ordered pizza with a group, the girls want the one with the veggies and the guys want all meat."

Germain grunted and thumped his chest. "Me like meat!"

As our laughter died away, we heard the front door opening again. Germain was instantly on his feet, dropping his pizza and drawing a gun that I hadn't known he had concealed at his back. He stepped casually through the kitchen doorway, holding his gun out of the sight line of anyone entering the front room.

His shoulders relaxed. "Kane." He tucked the gun away again and came back to the table, picking up his pizza.

Seconds later, Kane filled the doorway, sniffing hungrily. "Thank you, God."

"You're welcome," Hellhound deadpanned.

Kane sank into the remaining chair and reached for a slice. He chewed in silence for a few bites before glancing around the table. "We're making progress, faster than I'd hoped." He went back to his pizza, and I realized he wouldn't elaborate in front of Hellhound.

"Good." I turned to Hellhound. "Are you going to jam at Blue Eddy's tonight?"

"Yeah. Wanna come an' be my groupie, darlin'?"

I grinned. "I don't know." I nodded at Kane and Germain. "Depends on whether Mom and Dad will let me go out tonight. I might still be grounded."

Kane's mouth crooked up. "If you're planning to go and be a groupie for that old lecher, you're definitely grounded, young lady."

Hellhound put on an indignant face. "Old lecher? We're the same fuckin' age, ya shit!"

"I notice he didn't bother to deny the 'lecher' part," Germain put in.

"I'm pretty sure that's established fact," I agreed. "Not much point in denying it."

"Last time I bring you bums pizza," Hellhound groused

good-naturedly. "I do somethin' nice, an' I get nothin' but shit an' abuse."

I waved a slice of pizza at him. "Want some cheese with that whine?" He shot me a scowl, its sincerity slightly marred by his grin.

"Seriously, though," I added. "You have no idea how much I appreciate this. Thank you."

Hellhound reddened slightly. "Darlin', ya know I'd do anythin' to put a smile on your face." He winked, making a joke of it. "'Course, bringin' ya pizza wouldn't be my first choice of how to do that."

"Yeah, yeah." I waved a dismissive hand. "The day I take you up on that, you'll drop dead of a heart attack."

"But what a way to go," he breathed.

The subject dropped as we all addressed ourselves to the excellent pizza. Finally, I pushed away from the table, groaning. "That was so good. There is nothing in the world more lethal than superb pizza. I think I hurt myself."

Hellhound got to his feet amid the general laughter and agreement. "I'm outta here." He winked at me. "See if ya can ditch the 'rents tonight, darlin'. I got a little somethin' special for ya if ya do."

I eyed him critically. "Well, if it's that little, I don't know..."

He shook his head ruefully and let Kane's and Germain's guffaws carry him out of the house.

Kane sobered. "We've got some new developments on the warehouse network. Webb and Smith have cracked the crystal already. Once they got to it, the circuitry itself wasn't that complex. As we'd surmised, it is designed to be a skeleton key. It's supposed to spoof an authentic user to any network, not just Sirius. The only strange thing is that it doesn't seem to work for Webb or Smith. A couple of other analysts tried it, too, but no luck."

He smiled at me. "You seem to be the only one who can make it work. And thanks to you, it's in the hands of the good guys, not the bad guys. The CSIS analysts are still trying to trace its origin. Judging by what we know so far, it appears to be a one-of-a-kind item, which is good news."

"So once you know where it came from, you might be able to figure out what to do next, and then I can go back to my real life?" I asked hopefully.

"That's the plan," he agreed. "In the mean time, though, I'm sorry to have to ask you, but Sandler wants to run some more tests over at the warehouse. Do you feel up to it?"

"You are looking at an intensely motivated woman," I assured him. "When do we leave?"

"They're over there now. We can go right away."

CHAPTER 38

The hallways were spotless when Germain and I trailed Kane through the warren of corridors in the warehouse. Wheeler nodded from beside one of the doorways, and we entered the bare room he'd indicated, leaving him on guard in the hallway. Sandler, Smith, and Webb were already seated around the large boardroom table.

Sandler glanced up as we entered. "Kane. How nice of you to come at last. It's reassuring to know that your personal convenience overrides issues of national security." He gave my clingy workout gear an up-and-down examination that made me wish I'd worn Kane's baggy T-shirt. "Ms. Kelly. I see you're dressed for action, as always. Let's see if we can find you some."

Kane remained silent and impassive. I concealed my distaste, and we all sat down at the table.

Sandler addressed me again. "Kane tells me you accessed this network last night. I want to see if you can do it again."

"I can't without the crystal. I tried."

"These are not the dark ages," Sandler sneered. "You accessed the network using micro-miniaturized processing technology, not by rubbing a magical crystal and chanting.

Webb, give her the key."

Spider slid a tiny plastic bag across the table to me with a half-smile. "Don't sneeze, or we could lose it forever."

I held the bag up to the light, studying the miniscule dot in its corner. "Wow."

"Oh, very eloquently said, Ms. Kelly," Sandler needled me.

Mindful that I was holding the skeleton key to a simulation network, I clenched my teeth and determinedly avoided dwelling on the thought of dismembering him with a blunt butter knife.

"Here is how we will proceed," Sandler explained condescendingly. "I will enter the network first. Then you will attempt to access it, Ms. Kelly. If you are able to gain access, we will conduct some tests within the network. These tests may take some time. Are you ready?"

I nodded. Goody. There was nothing I wanted more than to spend time with the most objectionable man on earth. Not.

Sandler fell silent and his face took on the blank stare that indicated he was inside the network. I sighed and concentrated on the void.

Nothing happened.

I frowned around the table. Sandler still sat blank-faced. The other four men watched me, unmoving. I tried again, with the same result.

Sandler blinked, returning to the real world. "I take it you were unable to gain access."

I shrugged. "I guess your new security must be working. Either that, or there's some change to the key as a result of its removal from the crystal."

He nodded smugly. "Excellent. I'm so pleased. And

now, Ms. Kelly, your usefulness is almost at an end." He turned to Kane. "Kane."

Kane rose. "Yes, Mr. Sandler." He walked around behind my chair, then suddenly seized my arms and pinned them behind my back.

I let out a cry of pain and shock and tried to pull away, but he twisted my arms until I sat still. Smith, Spider, and Germain watched, expressionless.

"What the hell?" I demanded, the first flicker of apprehension racing down my spine.

Sandler smiled. "Ms. Kelly, thank you for delivering the circuitry for the hacked fob. You have our sincere appreciation. However, your continued existence would be a tremendous inconvenience. I have taken the liberty of assuring my associates that you have been eliminated. I would hate to be made a liar."

"But I've done everything you've asked! I signed the non-disclosure agreement, and I've abided by the terms. Kane said he trusted me." I squirmed painfully around to look up into Kane's impassive face. "John?"

He stared down at me in silence, his face utterly blank. "John...?"

"Your precious Kane will do exactly as I say," Sandler informed me with satisfaction. "He knows who his master is. Isn't that right, Kane?"

"Yes, Mr. Sandler," Kane replied flatly.

"But..." I gulped at the dryness that suddenly parched my throat. Eliminated? As in... killed? Cold fear raised the small hairs on my arms. I appealed to the others, my voice a croak. "Spider? Carl?"

They sat silent and motionless.

Sandler smiled again, licking his lips. "Let's play." He

rose from his chair and approached.

Adrenaline suffused my body and I launched myself to my feet, simultaneously relieving Kane's pressure on my arms and driving the top of my head into his chin.   He staggered off balance, and I turned to flee as Sandler cried out behind me.

"Restrain her!"

I barely saw Kane's fist in my peripheral vision before a tremendous blow to my temple turned everything black.

I shook my head groggily.   Knives of pain stabbed my head and neck and I groaned, trying to focus. A hard, cold surface chilled my back. Dots floated in the blank whiteness in front of my eyes. I groaned again and tried to rub my head, but my arms wouldn't move.   When I began to struggle, I realized the white dotted surface was actually the ceiling.

The blurs in my vision resolved themselves into Kane, Spider, Smith, and Germain, standing at the corners of the table. Spider and Smith each held one of my arms, while Kane and Germain held a leg apiece. With a shock of terror, I realized I was naked, spread-eagled helplessly on the table.

Sandler stood between my feet. I peered down at him, my breath catching in revulsion when I realized that he was masturbating with my panties.

He smiled. "I understand you expressed an objection to me doing this earlier. Quite understandable. I know you'll prefer the real thing." He caressed his erection.

Kane spoke up obsequiously. "Please, Mr. Sandler, can I do her when you're finished?"

My panic rose while I struggled frantically. The four

men held me completely immobilized, their faces distant and emotionless.

This couldn't be happening. I had trusted Kane with my life. He was so careful to avoid any hint of sexual misconduct.

And I'd never figured him to suck up to anybody.

Through terror, the tiny voice of logic whispered.

My voice trembled despite my effort to control it. "This is a sim. We're in the network, aren't we? Kane, Spider, Germain, they're all just your constructs."

Sandler's erection grew visibly. "Oh, my dear, I do love bright women. Although bimbos definitely have their place. On their knees with their mouths open."

Keep him talking. Give Kane time to rescue me.

"How long have you been working for Fuzzy Bunny?"

Sandler moved closer, still fondling himself. Oh, God, please tell me that was the touch of fabric against my ankle, not...

I tried to jerk my leg away, but Kane held it effortlessly, his massive arms flexing.

"Don't trouble your pretty head about that." Sandler's gaze slid over my body, and I fought the urge to close my eyes to shut out the invasion.

"Why do they want the fob?" I blurted desperately.

"For this. Welcome to the future of interrogation techniques." Sandler smiled. "I'm so pleased that you'll be the one to help me with the final testing. And I'm sorry to say that it will be truly final for you."

Nausea flooded me along with comprehension. Keep him talking, dammit. Stall.

"The ultimate tool," I choked. "Your victims don't even know there's a network. You can do whatever you want, and there's no evidence of torture. Their physical bodies are undamaged. You can break them at your leisure."

"Yes, and today we have all the time in the world," he purred. "I've taken the liberty of disabling all network access and monitoring except mine. And as you may recall, I did say the network tests would take some time. No one will ever suspect."

Hope died. Kane wouldn't be able to save me this time. He didn't even know there was anything to save me from.

Sandler stroked himself more quickly. His erection expanded to inhuman proportions and he spoke jerkily. "And I can use the network to kill people undetectably. If you die here inside the sim, it looks like an unexplained heart attack in the real world. So sad. That's what will happen to you. I understand you had... increasingly bad reactions... to accessing the network. They'll all believe... it was just an accident."

He was beginning to breathe heavily. "I've always wanted... to make a woman... scream and bleed. And in the network... I can go on... as long as I want... Of course, it will be... quite painful for you... as I keep getting bigger... and bigger... until you finally... bleed to death." He stepped closer, sliding the head of his gargantuan penis slowly up my ankle, then past my knee.

"Open wide!" he sang merrily.

Kane and Germain jerked my legs further apart, and I clamped my eyes shut, my mind fleeing to a safe memory. Lying on the warm sand, laughing with Kane, the real Kane, about Hellhound's tattooed butt and whose expectation had created it.

Expectations create reality.

My wrists and ankles slipped through the constructs'

insubstantial grip, and I yanked the trigger of my newly-created submachine gun.

"*Not my reality, asshole!*"

The gun jerked in my hands and the butt slammed into my shoulder. The power of the recoil threw the muzzle upward, ripping a trail of destruction from Sandler's groin to head in an instant. Wetness splattered my face and hands. I wrestled the gun back under control and held the trigger until no resemblance to a man remained.

My feet slipped in gore, and I dropped the gun and collapsed to my hands and knees to crawl away, whimpering and gagging. A few yards away, I curled into a shivering ball, holding down the sobs that tried to escape.

When I regained a measure of control, I dragged myself shakily to my hands and knees again, then crept to my feet and tottered toward the portal for what I hoped and prayed would be the last time.

Pain. A hand on my shoulder. A bolt of agony shot through my head as somebody slapped my face. I opened blurred eyes to see Kane looming over me, his hand raised to hit me again. I screamed and jerked away from him, throwing up my arms to protect myself.

I toppled off the chair and sprawled on the floor, rolling and scrambling away when he came after me. My back fetched up against the wall with a thump, and I was cornered. Scuffling my feet under me, I launched myself at him with all my strength.

He reacted almost too late to deflect the punch I'd aimed at his throat. Pain tore my knuckles when my fist connected with his chin instead. He staggered back, and I shoved past him toward the door.

Germain lunged to his feet from beside Sandler's crumpled body, his eyes widening as I charged. He made a grab for me, and I ducked to slam a shoulder into his unprotected rib cage. Rebounding off his hard bulk, I used the vector to propel myself into a desperate dash out the door.

Kane caught me two steps into the hallway, his huge hand clamping around my bruised wrist like a vise. I shrieked and swung on him, tearing savagely at his hand and kicking at his crotch. An instant later, he locked my arm in a painful submission hold. I fell to my knees, still screaming and thrashing as he yelled.

"Wheeler! Trank! Shoot her, dammit, shoot her!"

Wheeler whipped out a small gun and fired from point-blank range.

CHAPTER 39

I floated in warm, soft semi-darkness, wavering between muddled wakefulness and drifting sleep. I couldn't seem to open my eyes. My limbs were too heavy to move.

At last, full awareness returned, and I realized with a flood of terror that I was lying in the bunkroom in Kane's secret hideout.

I dragged myself into sitting position and hurriedly explored my body by touch in the dimness. I was clothed. That was good. I found no injuries other than those I'd had earlier. That was also good. Absorbed in my examination, I yelped and recoiled into the far corner of the bed when I realized the opposite bunk was occupied.

Kane leaned back against the wall, his legs stretched out on the bed. He spoke quietly, his deep voice soothing. "Aydan, you're safe. Don't be afraid."

"What kind of mind-fuck is this?" I tried to growl, but my voice was thin, trembling with the rapid pounding of my heart. "What do you want from me?"

"We need to know what happened in the network. Sandler is dead. You came out completely hysterical. You were so out of control we had to tranquilize you. What happened?" He leaned forward, and I strained away from him against the wall, my fists bunching.

"You hit me. You grabbed me. You shot me. And now I'm trapped in your secret bunker and nobody knows where I am." My voice was rising despite my best effort at control. "I trusted you."

He leaned back against the wall, raising his hands. "I won't hurt you. Nobody will hurt you. You're not trapped here. You can leave whenever you want." He reached toward me beseechingly, and I flinched away from the gesture before I could stop myself.

"That's what you were screaming when you came out of the network," he said. "You kept saying 'I trusted you'. What happened?"

"I'm not a prisoner here?" I asked, my breath fast and shallow.

"No."

"Good, then I'm leaving." I dragged myself out of the bed, staggering against the wall before I regained my balance. Kane stood quickly, his hand darting toward my elbow. I jerked away, my fingers stiffening into claws. "Don't you dare touch me," I hissed.

When I forged through the meeting room, Spider, Germain, and Wheeler twisted in their seats at the table to stare. Spider started to rise, his mouth framing a question, but I was already through the door and struggling up the stairs. Kane followed, but he made no attempt to stop me.

I reached the main level of the house and headed straight for the door. When I whipped around to face Kane, he halted instantly, swinging out a restraining arm to stop the others. They stood behind him in a knot, looking puzzled and worried.

"Can I have my jacket, or do I forfeit it as terms of my

release?" I snarled.

Kane's eyes widened. "It's minus ten outside. For heaven's sake, take your jacket." He picked it up from the chair beside him. "And here's your waist pouch."

He started toward me, but I backed away. "Throw them to me."

He frowned and lobbed me the pouch. I strapped it on stiffly and caught the jacket when he tossed it.

"Don't follow me." I stepped out the door and ran until my strength and breath failed me. At the edge of the neighbourhood, I hunched over with my hands braced on my knees, gasping and trembling. The icy air abraded my throat, but it felt clean and fresh, scrubbing away the last remnants of the filtered underground air. I gulped it greedily, ignoring the pain.

When my breathing steadied at last, I hauled myself upright and forced my shaking legs into a slow walk in the direction of the farm.

Sandler was dead. He'd told his bosses I was dead. I was as safe as I was likely to get in the foreseeable future, unless Kane decided to recapture me and beat some information out of me.

The crisp air cleared the last of the cobwebs from my brain. I shook my head vigorously, trying to drive off the traumatic memories and view the situation objectively. As I did, my peripheral vision caught a vehicle moving slowly behind me. Without looking at it, I took a hard right and stepped up my pace. The vehicle turned the corner and followed me.

I whirled to stride over to the Forester, stiffening my legs and squaring my shoulders to hide my tremors. Hellhound grinned at me from behind the wheel.

"Hey, darlin'. Wanna ride?"

"No. Kane called you, didn't he?"

He shrugged. "He's worried about ya."

I scowled. "Sucks to be him."

Arnie met my eyes. "I'm worried about ya."

"Sucks to be you, too, then." I turned and walked away.

I heard the SUV's door open and close. A few seconds later, I felt a gentle hand on my arm. I pulled away, spinning to face him. "Keep your hands off me."

He took a slow step back, surveying my face with a troubled gaze. "Coupla days ago, ya trusted me enough to come home with me an' fall asleep on my couch," he said quietly. "Few hours ago, ya still trusted me enough to be jokin' around. What changed?"

Remorse flooded me, and I couldn't meet his eyes. I wrapped my arms around my body and studied the Forester instead. "I'm sorry. I... can't talk about it."

"Can't talk about it at all, or can't talk about it to me?"

"Both. I'm sorry," I repeated. "I just need to think."

"Come sit in the truck an' think," he invited.

"No. I need to walk." I turned away.

He matched my pace, strolling by my side without crowding me. "Who'd ya hit this time?" He indicated the fresh damage on my knuckles.

"Kane." I kept my eyes on the sidewalk.

"Oh." I ignored the implied question, and after a few moments, he added, "You're hell on the good guys, darlin'." He walked with me in silence for a few more paces. "Where ya walkin' to?"

I sighed. "The farm."

"Where's the farm?"

"About ten miles from here. You'd better think twice

about walking with me unless you're starting a serious fitness plan."

Arnie stopped. "Aydan, ya can't walk ten miles. You're shakin' like a leaf. Come sit in the truck, an' I'll take ya wherever ya wanna go."

I rounded on him, fists clenched. "I can do whatever I have to do," I snarled. "I don't need you or anybody else to babysit me. I can take care of myself. I always have. I always will."

His face softened. "Aw, darlin'. Whatever happened this afternoon, it musta been bad."

I spun away, swiping angrily at my eyes. "Don't give me sympathy!"

He came to stand in front of me and reached slowly to fold me into his arms. I held myself rigid, fighting tears with all my strength while he stroked my hair. He murmured nonsense, his soft rasp crumbling my defences, and at last I lost the battle and buried my face in his shoulder.

Wrapped in the safety of his embrace, I drew a few ragged breaths before pushing him away and turning my back so I could wipe my eyes.

I held my chin up when I turned back to face him, but my smile trembled despite my best efforts. "I told you not to give me sympathy. All that does is get you a wet shoulder."

He regarded me searchingly, his ugly face worried. "Aydan, ya don't always hafta be strong. It's okay to lean on a friend."

"Yes, I do have to be strong. Now stop with the mushy stuff. I mean it." I planted my fists on my hips and gave him my best glare.

He chuckled, but the smile didn't reach his eyes. "Okay, darlin', whatever ya say."

I reached out to squeeze his hand. "Thanks." I turned away. "I really have to walk now."

"Okay. I'll pick ya up when ya fall down." A few seconds later, I heard the slam of the SUV's door and the engine turned over. I wandered down the sidewalk, reassured by the vehicle idling slowly behind me and by the presence of a friend I hadn't even known a week ago.

I gave myself over to deep thought, letting my feet take me where they wanted. I trusted Hellhound to watch my back, and as that thought occurred to me, I slowed to a stop.

Trust. Always the hardest thing for me.

I started walking again, separating myself from the events of the day and turning over the pieces in my mind. I tried to put away the nightmare memory of the constructs' soulless faces. That wasn't Kane or Germain or Spider. That was Sandler. They were all Sandler.

Other than the slap in the face this afternoon, Kane had done nothing to betray me. I'd been around him long enough to believe he wouldn't hit me without a reason. And he'd pretty much been forced to tranquilize me. I'd been ready to rip my own arm off to escape.

And he had let me run away, carrying highly classified information in my head. He was taking a huge chance.

Trusting me.

I sighed.

Turning back to Hellhound's cruising Forester, I shot him a smile and stuck out my thumb.

CHAPTER 40

When we pulled up in front of Kane's office, Hellhound reached for my hand and held it gently. "D'ya want me to come in with ya?"

"No, I'll be fine. But thanks for rescuing me. Again. That's getting to be a bad habit."

He gave me a cheerful leer. "Darlin', your debt's pilin' up. Ya better start thinkin' about payin' me back in sin pretty soon, or you're gonna hafta marry me."

I laughed. "A fate worse than death."

He laughed, too. "Amen."

I got out of the SUV and went up the walk. When I closed the door behind me, the Forester was still idling at the curb. Still watching my back.

I took a deep breath and faced Kane's worried expression. "I'm sorry about running off. I was messed up. I'm better now. We need to talk."

He smiled, his shoulders easing. "I'm glad you're back. Do you mind going downstairs?"

"Can we do it up here?"

His expression answered the question before he even spoke. "Aydan..."

I squared my shoulders and gathered every shred of

courage I had left. Avoiding the source of fear only gave it more power.

"Okay, let's go."

I did my best to hide my white-knuckled grip on the handrail in the stairwell, but I knew Kane's perceptive eyes didn't miss the trembling of my knees. I held my mind and my breathing under iron control. Ocean waves. Not trapped.

When we entered the subterranean meeting room, Spider, Germain, and Wheeler looked up from three corners of the table. One corner left for Kane. The table top for me. A shudder ripped through me, and I forced the thought from my mind. That wasn't real. That was Sandler, not these men.

"Aydan?" Germain's normally humorous eyes were worried. "Are you okay?"

I kept my voice light. "I'm fine. Are you okay? I'm told I'm hell on the good guys."

He laughed, relaxing. "I'm fine. But I haven't taken a hit like that since college football. There's a great career out there for you if you get tired of bookkeeping."

Spider snorted. "She went easy on you. She tossed me about six feet in the air."

"Hell of an uppercut, too," Kane teased, rubbing his chin.

I flexed the split skin across my knuckles, wincing as I turned to Wheeler. "See, you're lucky you haven't had to spend any time with me. You're the only one I haven't taken a swing at."

He frowned. "And I'm the one who deserves to have you take a swing at me."

"Oh, for cr..." I regarded him helplessly. "We had this conversation. You didn't do anything wrong. You couldn't have done anything differently."

"Agreed," Kane said firmly. "Now punch him so he can get over it, and let's get on with this briefing."

I attempted a laugh and gently socked Wheeler on the shoulder left-handed. "All better now?"

He gave me a sheepish smile. "Okay. I'll drop it."

We sat down, and I frowned in silence for a moment, wondering how to start. Start with the good news. "I guess I'm clear of Fuzzy Bunny. Sandler told them I was dead."

There was a short, shocked silence before chaos erupted as four men asked questions at once.

I couldn't decipher any of them, so I waved them to silence. "Sorry, that was a bad place to start. I'm trying to get my thoughts organized."

I rubbed the frown lines out of my forehead with trembling fingers, trying not to let the tension in my audience feed my own discomfort. "Okay. Point one. Sandler was not a good guy."

Spider snorted. "He was an ass."

"No, I mean he was one of the bad guys. I'm pretty sure he was working for Fuzzy Bunny."

Kane jerked forward. "How do you know?"

"He was involved in the creation of the warehouse network. They were developing it as an interrogation tool."

I shuddered, nausea climbing the back of my throat again. "It's a perfect setup. Create a network environment that exactly matches the room where you're holding your prisoner. Bring your victim into the network. He or she doesn't realize they're not still in the holding cell. Torture them, as much and as long as you want. If they get too close to death, pop them out of the network. Their physical bodies are well fed and well treated. Only the memory remains."

My throat closed, and I wrapped my arms around myself, staring at the table. "And then do it again. Over and over. Whenever you want. As long as you want." My voice came out in a harsh whisper, and I cleared my throat. "No physical evidence at all. They could be tortured for days, weeks, years even. It would break anybody."

Silence blanketed the table. "How do you know this?" Kane asked quietly, his voice vibrating with restrained tension.

I didn't look up. "Sandler confirmed it after I figured it out. I was his field test."

"But." Spider's voice trembled, and he swallowed audibly before continuing. "He replicated the meeting room exactly? But didn't you notice we weren't there?"

"You were there," I said as matter-of-factly as I could. "Constructs of you. He made you do," I paused, searching for words. "Uncharacteristic things. That was how I figured it out."

Kane's voice was so harsh I started in my chair. "Exactly what uncharacteristic things?"

I met his eyes. "I don't think it's productive to discuss that."

Kane's shoulders bunched as he leaned across the table. "If wrong was done in my name... no, in my image, then I deserve to know."

I looked around the table, stalling. Spider's face was chalk-white, faint freckles visible. I'd never noticed he had freckles.

I did my best casual shrug. "It was no big deal. Don't worry about it."

A glance at Kane's face proved to be a mistake. I quickly averted my eyes and added, "It was just a sim. I knew it wasn't real almost right away."

Germain's dark gaze burned into me. "We need to know what we did," he said with quiet intensity.

"You didn't do anything. You weren't even there. It was just Sandler's constructs. It was all him. Let it go."

Spider spoke almost inaudibly. "Aydan. Please. I have to know. Imagination is worse."

I dropped my head into my hands with a long sigh and spoke to the tabletop. "Fine. Five men. One woman. You do the math." Then I realized how it sounded and hurriedly added, "But none of you did anything bad. You just held me down."

Apparently that didn't help. Kane slammed his fist on the table with such force we all jumped. He surged up from his chair, turning away. His T-shirt strained across the knotted muscles of his back as he locked his arms across his chest.

Spider sprang up, too, and dashed in the direction of the bathroom. Germain sat as if carved from stone. His only movement was the flexing of his fist, the knuckles glowing as white as marble.

I didn't know how to make it better. "But, guys, it wasn't you," I pleaded. "You couldn't know what was happening. You couldn't have done anything. You were sitting in the meeting room, watching the two of us staring off into space. And anyway, I got away in the end. It's no big deal."

Kane turned back to the table, his face rigid.

"What exactly happened?" His voice sounded like steel cables parting.

I hesitated. "Well, I should have realized what was going on right away, but you..."

I revised what I was going to say. "I took a hit and got

knocked out for a while, so I was a little out of it. By the time I recovered enough to know what was going on, I was naked and held down on the table, so I was a little distracted..."

I glanced at his expression and blundered on, completely rattled. "I got suspicious because you... your constructs were acting so... Anyway, Sandler grew this enormous..." I started to gesture with my hands before thinking better of it.

"He planned for me to bleed to death slowly," I explained.

A muscle jumped furiously in Kane's clenched jaw.

"So, anyway, I knew it had to be a sim," I continued hastily. "And then I remembered that you create your own reality in the sim."

I bared my teeth. "It turned out my reality had an automatic weapon in it."

Spider had crept back to the table, his face ashen. "You shot him?" he quavered.

"To bleeding, twitching ribbons," I snarled.

"And he died in real life," Spider whispered. "I didn't think that could happen."

"He told me if you die in the sim, it looks like a fatal heart attack in real life. That's why he planned to kill me in the sim. No evidence. He would have gotten away with it, too, if he'd been smart enough to just shoot me right away. I'd have died without ever knowing it wasn't real. Lucky for me he decided to play out his elaborate little fantasy."

"Lucky," Kane echoed, his face like granite.

I dropped my head into my hands again. "I really hope that double-oh-seven license you granted me last night is still in effect," I mumbled to the table. "Because I just confessed to murder in front of four witnesses."

"No," Kane said. "You described a virtual self-defence

simulation. Four witnesses sat in the meeting room with you and watched Sandler keel over of natural causes while you sat unmoving at the opposite end of the table. There's no stronger alibi than that."

I gazed around the table at their grim faces, all nodding agreement. "Thanks," I said inadequately. "And I'm sorry I freaked out and attacked you when I came out of the network. But why did you hit me?"

Kane's brow furrowed. "When? I didn't hit you."

"When I came out of the network. You hit me in the face. And you were winding up for another one when I fell off the chair."

He shook his head, still frowning. "I didn't hit you. Sandler had collapsed a few minutes earlier. Germain was doing CPR. We knew something had gone seriously wrong in the network test. We tried to access the network, but we were locked out, so I was trying to wake you. Usually all it takes is a touch or someone calling your name, but you weren't coming out. I was just patting your face, trying to wake you up."

Understanding dawned. "And I had my usual shot of pain from leaving the network at the same time. So I thought you were beating me." I met his eyes, embarrassed. "I'm sorry. I should have known better, but I was pretty messed up by then. That's how the sim started..." I trailed off as his face hardened again.

"And then you tranked me," I went on. "I understand now that you didn't have much choice. But from my standpoint, one second I was in the sim, the next second I was in the warehouse with you hitting me, then you yelled 'shoot her' and seconds later I was in the bunker. I didn't know what was real anymore."

"I'm sorry," Kane said. "You were fighting so hard, I couldn't hold you without hurting you. And we didn't know what had killed Sandler. I was afraid you'd snapped because of a problem with the network interface."

"Now it makes sense," Germain said quietly. "You kept screaming 'I trusted you', and we couldn't understand why."

"I should have checked the network access," Spider mumbled. "I should have caught that." He met my eyes miserably, and then stared down at the tabletop.

Kane's face darkened. "And I should have gone in with you," he added. "I'm sorry. This should never have happened."

I knotted my fists in my hair. "Guys. It's okay. It was just a sim. Forget it."

Kane cleared his throat before speaking again. "So the warehouse network was never intended to connect to Sirius."

"Not that I could tell," I replied, grateful for the topic change. "If it was, Sandler didn't mention it. But I don't know why the key worked to get me into both networks. And I still don't understand where it came from, or what good it is if only I can use it."

"I might be able to answer that," Spider spoke up. "Using your timeframe for when the crystal showed up in your back yard, I went back over last October's records. It seems Fuzzy Bunny was expecting an important delivery around mid-October. One of our agents intercepted the courier."

"And get this," he looked around the table, his eyes sparkling. "Our guy cornered the courier close to Aydan's neighbourhood. The courier suicided, and nothing was ever recovered from the body, so it was assumed that he hadn't made the pickup yet. But if the delivery was the crystal, he could have tossed it over your fence, intending to go back and recover it later."

I rubbed my aching forehead. "But what good is it if it only worked for me, not for anybody else?"

"It looks like it was designed to be used along with a brainwave modulator," Webb explained. "You remember how Smith said earlier that a few people may use the right frequency naturally? Coincidentally, you do. The rest of us don't."

"Oh, so that's why they were hacking the fob instead."

"Right," Spider agreed. "The key that was inside the crystal can get you into any network invisibly, but it won't work for most people. The fobs can get anybody in, but they're coded to individuals, and they're traceable. We think they were trying to develop a generic fob that wouldn't have to be coded to an individual."

"Making it easy to infiltrate a network, or to send captives into the network without their knowledge," Kane concluded. "All right, we have a lot of loose ends to tie up. What was the relationship between Sandler and Ramos? Was Fuzzy Bunny really their purchaser for the hacked fob? If so, can we nail them with anything? Who was the supplier of the crystal? Who else knew about Aydan's ability to access the network, and is she in any further danger now that Sandler's associates, whoever they are, think she's dead?"

"And can I go home and get a change of clothes?" I added. "I realize it's insignificant in the big picture, but it'd really make me feel better."

Kane nodded. "I'll take you."

"I'll keep digging into the crystal and its suppliers," Spider volunteered.

"I'll start looking into Sandler," Germain said. "Can I

pull in those analysts you requisitioned earlier?"

"Yours," Kane agreed.

Wheeler stood.   "I'm going to go and continue questioning the detainees.   Now that we know about Sandler's involvement and the purpose of the warehouse network, I can ask better questions."   He turned and left, followed by Spider.   Germain sat down at one of the terminals that lined the walls and started clicking keys.

Kane turned to me. "Ready to go?"

"So ready."

CHAPTER 41

"Stay in the vehicle," Kane cautioned when we got to the farm. "We're going to follow the standard clearing procedure."

"Do you think it's still necessary?"

"Better safe than sorry. I won't get complacent until we have all the research done and the loose ends are tied up. If we've missed a single detail, it could change everything. Slide over and get ready to drive, just in case."

He closed the door and I slid over as instructed, watching him circle the house. I didn't know how he could stay so calm, putting himself in danger over and over. I was vibrating with nerves. Then again, he got to carry a gun. Maybe that helped.

He waved me the all-clear, and I got out of the SUV to join him on the front step. He opened the door and repeated his systematic search of the house. When he nodded, I headed for my bedroom, hands shaking.

"Do I have time to take a shower?" I asked over my shoulder. "Or should I just grab my stuff and go back to your office?"

"I'd prefer not to stay here too long."

I sighed. "Okay."

I upended my backpack over the laundry basket before repacking it with several changes of clothes, afraid to assume I might be back anytime soon.

I stripped off my clothes and dumped them into the laundry, too, regarding my panties with a shudder. I wasn't ever going to be able to look at them again without seeing Sandler's dick poking out of them. I picked them up with my fingertips and dropped them into a small paper bag. I dressed in fresh clothes and brushed my hair before going out to meet Kane in the living room.

"Looks like you have messages." He pointed to the blinking light on my machine.

When I pressed the button, Cheryl's worried voice filled the room. "Aydan, it's Cheryl. Where are you? I've been calling and calling your cell. I went to show the house today, and it looked like there had been a break-in. The door to your bedroom was kicked in. Are you okay? Call me."

"Shit." I checked the date. Sunday afternoon. "Shit!"

Next message. "Aydan, it's Cheryl again. It's Tuesday evening. I was over at the house again, and your car's in the drive, but I couldn't find you. I'm worried about you. If I don't hear from you by tomorrow, I'm going to file a missing persons report with the police. Call me. I'll leave this message on your cell, too."

I shot a frown at Kane. "*Shit!*"

I pressed the button again. Cheryl sounded tearful. "Aydan, where are you? It's Wednesday afternoon, and I'm so afraid something bad has happened to you. The police are looking for you. Hang on, wherever you are. Call me if you get this."

I flopped into a chair, making fists in my hair. "Son of a *bitch*! What the fuck am I supposed to do now? Phone her up and say, oh gee, sorry, it was all a misunderstanding, silly me?"

Kane was already dialling his phone. "The first thing we're going to do is cancel the missing persons alert. After that, we'll do damage control." He made several calls while I perched anxiously on the edge of the chair, racking my brain about how to deal with this latest problem.

Kane hung up. "That wasn't as bad as it could have been. When Eddy phoned in the 911 call about you on Wednesday night, they ramped up the search, but then the whole thing got called off when we reported we'd recovered you. We fed the police the stalker-ex-husband story, and they've passed it along to Cheryl already. She'll be upset, but not frantic that you haven't called her yet."

I slumped back in the chair. "Thank God. Poor Cheryl. I guess I'll just have to tell her I lost my cell phone. That'll explain why I didn't return her earlier calls. I'd better call her right now, though."

He nodded. "Remember, keep it simple. The more elaborate your explanation, the more complicated things get down the road."

I grimaced and dialled Cheryl's number. She picked up on the first ring, and I spent the next several minutes reassuring her and explaining as little as possible. When I finally hung up, I thudded the handset against my forehead. "I swear, in my next life, I'm going to be a hermit."

Kane looked bemused. "Isn't it a good thing that you have people in your life who care about you?"

"Yes! I guess. But I wish... I just hate upsetting people. I wish people didn't care so much about me that they tie themselves in knots like that. I feel so bad."

"So you'd rather die a horrible death than upset people."

"No!" I yanked a handful of my hair. He clearly wasn't getting it. Hell, I wasn't sure I got it myself. "Never mind. Forget it. I've just had too much emotional bloodbath lately."

I turned away from his scrutiny and made for the kitchen to grab matches and a bottle of fondue fuel before heading out the back door to the firepit. Kane stuck close beside me, scanning the landscape.

I'd forgotten he'd have to shadow me. Shit. Well, too late now.

I dropped the small paper bag into the pit and sloshed some fuel over it. "Stand back." I tossed in a match, and the bag caught with a whoosh.

The paper burned away first, and we stood in silence watching the flames consume the turquoise lace. I could feel Kane's eyes on me, and I stared into the firepit.

"You didn't tell us the whole story, did you?" he asked quietly.

"I hit the high points."

"The high points. When I cut you loose after you'd been tortured, you said 'Help me up', like you'd tripped or something. When you came out of the network, you were hysterical. It must have been bad."

I shrugged, watching the flames. "I just freaked out because I was disoriented."

"Aydan. I understand you don't want to talk about this, and I won't ask you again. I just want you to remember you don't have to deal with it alone. Don't try to do it yourself."

"I'll be fine. Dr. Roth gave me the name of a psychologist."

He sighed. "I've experienced post-traumatic stress first-hand. Don't wait. It only gets worse."

I looked up finally and met his eyes. "I have a bit of experience in that area myself," I told him gently. "I dealt with it the first time with the help of an excellent psychologist. If my coping skills aren't up to it this time, I definitely won't wait. I don't want to go through that again."

He studied my face. "Was that after your divorce?"

"No. I... had some problems. After the accident. I told you I was pinned..."

He nodded, his face clearing with comprehension. "Trapped. And you're claustrophobic."

"That was part of it. But... well, we were out in the middle of nowhere. It took a long time for the emergency crews to arrive. I was pinned right in front of the biker. Watching him suffer and not being able to do anything. And those horrible screams. And the smells... His intestines... well, you saw. Anyway."

I took a deep breath. "It was more than an hour before they finally took him away. They had to cut the post and take it along with him. When they started with the chainsaw, the screaming was just..."

He took my hand and held it, and we stood in silence for a few seconds. I shook myself. "Anyway, the psychologist got me over the flashbacks and panic attacks. He was amazing. And I still have the skills he taught me."

"I thought you seemed pretty blasé about the screaming nightmares."

I gave him a half-smile. "I don't do that very often any more. I've probably got a few more in me after the last twenty-four hours, but it shouldn't last too long. I usually have a couple of bad nights and then I get over it."

His gaze sharpened. "Usually?"

"I mean, if something scary or stressful is going on in my

life. You know. Shit happens to everybody."

"Mmm." He fell silent, staring at the smoking ruin in the firepit. After a moment he turned to me. "Ready to go?"

"Yeah."

We turned back toward the house, and I reached to touch his arm. "Thanks." I met his eyes, trying to make him see I really meant it, that I wasn't just blowing him off.

He smiled. "You're welcome."

CHAPTER 42

When we pulled up in front of Kane's converted office, I slumped in the seat, toying with my seat belt. "Back to the cave, eh?"

He shot me a sympathetic look and a nod.

I sighed heavily before straightening in my seat, running a hand over my abs. The pain was beginning to ease. Or maybe the rest of my body just ached so much it was fading in comparison.

I got out of the SUV and dragged my feet up the walk, already beginning my internal monologue.

Fine. I'd be fine. So I'd be below ground, so what? No big deal. Lots of ways out. Not trapped.

Fine. I was fine...

The stairwell seemed to shrink around me when the door clicked closed above and I muffled a panicky squeak, my hand clenching on the handrail.

Get a grip, dammit! Just breathe. Ocean waves. Think ocean waves...

I successfully held back my shudder at the sight of the big table in the work area and shuffled in the direction of the bathroom, leaving Kane and Germain leaning over one of the computers.

I stood in the shower for a long time, hoping the hot water would ease the aching tension in my shoulders. Determinedly rerouting my mind, I concentrated on recalling the open fields around my farm. How would they look once winter lost its grip?

I leaned my forehead against the wall, eyes closed while I visualized sweet, sun-warmed hay under a wide blue sky. The heat of the water warmed my back like summer sunshine, and my tremors gradually diminished while I drew deep breaths of imagined fresh air.

My serenity was short-lived. Back in the long corridor, the knowledge of the heavy earth above me tightened like a noose around my throat. I shook my head vigorously and headed for the work area, clinging to my vision of summer.

Claustrophobia was all in my head. I was doing this to myself. I wasn't trapped, anyway, for shit's sake. Stupid. Just get over it.

When I rounded the corner, the sight of two smug faces made hope soar in my heart. "What?"

Kane grinned, the tiredness around his eyes crinkling into those sexy laugh lines. "Sandler was the key. This thing is blowing wide open. We don't have the whole picture yet, but we will, and soon. Thanks to you."

I beamed at him. "Can I request a reward?"

Wariness crept into his eyes, the cop face closing down his expression. "Maybe. What did you have in mind?"

"A chance to get out of the bunker for beer and blues at Eddy's?"

His face relaxed again and he leaned back in his chair, smiling. "That could be arranged. I think we're all ready for that kind of reward."

I hid my surge of relief in a joke. "Good, 'cause I'm

starving."

Germain laughed. "The woman is a bottomless pit. Why don't you weigh three hundred pounds?"

"It's this new workout plan I'm on," I explained. "It's called the Spy Workout. Maybe you've heard of it. It involves a lot of punching good guys and running."

His eyes twinkled. "I've heard of that one. Tried it myself a few times, but I never got good at punching the good guys."

I laughed. "I'm glad to hear that. I'm planning to switch workouts pretty soon, too. The Spy Workout gets old fast."

"Smart choice."

Kane glanced at his watch. "Okay, we'll wrap up a couple of things here, and then we can go." He and Germain turned back to their terminals, and I retreated down the hall to pace in the bunkroom, not wanting to hover anxiously.

I was beginning to wear a path in the floor by the time Kane called me, and I feigned calm when I joined him in the work area.

Germain looked up from his computer. "I'm just tracking down a hot lead here. You two go ahead. If I get this tied up in the next little while, I'll join you, but I might just stay here and eat the leftover pizza from this afternoon."

Emerging from the basement felt like being reborn, and I sucked in a surreptitious breath of relief.

When we arrived at Blue Eddy's, most of the tables were occupied and the stage was set up. Three waitresses circulated, and Eddy was busy behind the bar. When he saw us, his face lit up and he put down the glass he was filling to hurry across the room.

He took my hands in both of his. "Aydan, thank goodness you're all right. I was worried about you."

I smiled at him and squeezed his hands. "No need to thank goodness, thank *you*. I would have been in serious trouble without you."

"What happened?" he asked, examining my bruised wrists. "They wouldn't tell me anything when I called the hospital, but there was blood down the hallway from where you got dragged out. Did they catch the women who attacked you?"

"In a manner of speaking. Those weren't women. They were my crazy ex-husband and one of his low-life buddies in drag. I moved here to get away from him, but he found me anyway. I'm really glad you called the police. He won't bother me again."

"But where have you been?" he persisted. "I called the hospital and they said you'd been discharged, but I called your home number and got no answer last night. I was afraid something might have happened after you left the hospital."

"Oh," I said in confusion. We'd figured out a cover story, but I hadn't expected he'd try to call me. "I was... I didn't go home. I, um..."

I felt Kane's hand at the small of my back. "She stayed with a friend," he said blandly, looking Eddy square in the eye.

Eddy's sharp gaze took in the two of us standing close together, Kane's proprietary hand on my back. "Oh." He nodded. "Well, I'm glad you're okay."

"Thanks, Eddy, and I'm sorry you were worried. I'll give you my cell number the next time I'm in."

"That would be good." He winked at Kane. "You take good care of her, John. I can't afford to lose my bookkeeper."

He went back to the bar, and I churned my fingers in my hair. "Gah. Looks like Spider's scenario wins after all. Sorry, I froze. Now what do we do?"

"Let it go," Kane advised. "Eddy made an assumption. If we play it cool, that's all it will be. It will just go away eventually."

"Good enough," I agreed. We both scanned the room, and I could tell that, like me, Kane was scoping out the best strategic position in the crowded bar.

A familiar burly figure wove its way through the crush. "Hey darlin'. Cap," Hellhound greeted us. He turned to me. "Thought ya were gonna give him the slip so we could play some wild music together."

I grinned, giddy with my reprieve from captivity. "How do you feel about threesomes?"

Kane's eyebrows rose as his mouth quirked in amusement. Hellhound leered. "Darlin', if you're talkin' two chicks an' me, I'm happy to oblige, but this big galoot would throw me off my game somethin' fierce."

I shrugged. "Darn. Guess you'll just have to play with yourself, then."

He pulled a mournful face. "Story a' my life." The sound of guitars floated over the hum of conversation in the bar. "Gotta go, we're gonna start the set," Hellhound said. "I grabbed the table over there. My jacket's on the chair." He jerked a thumb toward what I was beginning to think of as 'our usual table' before turning to make his way back to the stage.

Kane and I exchanged a smile as we slid into chairs with our backs to the wall. The waitress arrived quickly, and we ordered drinks, lime and soda for Kane and Corona for me. When the icy bottle arrived, I squeezed in the lime and lowered the level down to the bottle's shoulders in a long, blissful swallow. I sighed and lolled back in the chair, stretching out my legs and cradling my bottle lovingly.

"I'm getting spoiled by being chauffeured around all the time," I told Kane. "I've had more beer this week than in the last six months."

He laughed. "I'm feeling sorry for myself watching you enjoy it. I could go for some cold suds right now. It's been a long week."

I nodded. "I hear you."

The first set started and we sat in companionable silence, enjoying the excellent music. I smiled and moved with the beat, soaking in the freedom and normalcy. When the menus arrived, I ordered a burger and onion rings. Might as well go for the gut bomb. My normally healthy diet was nothing but a distant memory anyway.

The musicians took a break and Hellhound ambled over to the table, regarding the remaining chairs with disgust.

I smiled up at him and scooted my chair over closer to Kane. "Pull one around beside me. There's room."

"Thanks, darlin'." He dragged one of the chairs over and straddled it backward, facing the stage. He rested his arms across the back, dangling a half-empty beer bottle between his fingers.

"You guys are amazing," I complimented him. "Do you play up here often?"

"Every now an' then. Whenever I'm up here on a Thursday night. I been comin' off and on for a while, so I know some a' the guys."

We were interrupted by the arrival of the food, and I dug into the burger with enthusiasm. After a few minutes of intense concentration, I sat back with a sigh and drank some more beer. As I did, I realized both men were regarding me with amusement.

"What?" I asked.

"You eat every meal as if it was your last," Kane observed.

I gave him a half-smile and a shrug. "Some day it will be. Nobody will ever say I didn't enjoy my last meal."

He sobered. "True. You've come close enough to your last meal a few times this week."

I grinned. "Yeah, well, tonight I'm eating a fabulous burger, drinking ice-cold beer, and listening to the best music I've heard in a long time. I win."

Both men laughed. Kane raised his glass. "To winning."

Hellhound and I clinked our bottles against it. "To winning," we agreed.

The musicians were gathering onstage again, and Hellhound got up to join them. They put their heads together for a few seconds before taking their places. Hellhound pulled the microphone close. "I wanna do a song for a special lady tonight," he rasped, the mike deepening and enriching his voice.

They launched into a classic blues lead-in, and Hellhound leaned into the mike and began to sing. "I want this long-legged redhead woman, oh, but she won't treat me right. Oh, I want a long-legged red-head woman, y'know, but she won't treat me right."

He sang a couple more verses and then slid into a refrain, his voice growling into a rough-edged low note like the brush of whiskers against sensitive skin. The small hairs stood up on the back of my neck.

"Please, oh baby please, lay some sugar on a dyin' man. Hot sugar for your sighin' man."

I tried to control a shiver of pure desire as that low note hit my ears and headed straight south. After my experience in the sim, I thought sex would be the last thing on my mind, but instead, every inch of my skin begged for healing touch. Like eating a candy to take a bad taste out of my mouth.

Hot sugar.

Kane turned a concerned face toward me. "Are you okay?"

I lowered my beer by an inch or two. "I'm fine," I croaked. I shook my finger at Hellhound, who grinned unrepentantly. The set continued, and I squirmed in my chair, my body on fire.

Kane leaned over. "Do you want me to talk to him?"

"No. It's okay." I drained my bottle and nodded to the waitress's questioning look. When the fresh bottle arrived, I deliberately stretched out in my chair again, schooling my body into repose and concentrating on the blues. By the time Hellhound returned at the end of the set, I was down a half-bottle and moving to the music again.

When he took his seat, I reached over and shoved gently at his shoulder. "You old lecher. No wonder Kane won't let me go out alone." Both men laughed. "I didn't know you composed your own music," I added.

He bounced his eyebrows. "Only when I'm inspired. An' who're ya callin' old? I'm only forty-eight. 'Experienced' is the word I prefer."

I grinned. "I bow to your superior experience."

"Ow. Come on, darlin', there can't be more'n ten years between us."

I raised my eyebrows at him. "Oooh, flattery will get you everywhere. Try two."

He stared at me. "Now that, I don't believe."

I poked at his empty beer bottle. "Never underestimate the transformative power of beer goggles and bar lighting."

He shook his head. "Darlin', I've seen ya in the light of day."

I gave him a smile and dropped my eyes, pleased but a little embarrassed by his openly appreciative gaze. "Don't you have music to play?"

"I do indeed. An' I'm feelin' inspired all over again." He got up and headed back to the stage.

By the time I'd finished my second beer, I could tell Kane was getting restless. I knew he'd want to be in the thick of the investigation, and although I was enjoying the music, I had a feeling more beer would be a bad idea. I shot him a glance. "Ready to go?"

He nodded. "I'd really like to get back to work."

I nodded understanding, and he signalled the waitress. We split the bill and headed for the door, giving Eddy and Hellhound a wave as we left. They smiled from the bar and stage respectively, and we emerged from the heat and music into the crisp air of the parking lot.

I stood for a few seconds drinking in the silence and spacious coolness. I gazed up at the stars as I spoke to Kane. "Any idea when I can start living at home again?"

"I'll have a better idea tomorrow morning. The way things looked when I left, you might even be able to go home for tomorrow night. Everything I've seen so far indicates that you're in the clear."

I drew a deep breath of the fresh air. "That would be so good."

My hands were shaking by the time Kane stepped

forward to activate the breakers below the house. I drew a deep breath as the door swung open, and he eyed me with concern.

"Are you all right?"

"Fine." My voice was a little too loud, and I stood straighter and met his eyes with all the bravado I could muster.

His face softened, and he half-reached a hand in my direction. "Aydan, I'm sorry this is so hard for you," he said softly. "But it's for your own safety-"

"I know, and thanks," I interrupted. "It's just my stupid claustrophobia. It's okay. I'll deal with it." I turned and strode down the stairs to stand waiting at the lower door, staring into middle distance and repeating my internal mantra.

Fine. I was fine. Not trapped.

Webb and Wheeler had returned while we were gone, and suppressed excitement crackled in the air. Kane immediately joined the huddle in the meeting room, and I waved a general good-night and departed for the bunkroom, glad to be free of his too-perceptive scrutiny.

Once in bed, I lay still, concentrating fiercely while I did every relaxation exercise I knew.

CHAPTER 43

My eyes flew open and I peered at my watch for the umpteenth time. It was only six A.M., but I couldn't face the thought of tossing and turning any longer. Only sheer obstinate pride had prevented me from begging the men to shoot me with a trank so I could get through the night. The jagged blades of an incipient panic attack vibrated ominously near the edges of my mind.

I groaned my way out of bed, the aching tension in my muscles completely eclipsing the discomfort from my injuries.

In the shower, I breathed myself into a semblance of calm again, letting the hot water soften my knotted shoulders. Diverting my mind with a cursory examination, I was pleased to discover my bruises were blossoming into yellow, green, and brown. They actually looked worse than when they were fresh, but I'd had enough bruises over the years to be reassured by their colourful display of healing.

By the time I arrived in the meeting area, a paper bag was already perched on the table. Spider looked up as I came in, the dark circles under his eyes belied by his buoyant smile.

"Breakfast's ready." He pointed to the bag, and I grinned

at him, clasping my shaking hands under the table.

"Thanks, Spider, you're the best!" I sat down and pulled the bag over, purring my approval at the contents. "Mmmm-mmmm! I owe you big-time for this," I told him as I retrieved another bagel with peanut butter, taking secret comfort from its heat and aroma. "How did you know peanut butter is my staple breakfast food?"

"Lucky guess," he beamed. "And anyway, you don't owe me. It's on the department expense. After all you've done for us, a little peanut butter is the least we can do for you."

I glanced up eagerly. "Does that mean things went well last night?" I mumbled around a sticky mouthful.

He nodded. "Better than well. We're just tying up the last loose ends now." As he spoke, Kane strolled in, rumpled and stubbled again, the lines on his face etched deeper by lack of sleep. He set his coffee down on the table and dropped into a chair.

"How late did you guys work, anyway?" I asked. "You look like death warmed over. No offence."

"None taken," Kane growled in his morning voice. He cleared his throat and took a gulp of coffee before continuing, his deep baritone husky. "We've made some excellent progress. Once you identified Sandler's involvement, the rest of the pieces started to fall into place. There are still some lingering questions, but we'll get there."

I hid my desperation in a casual tone. "Does that mean I can go home today?"

He frowned. "You should stay here until we have time to search out the last of the details."

Stay calm. Breathe. Not trapped.

"But Fuzzy Bunny thinks I'm dead. Surely I'm in the clear now." I gave him my best pleading big brown eyes.

He shifted in his chair, looking troubled. "Aydan, I know it's been hard on you to stay underground. And you're right, so far it looks as though you're in the clear. But do you really want to take that chance?"

"*Yes*, for-" I bit off the harsh voice that issued from my throat, squeezing my hands together under the table and drawing a deep breath.

"But how much of a chance is it, really? And when would you ever be sure?" I argued instead, holding my tone calm and reasonable. "You'll never be a hundred percent sure."

He dropped his head into his hands and stared at the table. "That's true, but..."

"I need to get out of here." I tried to hold onto my calm voice, but it vibrated with desperation and my shaking fingers dug into my thighs.

He looked up to appraise me for a moment before blowing out a tired breath. "All right. If you're sure. I'll take you home, and clear your place one last time. Here's your cell phone, too." He pushed it across the table.

Germain arrived, the shadows under his eyes matching Webb's, his stubble even more rampant than Kane's. His eyes crinkled when he saw me. "You look like a kid on Christmas morning. Somebody must have fed you."

"Yes. And even better than that, I'll be out of your hair today." My relief bloomed into a grin. "Not that it hasn't been a slice, but..."

Germain laughed. "Fickle woman." He drifted toward the kitchen.

Kane leaned back in his chair, hands clasped behind his head. His shirt sleeves strained around his bulging biceps, and I sighed inwardly at the realization that this would be my last glimpse of that eye candy. As scary as the past few days had been, I had thoroughly enjoyed the view when I wasn't being frightened out of my mind. Too bad he was so scrupulous about propriety within the team.

He rose, stretching. "I need to grab a shower and a shave, and then we can go."

"Okay." With freedom in sight, it was all I could not to spring up and pace. I turned to my breakfast bag instead, concentrating on eating slowly.

Almost there. Almost free. Just breathe.

After a while, Germain appeared with his coffee and slid into the opposite chair. "So what do you plan to do with your first day of freedom?"

I turned gratefully to the distraction. "First, I'm going to go and stand at the top of my hill for about an hour or until I freeze, whichever comes first. After that, I guess I'll get organized and pack up some tools to take to Calgary, if I can figure out how to get them down there on the bus. And then I can bring my car back."

A clean-shaven Kane returned as I spoke, his short, still-damp hair neatly combed. A whiff of shampoo made my stomach drop with the memory of the delicious body under that black T-shirt. And those jeans... I kept my eyes above his waistband with an effort.

"Why don't you give Hellhound a call?" Kane suggested. "I think he was planning to go back today. He'd have room for your tools in his SUV. Are you ready to go?"

I jumped up, only wincing a little, and made a beeline for the door. I snatched it open before remembering my manners and forcing myself to turn with a smile.

"Thanks for everything. You guys were great, and I really appreciate all you did for me."

Germain rose and offered me a handshake that turned

into a hug. "Let's do it again sometime when you're not in mortal danger."

"Good plan." I smiled. "Spider, thanks."

He got up and hugged me, too. "Take care."

"You, too. Be safe, you guys. Say goodbye and thanks to Wheeler for me."

"Will do."

My rigid muscles threatened to give way with shaky relief when we stepped out into the cold gray light of dawn. I leaned heavily on the handrail beside the front step and drew in a long, trembling breath. "I'll never take liberty for granted again."

Kane gave me a half-smile. "Did you ever?"

"Once, a very long time ago. Not in the last few decades."

He nodded, looking thoughtful, and we drove to the farm in silence. He cleared the house one last time, and we said an awkward goodbye on the front porch.

Hellhound arrived in the afternoon, and we loaded my tools and got on the road. Less preoccupied with my own problems than on the previous trip, I gradually discovered the keen mind he camouflaged with his habitual bad grammar and ribald humour. The two-hour trip flew by while we conversed easily. When we pulled into my driveway, he glanced up at the house. "Nice place."

"Yeah, I can hardly wait to sell it."

"Why, darlin'? Bad memories?"

I smiled, feeling wistful. "No. Good memories."

He looked puzzled, but I didn't elaborate as we carried the tools inside and upstairs. I stopped at the top of the landing.

"Shit."

The door was split, hanging off a single hinge at the top. The jamb and casing were splintered on the latch side, but the latchset still seemed intact. I tried to turn the knob, and the latch jammed.

"Shit!"

"Somebody hit this door hard," Hellhound observed. "Musta been a pretty big guy."

"Yeah, glad I didn't meet him," I replied absently, examining the wall with growing irritation. "Damn. That asshole buggered up the drywall, too. Now I'm going to have to buy an entire new sheet of drywall just to repair this one little spot on the wall because I didn't think to bring one of the million fucking pieces I just moved up to Silverside. Goddammit!"

I scowled up at the remaining bent hinge. "New door. New jamb. New casing. New stop. New hardware. Bodywork for my car. New fucking drywall. Fill, sand, paint. A week of my fucking life gone. Thank you, Fuzzy Fucking Bunny. Aargh!"

I snarled and wrenched the door off. A chunk of wood splintered out of the frame with a crack. I swore some more as I staggered over and threw the broken door down on the bed, hunching over to support myself beside it while I nursed my protesting bruise.

"Ow! Not to mention getting the shit beat out of me by some fucking lowlife buttcrack..."

I paused in my tirade at the sight of Hellhound's expression. "Darlin', are ya feelin' okay?" he asked cautiously.

I breathed deeply, reaching for calm. It eluded me.

"No, I am not feeling okay! I am feeling pissed off! And if that asshole Sandler was still alive, I'd shoot the fucker to ribbons all over again, starting with his big fucking ugly dick, the smarmy self-important asswipe! This is all his fault! And I have to clean up the fucking mess!"

Hellhound moved into the room and sat on the bed, reaching to stroke one of my clenched fists. "Darlin', ya ain't makin' much sense."

"No, and I can't, either. Fucking NDA. Forget everything I just said."

He frowned. "NDA. Oh, the non-disclosure agreement. So you're sayin' this'd make sense if ya could tell me about it."

I did some more deep breathing. This time I managed civility. "Yeah. Sorry, you didn't need to listen to all that. This is why I live alone."

He shrugged. "Ya had a tough week. Come on, let's go get somethin' to eat. It's dinner time, and I know ya gotta be hungry."

My stomach agreed with an audible growl, and he laughed. I let him shepherd me out of the room and down the stairs, still trying to get my temper under control. When we walked by my car, the sight of the bullet holes made me clench my teeth to keep the profanity from spilling out again. I stalked to Hellhound's SUV and got in, breathing deeply. In. Out. Ocean waves.

He eyed my clenched fists with concern. "Let it go, darlin'. It's just things. What matters is you're okay."

"Yeah," I gritted. "Just things. Things I have to pay for out of my own pocket."

I closed my eyes and took a deep breath, letting it out slowly and concentrating on relaxing my hands. I rolled my neck and shoulders and took another slow, deliberate breath.

"You're right," I told him after a short pause. "The good guys are undamaged, despite my best efforts, and the bad guys took some serious losses. That's about as good as it's going to get. Sorry for the whining. I'm all better now."

He smiled. "No problem. Ya just gotta blow off steam sometimes. What d'ya wanna eat?"

"I don't know. I don't want to go to Kelly's, because my friends will all be there tomorrow for lunch, and I'm going to lie low. I don't want Alanna to tell them I'm here. Take me wherever you like to go. I like everything."

"Ya avoidin' your friends?"

"Just for this week. I really don't want to deal with the 'how was your week' question right now. And by next weekend the bruises should be gone."

He nodded and put the SUV in gear. "D'ya like sushi?"

"Love it! And none of my friends can stand it. I'm in serious withdrawal."

"You're gonna like this, then." He drove for a few minutes before steering the SUV into a small strip mall. When we walked in, the sushi chef greeted him warmly by name. We took seats side by side at the back of the sushi bar, overlooking the entrance and the rest of the tiny restaurant.

"The one good thing about this week has been that I don't have to explain my seating choices." I grinned at Hellhound. "Nice to hang out with a bunch that's as paranoid as I am."

He eyed me appreciatively. "Nice to hang out with a woman who gets it. My question is, why?"

"Why, what?"

"Why d'ya always sit with your back to the wall?"

I laughed and explained the bar scenario to him. From

there, the conversation wandered to biker bars, then motorcycles and music while we drank hot sake and enjoyed the delicate, flavourful sushi.

Finally, I pushed the last plate away. "That was amazing. I can't believe I never knew this place was here. I'm definitely coming back."

"Call me if ya do," Hellhound urged. "I get better service when I got a gorgeous redhead with me."

I laughed and handed the server my credit card. "This is on me. Thanks for everything. I'd have been dead a couple of times over if not for you. A sushi dinner isn't much of a payback for saving my life, but it's a start."

He gently captured my hand, turning it over to stroke lightly down the inside of my wrist and palm. He gave me an intimate smile.

"Ya know how ya can pay me back, darlin'," he growled, his voice hitting that low note that vibrated through my body.

I shivered, all the heat and desire rushing back in an instant.

Goddammit, you only live once. And I'd come damn close to not living through this at all. My heart sucker-punched my ribs before launching itself up to beat a hasty tattoo in my throat.

"Yes." My voice came out in a hoarse whisper, and I pulled away to sink my face into my hands. "God help me. Yes."

Silence.

"Aydan, I was just jokin' around. Ya don't owe me a thing. An' I don't want anythin' ya don't wanna give."

I sighed and raised my head. He was frowning at me.

"What kind of an asshole d'ya think I am?" he asked.

I took his hand, stroking his lean, strong fingers. "I don't think you're an asshole. I know you were only joking around. But you got me wrong. I didn't mean 'God help me, I don't want to do this but I have to'. I meant 'God help me, I want this so much and it's probably a really bad idea'."

I met his eyes, willing him to understand. "Arnie, I really want you tonight. But I'm so fucked up I should come with a warning label. The smartest thing you could do is take me home, kick me out of your truck, and drive away as fast as you can."

He grinned. "I never did the smart thing before, so why start now?" His smile faded, his brows coming together. "Ya kinda surprised me, darlin'. I got a few warnin' labels a' my own, so if you're serious, we gotta talk."

I gave him a faint smile. "I'll show you mine if you'll show me yours."

He chuckled. "Let's get the warnin' labels outta the way first an' see how it goes."

"I was talking about the warning labels," I said with dignity.

"Come on," he said. "I gotta go home an' feed the cat anyway, an' there's beer at my place." When I eyed him uncertainly, he added, "No hard feelin's, no strings attached. Whichever way it plays out."

We left the restaurant holding hands.

CHAPTER 44

At Arnie's apartment, Hooker greeted us with purrs and hoarse meows, winding around our ankles until his dish was filled. Reaching into the fridge, Arnie pulled out a couple of bottles and handed me one. "Sorry, no Corona."

I shrugged. "Beer is beer."

We went into the living room, and he sat in his chair while I curled my feet under me on the couch across from him. We drank a few swallows of beer in silence and assessed each other awkwardly.

Arnie cleared his throat. "Aydan, I like ya a lot, so I'm gonna be straight with ya. If you're lookin' for a little romp an' a few laughs, I'm your man. But if you're the type to get attached, you're gonna get hurt. 'Cause I don't do attached."

I let out the breath I'd been holding. "Thank God. You took the words right out of my mouth. I've done attached. I don't want to do it again."

His face brightened. "It's not that simple, though," I warned him. "I don't have any gifts that keep on giving, and I don't want any. Is there anything you need to tell me?"

He laughed. "That was gonna be my next question for ya. I got a clean bill a' health, too, darlin'. I done a lotta dumb things in my time, but bein' dumb about protection ain't one of 'em."

I relaxed. "One more thing then. I'm not offering you any kind of commitment, and I don't want it from you, either. Strictly casual. No expectations, no strings attached."

"Darlin', we're on the same page. No possessive, needy bullshit. No lies."

"Deal, as long as you promise not to lie to me, either."

He nodded, and we smiled at each other in the short silence.

"Any other warning labels?" I asked.

He shook his head, his smile becoming more intimate. I dropped my gaze to concentrate on my beer bottle while I picked at the label. "I have one really, really big warning label left." I met his eyes, making sure he was listening.

He sobered. "What is it?"

I paused, fumbling for words. This was harder than I thought it would be.

"My husband..." I began.

"You're married?" He leaned back in his chair, frowning.

"Let me finish. My husband died two years ago."

"Oh. Sorry, darlin'."

I sighed, wrapping my arms around my knees. "It was a heart attack. He was only forty-eight. Your age."

I paused again, staring at the carpet. I took a deep breath. "He had a massive heart attack while we were having sex. He died in my arms. Fair warning. I wasn't joking when I made that crack about you having a heart attack if I took you to bed. The last man to get on this ride didn't get off alive."

The couch dipped as Arnie sat beside me, and his arm closed around my shoulders. "Darlin', when it's your time to go, it's your time. That hadta be tough. But my heart's just fine. Nothin' to worry about." He stroked my hair, then tilted my chin up to study me. "So, what d'ya say?"

I smiled up into his ugly face and gentle eyes. "Yes."

He ran his fingers slowly through my hair and kissed me softly. "I been wantin' to do that for days," he breathed.

I kissed him back harder. Our kisses heated up, hands beginning to explore. His fingertips traced the curve of my breast as his tongue brushed my lips. Lightning shot through my body and started a three-alarm fire in the underbrush. I sucked in a breath of pure hot lust and pulled him closer.

I felt his smile against my lips. "I'm a little too old to be makin' out on a couch, darlin'. Let's adjourn to my office." He stood, raising me with him, and we exchanged a few more blazing kisses on the way to the bedroom.

Inside, he swung the door shut with his foot. "No need to corrupt the cat."

I giggled. "Or risk him taking a swing at the dangly bits."

I linked my arms around his neck and he kissed me slowly, sliding his hands under my T-shirt. When he lifted it over my head, I arched my back to press against him. My breath caught when I made contact with the hard bulge in his jeans, and a shiver of hunger shook me.

His hands slid down to cup my ass and pull me closer while he kissed my throat. I couldn't hold back a moan when the kisses trailed down to my cleavage, his whiskers an erotically rough counterpoint to the smooth heat of his lips.

He paused, his breathing almost as unsteady as mine. "I don't wanna hurt ya. You're so beat up." His fingertips glided over my black and blue stomach.

I giggled and pulled away. "Don't, I'm ticklish."

He gave me a slow smile. "I got a cure for that." He

reached over and undid my jeans, sliding them slowly down my legs. "Darlin', ya shouldn't hide a body like that under clothes," he said hoarsely as I stepped out of them.

"Then you'd better hurry and get them off me."

He pulled me close and kissed me deeply as he backed me further into the room.

My God, the man knew how to kiss. If I'd actually needed any convincing, those lips and that tongue would have been more than enough to do it. My knees went liquid with anticipation, my breath coming faster while his strong musician's hands slid over my body.

When we reached the bed, he lowered me to it, still giving me those magical kisses until I lay on my back, smiling up at him.

He straightened, his gaze fixed on me. When he peeled off his T-shirt, I moved my hips in sensuous invitation and parted my legs, and his eyes blazed hotter. He dropped his jeans at the foot of the bed and knelt between my feet, his hand skimming lightly from my ankle to my thigh.

And I froze at a horrid glimpse of Sandler at my feet, his loathsome touch slithering up my leg.

Arnie hesitated, then stretched out on the bed beside me without touching me again. He propped himself on one elbow and scrutinized me, looking puzzled and uncertain. I quickly shook off the bad memory and reached to pull him to me.

He refused to be pulled. "Aydan, what's wrong?"

"Nothing." I scooted closer to make contact between our bodies and reached to fondle him, but he caught my hand and held it.

"If ya don't wanna do this, just say so."

I moaned frustration. "I want this. I want you. Now.

Please."

He frowned. "Then tell me what I'm doin' wrong."

"You're not doing anything wrong. Don't stop."

"Bullshit." He shook his head, confusion turning to hurt in his eyes. "Ya went stiff as a board. D'ya think I wouldn't notice? I thought we promised no lies."

I debated arguing further, but I could tell from the stubborn set of his jaw that he wouldn't buy it. And the way his expression was closing down, I was pretty sure if I didn't come up with a plausible story, I'd be spending another frustrated night flying solo.

Goddammit!

I sighed and gave up hope for easy, uncomplicated sex. "I... Like I told you earlier, I'm a little messed up right now." I searched for words. "I was just... dealing with some shit from yesterday. That's all. Nothing to do with you."

The wheels turned behind his shrewd eyes as his brow furrowed. His face darkened, and when he spoke again, his voice was like flint. "That fuckin' asshole Sandler. He tried to rape ya yesterday."

Shock convulsed my body. "What?"

His expression hardened. "Tried? Or succeeded?"

"Tried," I said dazedly. "What... how...?"

"Aw, darlin'," he rasped. He cuddled me close and stroked my hair. "It ain't rocket science. Ya already told me, I just didn't get it right away."

"What? I didn't..."

"Ya said, 'if that asshole Sandler was still alive, I'd shoot the fucker to ribbons all over again, startin' with his big fuckin' ugly dick'," he quoted my own words back to me verbatim. "Ya were in rough shape when I found ya yesterday. An' the way ya tensed up when I touched ya just now, it ain't hard to figure out."

I pulled away, gaping at him. "That's the last time I mouth off to you. I keep forgetting you're a P.I. Do you have a photographic memory or something?"

He raised his eyebrows, his expression wry. "That's why I'm good at what I do, darlin'. Nobody expects a dumb, ugly biker to be payin' attention."

I gathered my scattered wits. "I certainly never thought you were dumb." Which was true. But I hadn't recognized exactly how smart he was, either. Chalk one up for the dumb biker disguise.

Suddenly realizing what I'd not said, I added, "And there's nothing wrong with the way you look. It works for you."

He chuckled. "No need to be tactful, darlin', I look in the mirror every mornin'. That's why I was surprised when ya said ya wanted me."

I poked him in the ribs. "As if. I bet you've got the ladies falling all over you. All you have to do is pick up your guitar and sing them a song, and down they go."

He gave me sly grin. "That might've happened once or twice." He sobered. "But... Are ya okay? That asshole Sandler..."

I hesitated. "Arnie, I shouldn't have said anything about Sandler to you. I shouldn't have even said the name. I was... out of control. Not thinking. Could you do me a big favour and forget you heard that?"

"Darlin', it's already forgotten. But are they still investigatin'? What-"

"I'm fine," I interrupted. "There won't be an investigation. His official cause of death will be a heart attack."

Arnie drew back slowly. "They're coverin' it up?"

"No. It's not a cover-up. Kane and the team know the truth, but there's nothing to investigate. Nothing to prosecute. He's dead."

"It's pretty fuckin' hard to convince the medical examiner a guy died of a heart attack when he's full a' bullet holes."

"NDA. I can't explain. I'm sorry. I just need you to forget it."

He scowled. "Okay," he agreed slowly. "Long's he's dead. 'Cause otherwise I'd hafta hunt the fucker down myself."

I shuddered at his expression. "Can we please not talk about this? It's kind of spoiling the mood."

His face softened and he stroked the hair back from my face to brush gentle lips across my forehead. "Maybe ya should forget about bein' in the mood tonight. Ya might wanna give yourself some time."

I slid my arms around him. "I don't want time. I want you. Now. I want you to make dirty jokes and laugh and kiss me and touch me and fuck my brains out. That's why I didn't want to tell you in the first place. Now you're all serious and I'm not getting laid," I joked, trying to make him smile.

He searched my face, his expression troubled. "Arnie..." I pleaded. "It's fine. Everything's fine. Let it go. Please."

I kissed him and trailed my lips around to nibble his ear. "Please, can we finish getting naked now?"

He drew back to study me, smiling, but his eyes were serious. "Ya sure that's what ya really want?"

I dragged him over on top of me. "I want it so much, you have no idea. I haven't had sex in two years. If you don't start giving me some action soon, I won't be held responsible for the consequences."

Arnie chuckled. "Sounds dangerous, darlin'. Lucky I'm a brave man."

He kissed me slowly, and I reached for him with demanding hands. He pulled away, teasing. "Slow down, darlin', we got all night. Don't rush a good thing."

"Rush? It's been two damn years!" I panted.

"Lemme take a coupla seconds to enjoy the view."

His hands drifted across my thighs with feather-light touches that chased hot shivers over my skin, making me moan with sheer need.

He grinned, his eyes devouring me. "I wanna see how hot ya look in my bed, with your gorgeous hair spread out on my pillow an' your long legs open for me. 'Cause ya know I'm gonna remember every detail."

He propped himself above me on one elbow and leaned down to kiss me again, his magic tongue seducing mine with sensual promises.

"I'm gonna find out how to make ya come your brains out, seven times," he murmured against my lips. "Or more." He kissed me again, harder and deeper, sending electricity sizzling through me.

"I'm gonna chase those bad memories away," he whispered as he unfastened my bra with a deft hand.

"An' by mornin'..." He made the bra disappear.

"...the only thing you're gonna remember..."

His lips moved lower. "...is me," he rumbled against my breast.

Thought evaporated as he explored the new territory lingeringly before working his way down my body, hands and lips and tongue and whiskers combining in mind-melting harmony. By the time he hooked his fingers under the sides of my panties and eased them off, I could barely breathe.

He ran a strong hand down my leg and lifted it over his shoulder to trail spine-tingling whiskers up the inside of my thigh.

Moments later, he began to deliver everything his kisses had promised, and more.

Two years of deprivation washed away in the torrent of exquisite sensation, and I gave myself up to it, almost weeping with gratitude. Rising moans escaped me while the sweet pressure built.

Time slowed. Turned lazily in on itself.

Stopped.

I lost myself, drowning in waves of ecstasy that went on and on while my body bucked under his hands and mouth.

When I gasped my way back to a semblance of awareness, he was kneeling between my legs, watching me with hot eyes.

"Oh... God... Arnie... please... *now!*" I begged, barely able to form the words. The hard promise of his erection pressed against my thigh when he leaned across me to reach the condoms on the bedside table, and I couldn't suppress a whimper of ravenous anticipation.

My breath stopped when he slid into me. My arms clenched around him, my body arching up to meet him. He let out a startled grunt, and I loosened my grip and panted, "Sorry."

"Don't be," he rasped, rocking into a perfect rhythm. I matched it with unthinking delight. My world contracted to a hot, hard centre, and I absorbed every ounce of pleasure while Arnie played my body like the gifted musician he was.

Rhythm, tempo, crescendo, he carried me effortlessly to the edge. A breathless second held me immobile before I toppled into free-fall, my body spasming gloriously out of control.

When I came back to myself, he was barely moving, still stroking slow, delicious heat into me. "Oh God don't stop!" I implored, and his smile blurred above my half-closed eyes as he rocked into motion again.

Everything melted away but sound and sensation, tension and release. I wrapped my legs around him when the mindless ecstasy claimed me again, and his breathing grew harsh above me. His last few hard, deliberate thrusts drove me higher still. His groan underscored my cries as his body strained against mine before collapsing on top of me.

We lay locked together, panting and sweating. At last, I sucked in a few deep breaths and gasped, "Ohmigod."

My brain steadfastly refused to supply anything more original.

"Ohmi*god*!" I repeated.

After a few more moments, I ran a trembling hand down his back and managed semi-intelligent speech. "Are you still with me?"

His hoarse chuckle vibrated my collarbone, and he dragged his head up from the hollow of my neck. "Jesus Christ, darlin'. That was some ride. Ya got some serious muscles."

I peered at him anxiously. "Did I hurt your back? I didn't mean to squeeze you so hard."

He laughed, still breathless. "My back's fine. An' I wasn't talkin' about your arms."

"Oh." I gave him a wicked leer. "Well, in that case, I did mean to squeeze you that hard."

He laughed again, untangling his hands from my hair. Then he gently disengaged himself and rolled over onto his back, pulling me close beside him.

I laid my head on his chest, tracing the lines and colours with my fingertips. "Tell me about your tattoos."

We touched and whispered and laughed for a long time, until finally he turned out the light. I let his quiet snores lull me into a doze, waking every time he moved. He got up once, and when he returned, I reached for him in the darkness. "Are you up?"

His knowing hands teased my body. "I can be."

I pulled him close and let him carry me away again.

I woke to sunshine streaming through the cracks in the blinds. Arnie lay on his back, snoring softly. He'd left the door open when he returned in the night, and Hooker was curled in a furry ball at the foot of the bed between us. I stretched luxuriously, feeling the lingering ache in my bruised muscles, along with the satisfying heat lower down.

I rolled off the bed and padded naked to the bathroom to work the knots out of my hair and borrow a dab of toothpaste on my fingertip. When I crept back into the bedroom, Arnie opened sleepy eyes.

"You're the hottest thing that's ever come through that door, darlin'," he croaked. He flipped the blankets open. "Comin' back to bed?"

I smiled and knelt onto the bed beside him, bending to trail my hair down the length of his body. He groaned and tensed as I worked my way back up from his toes, kissing and teasing him. I straddled his body and moved slowly against him as I slid up to brush my lips against his ear. "Oh, Hellhound, oh baby," I whispered. "You know what I'd *really like* right now?"

I sprawled bonelessly on the bed, my face still buried in the pillow that had muffled the sounds of my last stupendous orgasm. I felt Arnie lean up on one elbow, his ragged breathing slowing. His hand stroked over my back and down one outflung leg. "Aydan? Are ya okay?"

I flopped over limply so he could see my beatific expression. "I am so much better than okay," I panted. "I may not walk for a while, though."

He gave me a twisted leer, managing to look smugly satisfied and rueful at the same time. "Darlin', I may never walk again." He shook his head, still winded. "First I'm gonna sleep for a week, an' then I'm startin' a fitness program so I can be ready for next time."

I laughed. "Skip the fitness program. I won't be able to keep up. You wore me out."

He sobered. "Are ya really okay?"

I beamed satisfaction at him. "I am fabulous. But I'll probably be sore as hell when I come down off this high."

"Darlin', I didn't wanna hurt ya. Ya shoulda told me to stop."

"No way. I'll take as much as you'll give me." I shivered and ran my hands down my body, my breath coming a little faster. "I'm going to feel you for days. Mmmm."

I heard amusement in his voice. "Did ya just come again?"

I opened my eyes and gave him a slow smile. "Maybe."

"Stop it, you're gonna gimme another hard-on," he chuckled.

I reached for him. "Let me help you with that."

He caught my hand and kissed the palm. "Sorry, darlin', I'm done. I gotta be at a client's in an hour, so I gotta take ya home. D'ya wanna shower first?"

I shook my head. "You go ahead. I'll shower when I get home. I need a change of clothes, and besides, I'm not ready to stand up yet."

He grinned and headed for the bathroom.

CHAPTER 45

When we pulled into my driveway, Hellhound parked the SUV and reached for my hand. "I'm gonna be tied up for a while, but I'd like to see ya again sometime." He looked into my eyes. "I know ya needed somebody last night an' I was there. Was this a one-time thing?"

"I don't know," I told him honestly. "You were exactly what I needed. Thank you. Now I need to get my shit together and then I can figure out what comes next."

He nodded. "Take care, darlin'. If I see ya again, I'll ask ya then. No hard feelin's if the answer's no."

I smiled. "I'd be disappointed if you didn't."

We shared one last lingering kiss before I got out and oozed into the house, heading for the shower on still-rubbery legs.

Almost melting in the hot spray, I reflected that my first try at casual sex had turned out far better than I could have hoped. Making peace with my old ghosts felt good, but accomplishing it with multiple orgasms felt even better. I failed utterly to suppress the idiot grin that kept creeping onto my face.

Hours of construction and a crummy night's sleep later, I made the bed, gave the bathroom a quick cleaning, and called Cheryl to give her the go-ahead to show the house again. I locked up and left with a profound sense of relief.

Back in Silverside, I made the rounds of clients, hardware store, grocery store, and credit union. Finally heading home, I turned off onto my gravel road, mentally laying out the tile pattern for my bathroom.

As I crested the gentle hill a mile from my farm, I spotted a half-ton truck pulled over at the side of the road with its hood up. I slowed as I approached, and a man stepped out to flag me down.

I rolled the window down a couple of inches. The two black eyes in his bruised face didn't exactly inspire confidence.

He greeted me cheerfully. "Hi, can you give me a boost? I've got a dead battery."

"No problem. I'll just turn around on the crossing up there and come back." I drove down the road slowly, thinking. Even in the city, I normally wouldn't think twice about helping somebody out. In the country, refusing to help would be the height of rudeness.

I calmed my jittery nerves with the decision that I wouldn't get out of the car. He could hook up the cables himself. I'd play the girly-girl and pretend I didn't know anything about it.

I scowled, mentally cursing Fuzzy Bunny again. Two weeks ago, I would have pulled over to help without a second thought.

I nosed into a crossing to turn the car around, then pulled up to the front of his truck and popped the hood. He fumbled with the release for a few long moments before he looked up. "I can't get it to open. Can you help me out?"

Shit. Now what?

I weighed my options. You have to trust people sometime.

I was on the verge of getting out when the hood released. He gave me a jaunty grin.

"Got it!" He opened the hood and propped it on its stand, obscuring my view. Through the crack at the bottom, I watched him turn and go back to his truck, probably getting the booster cables.

I sat indecisively. What if he hooked the cables up wrong? I'd be really pissed off if he blew my battery.

He returned and bent over the engine. Seconds later, there was a bang and brilliant flash. My car's engine died.

"Shit!" I sprang out of the car and strode around to the front.

He shot me a shamefaced look. "Sorry. I accidentally dropped a wrench across the battery poles. I'll pay for a new battery for you."

As he reached into his pocket, I took a couple of fast steps backward. You don't need a wrench to boost a battery. And I didn't see any booster cables.

The hand that came out of his pocket wasn't holding a wallet. I'd never seen a stun gun before, but it wasn't hard to identify the electrodes on the device he swung at me.

Adrenaline burned my veins as I ducked back, slipping in the snow at the side of the ditch. He lunged and jabbed the weapon at me. Dammit, I wouldn't be able to outrun him in my heavy hiking boots. I jumped away and kicked wildly at the stun gun instead.

He dodged, and the momentum of the missed kick flung me off balance to tumble into the ditch.

Heart hammering, I flailed onto my back and spun as he pounced. My boots glanced off his chest and he fell with a grunt.

I scrambled up to charge for my car, my feet slithering on the snowy slope, my breath coming in sobbing gasps. If I could get to the car, I could lock myself in. Maybe the engine would still start...

I snatched at the door handle, but there was no time to open it. I spun to kick at him again as he leaped, his arm swinging around. The prongs of the stun gun hit my leg. I crumpled helplessly, every nerve sizzling.

Dim terror crawled through my addled brain while he bound my wrists behind me and my ankles together. He dragged me to the truck and heaved me into the box, the hard steel bruising my hip and shoulder. The cover slammed, plunging me into darkness.

I lay in helpless terror while the truck bumped over the gravel road. Then came the smoothness of pavement, and minutes passed at highway speed.

My mind raced in panicked circles. Fuzzy Bunny must have discovered I was alive, and now I was in their clutches. Kane and his team didn't know there was anything to worry about. Hellhound wouldn't call. I'd just seen my clients. My friends wouldn't expect to hear from me until the weekend.

It would be at least a week before anybody even started to look for me, unless some passerby got curious about my abandoned car.

By then, if I was very lucky, I'd be dead. If I was unlucky...

I stifled the thought and tried to force my flaccid muscles to struggle. I managed a spastic twitch.

The truck slowed and turned. Several other turns at low

speed told me that we were likely in Silverside. My body flopped helplessly from side to side as the truck cornered. We made one final turn, and the truck stopped. I heard the unmistakeable sound of a garage door rolling up, and then the truck moved forward again. The door rattled again as it closed.

The cover opened and I blinked and squinted in the sudden light. I got a confused glimpse of the inside of a garage and my captor's face as he reached into the truck box.

"Let's just make sure you're out," he said genially. Another jolt reduced my muscles to jelly.

The truck's suspension bounced sickeningly when he climbed in beside me. Barely conscious, I dimly registered a bumpy ride as he dragged me out of the truck and down a flight of stairs. Another short drag, and he dropped me to the concrete floor.

"Stay there," he panted. Then he chuckled and patted my shoulder briskly. In the sliver of vision afforded by my half-turned head, I saw his feet stride out the door.

A couple of minutes later, he was back. A wooden chair clattered on the floor beside me. I felt him cut the ties that bound me, and he rolled me onto my back. I whimpered and tried uselessly to force my body to struggle while he unzipped my jacket and pulled it off.

He knelt beside me, his eyes dilating as he eyed my splayed limbs. Utterly helpless, I could only lie watching him. My heart pounded so hard my vision blurred. My breath came in shallow gasps.

The corner of his mouth quirked up. "No, I'm not that stupid."

He manhandled my rubbery body up into the chair and I heard the high-pitched zip of nylon ties as he secured my wrists and ankles to the chair's arms and legs. Then he stood watching me for a few moments before turning to leave the room, closing the door behind him. His footsteps climbed the stairs, followed by sounds of movement overhead.

Strength returned in the form of uncontrollable tremors. The chair jerked and shuddered while my body spasmed.

The trembling gradually diminished and I clamped down on terror. Breathe. Just breathe.

By the time I heard my captor's feet on the stairs again, I had regained muscle control. The door opened and I sat up to face him.

Begging would be a waste of time.

"What do you want from me?" I demanded, pleased that my voice was steady despite my pounding heart and quivering body.

"Personally, I don't want anything from you. My associates, however, will be eager to find out who you're working for and how you knew Ramos. And where you've hidden the second hacked fob. You'll find them very... persuasive." He studied me, smiling. "I expect I'll be rewarded handsomely for capturing such a valuable agent."

"I'm not an agent. I don't know what you're talking about. You've got the wrong person," I argued without much hope.

He was beside me in a couple of quick strides, the cold muzzle of his gun pressing hard against my temple. "If you're just a civilian, you're useless. I'll kill you right now."

Fresh panic flashed through me. I clenched my teeth, weighing my options. I knew what awaited me. Prolonged, horrible suffering, and ultimately, death when they realized I couldn't access the network. If I'd thought there was a chance of rescue...

But there was none. Kane wouldn't even know I was missing until much too late. Better to die now, quickly and mercifully. And the secret of the key would be protected.

I stared straight ahead, trying to hold myself still while my heartbeat rocked my body.

"I'm just a civilian." My voice quavered despite myself.

I flinched at his movement, but instead of an explosion and oblivion, the pressure at my temple vanished.

"Thank you. Now I know I have the right person. Only an agent would choose instant death."

I glared up at him, shaking. "Or a total chickenshit."

He laughed. "I don't think so." He removed a small vial and a syringe from his shirt pocket. "Now, I'm just going to make sure you stay safe and quiet until my associates are ready to pick you up. How much do you weigh?"

"None of your business."

He drew up a dosage of clear fluid in the syringe. "That's all right. I'm a good guesser."

I made a desperate attempt to jerk away when the loaded syringe approached my arm, and he shook his head reproachfully. "Now, now, this will be much better for everybody if you just hold still."

The stun gun touched me again. I could only watch through blurred eyes while he injected me. My racing heartbeat slowed and the room faded.

CHAPTER 46

I struggled to open my eyes, driven by a sense of urgency I couldn't identify. My eyelids wouldn't cooperate. I managed to crack them partway open, and a blurred room spun around me. Overcome by effort and vertigo, I let them fall closed again.

Several attempts later, I managed to focus briefly before my eyelids won the battle once more. My mind slogged laboriously through memory.

I had to do something. What was it? It was terribly important.

I opened my eyes again. Tied to a chair. Trapped. My pulse raced, and I painfully raised my hanging head. The stiffened muscles of my neck screamed protest. With an effort, I pulled myself out of my slumped position and sat up. The room swam around me.

When I opened my eyes again, I was hanging halfway out of the chair, suspended by my aching wrists. I dragged myself upright again, successfully keeping my eyes open this time. The formless urgency resolved itself into the memory of my abduction. I was still in my captor's basement. How long had I been here?

I strained my ears to hear over the hammering of my

heart. There was no sound from outside the room or above me. What could have happened? Had he abandoned me to die? Or had he given me the wrong dosage, and I'd woken up sooner than he'd expected?

I shook my head, trying to clear the fog. The fear seemed to help. I wondered distantly how much adrenaline I'd need before it wiped out the sedative completely.

Sluggishly directing my mind back to my predicament, I tried to form a plan. My phone was in my waist pouch, probably somewhere in the garage. I knew I couldn't break the nylon ties that held me. I was in a basement, so screaming would be a waste of energy.

Giving in to blind panic, I yanked wildly at my bonds. The chair jerked and scraped across the floor with my efforts. The edges of the ties scored thin lines of blood around my wrists.

When the futility of struggling sank in, I held myself still, gasping and trembling. Think.

I drew a couple of deep breaths, trying to focus.

I leaned over and peered at the chair. It was a regular wooden dining chair with arms. A thought struck me, and I gripped the arms and heaved my weight back and forth. The chair swayed, ever so slightly.

Hope washed over me. In the warehouse, I'd been surrounded by enemies and tied to a steel chair. This time I was unsupervised, and wooden chairs could break.

I jerked from side to side. The ties cut deeper into my wrists, and I smothered a whimper of pain and panic. I slumped in the chair, working to slow my racing heart and control my shallow, rapid panting. Belly breathe. Stay focused.

Time for another tactic.

I shuffled the chair closer to the concrete basement wall. Hopping and twisting, I gradually turned it so my back was to the wall. After a couple of false starts, I managed to pitch my weight forward to stand teetering precariously on my feet with the chair legs off the floor. I flopped back down in the chair and gasped for breath while I planned my next move.

I backed up a little closer to the wall. Balancing carefully on my feet again, I slammed backward against it. The impact bruised my legs and back, throwing me sideways. The chair wobbled crazily. I twisted to maintain my balance and a cry escaped me when the nylon ties sliced deeper.

Stabilized in the chair once more, I shuddered violently and sucked in terrified breaths. If I fell over onto the floor, I'd never get free. I took another deep breath and tried to put aside the fear. I'd never get free if I didn't keep trying, either.

I gathered my courage and flung myself at the wall again. Then again. The chair was definitely starting to give. The extra laxness in its joints allowed me to put more force behind my efforts. Sweat trickled down my temples while my overworked muscles quivered uncontrollably.

I tried not to think about the noise I was making. If my captor was still in the house, he could be on me in seconds.

I slammed desperately into the concrete again, and was rewarded with a welcome crack.

Once more, with all my weight behind it.

The chair made a splintering sound and I thudded to the floor, pain jolting through me. A couple of sobbing breaths escaped before I clamped down on control again.

Kicking and struggling, I managed to jerk the legs loose, my jeans protecting my ankles from the sharp edges of the ties. I floundered awkwardly to my knees and knelt trembling for a few seconds. Then I heaved gracelessly to my feet, staggering sideways in my hunched position. My leverage was much better, and a few solid hits to the wall broke the arms loose from the chair back.

Gasping frantic relief, I yanked the broken wood through the bloodstained nylon ties. Shaking from head to toe, I salvaged a chair leg as a weapon and stumbled for the door.

For a few long seconds, I stood panting as quietly as possible, listening. Still no sound from above. What if my captor was waiting silently outside the door? I pressed my ear to it and heard only my pounding heart.

Ever so slowly, I turned the knob and tried to ease the door open. It wouldn't move. I pushed a little harder, but nothing happened. I stepped back and studied the door. There was no lock. It should open.

To hell with subtlety. I threw my weight against the door, pain jolting through my back, my bruised shoulder screaming. It might as well have been a solid wall.

Trapped!

I muffled a hysterical sob. Take a deep breath. Think.

I scanned the windowless room desperately. Concrete floor. Unfinished ceiling above, just the wooden joists of the main floor. Two walls were concrete. The remaining partitions were drywall. Faint hope rose again. I was used to dealing with drywall. It may look strong, but it's ridiculously easy to punch a hole in it.

Taking a deep breath, I kicked the wall, praying I didn't hit a stud. The drywall folded into a deep dent under my heavy hiking boot, and I kicked again to create a hole. I froze again, listening. Still nothing.

I wrapped my fingers around the broken edge and yanked a piece off. A couple more solid kicks and some pulling revealed standard sixteen-inch stud spacing. Thank God. I could fit through that.

Now the next step. I rested my elbows on my knees, head swimming. After a few moments, I hauled myself upright and kicked again to make a hole in the drywall on the outside of the wall.

I eased my head through, hoping it wouldn't be the last thing I ever did. I still hadn't heard any movement in the rest of the house, so I had to assume I was alone.

The basement was dark. My eyes seemed to take forever to adjust. When they did, I discovered why the door wouldn't open. My captor had dragged a heavy bookcase in front of it. Bastard. I pulled back into the room and aimed a few more kicks at the wall.

A wave of vertigo washed over me, and I found myself slumped on my knees and elbows, my forehead mashed into the dust and chunks of broken drywall on the floor. I struggled dizzily to my knees, shedding plaster crumbs, and squeezed out through the hole in the wall. Huddled in the darkness, I strained my ears. Still nothing.

Clutching my chair leg in shaking hands, I staggered as quickly as possible across the basement, making for the stairs. The tiny, high window showed only a square of darkness. How many hours had I been imprisoned?

A soft sound from the floor above triggered a fresh burst of adrenaline. I froze. Had I heard someone moving, or was it just the house settling as the outside air cooled? I shot a wild glance back at the window. I'd barely fit through. And I was too weakened to pull myself up anyway.

I stood in quivering silence for a few moments, but heard nothing more. Must have been my imagination. I tottered to the base of the stairs, hoping my shaking legs would carry me up them.

I carefully stepped onto the first tread as close to the stringer as possible, trying to prevent squeaks. As I gingerly transferred my weight to the step and straightened my knee, I fervently cursed my aging cartilage. It sounded like somebody was enthusiastically crushing bubble wrap under my kneecap.

I rose slowly onto the next step, then the next, clutching the handrail for precarious balance. I panted fear and exertion open-mouthed, trying to breathe as quietly as possible. The crunching of my knees was horribly loud in the silence.

At last, I made it to the top of the stairs and trembled on the landing, elbows braced on my knees. Should I go into the garage and see if I could find my phone to call for help, or just run for it? Or I could put in a 911 call from the house phone, if I could find it.

Better to just get out. I straightened and stepped cautiously into the dark hallway.

White-hot pain exploded in the back of my head and I crashed to the floor. My arm was twisted excruciatingly up behind me as a knee ground into my back. The familiar, unwelcome chill of a gun barrel crushed an expanding circle of pain into the base of my skull.

A hard voice grated next to my ear. "Give me answers, and I might let you live."

"...John?" I gasped.

"Aydan!" The agonizing grip released as he scrambled off me. "I'm sorry! Are you all right?"

I rolled over slowly and struggled into sitting position. "...Yeah..."

The dark floor seemed very far away, and I braced my

hands against it, trying to regain perspective.

"Can you walk?"

"Yeah..."

He helped me to my feet and the floor turned slowly under me. I focused all my concentration on staying upright.

I managed to stagger a couple of steps before Kane grated, "Dammit!" He scooped me up without apparent effort. My head spun nauseatingly while he carried me out of the house.

My feet touched the ground again beside his Expedition. I sagged in his one-armed grip while he opened the passenger door. His voice floated to my ears as if from a long distance.

"Stay with me, Aydan. Talk to me."

"Whaddaya wanna talk abou'?" I mumbled as he lifted me into the passenger seat.

When I dragged my eyes open again, he was driving one-handed, shaking my shoulder. "Aydan! Talk to me! What happened?"

"'Nother Buzzy Funny," I slurred. "F... Fuzzy... Bunny. Th... think I'm... agent. Drugged." The inside of the Expedition whirled around me and I closed my eyes to shut it out. "Ashosh... associates... They know..."

"They know what?" he demanded urgently.

"'Bout me... Didn... Didn' tell 'em." I fought to stay coherent.

His voice was very far away. "What didn't you tell them?"

"'Bout... key..."

CHAPTER 47

I struggled to open my eyes. There was something important...

Brilliant light flashed in first one eye, then the other. I groaned and tried to pull away. Must escape. I dragged my eyes open, blinded by afterimages. A dark figure loomed over me as I forced my leaden limbs to struggle. Strong hands closed on my shoulders.

"Aydan, you're safe. Don't fight, it's all right. You're safe."

Kane's voice. I sighed and let the darkness claim me.

The next time, my eyes opened more easily and I lay still, taking in my surroundings. I recognized the cubicle curtains. Back in B Wing. Déjà vu.

Kane smiled at me from the chair beside my bed. "Welcome back."

"Thanks, I think." I gingerly touched the back of my aching head. "Jesus. What did you hit me with?"

"Gun butt. I'm so sorry. I didn't expect you to be sneaking around in there."

"It's okay. How did you find me?"

"We'll talk later."

I nodded, wincing as my bruised head moved against the

pillow. Debrief in a secure area, right.

Dr. Roth bustled into the cubicle. "I'm glad to see you're conscious."

I gave her a rueful grin as I tenderly fingered my head. "Sorry I can't agree."

Her mouth quirked, and she checked the readouts on the machines and the level of the I.V. bag. Then she bent close, shining her small flashlight in each of my eyes. "That's better."

I blinked away afterimages again. "What happened? Why did the drugs wear off and then come back and knock me out? Is that going to happen again?"

The doctor gave Kane a severe look. "Not unless somebody hits you in the head again. You were probably able to overcome the effects of the drug initially with adrenaline and exertion. Then the head injury, combined with low blood sugar, made you vulnerable and you slipped back under."

She shook her head. "I'm surprised you're as alert as you are. There's still quite a high concentration of the drug in your bloodstream."

I gave her a grin. "That's my rock star metabolism. And I think the guy guessed my weight wrong."

"Well, you're not going to rock anywhere for a while. Rest," she commanded, and left.

I turned to Kane. "Did you catch him? Who was he?"

"Yes, we caught him. You heard the doctor. Rest."

"Roger that." I let my eyelids drift shut on his smile.

The next time my eyes opened, Kane was gone and Spider sat beside me.

"Hey, Spider." I squinted at my watch. "It's four in the morning. Don't you guys ever sleep?"

He chuckled. "I grabbed a couple of hours while Kane was sitting with you. He's sleeping now."

"They don't pay you guys enough. I don't know how much they pay you, but it can't be enough."

He smiled. "It's not about money. It's about keeping good people safe. And making sure bad people can't hurt anyone."

"Ordinary people don't know how lucky they are to have guys like you and Kane and the team working behind the scenes."

He flushed. "It's probably better that way," he said quietly. "Go back to sleep. The doctor says you should be okay to leave in the morning."

"Thanks." I closed my eyes again, trying to hide my discomfort at being watched. The drugs must be wearing off. I hadn't cared earlier.

By the time Kane reappeared at eight o'clock, I was antsy after several hours of fitful dozing. When the doctor finally cleared me for takeoff, I breathed a sigh of relief.

I stood slowly, but there didn't seem to be any lingering ill effects other than the sore place on the back of my head. I stretched the kinks out of my muscles and followed Kane and Spider out to the Expedition.

CHAPTER 48

"Breakfast," I begged as Kane pulled out of the hospital parking lot.

Both men laughed. "Good to have you back," Kane said. "We kept forgetting to eat after you left."

"Well, everybody needs a purpose in life. Mine is to make sure everybody around me knows when it's mealtime."

At the coffee shop, we carried our various food and beverages to a table. I bit blissfully into my crispy toasted bagel, the hot peanut butter melting in my mouth. I opened my eyes to two amused faces. "Where there's peanut butter, there's hope," I quipped.

"I'm really glad you're safe," Spider said.

"Thanks. Me, too."

We finished our food in silence. Both men looked exhausted, and I doubted if I looked any better. As soon as I swallowed my last bite, we all rose.

Kane drove directly to their shared office. Inside, he turned down the hallway toward the meeting room. I eyed him questioningly as Spider quickly swept the room with his electronic scanner and pronounced it secure.

"We should be fine upstairs now," Kane said. "You asked earlier if I would ever be sure. The short answer is no, but the long answer is that right now, I'm as sure as I'm likely to get."

I studied the table while heat rose in my cheeks. "I owe you an apology. I should have listened to you earlier and stayed here. You shouldn't have had to risk your neck to come and rescue me. Again." I met his eyes. "I'm sorry."

"Some rescue, when you'd already escaped. I just showed up in time to beat you senseless." He shook his head. "No. If I had believed at the time that there was significant risk to you, I would have made it clear. And I would have made sure you were protected. I'll accept your apology if you'll accept mine."

"Of course. No apology necessary. So what happened?" I swallowed hard. "Am I back in Fuzzy Bunny's sights now?"

"No. Fuzzy Bunny definitely thinks you're dead," Spider reassured me.

"But... who was the guy who grabbed me, then?" I stammered. "Jeez, please don't tell me I've run afoul of some other nutcase criminal organization now."

"No. That was Eugene Mercer," Kane said. "He was working with Fuzzy Bunny."

"Eugene Mercer? The analyst from Sirius? But I thought Fuzzy Bunny captured him and beat him up. I thought you suspected Mike Connor. Why...?"

"It was more complicated than we first thought," Kane said. "It turned out Connor was innocent of everything except poor judgement. Mercer encouraged him to bypass the alarm on the door, and when Connor sneaked out for a smoke, Mercer disabled the jamming devices so Ramos could test the hacked fob. Then Connor concealed the breach because he didn't want to get in trouble with Sandler."

"I'm glad he wasn't involved," I said. "He seemed like a

nice kid."

"Ramos and Sandler were Fuzzy Bunny's direct contacts," Kane explained. "Sandler had been employed at Sirius for a number of years. It seems Fuzzy Bunny got to him and turned him sometime in the last year or so."

"So he wasn't a spy to start with?"

"No, it doesn't look that way. We don't know what they offered him, but he was in deep. Sandler faked security clearances for both Ramos and Mercer to get them into Sirius. Ramos had access to all the restricted areas in Sirius because of his janitor's role. Mercer had the know-how to hack the fob. Mercer was also smart enough to never make direct contact with Fuzzy Bunny."

Spider picked up the tale. "The only reason we connected Mercer at all was because of that one phone call from Ramos. And the fact that something seemed to be missing when we put together what we had. Neither Ramos nor Sandler had the skills to hack the fob. Ramos was an agent, not an analyst, and Sandler was only a manager. There was just something off about the whole thing."

"But how did you ever figure it out from one phone call?"

"We didn't," Kane replied. "There was more than that. And thanks to Webb's good work, we found it."

Spider flushed and smiled. "I dug into Mercer when I was following up on that phone call. I ran across an email that didn't make sense. It was just a one-liner, sent to an obscure email address. It didn't mean anything to me, and I didn't catch it right away."

"At the time you left on Friday morning, we still hadn't been able to question Mercer in the hospital," Kane added. "He had been there since JTF2 pulled him out of the warehouse on Wednesday night. He was incoherent, apparently suffering some kind of drug reaction. When we finally talked to him late Friday morning, he told us he'd been abducted from his home at gunpoint. He said they'd beaten him and tried to force him to divulge information about the fobs, but he'd stood up to them and refused to tell them anything."

"He was pretending to be such a hero," Spider scoffed. "The noble martyr. It was enough to make you puke."

Kane nodded. "And that was another thing that made us suspicious. Actually, it was Wheeler who nailed it. Thanks to you."

I frowned puzzlement. "Me?"

"You made some comment to Wheeler. Something about the dramatic effect of a nosebleed."

"Right," I agreed. "Minor injury, major drama."

"Exactly. It made Wheeler think. We had another look at Mercer's hospital records. His only physical injury was a broken nose and two black eyes. It just didn't feel right. Considering what they did to you in the short time they had you..."

Kane glanced at Spider's haunted face and altered course. "Anyway, it was one more thing to make us suspicious. And that's when Webb hit paydirt."

"I went back over the records," Spider explained. "And I noticed that same one-liner email repeated at random times. It was a signal. Any time Mercer needed to communicate with Fuzzy Bunny, he sent an email with an encoded date, time and meeting place. He had all his meetings in person. No phone records."

"Smart," I said slowly. "But why would he keep the old emails?"

"He didn't." Spider gave me a mischievous wink. "I have

ways."

"Remind me never to try to hide anything from you."

"The problem was, I couldn't identify his contact," Spider said ruefully. "Different email address each time, and each time a dead end. I figured out the code for the meetings, and I could do a traceback on the email, but I couldn't get solid proof that he was contacting anybody at Fuzzy Bunny."

"So we lay low and kept tabs on him," Kane said. "And sure enough, another encoded email went out yesterday afternoon. Spider cracked the code to identify the time and location for the meeting, and Germain and Wheeler got into position to secretly monitor it. We didn't realize at the time that Mercer had captured you."

"He said he was going to deliver me to his associates," I said. "He said they wanted to find out who I was working for and where I'd hidden the hacked fob. He thought I was some kind of secret agent. I played dumb, but he didn't believe me."

"You're probably lucky he didn't," Spider commented. "He likely would have killed you otherwise."

"Yeah, that's what I was hoping for." I looked up to meet Spider's horrified eyes. "Well, it was better than the alternative."

He swallowed. "I guess..."

"But he knew who I was," I told Kane. "His associates knew who I was. They know I'm alive. They'll still be looking for me."

"No, I'm quite sure you're safe," he countered. "Don't forget, Mercer didn't have any contact with Fuzzy Bunny between Wednesday evening and yesterday afternoon. Sandler told them you were dead. Fuzzy Bunny received the message from Mercer, but as usual, there were no details in the email, just the meeting time and place. And we picked up both Mercer and his contact. As far as Fuzzy Bunny knows, you're still dead."

I breathed a sigh and sat back in my chair. "Thank God. So Mercer was just acting of his own accord when he kidnapped me. That's what he meant when he said he expected they'd reward him."

"Yes. We think he'd decided to lie low at Sirius and maintain his cover. That would allow him continued access to the facilities, and he could have reproduced the hacked fob later."

"That would be the smart thing to do," I agreed. "He already had all the clearances. But I still don't understand how he ended up in the hospital."

Kane nodded. "We haven't finished questioning him yet, but we think he was monitoring the network at the warehouse Wednesday night, in case you were forced to access it. He would have wanted to analyze the data record. We suspect when he heard gunfire and realized something had gone wrong, he decided to cover his ass. If he was tied to a chair and covered with blood, he could claim he was an innocent victim."

"So he tied *himself* up? And punched his own nose?"

"We think so. It would be easy enough to do. Nylon ties are easy to tighten once they're started. He could have secured both his legs and one wrist to the chair, and then just slipped his other wrist into a loose tie and tightened it by pulling on the end with his teeth."

I shook my head in disbelief. "So he lay around at the hospital a couple of days to divert suspicion. And went back to work a hero."

"Yes. But he must have seen you yesterday."

"Yeah, I was all over town yesterday. I would have been easy to spot. He would have had lots of time to go and set up on my road. Thank God I was in Calgary..." Heat spread at the memory and I went on quickly, "...or he'd have known I was alive earlier and told Fuzzy Bunny."

"Yes. Wheeler and Germain contacted me as soon as they overheard him tell his contact he had you," Kane said. "We had no idea where he might have taken you, and he wasn't talking after they took him down."

"How did you find me, then?"

"We tracked you through your cell phone. Luckily, Mercer made the mistake of leaving it in his garage. I didn't actually expect you to be there, but I got over there as fast as I could, hoping I'd find a clue. That's why I hit first and asked questions later." He grimaced. "In the end, I did more harm than good."

"No, you didn't. I don't know how much longer I'd have stayed on my feet. I'm glad you were there. So you have Mercer and his contact?"

"Yes, Germain and Wheeler are taking them to Calgary now."

"So it's over. That's the last of the loose ends."

"Yes."

"Thank God." I sagged back in my chair. "So does Fuzzy Bunny even know the key has been found?"

"We don't think so. Sandler had been at the warehouse half of Wednesday night after I called him in. He was pretending to research the network. In fact he was locking it down, as we discovered too late. We found a call record from Sandler to his contact around four o'clock that morning. There was another call record just around noon Thursday. That must have been when he told them he'd killed you.

With an ego like his, it must not have even occurred to him that he might fail."

Kane leaned back, grinning. "He made the call from home, and he didn't come in to work until just before he went to the warehouse for the last time. So he wouldn't have had time to tell them. As far as they know, you're dead, and the key has never been found."

His gaze sharpened. "That's what you meant last night. When you said you didn't tell Mercer about the key."

"Yes."

Spider broke in. "But they must have suspected you had the key, or they wouldn't have tried so hard to capture you."

I shook my head. "No, Mercer said they thought I'd been working with Ramos and I had another hacked fob."

"Good." Kane rubbed his forehead tiredly. "I don't even want to think about what could have happened if they got their hands on that key. Without your help, we never would have even known it existed. And if you hadn't made it out of Sandler's sim, he could have told us that accessing the network had killed you, and we would have believed him. Then he could have stolen the key at his leisure. Who knows when, if ever, we would have started to suspect anything."

"So will you be able to nail Fuzzy Bunny this time?" I asked.

He nodded. "We'll get a piece of them. They're far too big and too smart to put all their eggs in one basket, but we did some serious damage. Almost a dozen of their people were killed outright, and we have more in custody."

We sat in silence for a few seconds, each occupied with our own thoughts.

I sighed. "So I can go home. And go back to my normal life."

"Yes."

"You guys are the best," I said inadequately. "I don't know how to thank you."

"No need to thank us," Spider said. "This is our job. We should be thanking you."

Kane reached across the table. "Yes. Thank you."

I took his hand and returned his gentle squeeze. "I'd say, 'my pleasure', but I'd be lying."

CHAPTER 49

I let myself in the gate at the end of my lane and locked it behind me with a feeling of pulling up the castle drawbridge. The world outside could go fuck itself. I was home, and I intended to stay there for a while, working on my house and enjoying my freedom.

The day flew by while I absorbed myself installing the in-floor heating system and the first of the floor tiles for my bathroom. By the time I called a halt, there was still time to bake some bread, and I relaxed and enjoyed the therapeutic yeasty smell while I kneaded. Around nine o'clock in the evening, I patted the smooth, hot loaves with satisfaction and inhaled the delicious fresh-baked aroma, basking in normalcy.

I was just turning away when a muffled thump from the front yard pumped terror through my veins. I dashed to the bathroom for my crowbar, my mind rocketing through the possibilities.

I'd locked the gate. Nobody should have been able to drive up. I was miles from town, so nobody should be arriving on foot.

As I crept toward the front door with the crowbar clenched in my fist, I cursed the fact that the interior lights were on. The blinds were closed, and I couldn't peek out without being in full view of anyone outside.

The sound of the doorbell convulsed every muscle in my body, pain scoring my too-tight grip on the crowbar. I forced myself into analysis mode, trying to ignore the panicked thudding of my heart.

At least now I knew there was definitely somebody out there, and they weren't making any attempt to sneak up on me. I took a deep, steadying breath, berating myself for not installing the fisheye lens that I'd left lying in its package on the table. I was definitely going to do that. Tonight. If I lived.

The doorbell rang again, followed by a knock. Pulling myself together, I moved closer to the door and called out, "Who's there?"

"John Kane," the deep voice replied.

I gasped relief, immediately tempered with suspicion. Anybody could call out a name. I clutched my crowbar, opening the door left-handed as I stood away from the path it would follow if somebody kicked it from outside.

The door swung open to reveal Kane himself, and I blew out a breath. He frowned, taking in my white-knuckled grip on the crowbar. "You need a fisheye lens in this door. I meant to mention it the last time I was here."

I nodded vigorously, sheer relief making me babble. "Come on in. You're right. I've got one already, right there on the table. I'm going to install it tonight."

He came in, sniffing the air, and I locked the door behind him.

"It smells good in here." He zeroed in on the loaves. "Is that fresh bread?"

Taking a deep breath, I pried my stiff fingers loose to set

the crowbar down, and gave him what I hoped was a casual smile. "Want some? It never gets better than this."

He glanced at his watch. "I've got time for fresh bread."

I got out a plate and turned away to hide my shaking hands while I cut a couple of thick, warm slices. I set the plate on the table along with butter and a knife, and he dropped into a chair and wolfed down the bread.

"More?"

He nodded. "Please. I missed supper."

"Don't you ever eat regular meals or sleep regular hours?" I asked as I passed him the loaf and the knife.

He shrugged, slathering on the butter. "We've been busy tying up the last of the loose ends and writing reports. I've been pressed for time because I have to fly out tonight to deal with some critical business overseas. I'm glad you were here. I wanted to touch base with you before I left."

I watched him warily. "I need to ask you something."

He gestured at me to continue, swallowing a mouthful of bread.

"Is there any chance of legal repercussions for me as a result of all my various, um, adventures?"

He shook his head. "No. The only thing that was working against you was your possession of the key. I'm satisfied you were telling the truth about how you got it. Everything else... you'll be considered to have been working as part of the team, under my orders. The only place that information will appear will be in my classified reports."

I sank into a chair, surreptitiously letting the tension leak out of my shoulders. "Thank God. Thank you, too."

He leaned back, stretching out his legs and locking his hands behind his head. I stole an appreciative look at those bulging biceps again. Yum.

I realized he was speaking, and dragged my attention back to what he was saying.

"Because of you, we were able to uncover a potentially disastrous situation before it happened. Our government owes you, and I've put that in my report. I'm sorry it came at such a cost to you, though."

I shrugged. "I'm just glad it's resolved. And I'm glad none of the good guys got hurt. Much," I added sheepishly. "Has everybody recovered from my kind attentions?"

He laughed as he rose. "No permanent harm done." As I stood, too, he nodded at my scabbed knuckles. "Next time, aim for a softer target," he advised, rubbing his chin.

I gave him a wry smile. "I was going for your throat. I just had lousy aim. Luckily." I trailed him as he headed toward the door. "That pretty much sums up this whole episode. Luck."

He hesitated and turned back to me. "Aydan..." He frowned. "The reason I came by... I... wanted to ask you something. Completely off the record. Just between the two of us."

I glanced up at him. He'd taken me by surprise when he turned, and I was standing a little nearer than I would normally have chosen. That close, he was very tall and broad-shouldered, and I resisted the urge to step closer. Quite a bit closer.

Modulating my voice to casual interest, I replied, "Okay, shoot."

He looked down at me, his grey eyes piercing. "Last night, when you were drugged, you said 'They know about me'. And you were ready to lay down your life to protect classified information."

I held up a hand to stop him. "No, I was ready to lay

down my life because I'm a coward. I fear being tortured and maimed more than I fear death."

"You're no coward," he said softly. "And I don't believe in coincidences. I want to know. Aydan, are you an undercover agent?"

I met his eyes, trying to make him believe me. "John, I'm just a civilian. The whole thing was coincidence. Pure dumb luck."

He searched my face. "There's no other answer to that question, is there? If you're an agent, you'd have to tell me that."

I didn't know what else to say, so I just gave him a half-smile and a shrug. No way to prove a negative.

He reached for my hand and held it gently. "All right. If that's the way it has to be. But if you ever need help, you have my number." He leaned down and kissed me lightly, his lips barely brushing mine.

The touch jolted through me, and my grip tightened on his hand. Our eyes met.

"Tell me if you feel sexually harassed by anything I'm about to do," I said.

I pulled him down into a hungry kiss and felt his lips curve up against mine. He kissed me back, hard, his hands knotting in my hair. I ran trembling hands over his massive arms and chest, the heat of his muscles burning through his T-shirt and igniting my body.

Breathless with lust, I teased his lips with the tip of my tongue. He growled and backed me up against the wall while we devoured each other. His knee pushed between my legs, and fire spread low and fast while I made slow circles against his hard thigh.

When he pulled away abruptly, I let out an involuntary

whimper and braced myself against the wall to keep my knees from buckling. His chest rose and fell with his unsteady breathing, his eyes dilated black.

"I can't do this," he said hoarsely. "I have to catch this flight. National security. No choice. I'm late already."

I swallowed hard and straightened, trying to catch my breath. "Okay," I said, my voice almost as husky as his. "Take care. Stay safe."

He nodded. "You, too."

He hesitated, then turned on his heel. I propped myself against the door to watch while he strode to his SUV. He swung into the vehicle and drove away without looking back.

Damn.

A Request

Thanks for reading!

If you enjoyed this book, I'd really appreciate it if you'd take a moment to review it online. If you've never reviewed a book before, I have a couple of quick videos at http://www.dianehenders.com/reviews that will walk you through the process.

Here are some suggestions for the "star" ratings:

Five stars: Loved the book and can hardly wait for the next one.

Four stars: Liked the book and plan to read the next one.

Three stars: The book was okay. Might read the next one.

Two stars: Didn't like the book. Probably won't read the next one.

One star: Hated the book. Would never read another in the series.

"Star" ratings are a quick way to do a review, but the most helpful reviews are the ones where you write a few sentences about what you liked/disliked about the book.

Thanks for taking the time to do a review!

Want to know what else is roiling around in the cesspit of my mind? Visit my website at http://www.dianehenders.com. Don't forget to leave a comment in the guest book to say hi!

About Me

By profession, I'm a technical writer, computer geek, and ex-interior designer. I'm good at two out of three of these things. I had the sense to quit the one I sucked at.

To deal with my mid-life crisis, I also write adventure novels featuring a middle-aged female protagonist. And I kickbox.

This seemed more productive than indulging in more typical mid-life crisis activities like getting a divorce, buying a Harley Crossbones, and cruising across the country picking up men in sleazy bars. Especially since it's winter most of the months of the year here.

It's much more comfortable to sit at my computer. And hell, Harleys are expensive. Come to think of it, so are beer and gasoline.

Oh, and I still love my husband. There's that. I'll stick with the writing.

Diane Henders

Since You Asked...

People frequently ask if my protagonist, Aydan Kelly, is really me.

Yeah, you got me. These novels are an autobiography of my secret life as a government agent, working with highly-classified computer technology... Oh, wait, what's that? You want the *truth*? Um, you do realize fiction writers get paid to lie, don't you?

...well, shit, that's not nearly as much fun. It's also a long story.

I swore I'd never write fiction. "Too personal," I said. "People read novels and automatically assume the author is talking about him/herself."

Well, apparently I lied about the fiction-writing part. One day, a story sprang into my head and wouldn't leave. The only way to get it out was to write it down. So I did.

But when I wrote that first book, I never intended to show it to anyone, so I created a character that looked like me just to thumb my nose at the stereotype. I've always had a defective sense of humour, and this time it turned around and bit me in the ass.

Because after I'd written the third novel, I realized I actually wanted other people to read my books. And when I went back to change my main character to *not* look like me, my beta readers wouldn't let me. They rose up against me and said, "No! Aydan is a tall woman with long red hair and brown eyes. End of discussion!"

Jeez, no wonder readers get the idea that authors write about themselves. So no, I'm not Aydan Kelly. I just look like her.

Bonus Stuff

Here's an excerpt from Book 2: The Spy Is Cast

The ring of the phone made me swear. Extricating one arm and half my face from the toilet tank, I stumbled over the tools strewn on the floor. On the fourth ring, I snatched up the receiver with a dripping hand just as my answering machine kicked in.

"Hang on," I advised the caller, waiting for the message to finish playing. I held the phone to my ear with my shoulder and dried my hands on my baggy jeans while I waited.

"Hello?" I inquired when the line was clear.

"Is this Aydan Kelly?"

"Speaking."

"Aydan, it's Clyde Webb calling..."

"Spider!" I interrupted, smiling. "How the hell are you?"

He sounded pleased. "You remembered!"

"Of course I remembered. You never forget your first."

"Your first what?" he asked warily.

"The first guy you hit 'til he pukes. I still feel bad about that."

He laughed. "It's okay, it wasn't your fault... but, uh... about that..." His voice took on a wheedling note. "Aydan, how would you like to go to a gala affair? Dining and dancing, fabulous food and drink, rubbing shoulders with the cream of society?"

I looked down at my sweaty T-shirt and grubby jeans. "Um, Spider, I think you've got the wrong number."

"No, I haven't," he insisted. "It would be a thank-you for all you did for us back in March. You deserve a luxurious evening out!"

"Spider..." I paused, trying to be tactful. "I hate dressing up. I hate crowds. I hate making small talk with strangers. And I hate to remind you, but I'm the same age as your mother." I thumped my forehead with my free hand. I don't really do tact well.

"Oh, I wasn't asking you to go with me. Although I'd be proud to go with you," he added gallantly.

I laughed. He was such a nice kid. Well, twenty-something. Not really a kid.

"Okay, what's this about, then?" I asked.

"I'm asking you to go with Kane."

"What, you're Kane's social secretary now? Tell him he can ask me himself. He's a big boy."

I grinned, remembering tall, muscular John Kane with salacious appreciation. He was definitely a big boy. Too bad I'd never gotten the opportunity to find out exactly how big.

"Oh, he doesn't know I'm asking you," Spider replied.

"Whoa, hold on, Spider. What's really going on?" I asked, instantly suspicious.

"I can't tell you over the phone," he confessed. "I was hoping you'd be able to meet me. It's important."

I churned my free hand through my tangled hair, pulling the elastic out of my ponytail and yanking the knots out of the curly bits at the nape of my neck. "Important, as in 'national security' important?"

"I really can't talk about it over the phone," he repeated.

I sighed. "Okay. Where and when do you want to meet?"

"Can you meet now?"

"Why, are you standing on my front step?"

"No," he replied sheepishly. "I meant, how soon can you

get here?"

"I presume 'here' means your office in Silverside?"

"Yes. Sorry, I'm just... Can you come? I hate to bother you, but it's..."

"Important. Yeah, I got that. Okay," I agreed reluctantly. "It'll take me about half an hour to get there, though. Unless you really want me to show up in the same clothes that I wore to fix the toilet."

"Um, no." He sounded uncomfortable. "Business attire would be better."

"What the hell, Spider?" I demanded. "Business attire? Since when?"

"Just... can you? Please?"

"Okay, for you. I'm on my way."

I hung up the phone, frowning. The disorganized and stilted conversation was so unlike Spider that a tingle of apprehension made me hurry to my closet.

I scowled at my business clothes, hanging clean and pressed, neatly organized by colour.

I really hate dressing up.

I swallowed a growl and stripped off my dirty clothes, yanking on a pair of slim cream-coloured pants and a short-sleeved green blouse.

Doing a quick mirror check, I flapped my hair up and down in an attempt to dry some of the sweat, and reassured myself the blouse adequately camouflaged the extra ten pounds around my waist. Someday I'd lose that.

Right.

I dragged a brush through my hair and decided to leave it loose. If Spider thought I needed to dress up, it probably meant I'd be meeting somebody important. My long red hair was my best feature. Well, mostly red. The grey wasn't too noticeable yet.

I put on a pair of flat shoes and stuffed my waist pouch inside one of my enormous handbags. Normally, I wear the waist pouch everywhere, but even I don't have enough chutzpah to defy the fashion police and wear it with business clothes.

On my way across the yard, I slicked on a bit of tinted lip gloss, managing to keep it in the general vicinity of my lips.

Despite my growing sense of urgency, I let my steps slow while I enjoyed the view. I'd moved onto my farm in March when everything was winter-brown, and the greens of July were still a delightful novelty. I let my eyes rest on the long vista of rolling farmland and took a deep breath of country-fresh air before hurrying into my beloved four-car garage, patting the hoods of my automotive friends as I passed.

My faithful '98 Saturn waited in the last bay, and I skimmed my fingertips over its front quarter panel as I made my way to the driver's door. The local body guy had done an excellent job. You'd never know there had been a bullet hole in it.

Turning off my gravel road onto the pavement, I headed for town, curiosity warring with nervousness. The last time I'd gotten involved with these guys, it had cost me in blood. Spider's agitated demeanour hadn't reassured me one bit.

In the tiny town of Silverside, I navigated through the two-block business district and turned into the semi-residential area that housed Spider's and Kane's shared office. Pulling up in front of the small house, I swallowed a faint queasy sensation.

In the summer, the yard was mowed and well-tended. Perennial shrubs framed the house and accented the modest sign that read 'Kane Consulting' and 'Spider's Webb Design'.

It looked welcoming and benign. I wasn't fooled.

I took a deep breath before walking up to the front door. Tapping the knocker, I stuck my head inside. The shared office space in the converted living/dining area was empty, but I went in anyway, calling out a hello.

Spider appeared from down the hallway, his tall, skinny body and lanky limbs clad in a dark suit, blue shirt, and tie. My mouth fell open.

"Who are you and what have you done with Spider?" I ribbed him.

He grinned and twitched his shoulders in a nervous shrug. "Aydan, it's great to see you. You look great. As usual." He gave me a quick, awkward hug. "How are you?"

"I'm fine," I replied. "You?"

"Great!"

I frowned. "I keep hearing the word 'great'. Why does that make me nervous?"

He shuffled his feet. "We need to go into our meeting now. Would you like something to drink?"

"Just a glass of water, please." My trepidation cranked up a notch while I waited for him to return from the kitchen. Something was definitely up.

He handed me the glass and ushered me down the hallway to the converted bedroom that served as a meeting room. I paused in the doorway, surveying its two occupants.

One dark suit, white shirt, quiet tie. One military uniform, loaded with braid.

Oh, shit.

When I stepped cautiously into the room, both men rose. Neither was as tall as Spider's beanpole six-foot-two, but they shared an almost-palpable air of authority. While Spider made the introductions, I assessed them, trying to figure out what this was all about.

"General Briggs, I'd like you to meet Ms. Aydan Kelly," Spider mumbled without making eye contact. The general stepped forward, stretching out his hand, and I received a firm, dry handshake.

He was a fit-looking man with piercing blue eyes, his short grey hair in a precise cut. His seamed face gave the impression of too much time outdoors rather than advancing age. I placed him in his late fifties at a guess. His ramrod-straight posture made him seem tall, but in fact he stood only about an inch taller than my five-foot-ten.

"And this is Mr. Charles Stemp," Spider introduced the other man. Stemp extended his hand, too, his movements as sinuous as a snake. He looked fit as well, and very tanned. His short-cropped sandy hair was almost the same colour as his skin, and his eyes were an odd shade of light brown, almost amber. His monochrome colouring and flat, expressionless eyes reminded me of a rattlesnake. Jeez. No wonder Spider was nervous.

"Mr. Stemp is the civilian director of our INSET team," Spider explained, referring to the counter-terrorism unit to which he and Kane ostensibly belonged. "General Briggs is Kane's commanding officer."

That was where things got a little more complicated. In lighter moments, I had nicknamed Kane 'James Bond'.

Spider drew me further into the room. "Have a seat," he invited. I perched warily, wondering why the big guns were here. The others resumed their seats as well.

"Ms. Kelly," the general began. "So nice to meet you at last."

I wasn't quite sure how to respond to that, so I put on my best pleasant smile. "It's nice to meet you, too, General

Briggs."

"Thank you for meeting with us on such short notice," he continued. "This meeting is rather overdue, and I apologize for the long delay. Our country owes you a debt of gratitude, and we would both like to offer you a sincere thank you for your assistance in March. Your bravery and self-sacrifice did not go unnoticed."

I squirmed. "I appreciate the kind words, but I didn't really do anything. I was a dumb civilian in the wrong place at the wrong time. I'm just glad everything worked out all right."

The general's eyes bored into me. "I read the reports. I beg to differ. You uncovered a potentially disastrous security breach. You withstood torture to protect our national security. You saved the life of one of our top agents."

I shook my head. "It sounds good when you say it like that, but really, it was your team who pulled it all out of the fire. I was just along for the ride."

He smiled. "That may be true, but the entire operation would have failed without your unique talents."

"The whole thing was pure dumb luck on my part," I muttered. "Your team did all the work."

"I'm glad you're loyal to the team," Stemp said, his voice betraying no emotion whatsoever. "How would you like to help them again?"

Warning bells clamoured in my brain. "Help them how, exactly?" I asked slowly.

"We are chronically understaffed," the general explained. "We have a situation in which a female agent is required, and we have none currently available. The mission would entail almost no risk. In fact, you would probably find it quite enjoyable. We thought of you because of your excellent performance this spring, and because you already have the sufficient security clearances."

I hid my surprise and suspicion in a casual tone. "When did that happen? I'm just a bookkeeper. A civilian. I don't recall doing any applications for security clearances."

"You were thoroughly investigated in March," Stemp replied. "And your knowledge of our secured facilities and clandestine activities in effect gives you a top-level clearance. You already know more than many of our agents."

"Oh." I attempted to rub the frown away from my forehead. "Exactly what do you want me to do?"

"John Kane will be attending a formal function in Calgary the day after tomorrow." General Briggs picked up the narrative. "While there, he will be researching the layout and security of the venue in which it is held. A man doing this alone would be too obvious. He needs a female companion to attend with him." The general gave me an encouraging smile. "I'm told the food and entertainment will be quite magnificent."

"I'm not sure Kane would want me tagging along," I objected. "I don't have the first clue about spy stuff. I'd probably put him in danger just through my own ignorance."

"You would be fully briefed, of course," Stemp said. "We would also compensate you for your time. And there would be an allowance for your wardrobe and accessories for the event." He added that last bit as though it was an irresistible inducement.

I did my best to control my face. He really thought I'd want to go if he bought me a new dress. Poor deluded man. Little did he know I'd happily pay him if he'd let me go in jeans and a sweatshirt.

I shrugged. "If Kane thinks it's a good idea, I'll go with

him. I'll help if I can. But if he thinks he'd be better off without me, then I don't want to be foisted on him."

"Excellent." The general nodded with obvious satisfaction. "Please come here for your briefing tomorrow morning at ten o'clock. You should be prepared to leave for Calgary immediately afterward so that you have time to purchase whatever you need for the following evening." He rose. "It was a pleasure meeting you, Ms. Kelly."

I recognized a dismissal when I heard it. I got up and shook hands again with him and Stemp, and turned to leave the room.

"I'll see you out," Spider said, his first words since the introductions. We went down the hall together, and he followed me out onto the front step.

"What the hell, Spider?" I demanded. "Those two big brasses came here just to blow sunshine up my ass and ask me on a date? I don't think so. What's really going on?"

He shook his head. "Later."

"Will they be here for the briefing tomorrow?" I asked.

"Yes." He regarded me tensely, and I could see I wouldn't get anything more out of him.

"Okay." I sighed. "See you tomorrow at ten. Do I have to dress up again?"

"Yes."

*** End of The Spy Is Cast, Chapter 1 ***

CPSIA information can be obtained at www.ICGtesting.com
Printed in the USA
LVOW11s1822260215

428495LV00001B/4/P